GW00570223

SAILOR'S
HEART

SAILOR'S HEART

by
MARTIN CAMPBELL

**"TRUE COURAGE IS IN FACING DANGER
WHEN YOU ARE AFRAID"
L. FRANK BAUM**

SAILOR'S HEART
By
Martin Campbell

Published by MIGHTY PENS LTD

ISBN: 978-1-5272-5482-4

Copyright © 2020 Martin Campbell.

Martin Campbell is recognised as author and copyright holder
of this book and its full contents. All rights reserved.
No reproduction is allowed of part or whole of this book for
any purpose without prior permission.

First printing, 2021.

Page design: Pageset Ltd, High Wycombe, Buckinghamshire.

Printed and bound by Print2Demand Ltd, Westoning,
Bedfordshire.

Cover photograph by Malcolm McCandless.

Prepared by Mighty Pens Ltd.
Mightypens.co.uk

CHAPTERS

FOREWORD

When I first looked at Sailor's Heart I wasn't sure what to expect. I knew it would involve the sea which was a plus and I also knew there was a circus connection which was a big plus because I have circus connections myself and looked forward to seeing how Martin Campbell coped with it. Few people have succeeded in actually presenting circus properly in non-fiction, let alone fiction.

Having read the book I have to say, "Martin – you nailed it!"

This is a story you will want to read more than once. It is gripping, it is painful, it has humour and it has a raw reality that only those who have been there will fully recognise. That is why you will want to read it more than once. The first time will be as a spectator, the second time will be to experience it, the third time will be to feel it under your skin and beyond that you will read it once again live alongside those comrades you have come to know from the very start of immersing yourself into this particular window into how human beings can find themselves in the most horrendous of situations but survive.

The reader will go on this roller-coaster of emotions and emerge from it a little bruised but happy to still be alive.

Sailor's Heart is not just a good story, it is a very well-written good story created by a man who is an expert on human psychology and knows how humans can suffer mental as well as physical torment and yet survive and perhaps even smile about it one day, whether it is a smile of satisfaction at having made it to the other side or a smile which is simply a warm mask concealing the frozen waste that was once a Sailor's Heart.

Bernard Bale

INTRODUCTION

Sailor's Heart, some call it. A combination of circumstances, all with the same end result. A man at sea loses his interest in the battle, then in the will to fight, or the will to live. He comes in from a cold deck, with no desire to go back.

On a fighting ship he becomes a liability; a worn-out, malfunctioning or broken part. But can he be repaired?

Can Sea Broth or the Stone Frigate Approach bring back men who are lost, and at what price?

PROLOGUE:

SAVED BY SEA BROTH

Special Block F was the first to contain naval maniacs. These were men, ordinary men, who had sailed off to serve King and Country at sea and returned, changed irreparably. The shuttle boat ferried men from ships anchored in the bay to the hospital jetty at Haslar Creek, where they were ushered or carried into boxcar ambulances, converted goods carriages that ran on the rusting railway tracks from the jetty to the covered transit area of the hospital.

At the sea end of the jetty, the outflow pipe of the hospital sewer emptied into the bay. Years of plopping deposits had sustained bottom-feeding fish and left a fifty-yard crescent of deep sludge, with the consistency of mud and a smell that brought hands to mouths. Before iron bars were set into the red brick of the sewer, men who were slim and strong enough had escaped from Haslar Hospital by lowering themselves into the hospital bogs, then down into the main sewer before swimming out into the creek.

The outflow spot passed into the English language as the creek where you didn't want to be caught, especially without a paddle. Sailors said to be 'up the creek' were in trouble, on their way to insane confinement in Haslar, where exit was more often by death than by escape or recovery. Sailors who had been in one battle too many or on one voyage too far were rarely cured of their afflictions.

Two hundred and fifty years later, the creek and the hospital would be reborn as a luxury waterfront residential village overlooking Portsmouth, all shit removed along with memories – mostly.

The red brick front of the Haslar hospital was longer than ten of the ships on which the men had sailed, and inside the there was a central spiral staircase, down which one of those ships could have been launched.

Block F of the hospital was set aside as an asylum. The need for an entire block acknowledged the fact that sailors in the British Navy were seven times more likely to suffer from lunacy than the general public. *Calentura,* the Spanish called it, a fever that drove men at sea mad. But there was more to it than that, much more.

Like parts of the ships, some men at sea malfunctioned, broke or became worn. Most of those who lost their sanity at sea to heat stroke or scurvy or isolation or alcoholism never set foot on land again. The oceans were a welcoming receiver for those souls who had lost their way, instant relief to all troubles guaranteed, available 24 hours a day and accessible from the deck in fewer than ten steps in the right direction.

In its original construction, Haslar was three sides of a quadrangle in a double row of buildings, one within the other. The walls of the buildings were four feet thick at the base, to support the floors above, tapering to one-foot thickness in the attics. There was no ornamentation, except over the main entrance. Visitors passed under the unlikely sight of a female on board ship. It was a plain stone sculpture, a 12-foot woman wrapped in what looked like a bed sheet, one arm fused to the ship's rudder to guide, the other pouring soothing oil on the wounds of a sailor at her feet. She promised succour and strength to all those who had been damaged at sea. The reality inside was different.

One part of the inner row of buildings was Block F, and within Block F was Number 4 Gallery, containing the worst cases. The Gallery itself was further divided into five small dormitories, each with five or six men. There was nothing to distinguish Number 4 Gallery from the rest of the corridors in Haslar, built to the same plan, other than the locked doors on each dormitory. Men in Gallery 4 were all classed as furious or fatuous persons, or lunatics, but other than having all served before the mast, they had little else in common. They had all arrived at Gallery 4 by different journeys, little of which they could remember.

The corridors of Block F, like much of the hospital, smelled of wood smoke. Men first admitted had what little clothes they stood in removed and fumigated over oak chips in the smoke room. To further reduce infestation of lice, all bedding as well as patients' clothes were smoke-fumigated regularly, but washed rarely. There were no baths in the hospital, and many men in Block F refused to be washed in the few tubs available because they associated them with scrubbing, a stiff brush punishment for misdemeanours on board ship.

Once a day, a whistle blew and a line of doors was opened. A long crocodile of men in Block F were led in to the airing grounds, the open side of the vast quadrangle, which stretched to 30 acres. Depending on weather and the number of assistants on duty, men were allowed to wander for one or two hours, "taking the air", a regular form of therapy, deemed by all physicians to benefit the spirits of the afflicted men. It was a treatment that cost nothing and did nothing, other than let the men breathe air that didn't smell of smoke or piss and ease the consciences of medics. Some other treatments in Block F were less benign.

A high, red brick wall, over a mile in circumference and guarded at nine points, marked the boundary line of the grounds. The wall was topped with metal spikes and had taken almost as long to build as the hospital itself. Men had escaped through the sewers in the past, but no one had ever tried to go over the wall.

* * * *

Sir Francis Drake was due some credit for the hospital, through his actions many years before. Timing was important. Drake asked for money for a scheme at a time when he could do no wrong in the eyes of Queen Elizabeth, having just defeated the Spanish Armada against the odds in summer 1588.

Drake and his cousin, Admiral Sir John Hawkins were Sea Dogs and unlikely philanthropists. Before defeating the Armada, they sailed together for years, looting Spanish ships for the Queen;

authorised piracy without the excuse of being at war with Spain. They may have been knights and gentlemen, but they were no humanitarians. A decade earlier they had been slave traders, abducting bewildered West Africans and cramming them into disease-ridden ships, selling those who survived the voyage to plantation owners in the Spanish Caribbean.

It was cosmic payback of some kind, perhaps, that both Drake and Hawkins died of dysentery in those same slave seas, eight years after defeating the Spanish. At the end, when he realised that his time was near and he was to be buried at sea, Drake insisted on a lead-lined coffin. In his voyages from Africa he had seen the sharks following the slave ships for the regular supply of bodies tossed overboard. So what Drake and Hawkins hoped to gain from their naval philanthropy remains a mystery. They were motivated more by ego than by heart.

What began as an appeal for money, by two opportunist sea captains, to support navy men maimed in body or mind by the Spanish Armada, became an Act of Parliament that then evolved into an iron box containing the funds.

The Chatham Chest was a metre-long, multi-lock box, which could only be opened by five men with different keys, to prevent the temptation of theft that came with such a large hoard of silver coins. The compulsory contributions taken from navy wages were used to provide for sick and wounded sailors and the surplus was added to the chest weekly. That large box containing the coins evolved ultimately into the massive building, containing the sailors, long after the Caribbean seawater had dissolved Drake's coffin.

Haslar Hospital was opened for its first patients in 1754 as the largest brick-built structure in Europe. Its construction was championed through parliament by another man better known for other exploits. Like Drake, John Montagu, Fourth Earl of Sandwich, and First Lord of the Admiralty was an unlikely do-gooder, more associated with salt beef than the first Royal Naval Hospital. His invention came through his devotion to the card table, where he would have two slabs of bread with a filling brought to him, to avoid taking a meal break from gambling on a big hand, which in his case was just about every hand.

* * * *

When Block F at Haslar finally opened, it filled up so quickly that the people living in ports on the south coast wondered how they had coped without it. Before Haslar, ships had docked, unloaded their cargo and left their unwanted human jetsam to wander the streets, begging, and dying of hunger and disease.

The first Commanding Officer of Royal Hospital Haslar was George Cuthbert M.D. and each Block was overseen by a Superintending Physician and Surgeon. For Block F, this was Dr James Dowden-Ballard. Like the majority of physicians at Haslar, he had never been to sea.

The closest Dowden-Ballard came to the great oceans was a pair of nose spectacles made of whalebone, carried in his chest pocket. These he used only when making his notes about patients, in handwriting so small that only he could read it. Although he did not know each man on Block F by sight, given a name by one of the attendants he prided himself in being able to give a detailed account of that man's condition, and how he came to be at Haslar.

The most common infirmity in the main part of the hospital, in Blocks A-E, was loss of function through battle or accident on board ship or, less commonly, injury while drunk onshore. There were hundreds of men missing limbs or eyes, and many others with spines that no longer worked. Creeping rheumatism was another common cause of admission, brought about by sleeping on damp hammocks and working in sea air for many years. In Block F, however, the distempers of the men were more varied and less easy to see at first glance.

Dr Dowden-Ballard considered himself a modernist, a true medical man and an innovator. He dismissed the long-held belief of his physician colleagues that there was more lunacy in sailors because of the number of times they banged their heads on low wooden beams on board whilst intoxicated on ship's rum. He read with disdain the writings of those who persisted in this simplistic and misguided belief. The navy's first attempts to explain the increasing number of sailors who had lost their mind had held sway for many years, even when he was a young doctor, training at Hoxton House in London.

In his own enlightened notes, if anyone had the patience and magnification to read them, Dowden-Ballard had expounded his own, unified theory of the causes that had brought men to Block F. He had specific ideas about those men in Gallery 4, the worse cases who came in wrist and ankle manacles, clanking in the make-shift boxcar ambulance from Haslar jetty.

All truly great physicians had one great innovation in diagnosis, Dowden-Ballard believed, and this was to be his. It would be his ground-breaking contribution to medicine. To be published in *Medical Observations and Inquiries by a Society of Physicians,* if he ever found the time to write it up. It would be the presentation he would make to the Royal Society in London, with panache, when his genius would be finally recognized.

Being isolated at sea in extremes of hot and cold, in the worst of weathers, in small, confined spaces all took its toll on men. Dowden-Ballard acknowledged that part of the accepted wisdom of his fellow medical men. Each man at sea had a limited store of fortitude and there was no way to know when that store was running low. Banging the brain on wooden beams repeatedly didn't help, but the real causes of madness at sea were more complex.

Dowden-Ballard proposed, in letters small enough to keep the secret, that the afflictions of men admitted to Block F could never be explained by just *one* precipitating cause. It was a two-stage process. Men first had to be taken to the very edge of their madness by one circumstance of body or mind, and then pushed over into one of the many sub-types of insanity by a second ordeal. He called his big idea the Chance Combinations Theory.

In his example, to be presented to the Royal Society, a diet of salt beef and pork resulting in scurvy could weaken a man, certainly. That man could then succumb more easily to madness, triggered by loneliness, by strong liquor or in the height of battle, by hearing the shrieks and seeing the pieces of the wounded men around him. The brave sailor with a heart of oak might be strong enough to withstand the close confines of a gun room in battle, never knowing where the next enemy cannonball would splinter through the hull, only to be reduced many weeks after the battle was over to a dribbling, incontinent wreck by what many would consider an inconsequential event; an argument or a disappointment in love or fortune, for example.

A combination of circumstances, all ending in the same end result. Besides having all served before the mast, all the men of Gallery 4 shared just one other trait, manifest in many different ways. Sailor's Heart, some called it. Men lost interest in the battle, then lost the will to fight, or the will to live.

For Dowden-Ballard, the root cause of the condition of men confined in Gallery 4 was always the Chance Combinations.

It was rare for a man to be admitted with any history or other evidence that Dowden-Ballard could use to support his quest for medical recognition. The single-page navy form, sometimes pinned to a man's tunic, might give, "head injury" for ordinary ratings, or "melancholia" for officers, as the cause of the man's affliction. Dowden-Ballard made it his mission to find out what was missing; exactly how a man's spirit had been broken. He had two ruler-drawn columns in his medical notes and he pencilled in his best guess at the Chance Combinations for each man in Block F. Counting through the cases, for nearly half of the men he had written "impressment" in the first column.

Despite legislation to ban it, press gangs still operated in the larger ports, snatching men from ale houses and the occasional wedding, to make up the chronic shortages of crew, especially in times of war, which was most times. For just a few cases in his Block F notes, Dowden-Ballard was able to trace a man's transformation fully, from town blacksmith or cooper to one-eyed alcoholic, returned to shore years later. Men were pushed into madness by the combination of impressment and one too many years at sea, or some unseen battle wound that did not bleed. The same pattern repeated again and again as Dowden-Ballard looked for it more and more.

One patient in Block F, Gallery 4, Alexander Robertson, was

Dowden-Ballard's proof of theory. Robertson was the case that he would present to the Royal Society when his moment came. If Seaman Robertson was still alive, he might even take him in person to present to the esteemed audience.

On his record sheet at admission, cause of insanity for Robertson was given only as, "paralysis by wind contusions". The man, now many years demented, had been narrowly missed by a cannonball that flew over his shoulder, killing three men on the other side of the deck. Seaman Robertson had felt, but not seen the passage of the cannonball, but he had seen the damage it inflicted, leaving severed limbs twitching on the deck behind him.

Dowden-Ballard would argue in his Royal Society presentation that no man could be so affected by such a non-injury alone. There must have been an unseen set of circumstances–shock, grief, poor diet–that would have caused the wind from a cannonball to be not the first, but the final push, sending Alexander Robertson into the catatonic state in which he was admitted to Haslar and in which he remained.

Was Seaman Robertson still in there somewhere, in the husk that was his body, shitting and pissing himself every day and opening his mouth only when a spoonful of food touched his lips? Could he be brought back from wherever he had gone, even part of the way back? For Dowden-Ballard, these were also critical questions to be answered.

But could he answer them or would that be for others? His main work would be spreading word of his great discovery, his Chance Combinations, around the country and being suitably lauded for it. Among the many physicians who would clamour to use his new diagnosis there would be some, innovators like himself, who would seek to discover restorative measures to alleviate the suffering of afflicted men like Seaman Robertson.

But what if he, Dr James Dowden-Ballard was able to complete the loop, to show not only how sailors' sanity was lost but how it could be *restored*? His name in history would be doubly guaranteed. He would be a legend like Thomas Willis before him, and his contemporary William Battie.

In his first two years at Haslar, he'd seen the steady flow of tortured misery from the jetty, the same disconnected men, again and again. They shuffled ashore. They were long, short, herring gutted and bacon-faced; all different, but all strangers that you would cross the street to avoid, on one look. Some men were interrupted from incessant, internal routines for a moment by the shock of the solid ground beneath their feet, but went back quickly to muttering, twitching and lip chewing before they boarded the box car.

Dowden-Ballard's intuition as a physician, having studied the men in Block F, was that the cure for many men's distempers, like the cause, would come from water. It was logical. Just as the men had lived on water for most of their adult life and had lost their sanity at sea in a combination of circumstances, they could find their way back to life with the aid of water – with that which was familiar to them.

Cold bathing was used at Haslar, for selected cases and when there were enough attendants. The shock of an icy plunge would sometimes have a silent man shout out or a catatonic man come to life and struggle, at least for a while. Dowden-Ballard had seen it and he had seen promise in the method. But the effects were short lived. If there were six rather than 60 patients in Block F, more could be done. With more time and more assistants Dowden-Ballard could select promising patients, test his ideas and perfect his techniques.

Dowden tried to keep up with innovations and trends in the Royal Society, but being so far from London and from medical meetings, he picked up only scraps of new ideas. He read in one pamphlet that among London's rich the practice of flesh brushing was a new treatment for nervous conditions and fevers of the mind.

Gentlemen and ladies could be stroked lightly with soft bristles dipped in purified water, to lead them to a state of calm. In consulting rooms and hospitals that did not smell of wood smoke or piss, where physicians chose their patients, those who could pay for it lay naked in coffin-like boxes, lined with the curative bristles. The practice was becoming popular. Even those with aspirations, but of restricted means, could administer the treatment to themselves using a special device that resembled nothing so much as a common hairbrush. The pamphlet claimed that flesh brushing with water could also cure limb paralysis and even diseases of the blood.

But flesh brushing wouldn't do for the men of Block F. No, no, it would not be suitable at all. Introducing the men to bristles and water? That would cause further agitation. Too many memories of back breaking work, scrubbing fungus off the deck, or seeing the very same scrubbing brush used to scrape the skin off a man, as a punishment to keep discipline on board a long voyage.

No, the cure for men in Block F, like the cause, would come from water but it would not come from brushes, Dowden-Ballard believed, all the more so with each new admission. It would be a genuine, therapeutic breakthrough, not some money-making scheme to fleece the rich and aspirational rich of London.

The men of Block F, curled up on beds, speaking to unseen figures all day, or walking until their feet bled, having to be tied down at night, would need something more powerful than what could be delivered by any soft brush. To bring them back from their death-in-life existence would need something at least as powerful as the experience that had broken their spirit in the first place.

Dowden-Ballard was aware of one such treatment, and had been since he took up his post at Haslar. It was a simple procedure that promised to make hopeless cases walk and talk again, but it was not without risk. It was not included in his *Pocket Medical Book* or published in any of the *Medical Observations and Inquiries by a Society of Physicians*. Nor did it appear in Battie's recent book on *A Treatise on Madness*. He had come across details of the treatment at Hoxton House in a tract of well-thumbed pages that had been passed around the younger medical men, like a salacious French pamphlet.

The writer had disguised his name, for fear of infamy or imprisonment, which was wise, given the content of the pamphlet. No great medical skill was required, nor was a knowledge of how the patient came to be afflicted. Some professional judgement was required, clearly, in identifying those patients most likely to benefit. The pamphlet was titled, *Swimming for the Shore: Saved by Sea Broth*.

The treatment it described was near death in saltwater. What was needed most, more than any number of years of medical training, was the physician's total and unwavering belief in the efficacy of the treatment. The patient need not understand the treatment and, indeed, it would be unlikely that agreement would be forthcoming if he did. This was no moral therapy, no fad being promoted in private London asylums of the time. By all means, the patient could be made comfortable and kept in a cheerful, loving environment before the treatment, but to effect the cure, robust mechanical means and strong hands were needed.

The dog-eared pamphlet reported "wonderous and amazing" results. Patients, carefully chosen, made instant recoveries, returned to their families after weeks or even months in fugues or hysterical states. From barking at the moon to sitting by the family hearth, smoking a pipe contentedly, sometimes after just a single session.

The pamphlet was four pages and the basic instructions for treatment took up less than two paragraphs. A physician and two male assistants were needed. With minimum fuss, the patient was seized and submerged, sitting or with knees drawn up, in a bath or wooden bathing cask of cold sea water. The patient's head was held under until no more bubbles rose to the surface. He was then pulled out and revived.

Timing was of the essence. When the last bubble broke the surface of the water, the patient was to be removed from the water promptly. All three men were needed to prevent the patient fighting his way to the surface during the treatment, but judging the exact moment when no more bubbles could be seen was the decision of the physician alone, according to the pamphlet.

The anonymous writer described patients brought back to life, vitality of mind reappearing with that first breath of resuscitation. Dowden-Ballard and his fellow junior medics had read the pamphlet as students, at first with incredulity and scorn. There were heated debates at night at Hoxton about whether a man could be brought back to his previous life by touching death.

The bigger question for Dowden-Ballard was who among them, as physicians, would be bold enough, confident enough to stake his standing, his very career on this perilous procedure to revive lost souls?

It took many years to build a solid professional reputation, but only minutes to destroy it. Sullying one's reputation was a constant risk for physicians, and young physicians in particular. Conduct was constantly scrutinised in and out of the hospital.

But the accolades from the medical world of perfecting such a treatment would be unprecedented and perhaps worthy of the risk. Bringing patients back from states of false perception and deep melancholia, demonstrating that a man's soul remained intact within, despite his mental afflictions, would guarantee inclusion of the achievement, of the physician's name in every medical school in the country and abroad. The pamphlet promised much for someone brave enough. But to take such a chance and to fail would be professional death.

Dowden-Ballard never saw the *Saved by Sea Broth* pamphlet again after he left Hoxton House. As his career progressed, treatments for the insane advanced from blistering and leeches applied to the temples to increasing hours of vigorous exercise and fresh air. Cold water treatments were still favoured by some doctors, but as an extended bath, never as treatment by near death in saltwater. With his appointment to Haslar, and the increasing number of patients in Block F, the details of the pamphlet came back to him. He began to consider what might be possible.

There were enough men in Dowden-Ballard's charge in Block F, in Gallery 4 in particular who would be missed by no-one. These were men now considered dead or lost forever by anyone who had ever loved them. There were no letters, parcels or Christmas visits for the lost souls in Gallery 4.

Some patients might die until he got the treatment just right. That would be a regrettable but acceptable price for the benefits to the many that would come with success. But on balance it would be too big a risk for someone like him, someone about to begin his ascent, leading to his presentation of the Chance Combinations Theory to the Royal Society.

One safe step at a time; that was how to proceed, he decided. That was how to work his way out of the hell hole that was Block F, to use it as a stepping stone. There was much more fame and fortune to be had in his position from a speculative diagnosis, convincingly reported, than from stretching for the stars too soon with the uncertain saltwater treatment. His new diagnosis by itself, properly presented, would have many believers. His Chance Combinations told a good story for those who would hear it. It fitted with recent advances and with the thinking of the day. It had the added benefit of being difficult to disprove.

First his paper, then the recognition of his peers, then the Royal Society and then? Dowden-Ballard rather fancied that his fame would be a stepping stone to even greater things. In his later years, he might establish an epistolary practice, the very antithesis of his life in Gallery 4.

It was a new form of medical diagnosis, exclusive to renowned physicians and rich correspondents. That would be the time in his career to find a town house in London, an address to which letters of enquiry with enclosed fees could be sent. One or two guineas would not be unreasonable for his services by then. From his desk, he would dispense his wisdom to concerned letter-writing clients and their relatives, giving them his diagnosis by return of correspondence, addressing the complaints and the symptoms described. Medicine at a distance, for those rich enough, but too embarrassed to visit a physician in person.

CHAPTER I

CLARENCE THE COWARD

Clarence Watson couldn't remember a time when he wasn't hairy. There must have been a period in his life, when he was a boy growing up, but he just had no memory of it. Even at school he noticed how he stood out from other boys because his dark hairline seemed to crawl further down his face, making it look like he was peeking out from under a canopy. When he was eleven and moved to secondary school, some of the older children called him Kong and pounded their chest when he walked past them in the corridors. The barber would make jokes about giving him a hot shave when his mother took him for a haircut. His hair was wiry and it was thick, more follicles per square inch than the average otter.

It was difficult for the seamen who worked with Clarence to imagine how he might have looked as a boy, other than like a smaller version of the hairy adult. The starched shirt of his dress uniform rubbed on his skin only in two patches, high on the sleeves, where his arms became his shoulders. Elsewhere, on his back, chest and forearms the cotton shirt rested on the thin carpet of tight-curled wiry wool that covered Clarence's body. When he buttoned his collar, his chest hair curled over it, looking like a narrow ruff worn around his neck. It was a relief to him that most of the time on board ship he was required to wear nothing but underwear under his engineer's blue overall, with socks and standard issue navy boots.

When he shaved, the hair on his face didn't grow back any faster than on any of the other men, but the base layer was there, permanently. He looked like a miner who had emerged from the pit and splashed some water on his eyes and nose, leaving a layer of coal dust on his cheeks, chin and neck. The dark stubble underlay that grew all the way up his cheek bones seemed to absorb light, making his eyes stand out like beacons in his face. His low hairline, coming to a point in line with his nose, started at the top of a permanently furrowed block of a brow.

Clarence didn't think about it much. The only hair that caused him any problems was the growth of hair on his hands. Long hairs, the length of fingernails, covered the back of his hands and middle segments of his fingers, sprouting in every direction. The difficulty came when Clarence was doing fine work on his bench or reaching into machinery on the ship. Anything with parts that could move seemed to seek out the hairs on his fingers. Springs were worst. They would grab the hairs and rip them out before he had the chance to disentangle himself. Anything with cogwheels was the same. He'd be reaching in to make a fine adjustment and there would be a quiet pop; metal teeth meshing together and pulling out a few more hairs. The shock of the pain as the hair was torn out was worse because he never saw it coming. At night in bed, Clarence chewed through the longest hairs on his fingers to save on future pain, but within days new hairs would appear, to replace their fallen comrades.

Clarence had drifted into engineering rather than chose it. As he got to the end of his schooling he was keen to drift into just about anything except banking, where his father had worked since leaving school. Clarence could do straight numbers, getting to the right answers, and he was very good at it. But he didn't enjoy it much. It made him think about when he had to wash dishes at home, one of his chores as a boy. The plates in his mother's tidy kitchen were cleaned, dried and stacked with precision – "gleaming" she would say – but the task brought him no satisfaction, even though it was necessary and helped his mother.

He was good at more tricky numbers too, the ones he had never heard of in real life outside school; natural cosines, reciprocals and calculating resolution of forces. In engineering tests at school, there always seemed to be someone, usually a man, throwing a brick down a well for no reason other than to calculate its acceleration, or the same man pulling a 400-pound barrel up a smooth inclined plane desperate to know the least pull that he had to exert. Conical pendulums also featured a lot in school maths and mechanics; balls on the end of a string, swinging in a circle. Clarence had never seen one in real life. They seemed to exist only on blackboards. He could work out the angles and the forces as the ball spun around, but what was the point? And how could you tie a metal ball onto the string in the first place?

Clarence would hold back in class when he knew the answers, reluctant to show what he could do. Keeping quiet came from the fear that being identified as one of the clever boys would make more certain his career path into his father's world of suits and banking. He had, by age 15, resigned himself to the inevitability of life in a bank straight from school. Such was the well-trodden path before him and the lack of alternatives that he had seen. As the time got closer, he became more panicked about swapping one desk for another and a life spent filling books with scribbled numbers, just as meaningless as cosines and tangents.

To be fair, his father had never said it was banking or nothing. But during his teenage years there were enough hints and comments at home to make it clear that if it wasn't banking then it had to be something equally prestigious and respectable, in the eyes of his parents and the neighbours.

In the end, it wasn't his schooling or a careers officer or even the war that saved Clarence from banking. It was the Benson family, previous owners of his parents' new house. When his father was promoted, moving up meant moving out of their modest family two bedroom semi-detached to something more befitting an assistant bank manager.

Clarence had never heard his mother swear, but more than once in that first week she said the Bensons had left the property in a hell of a state. His parents had been to see the house one dark night when the family was still there and the house was still furnished. They came home talking about how warm the rooms were, how much space there was, and what a respectable neighbourhood they would be moving to.

The Bensons cleared everything when they left, and the empty house was less impressive. The carpets in every room were stained, patches dark and sticky where the furniture had been moved to hide them. The inside of the windows and the ceiling were coated with the nicotine of many years smoking, layers of a gummy yellow emulsion that took some serious scrubbing to remove. Cleaning the grime and cobwebs from the skirting boards took his mother three whole days on her hands and knees. You could hide a car in the grass in the back garden, his father had said, which was an exaggeration, although the grass was so long that a scythe would be needed before any lawnmower would be of use.

If the Bensons had a car it would never have fitted in the garage at the bottom of the garden. When Clarence's father found the key to the garage padlock in the kitchen, three days after they moved in, the Watsons discovered why the only trace of the Bensons inside the house had been stains, dust and dirt. Every piece of unwanted furniture, broken appliance, and household junk had been piled high on the garage floor. It was a pyramid of domestic leftovers that touched the beams of the garage roof.

It took Clarence and his father two weekends to move enough of the pyramid to the local rubbish tip to make the space needed to store their own family junk. It was only then that they found the heavier stuff that had been left by the Bensons, tucked under the benches which lined the garage walls.

Whether Mr Benson had been a motor enthusiast, a scrap metal dealer or just a hoarder was difficult to tell. The spaces were crammed with discarded machine parts, big and small. The bottom layers had rusting spares too heavy to lift without a hoist: a whole engine block with a crack running through it, two sets of leaf spring suspension, the steel leaves separated and a mechanical jigsaw of gearboxes and clutch plates. Balanced on top were the smaller pieces; starter motors and dynamos, a broken Smiths speedometer, an ignition magneto from another

4

motorcycle, or maybe the same one, and a rear axle differential, all crusted in rust.

None of the parts would ever run again. The task Clarence set himself over the following year, before his father found a scrap dealer willing to take the lot, was to work out what each of the components had done when they were new. He spent hours in the garage, wrapped up against the cold, taking the guts out of the machines, using only the discarded tools that the Bensons had also left behind and the three spanners his father owned.

He started by opening up anything held together with screws, to find out what was inside, saving magnets and copper wires for no reason other than he knew what they were. When he ran out of parts to deconstruct, he moved onto connecting units that might have worked together at one time, guided only by a grease-stained copy of *Instructions For The Upkeep & Management Of The Rover Meteor Car*, left in the back of a drawer. His parents neither approved nor discouraged his hobby, as long as he wiped his shoes before coming back into the house and used a nail brush to remove the black rings around his fingernails before sitting down to meals.

It was that year, wrapped up in three jumpers and a woollen hat, messing about in the garage that decided him. Clarence went for engineering, not banking, when the day came. He went up to Glasgow University on a combination of a bursary awarded by his school and fees, shouldered by his father, who still ambivalent about where engineering came in the hierarchy of occupations. Most of the other boys becoming men on the university programme were sons of garage and mill owners, studying engineering so that they could take over the family business. The choice had been made for them.

To neighbours and friends, Clarence's parents played up the respectability of having a son going to university and played down the connotations of overalls, grease and machines associated with full title of the course, which was Mechanical Engineering. The course was new, and taught by academics from physics, chemistry, maths and aeronautics. The emphasis was on engineering science, from first principles to advanced theory, rather than the practicalities of how to be an engineer. This was to play up to the strengths of the university staff, and to compensate for the fact that there was nobody on the staff who had worked as an engineer.

The first year of the course was a patchwork, and some of the second-year lectures would have made more sense earlier in the course, but Clarence was fast on his feet and adapted. He attended lectures, took notes and then read them later, trying to work out how the lecture topics connected to each other. It was a question that no one asked, for fear that everyone else knew the answer. Students were told that the course would equip them to work professionally in mechanical, thermal and the newly emerging electrotechnics systems. Each of the lecturers knew a lot about his topic, and could cover a board with hydraulics diagrams, or formula on the theory of elasticity, without pausing for breath, or for questions. Lectures were delivered.

It was only when the university brought in a real engineer, once a month, that Clarence was able to piece together sections of his notes into something coherent that might get him a job. Mr Miller – the "Mr" was always emphasised by the Professors and Doctors of physics and maths who introduced him – had worked in general mechanical design and production since leaving school. He did his lectures the only way he knew, as a series of case studies showing the students how real-life problems were solved by application of engineering. As well as being the only lecturer who didn't try to hide his Glasgow accent, he was the only person put in front of the class who asked if what he was explaining had been understood. He would take the time to backtrack if he saw that he had lost his audience.

He always left time for questions. At the end of one of his lectures, he got through what was needed quickly and finished earlier than usual. None of the boys was bold enough to ask detailed questions about the engineering from the lecture in a full class of their peers, but news had come through that day about Hitler marching into the Sudetenland and in a silence one wit in the class had shouted out, "*Will there be another war sir?*"

This got an uncomfortable laugh from some of the boys and

a smile from Mr Miller. He paused for a moment, looking at the floor and then turned without replying, picked up his chalk again and started to draw lines on the board. The boys went quiet again as the shape of a Vickers machine gun, complete with tripod and belt-fed ammunition took shape. When the drawing was complete, he turned and faced the class.

"*Well boys, to be honest, I don't know if there will be another war. I hope not. But if there is, your engineering may be put to good use.*"

There was silence.

He turned back to the board and chalked some numbers and arrows onto the diagram.

"*We've got five minutes left of the class. Let's see if any of you budding engineers can put your heads together and calculate the pressure necessary to prevent recoil on this Vickers automatic gun if it's firing 300, one-pound bullets per minute.*"

There was a brief pause, then excited chatter and rustling of paper as the students went into twos and threes to race for the answer. A few boys came close, including Clarence.

From that day, Clarence was hooked on engineering, real engineering. The war, and his first real job came sooner that he had anticipated. When Hitler moved onto invading Poland, Britain responded and all plans and bets were off. Clarence and most of his class were hurriedly awarded a "War degree", something created by Glasgow University to allow students who had completed two years of their studies to fast track into any the forces.

In the push to get men to the front, what would have taken months was condensed into weeks. Clarence was whipped through naval recruitment and assignment in record time. After basic naval training at Portsmouth and then an engineering refresher back in Scotland, he found himself working on the engineering bench on board HMS *Perseus*.

His supervisor and senior officer, Chief Engineer Jimmy Morgan, recognized quickly that Clarence was special. He had an intuitive sense for repairs, needing only to examine the parts once. He was able to come up with patch-ups for broken bits of machinery using what was on the ship, until the specialist parts needed could be supplied, back in port. The technical manuals were good for the regular inspection checklists to be followed to keep the machinery operational, but no checklist was a substitute for a good engineer when machinery went wrong. Morgan also saw something else in Clarence that marked him out from other apprentice engineers in his charge. He was good without being flash, his reward coming from the success of the repair, rather than the commendations from others that went with it.

Clarence was not religious. He had stopped going to church when he was old enough to tell his parents that it was mumbo jumbo to him. So, unlike many of the other men, he didn't have Christian beliefs to guide him or a God that he could call on when the war started in earnest. What he did have, that he had developed and refined over his teenage years and his training was his belief in the certainty of engineering. He kept to himself two tenets of faith about the work he could do with his hands. It was enough that he knew. First, he believed that given the right materials and tools, he could manufacture machine parts that would never need to be repaired. Second, if a machine had enough parts in it made by him, that machine could work forever. This is what he believed and what he aimed for on every job he did.

His apprenticeship on board HMS *Perseus* became active duty. It was not what he had pictured for himself, sitting through the lectures at university, but it was real engineering.

When he was working on jobs that needed all of his attention, which was most jobs, he had a routine. He would first position himself at the bench, between the fixed drill and his prized Adept power-operated shaper. Two feet of clean space either side of his shaper, that was all the space he needed to work his magic. The shaper was a basic vice with a set of adjustable wheels, cogs and levers, each capable of tearing out the hairs on the back of his hands. It was crude-but-good technology, but with Clarence it became more than the sum of its parts. He kept it dust, filing and grit-free, cleaning and oiling it after each use, then covering it with an oiled rag when he had finished.

Broken parts and worn-out fittings hobbled up onto one end of his bench on the ship and danced off the other, having received the healing hands. There were rods, hinges, connections and spindles that came to him beyond repair, unable to be resuscitated. The peripherals on the machine would still be sound, but the vital centre was gone, the one part on which all others depended for function. When those parts at the heart of the machine couldn't be saved, Clarence rebuilt a replacement from scratch, if he could find the raw materials. Other parts he stored, in boxes under his bench, so that they could give life to stricken machines that would come limping to his bench in the future.

Clarence's final stage of preparation in his routine for bench work was to turn around his blue cap and have the peak facing back. This put him in the zone. He would drop out the sounds of voices and the ever-present ship engine noises, then his peripheral vision would go. Everything around him, even his arms, went out of focus. The only things he could see in detail were his hands and what was in them. His strong fingers became hypersensitive to every wire, metal plate and surface that he touched, and in the zone he could repair or create what was needed, to tolerances of a fraction of an inch. Time floated. If he had an hour to finish the job, he would, but he was never aware of the clock hand turning. The men around him learned that the reversed cap served as a sign that he shouldn't be interrupted, and they would take a wide berth, as if he was an additional piece of working machinery, operating without safety guards. When he was finished, his ritual was to re-position his cap, tap the bench twice, and say, "*Three, two, one, job done.*" That brought all the noise and the bustle of the ship flooding back to him instantly.

The warship HMS *Perseus* did have two "real", highly skilled artificers. They were ranked as Petty Officers and above, well above Clarence, in recognition of the five-year apprenticeship served in engineering training. The artificers spent most of their time on electrical repairs or maintaining and fine-tuning instruments on the bridge and in the communications station. But if it was mechanical or engine room and it needed done fast, Clarence was the man.

He made running repairs to the draft fans that cooled the boiler room and he manufactured a reinforced patch in less than two hours, when one of the evaporators on board supplying pure water for the boilers sprung a leak, threatening the operation of the engines. When they were at sea he also maintained the auxiliary, or "donkey" engines used to power the anchor windlass and the bilge pumps. Clarence and the rest of the low-ranking engine room crew on the ship were thus known as donkeymen. It was a term of humorous affection rather than disrespect for the work that they did.

Although he was not a religious man, the parts that Clarence made with his hands, fixed and kept running were for a higher purpose. All that he did in repair and in maintenance was ultimately to serve the gods of the boilers and the engines that they powered. For without them, the ship, one of the fastest light armoured cruisers in the fleet, was just a floating shell, target practise for the next patrolling German sub.

* * * *

Clarence's dress uniform showed a straight stripe with a purple insert, confirming his engineer status as someone, "capable of raising steam". Raising the stuff wasn't as easy as it sounded, and it could be dangerous. Less than a cupful of the distilled water fed into the water tube boilers was enough to kill three men if it burst out from a faulty joint as super-heated steam.

Starting the boilers from scratch was called 'flashing up'. The boilers, pipes and turbines needed to be coaxed into action, with the steam worked up and fed in slowly over two hours. If the heat was cranked up too quickly, the face-to-face, flanged joints between pipes were the weak link in the chain between boiler and engine, liable to spring the kind of leak that could kill.

When the ship was at sea, Clarence and the other engineers had to be up before the rest of the crew. They were roused at the same time as the jankers – men under punishment for minor offences, who were allowed less sleep as part of the on-board disciplinary procedures. *"Engineers and defaulters feet on deck!"*

was what Clarence woke to most mornings, with his hammock being bounced off the side wall, just in case he hadn't heard the order.

Clarence had the rank "E" (Engineer Branch), as a sub lieutenant, temporary Royal Navy. This was given to university graduates who had joined up. His time at the barracks in Portsmouth, and the engineering back in Scotland had been a crash course. For Clarence, the useful bits at Portsmouth were seamanship training, naval discipline and knowing who ranked above whom on a ship. The constant kit inspections, daily scrubbing of surfaces and washing his clothes in a bucket he could have lived without. A few of the trainers at Portsmouth picked him out as a posh boy; a "90-day blunder" because he had not come through Royal Navy engineering college but through some Jockland university. The other recruits however, treated him as one of their own.

He travelled back to Glasgow to do two months of refresher experience with Clyde Marine Engineering, where he worked under men too old for war service. He looked on all of them as master tradesmen, surgeons of machinery. They could build an engine from scratch, or take turbines apart and give them new life, without once looking at the engineering plans he had become familiar with at the university. They could take plain sheets of steel or soft copper needed for a job and cut, shape, fit and join it with precision, first time. The seasoned marine engineers guided him through his fast track apprenticeship, but Clarence wondered if they would have been less patient and tolerant of his mistakes without the war as background, pushing everybody to do everything faster.

When he left Clyde Marine, he knew just enough to get the job as Sub-Lieutenant engineer on board HMS *Perseus*. But then he had to learn how to *do* the job. The ship was a newer, lighter cruiser, built for speed and manoeuvrability. He had seen or worked on most of the systems aboard before, although the three-drum water tube boilers on the ship were new to him. But he learned fast.

At sea, on escort duty, first in the Mediterranean and then on the Arctic convoy, Clarence and the other engineers were on the move, doing machinery checks on alternating, four-hour watches, monitoring the array of engine pressure and temperature gauges. There were no boxes to be ticked, just the chief engineer to be appeased for whatever checks he decided needed done to his precious engines that day. When HMS *Perseus* engaged in the Arctic, the engineers were forced to sit for long stretches, rigid at action stations, waiting for orders and listening to the sound of the ship's guns and enemy fire, loud even above the sound of the heavy turbines turning at high speed. There would be a break, then the explosions would start again, with no way of knowing when or how they would stop. Sitting there in the pounding of the turbines, Clarence looked around at his shipmates, wondering if he was the only one thinking about how many seconds it would take for them to die if a shell or a torpedo burst through the hull into the boiler room. Even near misses were powerful enough to spring the plates of a ship at the waterline.

During the two years he served, before it all went wrong, Clarence could only remember once having the same amount of shore leave as the rest of the ship's crew. It was when they put into Leith and the ship had to be fumigated to clear the rats that had come on board with the supplies. Fumigation was only ordered when there were so many rats on a ship that men were being kept awake by them, or when rat shit was found in the food supplies.

At all other times, Clarence's shore leave had been eaten up by swarf in the turbines. Fine corkscrews of metal built up in the oil that lubricated the pistons, sending the dials in the engine room into the red and taking two days to clear out. It was part of the engineers' duties to use the time in port to clear out the shavings before the ship set sail again. It was one of many maintenance tasks that stole shore leave from the engineers. Another was cleaning and sighting the boiler every three months. This was the last job that Clarence ever did for the Royal Navy.

The ship had docked at Rosyth for minor repairs to the radio tower, damaged in a storm. Time was always tight, whether the ship was at sea or in dock, and the routines were done to minimize the periods during which the HMS *Perseus* was not a fully operational, sea-going warship.

The water boilers were always fed with water distilled from the evaporators but despite this, impurities got through and the tubes furred up. The evaporators only removed some of the cocktail of chemicals in sea water and a crust would slowly accumulate on the tubes, reducing efficiency and eventually threatening to block the pipes.

Time had to be found while the ship was docked to clean the boilers. The process was long and repetitive, working in cramped conditions. The engineering crew dreaded and resented it, thinking about other crew walking off the ship and into town while they sweated in boiler suits in the lower decks.

HMS *Perseus* had four boilers, with just one bolted hatch for access to them all. The cleaning routine started with one man going in first to open up the boiler drums. All the baffles and other fittings were removed to get access to the boiler tubes. Then a long wire brush was pushed down each of the long tubes to scour it. This was hot, back breaking work; crawling, twisting, holding the brush at awkward angles and working it into the tubes. There was only space for two men at a time in the confined space of the boilers. The men kept a steady pace with each other, conscious that every minute spent on the job was a minute less on shore, drinking and forgetting.

When the wire brushing was completed, the tubes had to be sighted to make sure that nothing had been left in during the cleaning. Again, this was laborious, but necessary. If the boiler was started up again and steamed with an obstruction in one of the tubes, there would be no water circulation in that tube and it would heat to metal melting point, with a steam blow out. For the ship, that would be loss of power. For the boiler room crew, it could be a scalding.

Sighting the boiler was one task that had to be done right. It was a skilled job assigned to an officer, rather than a donkeyman. A steel ball bearing had to be dropped down each tube in turn, to make sure it was clear. A wooden board with indents, for 36 ball bearings was slid into the top of the boiler. It looked like a game of solitaire.

Petty Officer James Madden, one of the artificers on the *Perseus*, wormed his way in with difficulty, and lay on his stomach in his clean set of overalls in the upper drum. He positioned himself and dropped a steel ball down each tube, to be caught below by Clarence, who had crawled to the lower drum, with a small canvas bag clipped on his waist band. Madden chalk-marked each tube as he dropped a ball down it, leaving what he estimated was enough time for Clarence to catch one ball and reposition himself for the next. After all 36 balls had been dropped, the solitaire board was passed back to the hatch, then to Clarence in the lower drum. He transferred the ball bearings from his bag back onto the board. Clarence stretched and bent in the confined, dark space, feeling with his fingers for the few balls he had missed, as they shot out the end of the tubes. With the board filled again, he passed it carefully back up to the stoker at the hatch who passed it to Madden in the upper drum. Clarence and Madden moved onto the next set of tubes and the cycle started again.

The constant thrum from smaller engines around the ship blocked out all other sounds inside the boiler. The steel walls amplified the deep vibrations in the confined space and Clarence could feel his whole body quivering to the deep bass. The first he knew that another ball bearing was rattling through a tube was when it dropped into his hand. If a ball bearing failed to emerge, the signal from Clarence was four sharp thwacks with a spanner on a tube to alert Madden to stop. Banging hard with a spanner was felt, rather than heard by Madden. The hinged wire brush was then pushed down the blocked tube to clear away the remaining crust and ball bearing, and then they continued.

They had been at it for two hours straight. Madden had missed one of Clarence's spanner taps and kept feeding ball bearings. Two shot down the tubes and rolled off into boiler seams, where they were hard to reach. It was hotter than usual in the boiler and there was a swell in the harbour, making the ship shudder unpredictably, as she pulled against the ropes. The final set of pipes had three blockages, slowing the two men further when they were near the end, and one of the brushes had snapped off at a hinge, needing to be pushed through from the top, by a second brush, which had to be sent for.

When the tube check was completed, the men were ready to crawl from the drum for the boiler hatch to be bolted back into place. Clarence had spent an extra hour once, after all the tubes had been sighted, re-opening the hatch and crawling around blind to find the piece of chalk left behind by an officer.

Clarence crawled out the hatch, a pint of sweat lighter and the palms of his hands throbbing from the sharp rims of the tubes and impact of the ball bearings. He was calculating how long it would take for his saltwater shower, subtracting the number of hours he had already missed on shore before his next duty.

There were tannoy speakers at either end of the engine room; large, folded horn speakers, loud enough to blast out ship's commands above the noise of the engines. As Clarence straightened up, stretching his back, the speaker at his left ear crackled like a pistol shot, followed by the sound of the ship's bugler sounding Action Stations. The volume was painful.

He jerked his head away from the tannoy, cupping his ears in his hands and stumbled towards the centre of the engine room, his Action Stations watch. He had to push through wet boiler suits and underwear, hung on pipes to dry above the boilers while the ship was in port. The smell was a mix of carbolic soap and residual sweat from the bucket washed clothes.

It was a drill. He knew it was a drill and he resented it, but still moved as fast as he could, on trained reflex. There was no time for drills when the *Perseus* was at sea, and the men would have resented it even more, being asked to play at war in the short respites between doing it for real. So going through the dummy runs when the ship was in port was the time used. Fire stations, general alarm and various drills were all dutifully completed on the tacit understanding between men and officers that everybody could move faster when it was the real thing. Men were lined up and lectured about how the time had to be improved, but this was part of the drill too. The men and the officers knew that in the real thing, adrenalin would shave minutes off completion times.

There was a similar, unwritten understanding about shore leave. The regulation was that men had to return to the ship on time, and be capable of walking up the gangway unaided, but not necessarily fit for duty. Each man was trusted with factoring in his own recovery time, before his next watch, as a responsibility to his fellow crewmen, who might be dependent on alert decisions and actions to keep them alive. Shore leave was not compulsory, of course. In the down time, some of the crew would write letters home, or sit playing cards for money and cigarettes, or sleeping off the tensions of the days before. For crew ashore, no one kept track of who went where, except when they didn't come back.

When James Madden was missing on the roll call before breakfast next day, the first thoughts of those who knew him were that the reserved, by-the-book Petty Officer had at last grown some balls and gone on a bender in Rosyth, maybe sunk a few pints, and ended up in a bed more inviting than his own cramped quarters. There were raised eyebrows and smiles exchanged down the line of engineers, including Clarence. There was some satisfaction in seeing that it was not only the lower ranks who succumbed to the temptations of cold drink and warm women ashore.

It was only when the duty officer checked and found that James Madden's name did not appear on the list of men ashore that the alarm was raised.

When his body was found, four hours later, the ship's surgeon could not say with any certainty how the gash on his head had been caused. Only the skin contained by his overalls was still in place. The skin on his hands, neck and face was reduced to a white blubber, with yellow patches of fat, scalded by the steam. The wound on his head was a straight line, the only feature to distinguish it from the other breaks in the skin, where blood and fluids had boiled through. His tongue and tissue on the inside of his throat were swollen and filled the space where his mouth had been.

The first action of the captain was to absolve the boiler crew.

"When Action Stations sounded, you did your duty men and reported to your stations. That is what is asked of you on a ship

in times of war," he said, when he had assembled them on a lower deck.

"*When the two men responsible in the boiler room sealed the hatch, they were following the orders of the chief engineer and that is also what we expect of you.*"

The line of men stood at ease, but rigid, eyes forward.

"*What we could not expect nor predict was that Petty Officer Madden had fallen inside the boiler and was unconscious. The surgeon tells me that in all probability he banged his head, possibly startled by sound of the call to Action Stations.*"

Clarence was already ahead of the captain, picturing what had happened to Madden. He failed to stifle a sob. The Captain glanced at him and then continued.

"*We can be relatively certain men that the Petty Officer did not suffer. He would still be unconscious when the boilers were fired up, and he would be dead within seconds.*"

Except that Clarence and the other engineers knew different.

How long had he been unconscious for the two hours flashing up? Conscious and more aware than anyone on board of the slow process as the steam built up in the boilers. Banging with nothing but his hands on the boiler jacket and the hatch as the temperature crept up, knowing that the noises he was making wouldn't be heard, as he was cooked alive.

Yes, he would be dead within seconds, as the Captain said, but Clarence knew that those merciful seconds would only arrive after suffering minutes when Madden thought his pain couldn't get worse, then minutes when it did, again and again, over an hour, all in the inexorable agony of knowing how it would end.

Would he have sat in a corner and given up, or kept banging on the hatch until the end, believing even then that someone would hear, or would he have tried to find a way to end it quicker? Should engineers Barton and Cruikshank have checked the boiler before they sealed it, even though it wasn't part of their duties? Should Clarence have looked behind him for Madden when the call to Action Stations came? Would he have seen Madden fall or seen him lying there and gone back in, knowing that the Action Stations was a drill?

In the two days in port that followed, Clarence turned it over in his head, more and more in his long waking hours. Each time, the thought came back to what he did. That was the difference between Madden being alive and Madden being dead. The scene played over and over and he was unable to interrupt the loop of memory and pictures in his head once it started. Clarence came back to how he could have saved him, what he could have done differently. Then moving on to what he *should* have done differently.

He played out the timings, placing each of the crew in the replay; where he went when the alarm sounded, what each man did, then what he did. The dark realisation came that he was responsible for Madden's death. While he was wiping the drops of condensation from the side of his first pint in that Rosyth bar, the steam was being fired up to begin Madden's slow death in the boiler. His selfishness, thinking only about how fast he could get from Action Stations to the shower to the bar had cost a man his life. Five seconds it would have taken; a look over his shoulder for Madden following him out the hatch. In those five seconds he had condemned Madden to slow torture and death. It was on him.

Those five seconds, played over and over, taking up more and more of Clarence's time in the days following Madden's death.

The captain had left instructions with Chief Engineer Morgan, following Madden's death.

"Keep the men busy."

That was it. That was the extent of what the captain knew should be done to restore equilibrium in the engine room and get the ship operational again. Death in war had a script to be followed that both the captain and the men could lean on. The crew knew the words – died in the service of his country, brave crewmen, sacrifice that would not be forgotten, redouble our efforts to defeat the enemy, etc. But this was a death in port with no enemy in sight. This was different. The captain had no words, neither did Morgan.

Clarence got through his next few watches and did what was necessary. He cleaned, lubricated, checked, recording pressures and temperatures by rote. But some jobs needed him to be in the boiler room and his memory loop was just as fresh and raw each time he entered.

He was on autopilot for most of the jobs and could lose himself only in bench work, tapping nuts and die cutting bolts, any jobs that needed precision and concentration. The long hairs on his fingers were no longer a hazard for the fine engineering work. In the space of two days, he had chewed through all of them systematically, leaving red, swollen patches on the middle segments of his fingers. In his down time and in his bunk he had moved on to the hairs on the back of his hands, working his way to his wrists, sometimes grinding his way through individual hairs, or grabbing longer hairs and pulling the hair out whole with his teeth.

The pain was comforting in a strange way. He had control over when it came, and he knew just how it would feel. It was also private, something he could do without attracting the attention of the other men. When he was working, he made it look like a simple wipe across his mouth, catching and pulling a couple of hairs each time, until there were so few that they became hard to find.

Even when he was seen by others, yanking out an especially stubborn hair, nothing was said. Talking above the noise of the engine room was impossible. He noticed men look away when he came into the room. He knew they didn't blame him. But when they looked away it confirmed that they knew too. He didn't kill Madden but he was the only one who could have saved him. Nobody said, *"There was nothing Clarence could do,"* because the hard truth was that there was something Clarence didn't do.

He worked, ate and slept. The *Perseus* received new orders and put to sea. The route was known only to the captain and a few officers, but as they steamed north, all on board knew they were headed for Arctic convoy escort duty, rather than sunning themselves on deck in the Med. Three days out of Rosyth, HMS *Perseus* joined the rest of a screen of ships protecting a cargo convoy off Iceland.

Perseus was in the inner, close escort, fifth in a line of eight ships. The convoy was made up of a combination of ships that had been built to fight and a mishmash of coal burning ex-fishing boats and whalers, holds converted to mess decks and guns dating back to the World War I, bolted onto the main decks.

On the day that HMS *Perseus* reached the main convoy, Clarence disappeared.

* * * *

He finished a watch at 1800, as the ship sailed north with no enemy contacts, then failed to report for his next shift at 0600 the following morning. The Chief Engineer didn't report him missing right away. He took aside two men who worked with Clarence and sent them running. Jimmy Morgan had seen the effect of Madden's death on Clarence, or he thought he had.

An hour later the men returned to report an empty bunk, no sightings in the mess, or on deck. Morgan then had no alternative but to report Clarence missing, possibly overboard. More men were recruited in a general, systematic ship search and the call was put out on the tannoy.

The convoy protocol for 'man overboard' was an order to following ships to allocate spotters on port and starboard and pick up the man, dead or alive, unless stopping endangered the ship. The order to ships included details on where and when the man had gone into the sea. The last confirmed sighting of Clarence had been over 12 hours ago. His disappearance was included in the captain's log for the day and a note made to inform next of kin when it was possible.

The convoy continued on its route the next day, the formation of ships tightening in anticipation of attacks. The first ice on deck was seen at 60 degrees north, as the ships drew level with the Norwegian coast and started the wide arc that would take them to Murmansk to deliver supplies to keep the Russians in the war.

Later, the watch commander would record in the log that the incident had happened between the middle watch and the morning watch, in the minutes around 0400 when one set of crew was finding a warm bunk to celebrate sleep and bleary eyed colleagues were taking up their positions to see in the dawn.

One minute he wasn't there and the next he was. It was possible that he had been there longer, that men may have walked past him in the dimmed night lights. The man who found him was a Sub-Lieutenant, like Clarence. Dave Provan was stumbling off to his bunk after another nothing-much watch and his first words to Clarence as he squeezed past were, *"Pull that seat in a bit there engineer – you're blocking that passageway here."* He was on his way through the next hatch before he did a double take.

Clarence was slumped over his beloved bench, arms outstretched and fingers hooked on the far edge. His cheek was flat on the cold metal. He had been missing for 60 hours. When Sub-Lieutenant Provan spoke to him, then shook him by the shoulder there was nothing. When Provan shouted for help, thinking he was looking at a dead body, Clarence opened his eyes. It took three men to get Clarence standing, after prising his fingers from the bench. His hands remained hooked as he was half-walked, half-carried to the sick berth. Apart from his hands, his body was as floppy as a scarecrow.

Neither the ship's doctor, Robin Hamlin, nor the chief engineer got any answers from Clarence. He would turn his head to look as he was spoken to, but would then revert to an unblinking stare, straight ahead. When Chief Engineer Morgan grew desperate, he moved his chair in front of Clarence and took him by the shoulders, their faces less than a foot apart. He kept eye contact. The proximity got a response, of a kind.

"Clarence, we were worried about you. Where have you been hiding for two days?"
"...hiding for two days."
"You need to tell us what's up so we can help you."
"...help you."
Jimmy Morgan spoke louder, squeezing Clarence's shoulders.
"We all want to get you back to work."
"...back to work."
As Morgan moved in closer, putting his face inches from Clarence, Dr Hamlin put his hand on Morgan's arm.

21

"Some sleep needed, I think, Chief Engineer. I'll give Mr Watson something to help him rest and we'll talk again when he's awake."

What puzzled Morgan most was not why Clarence couldn't answer his questions; it was where his best engineer had been. He wanted to know why, of course, what had made the poor bastard want to disappear, but that was for later. Maybe for the ship's doctor or somebody else if they needed to get Clarence ashore for help.

Morgan knew every inch of the ship. That was part of his job. There were places for a man to hide on HMS *Perseus* if he was determined, but not many. It was a ship built for a function, lean and fast, not some cushy liner with spare space for passengers' trunks and stowaways. On the waterline, some dark hollows in the engine rooms would never be visited unless there was a leak. The noise in these spots was more throbbing vibration than sound, a combination of pounding engine pistons and sea thudding against the hull as the ship cut through the waves. Anyone hunkered down there would be shaken like a jelly. Clarence would have lost his hearing and the contents of his bowels. Storerooms in lower deck spaces aft were a quieter option, if he had buried himself behind enough crates of ship's provisions. There were also narrow crawlspaces where some decks joined the hull. These were irregular shaped, metal caves with no heating or lighting. Clarence would know many parts of the ship through his own maintenance schedules. But Morgan found the idea of Clarence wedging himself in any of these cramped, cold spaces for 60 hours hard to believe.

Had he been wandering instead? Walking in other parts of the ship unnoticed. An engineer carrying tools, as men went about their duties. Or had he been moving from one hiding place to another, one step ahead of the general search? In the state he was in, it was difficult to see how he could have done the planning and timing for that.

When he was found, his blue overalls were dry and in one piece. There was no oil or other stains to give a clue to where he might have been. His cap was never found. Whether from the sedative he was given by Hamlin or from the 60 hours on the run, Clarence slept for 14 hours straight in the sick bay.

He took the soup, bread and tea that was offered when he woke up, then curled up in the bed again, without a word. When the doctor left the sick berth for a moment later that morning and came back to find it empty, he reached for the speaking tube, about to raise the alarm. Just as he did, Clarence stumbled back in the door barefoot, with his overalls unbuttoned, wet patches showing a journey to the toilet. The doctor called for Chief Engineer Morgan on the blower instead. They spent another half hour trying to get through to Clarence, getting nothing back but the final echo of their questions.

* * * *

The Petty Sessions were held every three days on the ship, unless the ship was engaged with the enemy. The hearings were on-board justice for both requestsmen, who were "in good", and defaulters, "in bad." The ship's Commander, one rank below the captain, and the Master-at-Arms sat in democratic and public judgement, or as public as a small room on the lower decks could be. They decided if and how men were to be praised and advanced for their deeds, or punished for what they had or had not done.

The defaulter case to be sifted before Clarence was a man on a disciplinary charge for staying ashore at Rosyth for an extra three hours, asleep after a late night drunk. He was only now being judged or "in the rattle" because of James Madden's death in the boiler and all disciplinary hearings having been held over. The Commander had already heard three cases that morning before getting to the late returner and other defaulters. One man asked for compassionate leave (granted at next home port), one complained about sloppy food (heard out in full and dismissed) and a third man asked for the reinstatement of his Good Conduct Badge, lost when his conduct was less than good (also granted).

Morgan accompanied Clarence to the hearing and gently

nudged him forward when his name was called, whipping the replacement engineer's cap off his head and thrusting it into Clarence's hand before the commander glanced up from the papers he'd been lining up, making sure all edges were straight.

It had been a long morning.

The Master-at-Arms read out the charge sheet.

"Sub-Lieutenant Clarence Watson was missing from his post for 58 hours and 32 minutes, without leave, while the ship was sailing."

The Commander stopped tapping the paper edges and sat up in his chair, interested.

"Fifty-eight hours? While we were at sea? Mother of God man, where were you?"

Clarence looked first at Morgan, then at the Commander, then back to the floor. He sniffed but said nothing.

The Commander was used to men trotting out excuses a child would not believe, to escape punishment, or straight out admitting what they've done and asking for clemency. But having a man go dumb on him was new.

"Well, engineer, let's hear it. Where did you go?"

Clarence continued to look at the floor.

The Commander made a real effort to count to five, allowing for a reply from the rough looking engineer. Maybe he's a bag of nerves, caught in the headlights of the hearing, overawed at facing such senior officers, he thought. As the Commander stared at him, Clarence kept his head down and looked first to one, then to another corner of the room.

Having reached his count of five, the Commander gave up. He thumped the edges of his papers on the metal desk, put them down and crossed his arms.

"Right, does anyone else have anything to say on this man's behalf?", he announced in a louder voice, looking directly at Morgan.

Morgan came even more to attention than he already was.

"Yes, sir. If I may. In all the time that I have known him, I have found Sub-Lieutenant Watson to be meticulous in the discharge of his duties and in his time keeping. He is one of my

best engineers, sir. *You will see from his record that he has never had any disciplinary problems, and this lapse is totally out of character.*"

The Commander continued to stare at Clarence as Morgan spoke. He looked down at his papers again, and flicked through them once.

"*OK. Same question to you then, Chief Engineer. Do you know where he was for 60 hours?*"

"*No sir, I do not.*"

"*Mmm.*"

The Commander looked at Clarence.

"*Any final words Sub-Lieutenant Watson?*"

He counted only to three this time.

"*Right. We're wasting time here, yours and mine. Take Watson back to sick berth with you Chief Engineer and bring him back tomorrow, or whenever he decides that he is ready to tell us all about his game of hide-and-seek. Then we may be in a position to make a proper decision. Dismissed.*"

While Clarence slept, Morgan and the ship's doctor, Hamlin, hatched a new strategy. Hamlin would talk to Clarence again, using the information they have. This is what Morgan knows about Madden's death, and Hamlin's knowledge of clinical interviewing, which consists of what he can remember from two lectures he attended, four years previously, on "*Psychology for the Fighting Man*" and "*Talking to the Unstable and Insane.*"

The sick room was basic; two beds, a desk, two chairs, and some medicine cabinets bolted to the steel walls. There is a makeshift operating table in the adjoining room, with instruments, sterilizing equipment and a water supply.

Hamlin was keen for Morgan to sit in on the interview with Clarence. In fact, he insisted, "*In case the patient turns violent,*" he explained. His only experience with use of psychotherapy, he also explained had been during his training, when he saw a psychologist punched in the face for asking damaged people personal questions. What he learned from that experience, he told Morgan, is that leaving both the sick room door and the connection to the operating theatre open just an inch is wise, and the best position for his chair is close to the exit.

They decided to have Clarence sit on the other chair, with Morgan perched on the bed. Hamlin's plan is basic. Probe slowly, working up from the simple to the complex. Starting with questions that need just a "yes" or "no" answer and working up to the questions he really wants to ask: *"Where-the-hell-have-you-been-for-60-hours-and-why-are-you-acting-like-the-lights-are-on-but-nobody's-home?"*

What is needed as a starting point in cases like this, Hamlin knows, is establishing rapport with the patient. If he can get Clarence talking, he will be on safer, more familiar ground, with something to work with in finding out what is wrong and how it can be fixed. Hamlin and Morgan went back to other work and agreed to meet up in an hour.

They roused Clarence. He still looked like he needs more sleep, a lot more.

"So, Clarence, Mr. Morgan and I are here to help you. Are you feeling up to having another chat?"

Clarence looked up at the ship's doctor, then back to some midpoint between the two men, but said nothing.

"We're both keen to find out why you're so tired and what would be best for you. Are you feeling any better after your sleep?"

They wait for the yes or no answer.

This time Clarence looks across to the bed where Morgan sits, as if he might answer for him, then back to nowhere. Hamlin gives it a few more seconds, to see if Clarence replies, but there is nothing.

Hamlin smiled at Clarence, trying to be reassuring.

"It's been a difficult few days for you, I know. We were worried about where you had gone. You did give us all a scare."

He pulls his chair a bit closer to Clarence and touches him on the arm.

"Some of the men even thought you might have gone overboard."

Hamlin gives a short laugh, nodding to Morgan, hoping to draw out Clarence with the shared joke. He smiles at Clarence, looking for anything back. Clarence glances at him, then looks away.

The ship's doctor works through his list of openers to get Clarence talking. He's aware that it's a short list and he's already getting near the end of it. If he could get just one sign from Clarence about why he's clammed up, just one, he could work with that, build up a picture. Is Clarence being cagey, too afraid to talk yet because of what he's done, leaving his post, because of what might happen to him next? Or is it how it looks? There's nothing going on outside because there's nothing going on inside? Is he out of it completely, damaged by Madden's death and by whatever happened to him in the missing hours?

Hamlin considered one other possibility, but it's the most unlikely, given what Morgan has said about the man. Playing the sick card would be the smart way to go in Clarence's circumstances, faking it so that he's dropped off at the nearest port, taken to a cushy hospital bed and given time to recover. There would be no disciplinary charges to face, and a free ride back home, extra R & R guaranteed.

Hamlin changes tact, going from chatty to more formal, to see if Clarence reacts to talk of what might happen to him, or what might not.

"I'd like to reassure you first Clarence that if you're worried about any disciplinary charges, about being a defaulter, away from your post, don't be. Mr. Morgan has sorted all of that out with the Commander."

He looks towards Morgan for confirmation, keeping one eye on Clarence. Morgan plays along, nodding, even although he's had no contact with the Commander.

"So the only thing for us to concentrate on now is getting you well and fit again."

Dr Hamlin pauses again.

"In fact, you don't even have to tell us where you've been. Unless you want to, of course?"

He waits longer than is comfortable, allowing Clarence a bit of processing time, hoping that there will be an answer in the pipeline, something dislodged, just working its way from Clarence thoughts to his mouth.

Nothing.

"OK…we can understand that you might not want to talk about where you've been at the moment. Perhaps you would you like to talk to us about something else?"

From where Morgan is sitting, side-on to the conversation, Clarence appears to shake his head, just once, but it's difficult to tell. It could be just a nervous shiver. The doctor's gaze is fixed on what he can see of Clarence's face, the heavy hair growth of the past few days having made any changes in his expression even more difficult to read. He thinks he sees Clarence's eyebrow ridges furrow in the centre and his lips tighten. It isn't much, but he's had slim pickings on any response so far and it might be something. It might be a start. He follows up.

"We can have a chat about anything that's bothering you, or anything you would like to talk to me and Mr. Morgan about?"

Clarence looks down again, as if something has fallen from his lap and the doctor follows his gaze. Hamlin sits back in his chair. He looks up at Morgan to get his attention, then eye points urgently to the floor.

The painted white steel is wet, small rivulets running from Clarence's bare feet. Hamlin tries to ignore where the water might be coming from, his voice calm, conversational, still probing for an opening.

"What about before you went missing Clarence? Perhaps it would help to talk about what happened then? Can you remember what you were working on?"

Now Morgan sees the wet patch on the floor. It's a thin puddle, advancing toward Clarence's toes, then back again as the ship rocks gently. His first thought is that Clarence has peed himself, either lost control because of Hamlin's questioning, or so far out of it that he doesn't care. But when he looks more closely, the leg cuffs and the rest of Clarence's overalls are dry. The liquid is corralled between his feet.

Morgan watches Clarence more closely. He sees him lean forward, moving his shoulders away from the back of chair. His hands are pushed between his legs, fingers dangling below his knees.

Hamlin holds another long pause, waiting. But Clarence isn't looking at him any more, not even a glance. He is staring at the floor. The doctor decides that he needs to backtrack a bit to regain eye contact.

"*Clarence?*"

"*Clarence? Can you hear me?*"

Clarence raises his head and looks up at Hamlin on the second mention of his name, but without coming out of his hunched position on the chair.

"*I was asking about before you went missing?*"

Clarence mumbles, "*Missing...*". His tone is questioning, echoing Hamlin.

The doctor follows up, encouraged that Clarence has at least said something.

"*Yes, that's right, you were missing for a while. We were worried about you. We're glad that you found your way back to your bench. Mr Morgan needs you in that engine room you know. You're one of his best men. Isn't that right chief engineer?*"

"*That's right, Watson. We need you back on watch as soon as you are able. You're...*"

Before Morgan can finish, Clarence speaks again, louder this time.

"*Engine room?*"

Clarence has turned his head to the sound of Morgan's voice, but now it's Morgan who is looking down. The puddle on the floor has spread. A single, thin rivulet runs out beyond Clarence's toes, advancing towards Hamlin.

Morgan realizes with a shock that it is sweat. Clarence's face and his upper body are dry. There are no patches on his overalls. But the soles of his feet are pumping out sweat.

Morgan looks up, towards the doctor, trying to catch his eye and nod down to the puddle, draw his attention to it. But Hamlin is onto his next question, buoyed by his success in drawing Clarence into talking.

"*Yes, the engine room Clarence, that's right. Good. Now it's*" *starting to come back to you."*

Hamlin decides to take a risk, to strike while the iron is hot. The time is right. He's made a breakthrough of sorts. Clarence is coming back, he's hearing the questions, and responding in some way, even if it's only a word or two. But he might just as quickly drift off again, back into himself, closed down for the rest of the day. Then they'd be back to treading water, with the same routine of unanswered questions, trying to find an opening.

"It will help to talk about what happened to you Clarence. I can give you my guarantee on that. I've met with many men in your position," Hamlin lies.

"Just talking to me and to Mr Morgan privately now will make you feel better. Nothing you say needs to go beyond this room. You've been through a rough few weeks. We both know that."

Clarence has slumped even lower in his chair, his knuckles now brushing the inside of his calves. He raises his head again as Hamlin speaks, straining his neck to look up, like he's imitating a chicken.

Hamlin looks at Clarence, curled up, staring at him. Now he has his attention, all of it. This is the time to move him on.

Morgan is listening to Hamlin, but he is watching Clarence. Something has changed. His gaze is fixed on Hamlin for the first time, and he has stopped moving. The small movements, rocking back and forward in the chair, the threading and unthreading his fingers, the squeezing and releasing his knees have all frozen in place.

"I've seen many men in your position. In times of war, it's so hard to lose fighting men to the enemy. I've lost people I've come to know on other ships, killed by bombs and bullets."

Hamlin is winging it now, making it up as he goes along. He has an idea of where he wants to get to with Clarence now, to get him talking in full sentences, but he has no plan for getting there, other than saying what sounds right to him, moving from one sentence to the next without leaving any give-away gaps.

"Yes, to lose colleagues in battle is difficult, it takes its toll on us all, but to lose someone when we are not engaged with the enemy can be so much harder."

Hamlin thinks he sees Clarence nod in agreement. It's another breakthrough.

What Morgan sees is Clarence's head go down, closer to his knees.

"*We know that you had worked with Madden for a while...*"

Madden's name is the trigger. Morgan sees it hit Clarence as if he had been slapped.

"*...and you and the other men respected him as an officer.*"

Clarence rolls, rather than falls out of the chair. He doesn't have far to go to the floor. As Hamlin and Morgan watch, frozen, Clarence hits the floor and crawls the short distance to the wall of the room on his belly, moving fast for a big man.

His hands start feeling along the solid steel surface until they reach the first joint in the metal plates, marked by a column of painted-over rivets running to the ceiling. With his fingertips, he starts to claw at the joint, pulling his body closer to the wall with the effort. Blood appears, smearing on the white paint within seconds and there is the sickening sound of a fingernail snapping.

Morgan reacts first, jumping off the bed.

Clarence is now up on his knees, to get better leverage to claw at the steel joint. He barges Morgan aside easily with his hip as he tries to pull him away. Blood from both of Clarence's hands is now smeared on half a dozen of the rivets and it is running down the edge of the joint. Hamlin still sits transfixed in his chair.

"*Help me man. Get him away from the wall!*" Morgan shouts.

Taking one arm each, the two men are able, just, to hold Clarence down until he gives up pushing forward on his knees, trying to get back to the unseen hatch on the wall. As passing crewmen, alerted by the noise, come into the room Clarence stops as suddenly as he started, closes his eyes and curls into a foetal ball on the floor.

It takes four men to lift him onto the operating table in the next room. Hamlin bandages six of his fingers, where the nails had snapped off, after washing off the blood and lathering the hands with balm. During the procedure Clarence showed no signs of being conscious, remaining limp and breathing deeply. When Hamlin writes up his medical notes, he is careful to emphasise the care with which he questioned the patient, noting how Clarence's lunge for the wall had come without any warning. His diagnosis is based on a selection of terms he had picked up elsewhere, terms that he hoped nobody is going to question.

He understands less about Clarence's condition after his interview than he did before it.

"*The patient, Clarence Watson (Engineer, Sub-Lieutenant) is of an anxious and unstable temperament. Possible neurasthenia. His behaviour is a risk to the ship. Medical confinement for a period is strongly recommended.*"

The convoy was far from any port, and the needs of the many outweighed the needs of the few. Convoys did not divert for sick or injured crew. Men were treated on board with whatever and by whoever was available.

The captain of HMS *Perseus* read Hamlin's report and was too proud to admit that he didn't know the meaning of neurasthenia. To cover his ignorance, and his fear that Clarence might run amok on his ship, he requested Clarence's transfer to the convoy's rescue ship, HMS *Zenfranan,* with all haste and minimum delay to the convoy.

The rescue ship, as its letter in the alphabet suggests, was the last ship in the convoy. It carried additional lifeboats, cargo nets and well-equipped sick berths, and its principal function was to rescue as many survivors as possible if ships in the convoy were torpedoed or bombed. Taking on Clarence was highly unusual and against Navy regulations, as he was neither wounded nor dead.

In a briefly calm sea Clarence was lowered in a row boat and taken across to *Zenfranan,* where he was confined to a cabin. For the Chief Sick Berth Attendant tasked with guarding Clarence on *Perseus* until the transfer could be made, it was an education in how many hours a man could sleep, even in the roughest sea conditions.

* * * *

The convoy sailed on. The sea was wilder with every degree

further north, until the ships looked like children's toys in a rough pond.

Bear Island was midway between the port of Tromso on the Norwegian coast and the main Svalbard archipelago, a group of islands less than 650 miles from the North Pole. The island was a bleak teardrop of rock and ice, but strategically significant as a meeting point, where outgoing PQ and returning QP convoys crossed paths, or tried to. Critical equipment and information could be transferred between ships, if the convoys could find each other.

The Arctic gales and blizzards faced by both convoys split and scattered ships across the Barents Sea. The first and last ships of the convoy could be 60 miles apart. The number and type of ships that eventually crossed close enough at Bear Island was dependent on the weather and on how many ships had reassembled into the remnants of a convoy. The rendezvous point was also an attraction for the German wolf packs and Ju88 bombers, picking off isolated stragglers on convoys travelling in either direction.

When a storm isolated the Russian freighter *Dekabrist* early in the war, it was torpedoed north of Bear Island. Just four of the 80 crew on board made it to a lifeboat, drifting in the icy sea a further 170 miles further north, to Hope Island. There they survived six months by catching seabirds and harvesting beach jetsam washed up from the many other wrecks. The four survivors became heroes, the story of the *Dekabrist* told around ships' messes in the convoys. It was a tale of endurance and hope in the face of incredible odds. It was an inspiring story about the strength of human spirit. But in reality it was a survival fantasy; four lucky survivors in four thousand. Ships in the convoys caught by the Nazis during any storm or in darkness usually went down with total loss of life within 15 minutes.

HMS *Zenfranan* and Clarence reached the rendezvous at Bear Island, together with six other ships after another three days of rough seas. In poor light, the rescue ship signalled every ship they passed in the QP returning convoy, until they got a reply at last from a sister rescue ship *Zomalek,* a converted ocean-going tugboat. By that time, the sea had a six-foot swell, pushed on by high winds and the light was fading. The ships circled each other in the choppy waters and lined up on a parallel course to do a breeches buoy transfer of *Zomalek,* bound for Scotland.

Zenfranan shot a line across, then the ropes and pulleys were dragged through the water and made secure, as the two ships reduced speed to steerageway. The swell in the waves and the difference in height between the two decks made the transfer even more hazardous, with the risk of the ropes snapping as the two ships rose and fell at different rates in the waves. The captain of the *Zenfranan* ordered every man who could stand onto deck against the port rail, to lean the ship towards the *Zomalek* and reduce the steep angle of the ropes by even a few degrees. They waited until there was a brief lull in the waves and released the brake on the breeches buoy. Clarence, strapped in leg and shoulder harnesses, shot across the gap like he was on a zip wire, at a speed that caused rope burns to the men on *Zomalek.*

The returning ship that Clarence joined was already half full. Injured men from the cargo ships that had limped into Murmansk were bedded in the hold, together with 40 malnourished Polish soldiers, picked up at Kola Inlet. The Poles had been released from Russian prisoner of war camps, where they had been held for a year as counter-revolutionaries, until allegiances in the war changed and they suddenly became allies, released to join in the fight against the Germans.

The *Zomalek* continued, thrown about on the North Sea, with medics trying to keep alive as many men as possible until the ship docked in Aberdeen. Clarence was taken together with the physical casualties ten miles inland to the village of Newmachar and the largest naval hospital in the British Empire.

Despite, or perhaps because of its size, the Royal Auxiliary Hospital Kingseat had become ruthlessly efficient at processing incoming patients. The neuropsychiatric ward, like the rest of the hospital, operated on triage principles, with no exceptions; most urgent cases first, hopeless cases last or not at all. Non-urgent cases were treated when medical staff became available.

All of the psychiatric patients arriving at Kingseat had been referred by ships' doctors. The Admiralty guidance was that except in extreme and obvious circumstances, all men sent ashore as psychiatric cases should be given a diagnosis of "exhaustion" in medical notes, the implication being that rest could cure the condition. To the British Admiralty "exhaustion" was far preferable for public relations and war morale than "psychoneurosis", the term being used for the same combat condition by American psychiatrists.

Navy doctors were asked to use just two criteria when deciding if a man was to be sent ashore: What was his usefulness in battle in his present condition; and was a further, more severe breakdown in his mental state more likely than a recovery. Many of the so-called "exhausted" men being transferred to Kingseat from ships were so disturbed that they had to be first sedated, using soluble barbitone to keep them calm.

Clarence had made the breeches buoy transfer, but his notes had not, and he arrived at the Kingseat neuropsychiatric ward without a diagnosis or sedatives. The psychiatrist who interviewed him, or tried to, was Surgeon Captain H.C. Joy. He decided within twenty minutes that whatever Clarence's diagnosis, it could not be treated within a month at Kingseat. The standard procedure was to move these cases, troublesome and time consuming, without delay to the nearest psychiatric ward in a General Hospital, freeing up a bed for men who could be treated and sent back to ships more quickly.

H.C. Joy, took the unusual step however of requesting Clarence's transfer to a new facility. He was aware of the Royal Naval Camp at Kielder only because his fellow psychiatrist George Thurman had left Kingseat to start work there the previous week. H. C. Joy's referral was based partly on the best interests of the patient, as was appropriate, and partly on dumping George Thurman with a difficult case, as payback for leaving Kingseat with unprofessional haste, before a replacement could be found for him.

The decision to transfer Clarence met with some resistance from the administrative management at Kingseat. H.C. Joy's clinical recommendation could not be questioned of course but a car, a tank of petrol and two men for two days was needed to transport Clarence on the long journey south.

An arrangement was reached after a day's delay and Clarence was handcuffed to a hospital attendant in the back seat while an Aberdeen policeman drove the 200 miles route south. They stopped just once for food and fuel. During the long drive Clarence didn't speak. In the back of the car he slept or tied and untied a variety of navy knots on a piece of brown twine that he held in his free hand.

CHAPTER 2

MARCO THE MALINGERER

At 17, Marco was the youngest of the three Flying Brothers Craston, an act which toured the north of England and Ireland with Corbett's Circus. The circus piggybacked on what was left of a calendar of religious festivals and livestock fairs, dating back to the 14th century. For all that time, people had travelled to meet, to trade and to celebrate on the same patches of grass around the country on the same dates, interrupted only by war.

Little remained of the great Royal chartered fairs and massive horse-trading events, but the dates were still observed for the sale of farm animals and food, and for hiring fairs, where new servants for grand houses could be found. Since the earliest years, performers and showmen had materialized reliably each year on the same dates, on the fringes of these fairs, like migrating animals, finding sustenance in the gatherings of people.

Corbett's circus was a small operation; just 25 performers in total, including two horses and four dogs. Marco, Peter and Paul did a springboard and see-saw act that somersaulted them 30 feet over piles of tables and barrels. Their father and trainer, Joe "Pimpo" Craston, had been the circus clown since before the birth of the first of the brothers. He was always Joe, or Boss to the boys, never Dad or Pop. His ring act was old. It was solid ringcraft, built up over the years, slick and professional but with nothing spectacular or memorable. It did have the advantage that most of the audience had forgotten they'd seen it before by the time the circus came around next time. When he finally admitted that the waning laughs during his act and applause at the end were coming only from those in the tent who were simple-minded and those who would clap at any act, Pimpo realised that it was time to step down.

Joe loved all his boys equally, but he made the decision about his successor without favour, knowing what sold tickets and from his experience of times of both hardship and of plenty.

Marco had been the boy who would sit enthralled, watching his father transform himself from Joe, his father, into Pimpo, putting on his costume and layers of thick red and white, auguste clown make-up. Marco felt the same amazement every time. Joe sat down on the stool, and ten minutes later Pimpo stood up, immediately in role, his movements, like his eyes and mouth, exaggerated. He walked with giant steps and swinging arms, his head lolling on his shoulders.

As they all grew older, Marco was the only brother who showed any interest in how Pimpo got his laughs or what was new in his box of props. Joe loved him for it, but none of that sentiment came into his decision about how to sell tickets and keep the act running. If you were in the circus, you worked to live. That was why Joe chose Marco over Peter or Paul as his successor.

Hard-headed Joe had hammered the need for hard work into the boys, even though working to live had lost him the boys' mother. She had enough of being on the road year-round, juggling the three boys while Joe rehearsed or performed. There was a note one night after a show in Newcastle. She left and Joe never went looking for her.

Both of his older brothers were more skilled than Marco as tumblers. *"When in doubt, tumble,"* was what Joe had taught them all from the earliest days. Peter and Paul could keep the attention of the audience by filling the gaps between the real acrobatics to follow by doing punch fronts and back flips. They would entertain opposite sides of the ring while Marco set up the props for the next sequence. Peter could catch and hold the weight of both brothers and Paul alone had learned to juggle well enough to use it in the act.

Joe knew they could keep the Flying Brothers act going for a few more years at least, even if they had to poach a replacement "brother" from one of the other touring circuses when Paul was too old to tumble.

Necessity made Marco the logical choice to double up as acrobat and circus funny man, in Joe's analysis. Joe could have taught any of the brothers the mechanics to take on the mantle of clown and keep the act going, yes, but Marco was a rarity in floor acrobats who had started practising, rehearsing, and missing catches from a young age. He had something neither of his brothers did; a full set of teeth.

It was important that clowns could smile, and laugh, without reminding parents in the front rows about how much they had paid for a ticket and the money needed for their child's dental work or their own. Next to fire eaters, ground acrobats had the worse teeth in the circus. If a tumbler misjudged a jump or a catch, a knee or a shoulder or a springboard would often be what his face hit first. Air acrobats, on the other hand, had good teeth. Broken backs, necks and death were the main occupational hazards for them.

* * * *

Marco built it slowly. He did ten minutes of his father's old act, without changes, squeezed between two of the main acts, still using the Pimpo name and exaggerated make-up. Nobody in the audience questioned whether it was the real Pimpo, and none of the other performers cared, as long as Marco could fill the slot.

Watching Marco gave Joe more thinking time, and ideas for how his old act could be developed. He thought of how he could have changed the original Pimpo act when he was younger and fitter. He wanted to live what he could have done through Marco. Marco tried hard to incorporate Joe's recommendations in the act, but it was never right for either of them. Joe became frustrated when the new laughs didn't come, and Marco was stuck with an act that wasn't his.

With nothing to lose, Joe conceded to Marco's request to devise a new skit, allowing him just five minutes to begin with. Marco still had his rehearsals for the Flying Brothers Craston and his other circus duties to do, putting up and pulling down the tents, splicing ropes and loading up the acrobat props, moving from town to town. It was only in any downtime that Joe allowed Marco to work on his new act in the empty ring.

It had to be something that didn't come from Pimpo's routine, Marco knew, because it would never be good enough for his father. They both agreed that it was to be Marco's routine, but Joe couldn't help himself. He peppered Marco with what would be good for the act and good for the circus. The skits that all these "new" clowns in the principal circuses were doing, Joe said, were with buffers and prads – dogs and donkeys. Joe told Marco that he didn't want an animal to train, feed, cage and transport around the country. Having the spotlight on an animal when there was a human in the ring was just plain wrong. Marco wanted a new skit, but it didn't involve dogs on bicycles or donkeys wearing hats.

What Marco came up with was the Humpty Tumble. It came to him, the whole sequence of the routine, almost fully formed, when he was watching one of the circus dog acts rehearse, waiting for some time in the ring to run through his own act. It was the dogs' constant motion that gave him the idea. That, and the big build-up to jumping through the hoop of fire.

The Humpty Tumble began simply enough by impressing the audience with spot somersaults, starting and landing on an oversized, spotless handkerchief, taken from his pocket. Then the same routine repeated with another handkerchief, less spotless, from an audience member. A series of perfect tumbles around the ring followed, performing forward and back flips, back tucks and faultless cartwheels, all done with clashing cymbals, a smile and much bowing for applause.

Then he would set up the finale, building it up bit-by-bit, working the audience expectation. He threw a few bentwood chairs into a pile in the centre of the ring, miming his preparation for a giant leap over them each time, before stepping away and deciding to add one more. By the time he had the final, jumbled pyramid of the chairs in the ring, over eight feet high, he had built up his mime to the promise of a full air summersault over the enormous pile. His handkerchief, laid out with precision on the other side of the pile, marked the landing spot.

The next part of the routine was to produce his wristwatch, from a box. The watch was the size of an alarm clock. He got children in the audience involved in a countdown to his run up, getting louder as he urged them on. After three staged, false starts with aborted counts and drum rolls, he finally he took his run, tripped on one of his oversized shoes, flipped high in the air and landed on his back, giant feet in the air, hopelessly entangled on top of the chairs. There was a gasp from the audience before they got the joke and Marco took the laughter and applause.

The chair set up was the most difficult part of the act. He had to make it look like he was just throwing them together randomly, some over his head, but the centre of the pile had to be a flat "nest" that would cushion his landing, so that he didn't break a rib or puncture a lung on one of protruding legs.

The audiences loved it and even more so, he discovered, if they had seen the same routine the night before. They came back for more, bringing others, which was the reason, the only reason, Joe explained, that he let Marco keeping it in the act. Now being introduced as Young Pimpo, Marco extended the act from five minutes to ten, building the expectation and the chairs higher before doing his trip-somersault onto the pile.

In Pimpo's original act, he had never spoken a word in the ring in more than twenty years. It was old school. Circus clowns spoke little, if at all, communicating in the ring through movement and make-up. The truly great clowns however, Marco heard from his father's stories, were allowed a *motto*. It had to be earned, and it had to be short. It had to be something that belonged to that clown only, repeated until it stuck, until it was as much a part of the clown as his name. The clown could start it and the audience would finish it.

All the way back to Joey Grimaldi, through Grock the Swiss and Weary Willie, clowns who had made it big were remembered by their *mottos*. Grimaldi became so big that he had not one, but two catchphrases – *Here we are again!,* shouted out with the audience when he came into the ring, and *Shall I?* when holding a bucket of water or sawdust over a hapless victim.

Marco wanted his own *motto* to add to the act, to make it his alone, even when Joe dismissed it as nonsense for one so young and inexperienced.

"*Clowns that need to tell the crowd what's funny need to work more on their act son, and so do you,*" Joe said.

But like the strong-willed child that he had always been, Marco persisted. He tried out a few *mottos,* bouncing them off crowds for a reaction. Some were too silly, or too long, or had the audience looking elsewhere, thinking Marco was introducing someone else into the ring. Some had drunken guys in the crowd shout back their own *motto,* looking for a laugh, like Marco. He kept trying each night for one that would work, even when Joe started giving him the thumbs-down sign as he came out of the ring after another one had failed.

Then one night he came out with one without thinking about it, while he was splayed on his back in the nest of chairs. It worked for both adults and their children, and for his act:

"*Just a little tumble, just a little dance, Oob-dee-boop, fell on my pants!*"

He started shouting it to the audience between set-ups, with different inflections, depending on where he was in the act. The children picked it up fast. It was short enough to remember, long enough for the anticipation of the final line.

His solo routine became established and extended to twelve minutes. Corbett's circus continued to tour, setting up on Commons outside northern towns for three or four nights at a time, and keeping an eye on where competitors were moving. Most nights the main tent was over half-full, which was break even.

Then the war came.

* * * *

Two of the circus' three lorries were commandeered for the war effort, to move uniformed troops instead of troupes of acrobats. The showman's tractor, a cut down version of more grand traction engines used in larger circuses, was spared from wartime agricultural work as it was the only means of powering the side shows, lights and equipment in the circus, via a flywheel and belt. The chaotic lifestyle of the showmen meant that there was no paperwork to track and conscript them, but six of the able-bodied men, including Marco's brother Paul volunteered as soon as war was declared.

Unlike during the First World War, when the circus coming to town brought unwanted reminders of foreign cultures and languages to a country at war, the British government encouraged touring circuses to continue in 1939, to raise public morale. From September they were restricted however to daylight hours, or to performing under blackout tarpaulins. This hit the already slim profit margins of Corbett's Circus. There was no money for a new, two-pole black out canvas and the daytime shows meant long walks out of town for the main audience, which became women trailing children. By May 1940 the number of jossers – ticket buying public – turning up for the shows barely filled two rows of benches around the ring, and numbers continued to fall as the war abroad and the war effort at home overshadowed every aspect of daily life. Circus seemed an irrelevant luxury to many when news of casualties started to filter back from the front.

The circus tried appeals to the hearts of those left at home by posting signs around town.

"*Come See Corbett's Circus,*" in black lettering, then in red, "*Owing to many of our performers serving in the forces we are sorry that we are unable to put on the circus in the usual size. Trusting you will support our effort. Your ticket money will boost the Spitfire fund.*"

The Spitfire funds were a home front initiative that encouraged locals to raise money through organised events and personal donations for a fighter plane, to be named after their town. Corbett's signs were aimed at selling more tickets, but also an effort to counter growing mutterings in the newspaper columns, and increasingly on the streets, that travellers and carnies were cowards, shirking war duties. Circus performers and gypsies were two separate communities, travelling for different reasons, but this distinction was little understood. Circus slang was derived from Italian, not Romany, and performers saw themselves as bonnah homies – good men.

Stories about carefree travellers, dodging the draft by ignoring conscription notices or moving around the country to avoid having to join up, started in the cities and spread. The image of the pinching, poaching gypsy with no home country and no patriotic interest was added to weekly by newspapers, with rumours that they were using ration books in a number of different towns on the same day, or stealing extra petrol to maintain their travelling lifestyle. Letters to the same local newspapers complained about hired cars full of gypsies driving through town on their way to gamble at the few horse racing meetings still running.

Even cowardly gypsies who were traced and conscripted – or so the rumours went–had devised sneaky ways of failing the medical examination, or faking stupidity to fail the Army education standard.

Any accusation of shirking or malingering in times of war was a serious one. Families who had seen their men go to war to fight saw malingerers as the men who should have gone to share the load, to reduce the casualties, to allow their sons and brothers and fathers more of a chance of coming home alive. That these travellers were avoiding the war abroad and still living the same easy life at home made them an easy target in the first few months of war, when allies and enemies became quickly and clearly defined.

The total of the Corbett's circus contribution to local Spitfire funds from ticket sales would have paid for no more than a few rivets or a couple of spark plugs on a fighter plane, but the black and red signs around town were an effort to set the circus performers apart in the public mind from the urban myth of the malingering gypsies, living on double rations and cooking up hedgehogs on their campfires, laughing at the men who had gone to war. What the black and red signs really said was, "*Look, we are not gypsies and we have made sacrifices, just like you.*"

* * * *

At the same time as Corbett's circus was putting up its posters, the British government was constructing Nissan huts, surrounded by barbed wire; the first internment camps of the war. Foreign nationals, especially anyone living near the coast and considered capable of assisting the Germans with a planned invasion were being rounded up. Corbett's changed the established route for their circus pitches, moving to inland towns and avoiding the coast.

Paul was gone and when Peter told his father that he was signing up too, the Brothers Craston act ended. The big ring had to adapt again. Marco was given 20 minutes to fill the gap on the programme with his clown skits. He developed the Young Pimpo act further in the first month, doing the Humpty Tumble, still getting the laughs, still feeling the buzz. But more and more, with Paul and Peter gone, the times when he was tumbling and being Young Pimpo became the only times when he was not feeling the creeping guilt of being the only brother not fighting the Nazis.

He missed his brothers in the ring and out of it and came to dread speaking to other performers, just waiting for the question he wouldn't know how to answer. How come he was still there when his brothers were gone? He took to more rehearsing and perfecting his act between shows when the tent was up. He avoided whoever he could when they were on the road, travelling between towns.

When the circus pitched up on the outskirts of Carlisle, Joe sent Marco into town for supplies. By then, Marco was convinced that every shop keeper and passer-by on the street had the same question in their eyes. The same question he had asked himself, every day since Peter left. The answer to the question, by that time, was some confused combination of not wanting to let the circus down, not wanting to let the ticket-buying punters down and, the more thought about it, not wanting to see his father forced to squeeze back into the Pimpo costume. If Marco left, Joe would put on the make-up again, in the desperate belief that he could keep Pimpo alive, and earn his keep at the circus until his sons returned from the war.

If Marco hadn't taken a detour on his way back from town with the supplies, his life might have been different. He took a right instead of a left, just to make the walk back to the circus more interesting, and walked past the Royal Naval recruitment office in Carlisle. But then maybe if it had not been Carlisle, it would have been Manchester, or Preston or Durham.

He was inducted into the Royal Navy. It happened quickly. When he had taken that first hesitant step through the door of the recruitment office, it was like he had been swept up in a passing march of men. There was little time for contemplating what he was leaving behind or what was ahead, and no space left for thoughts about backing out. The march was one-way, quick time. Back to the circus with his arms full of the supplies, a quick, guilty farewell to Joe, then he was gone, straight into being processed as a recruit. The burden of decision making was taken from him as he moved up the line, examined, instructed, and then transported.

He learned how to sew, using a chain stitch and red thread to put his name on every article of his uniform and kit, and he learned how to do it again when his stitching failed inspection. He was issued with identity discs, given a medical inspection and vaccinations, and then queued with other eighteen-year-olds to make his Will and Testament. His father Joe had taught all his boys how to read and to count money, but there never was much call for writing. That had been a while back and Marco had little use for reading when he started performing. He could sign his name and sound out words, which was just enough to allow him to sign everything over to Joe in the event of his death.

Marco was given a travel warrant and squeezed onto a train headed for Euston with other new recruits. The 30 "nozzers" were told to sit as close to the rear of the train as possible in case it was bombed. There were more survivors at the back, they were told. Sweating young men were almost sitting on each other's knees in the back carriage as it pulled out. Up the line from Euston to Waterloo, from Waterloo to Portsmouth, then onward by naval buses to HMS Collingwood outside Fareham.

Marco made it through the next ten weeks of seamanship training by watching what others did and by being fitter than any nozzer the training officers had seen. He learned that you tied up your shoelaces, but made fast a ship in harbour. He learned how to march, and how to keep his mouth shut when he saw what happened to others who questioned what the hell marching had to do with being on a fighting ship. He learned how to sling a hammock, the names of decks on a ship, rope work and basics of navigating at sea. His greatest challenge was swimming. Most of the nozzers had been to the seaside as children or had messed about in pools. Marco had never been in deep water, in fact had never been in any water without a bar of soap. But if you were a sailor, you had to be able to swim, unless you wanted to die extra quick if your ship went down. He pushed himself hard, going under, being hauled out, spewing, getting back in, again and again until he could keep afloat from one side of the pool to the other. He made himself believe that he could swim.

The rest was routine, mostly. All that happened on a ship in harbour was timed routine. The times and the tasks changed for a sea routine, but everything was still a predictable sequence. There were shouts, bugle calls, whistles and pipes. Like sheepdogs, men responded, racing to their allocated spots, moving left or right or standing steady, ready to do the master's bidding. Marco took well to training in routines. Circus, the rehearsals, the shows, and the long stretches between shows that the public never saw, had been routines. Moving at the right time, doing the right thing, he could do. He sweated over the classroom sessions and paperwork, trying to copy others when he didn't know what was being asked, bluffing his way to the limit. There were times when he was lost, forced to admit he didn't understand and not too proud to ask one of the other nozzers what it had been about later. But he got through.

* * * *

There were choices at the end of basic training, or at least there were choices offered. Marco went for the motor mechanics course, because he had some experience in working on the lorries at Corbett's circus. He made his choice but what he got instead was gunnery training. Too many nozzers had opted for too few motor mechanics courses. The need for replacement crew on destroyers and battleships became great, very quickly, from the start of the war. A steady supply of new blood was needed.

The guns on the ships had an order. They went from 16-inch barrelled behemoths that could throw a 2000 lb shell over 20 miles to destroy anything it hit, down to two-pound quick firing pom-poms, which danced on deck as they fired at enemy aircraft. Marco learned fast that the power of the big guns, 15- and 14-inchers, and even the 8-inchers, would lift you off your feet or throw you against bulkheads or steel ridges if you were in the wrong place when the warning bell sounded and the guns fired. Where you ended up when the guns opened up depended on the rate of fire and where the other turret crew had found to crouch when the first salvo went off.

In his brief but intensive training, Marco learned the chain of control and why it had to be right. The shells would be transported from the shell room in gun loading cages, together with quarter charges. The loading cage was sent through flash proof doors into the gun house. Marco and other gun crew loaded the shell into the open breach of the gun. The chain rammer tamped it home, then did a final tamp up on the quarter charges in their silk bags before the breach was closed. It had to be done fast–one minute or less–but it had to be done right. When the gunpowder charges were being pushed into the gun, over-ramming could cause them to ignite prematurely. If they were rammed in too far, there would be a gap between the final bag and the primer, which would prevent the gunpowder from lighting, and the gun would misfire.

The same process was repeated by the other two gun loaders, then it was out of Marco's hands. The guns were directed by elevation operators and the gun-ready light came on in the director tower, where the order to fire would be given.

Sometimes the gun loaders got time to find a place to crouch after the bell rang, wedged against something solid, but sometimes not. They were drilled daily to load shells, but not where to take cover, or how to avoid running into each other in the seconds before the guns fired. If you found a solid spot, you stuck with it, unless somebody got to it first. At first, it was like a game of musical chairs in the gun room, until each loader found a nook to hunker down, to avoid being slammed by the sound and shock waves from the guns.

New targets were identified and range set. Marco could hear the creaky pedalling as the guns shifted direction and angle of fire. Loading the shells and tamping them up again and again, the five-man gun crew were moving parts. They worked well together, reliable and efficient as cogs, without emotion; turn, move, repeat, job and finish. Marco thought of himself on autopilot, which always made him smile, as he was on a ship, not on a plane.

Loading was like the circus ring. There was start, set-up, execute. Except there was no finish. There was no round of applause or any way of knowing when the last shell was being loaded. Sometimes it was rapid fire, the vibration of one shell fired still shaking the bulkhead as another shell came through in a cage, ready for loading. Then it could slow to one salvo every ten minutes, then fast again, then with a gap that made you think it was over, before it started up again. There was no way of telling when the last shell had been fired.

* * * *

Marco's first ship after gunnery training was HMS *Devon*. His turret officer was Petty Officer, First Class, Sam Berwick. Berwick treated all of the men in this charge well, knowing that each one of them – gun layers, sight setters and gun crew – needed to believe that they were vital parts of the machinery that was hurling the next shell that could destroy the Nazi ship they were chasing or being chased by. But to operate at their very best, willingly, they also needed to believe that they were more than efficient but replaceable parts. They needed to believe that they were valued, by him and by the captain of HMS *Devon*.

Berwick made it part of his job to read the mood of his men. He knew when things were going well and he knew when his men's morale was fragile, even when the men didn't. Some of it was basics, like checking there was good food in the mess room and the right gear to keep warm on deck on the coldest of seas. The difficult bit was making the men believe, being a convincing leader without looking like you were reading from a book of effective management.

Petty Officer Berwick knew first and last names and got to know each man well enough to learn what he could do to keep him going under pressure. For some men, it was a quiet word, delivered as they squeezed passed each other on a watch. *"Good job, Briggs," "Slick operation there, Davies."* For others, it had to be more public, and louder. For some men he had to ensure that other men were in earshot before dishing out the praise, like a teacher, picking out smart kids in the class who had done homework really well and bringing them to the front of the class. *"Great work, Bradshaw. What would we do without you?",* *"Keep it going, gunner. Great work."* Different strokes for different folks; each man's chest would swell with pride to a different approach.

Berwick could spot Marco from a distance, in a group of hooded gunnery crew, dressed identically. It was his speed and balance. Marco seemed to move on castors across a deck, and when he climbed through a watertight door or went over or around equipment, his head and shoulders stayed straight and level, while his legs did all the adjustments necessary to keep the wheels on his feet running smoothly. He stood out from the other men, as they stooped and twisted their way through the passageways to get to their stations.

Marco was not a talker or a joker, but he was reliable, respected by the men with whom he worked for doing the job, doing it right, every time, without fuss. Berwick learned quickly that Marco didn't need much encouragement to do a good job. Marco knew that he had done a job right without being told by a Petty Officer. A nod from Berwick when they passed and the minimum exchange by both men was enough: *"Craston." "Sir."*

Yes, Berwick knew his men, how they worked and what worked for them.

By contrast, Petty Officer, First Class, Michael Stephens, made a point of knowing men not by their names, or by their work, but by their background. Stephens was the turret officer for the port side gun, Berwick's opposite number on the starboard gun crew.

Stephens did his research by asking around, then using the information gained as a source of amusement for himself and, he fancied, as a source of entertainment for the men who laughed along with him. Some laughed out of ignorance or indifference of the feelings of those being targeted, and some laughed because Stephens was a superior officer and when officers made an attempt at humour, you laughed.

Stephens worked on building the loyalty of his men by drawing them in and isolating them from other ratings. When they were off watch, he would get them together in the mess to eat, or to find space to talk. In whispers, he would share information that he said he had heard from other officers, confidential orders about operations that only his gun crew were privy to.

Stephens also like a bet, to keep his crew busy in downtime, and to keep them tight as a group.

"Nothing to break the bank boys, just a bit of fun to keep the spirits up, and maybe win a few shillings while we're at it."

With dog racing restricted to one day a week back home and the form and results from the horse racing cards hard to come by, Stephens was reduced to friendly card games with penny antes, but there was one daily gamble where real money could be made, especially by him.

While the ship was sailing, there would be bets on the estimate of the ship's run for that day. Stephens would first announce to his crew the Captain's own distance estimate for the day. This was something he had learned from a confidential source on the bridge, he said. His men could then bet on any number, ten miles above or below the Captain's estimate. There was also a high-field and a low-field estimate to bet on. The high-field was any number more than ten miles above the Captain's estimate, the low-field was a bet on the number of miles travelled in the day being more than ten miles less than the Captain's estimate. Stephens would allow all of his men to choose their number before betting himself. There were no restrictions and more than one bet allowed on any number. Stephens' preference was the high or low field for his bet.

The miles travelled would be announced by Stephens the following morning, and monies paid out, after he had verified the mileage from his confidential source. Stephens won more of the ship's run bets than would be expected by chance, but not so many as to raise any suspicions about his source on the bridge, or the fact that only he could confirm how far the ship had travelled.

Another, riskier bet among the port side gun crew was on how many ships the convoy would lose in a day. Stephens restricted the bets to one number per man, and his crew were sworn to secrecy.

"Not everyone on this ship would appreciate that betting on this is just a bit of fun men, so best to keep this one among ourselves."

Playing cards were auctioned off in the mess, starting at the ten of spades and working down to the ace, the death card. The bidding was highest for lower numbers, but if there were no bidders for a card, a man might bid just to have a chance for that day. The rules were that winner took all, and more than one member of the gun crew had to witness the sinking for the kill to count. Stephens kept the book on who owed what, to be settled up after the next Pay Parade. When money was tight for any of the crew, Stephens would put up some betting money in exchange for a watch, a lucky medallion, or a cigarette ration, all of which could be redeemed when the man was again in funds.

At just an inch above the minimum height requirement, he may have had small-man syndrome, but there were many other men on board smaller who were less cruel and spiteful than Petty Officer, First Class Stephens. The Germans, who they were all trying to kill, might have called it *Schadenfreude,* but it was more than that. Yes, Stephens took pleasure from seeing stuff happen to others – a junior rating take a bollocking from an officer, or a crew member forgetting to duck and almost knocking himself unconscious going through a doorway – but he got most of his kicks from creating situations where a man was embarrassed or demeaned. For Stephens, the bigger the audience, the bigger the kicks.

He found out that Marco had been a performer, an acrobat, and started calling him *"monkey boy,"* conflating circuses and zoos. Every time they passed on the ship, Stephens would bend his arms and scratch each of his armpits in turn. If he was behind Marco, he would attempt to imitate his gliding walk, but with bowed legs and a swaying gait. If Stephens was in a group with his turret crew and Marco was in earshot, he would make casual but loud enough reference to how much he missed bananas when they were at sea or wondering when they would next see a tree.

Marco was not the only target for Stephens, but he was a frequent one. It irked him that Marco didn't respond, no matter how hard he pushed. There were no angry looks, no avoiding Stephens as they moved about the ship in their duties, no backchat to a senior officer, nothing. Stephens avoided the jibes and jokes at Marco's expense when Petty Officer Berwick was around, but when it was just Marco, he escalated, pushing him for a reaction.

Between the circus and joining up, Marco had limited experience of people from other classes. Audiences at Corbetts were people who worked, made a bit extra and chose to spend it at the circus. Naval officers were not the type who went to the circus. They didn't speak like him, they dressed and walked differently, and they were used to ordering others about. It was easy to fall into his place. Marco assumed that Stephens was some lower form of this upper class. He was Petty Officer, so not quite real officer class, but still above him in rank and status. He also assumed that Stephens' cruel streak was what some people of that particular class did, because they were able to.

He took it and kept taking it over the first two months on the ship because he didn't see that he had a choice. He was a traveller serving in the navy, even lower than most of the rest of the ratings around him and Stephens was a Petty Officer, First Class, with the privileges that gave him over lower classes.

As Stephens stepped up his harassment, Marco became aware

that it was getting to him more often. Not that he reacted, but each time he was the butt of one of Stephens' clumsy jokes he took a bit longer to pass it off and get his focus back on what he was doing. He looked like he was ignoring the provocation and he kept working, doing what was necessary well, but he started turning over what Stephens had said, what he might have said back, what he would like to have done.

He could've walked more like a monkey, bounced it back to Stephens, or he could have used one of the comebacks he'd heard in the mess room when crew were trading insults. But it wouldn't be him, it would be Stephens forcing him to pretend to be somebody else. The same jibes, over and over, became predictable, even in time and place. It should have become background noise, like other ship sounds that Marco could tune out. He knew that. Instead, the sound of Stephens' voice cut through other noises. It became grima, like a knife being scratched across a plate, or the sound of the dentist drill. Marco had only ever been in a dentist's chair once in his life, but the whine of the drill, or anything like it, still caused him to clench his teeth and had the tendons on his neck standing out like he was lifting something heavy. Marco started to tense up when Stephens was around.

Stephens kept picking away, angrier and more desperate with each day that he couldn't get a rise from Marco. He still got the laughs from his gun crew sycophants, dutifully reacting to his badgering of monkey boy, but it was the bigger laughs that he craved, the ones that would come only when Marco reacted and he had the satisfaction that he was getting to him.

* * * *

HMS *Devon* had to dock to refuel, rearm and have running repairs done at Greenock, prior to being part of the next PQ convoy via Iceland. To speed the process of preparing the ship, there was no shore leave. The Captain's orders to all his officers were simple; "*Keep the men busy at all times; keep their mind off going ashore.*" For some crew there was the monotony of radio and standing anchor watches, trying to stay awake or avoid being caught asleep, for others there were drills to improve battle reaction times. The standby jobs for the rest of the crew were cleaning and painting. Any part of the ship that had been touched by salt water was scrubbed and washed down, any piece of equipment that used grease or oil got checked and re-lubricated, and where patches of the ship's standard, medium grey paint had been chipped or flaked off, it was sanded and redone, in unskilled brushstrokes.

Most of the paint damage was at deck level, from feet, wheels and dragging crates. Around the base of the mast there was chipping, where wires had been used to run up signal flags at sea, to warn of incoming aircraft and keep radio silence.

Stephens was bored, in charge of a work party painting an area of deck that included the base of the mast. Marco was working on scrubbing down drainage channels on the port side of the ship.

Stephens first checked that Berwick was not around, then shouted Marco over.

"*Sir,*" Marco saluted.

"*Correct me if I'm wrong monkey boy, but it seems to me that you are at a loose end there, scrubbing clean paint. I've got a special job for you,*" he said, glancing about to make sure that he had the attention of the other men painting.

"*Thought we'd make use of your particular skills. Get yourself up the mast there, chop chop, and report to me on any damage to paintwork.*"

Marco looked around at the mast, propped his scrubbing brush behind a door, walked over slowly and started climbing the metal rungs, stopping every few feet to inspect the solid grey surface. He stopped at twenty feet.

"*No damage to report, sir,*" he shouted down.

"*Good job Craston,*" Stephens shouted up.

"*Now while you're up there, have a look at that yardarm. I think there may be some chipping and wear from the flags. Might need a paint touch up.*"

Stephens' shouting stopped the work of the other painters and a dozen other men in earshot, who raised their eyes to the mast.

Marco looked up at the yardarm, another thirty feet above him and paused.

Seeing his hesitation, Stephens shouted again, *"It's OK, we'll get some paint and brush up to you in a bucket, it that's what you're worried about."*

This got quiet laughs from two of Stephens' gun crew lackeys.

"Keep climbing Craston. I think you're a natural," Stephens continued, sniggering.

Marco sized up the handholds on the mast and started moving. It took him another four minutes to reach the cross piece on the mast, where the yardarm extended left to the shore side and right, pointing to the harbour. He looked both ways along the paintwork. Down below, there were now twenty faces looking up.

With one arm wrapped around the mast, he cupped his other hand, and shouted down, his voice steady, *"No damage to report on the yardarm, sir."*

Stephens had his crowd, and their attention, glancing from him to Marco and back, but he didn't have the laughs he had planned. Craston hadn't bottled it, as he'd hoped, hadn't thrown his arms around the mast, looking even more like a monkey, shaking and asking to come down. He hadn't refused the order to go any higher, hadn't begged Stephens to let him climb back down. Stephens felt panic growing at the thought that Marco would climb down, unaffected, and the crowd would pat him on the back. He knew he had to get them more worked up, back with on his side. He gambled, desperate to keep their attention.

"Check the yardarm for damage, Craston. Get yourself out there and inspect the paintwork for chips."

The upturned faces looked down from Marco to Stephens, questioning if this was a serious order to be carried out, or a joke. Was it something just to bring laughs? Marco had the same thought and paused again.

"Go on man, we can't wait all day!" Stephens shouted. *"Check it."*

All faces looked back up.

Marco kept his position for a moment, then started to climb

56

higher slowly until he was level with the yardarm. He paused then stood up, both feet on the yardarm, both hands on the mast, and looked left and right. His left leg began to shake, and he lowered himself to a sitting position astride the yardarm, facing the harbour, his back against the mast.

"*Don't sit down on your arse up there all day Craston, you lazy bastard,*" came the shout immediately, "*check for damage further out.*"

Shuffling forward on his bum and holding onto the stay wire, Marco edged carefully along the narrow pole, inch by inch. At eight feet away from the mast, he stopped. The yardarm was tapering and he was having to make more adjustments to his balance the further he went. He looked down between his legs and noticed that the wire stay had chipped the paint near one of the metal eyes through which it was threaded. It was at a point where the wind had brought the wire against the yardarm, again and again, over months, slowly wearing down paint that could withstand a hammer blow without damage. It was a chip that went down to the grey undercoat, but not to the metal beneath.

But hanging onto the stay wire, ten feet from the mast wasn't about damage to the paintwork. He knew that. Marco looked down again at the faces. They were still close enough to count, but too far away to recognise individually. He could spot Stephens by the circle of space around him. He was shouting again, but Marco couldn't hear what he was saying above the wind, and the rattling of the stay wire on the metal.

Below, some men started to drift away from the pack in ones and twos or moved to places on the deck where they could still see Marco, but not be associated with Stephens' show as it threatened to spin out of control. It was a laugh, harmless fun, to take a break from scrubbing and painting and cleaning that could wait, to watch Marco forced up the mast, climbing to a height of signal flags. It was something else to be around if things went badly wrong. You could be asked where you were, what you saw and what you did to try to prevent what happened.

By the time Marco had slid out to where the yardarm was thin enough for him to encircle it with both hands, only members of Stephen's own turret crew were left at the foot of the mast, together with a few slack jawed extras, all eyes fixed on Marco. He was leaning forward, chest almost on the metal, and pulling himself along with his arms. Stephens was now sounding hoarse. He shouted first to Marco, then appealed to what was left of the crowd.

"Deck to Craston, deck to Craston. Return to base."

He addressed the remainder of the crowd.

"See, that's the problem with monkeys, men. Getting them to climb a tree is easy because they do it every day. It's getting them down that's the problem."

Only the most devout of his followers managed a forced laugh.

Marco was now almost as far as he could go. Conditions in the harbour were calm, but there was incoming swell. On the mast, the ship's gentle roll at sea level was translated to six feet of see-saw movement on the end of the yard arm. Marco focussed on the blunt end point of the yardarm and watched it dip below then above the sea horizon, four miles out.

"Mission accomplished Craston. Stand easy!"

Stephens' shouting was through cupped hands.

He turned and pointed at the men standing around him.

"Remember, you men are all witnesses now. That was a direct order to disengage."

The men around Stephens shuffled their feet and looked anywhere but up.

Marco sat up straight, with one hand on the spar between his knees and the other holding the stabilising wire, angled from the end of the yardarm to higher up the mast. He heard the words of Stephens' last shout, and as the wind dropped he also heard his aside to the men below.

When he had joined up, he had put up with the discipline as a nozzer, in the belief that doing all the polishing, straightening, sewing, marching and standing was in preparation for fighting the Nazis, even if he couldn't always see the connection.

Somebody smarter than him, far smarter, had a master plan to get sailors ready. There was somebody who knew all the details. Somebody who knew that competence in both rope work and needle work would be needed to win the war. That the training seemed irrational to Marco was only because he wasn't high enough up to have an overview of the plan, to be able to see how all the pieces fitted together and moved. He was a very small piece in the plan. All he needed was orders to follow and a bus-load of faith that the plan would work.

But sitting at the end of a yardarm as the swell in the harbour increased was not in that master plan. He was pretty fucking sure about that.

Ignoring Stephens had been the line of least resistance. Marco had been close to *"bugger off"* a few times. Drawing a line in the sand to let Stephens know that he wouldn't take it, day after day. But then it wasn't day after day. It could be once a day some days, then a break for a few days when he never saw Stephens, then it started again. It was a comment, a joke at his expense, then it was over and he could ignore it, forget about it, and get back to the guns and what he was good at. But ignoring Stephens hadn't worked for Marco, and it hadn't worked for Stephens, who was now shouting again. It was loud enough to be heard by the small groups of men scattered around the deck, cleaning and painting forgotten.

"I hope you're not sleeping on duty up there Craston. Swing down from that tree any way you like now. You can't expect these other men to do all your work for you while you admire the view."

Stephens was now the only person laughing at his jokes.

The stabilising wire was tight, unlike the stay wire suspended on the yardarm. Marco held onto it with both hands and brought one foot then the other up in front of him, his ankles crossed. The rubber soled deck shoes gave him grip as he rose first to a squatting, then smoothly to a standing position, pulling hand-over-hand up the angled wire above his head to straighten up. There was only a light breeze as he stood up, looking from below like some ancient mariner trying to spot whales or land.

When he was at Corbetts, his balance wasn't something he consciously worked on. He'd seen other circus tumblers do hours of exercises, one-leg stands, one-hand stands, at floor level and at height. Rehearsing every day with his brothers he could hold his position, fly straight and make the quick adjustments when he landed. He always knew which way was up when he was in the air, and it was this ability alone, he believed, that allowed him to keep a full set of teeth.

Stephens started his hoarse shouting again when Marco stepped out to the end of the yardarm, holding the stabilising wire with just one hand. When Marco put his back against the wire and slowly extended his arms out from his sides, the shouting reached a new level. Below, it sounded like screaming. From above it sounded like a goat bleating.

"*Craston! Craaaston!*"

Marco looked down at his feet, adjusting so that his left was behind his right, forming an inverted T. He waited for the ship to roll again, until the tip of the yard arm was at its lowest point on the roll above the water in the harbour. Then he dived.

Some of the crew further down the starboard side of the ship, who had not been watching events on the mast, caught movement in the air and saw something fall, fast, followed by frantic "man overboard" shouts, then the tannoy blasting out the same alert. Most of the men went back to what they were doing, assuming that it was the "Dead Fred" kapok doll, thrown over the side for one of the monthly drills. Unless you were designated rescue crew or close enough to get sight on the body in the water, there was no action needed.

Marco missed the side of the ship by three feet and his dive was parallel to the hull all the way down. He brought his arms together above his head, fingers locked, just as he passed the now hysterical Stephens on deck. His entry into the cold harbour water would have had the Olympic judges reaching for the big number scorecards. There was the sound of paper ripping, a ring of bubbles and he was gone. From the height of the yardarm Marco knew the dive needed to be good to avoid knocking himself unconscious on impact, which he almost did as he panicked to get back to the surface and came up under the ship, banging his head. He pulled himself along the hull the last few yards and gasped a lungful of air, doubly shocked by the depth he had gone down and by the temperature of the water.

He had convinced himself that he could miss the deck if he pushed out hard enough as the yardarm dipped. From there, it was just getting his feet right, finding his point of balance and concentrating on going far enough out horizontally before gravity kicked in.

His navy swimming instructor had taught the nozzers to avoid gasping for air and thrashing about if they fell into cold water. The trick, the instructor said, was to take a minute to float, conserve energy and calmly assess the best way to get out of the water. Good advice, except Marco had planned no further than making the dive, and he was now slapping against the hull in the swell, kicking and feeling the weight of his wet uniform pull him down.

Marco heard a rope hit the water behind him, then saw a ship's life-ring as it flew through the air further out. He kicked off the hull and made it to the rope, already shivering. Linking his feet, he started to climb, hand over hand, until his feet cleared the water. Shouts and signs from above told him to wait, and a rope ladder rolled down the hull. He dropped off the rope, back into the cold water, going under again, before making it to the rope ladder with just his face above the surface. When he was on it, the speed with which he climbed surprised the men puling the ladder from above and he was back on deck just 15 minutes after diving. Wrapped in a blanket he was led through a curious but silent crowd to the sick berth.

Next morning, the watch commander convened a Captain's mast, an enquiry short of a full disciplinary hearing. Of all the men who could be identified as being at the base of the mast, none saw what happened. Stephens reported that Marco misunderstood his orders about checking for damage on the mast, and when Marco was called he said that he slipped and fell from the yardarm while checking for damage to paintwork. No offences committed, no disciplinary action needed, and all men returned to duty. End of hearing.

As they walked back to the gun stations, Stephens came up close behind Marco and muttered, "*You're a cocky little bastard*

Craston, and a lucky one. Don't think that I don't know it. You've gotten me the run around with the watch commander now, and I could have been in shit with that Captain's mast because of your Tarzan act."

"*Yes sir,*" Marco replied, as they turned in separate directions to re-join their respective gun crews.

* * * *

The ship went back to sea the next day and Marco went back to duty with nothing more than a mild ringing in his ears and some whispered pointing from other men to remind him that he had dived from the yardarm. But something had changed.

Stephens backed off a bit. Marco couldn't tell if there were fewer jibes directed at him, or if he was again more able to ignore them. Over the following three days, they sailed North West, colder each hour. The shells and charges came into the gun house, were loaded, tamped and test fired. The process was repeated, again and again, in readiness for the real thing.

Marco first felt the ache in his stomach when the guns fired at enemy ships for real. He had felt something from the first test firing, when he was unprepared for the terrible power of the 14-inchers blasting out their shells. He put it down to a nervous excitement, then as he learned to load and then find a space before the gun fired, he dismissed it as a stomach cramp from crouching fast, wedging himself in a corner. Turn, move, repeat. Down time wasn't down time. It was crouching, tense, waiting for the next shell, and hoping it was coming on wheels through the flash proof doors and not through the air from an enemy ship.

Outside the gun house his stomach never bothered him. The food he ate was one of the unexpected joys of joining up. Meals, such as they were, at Corbett's circus had been taken on the run. It was eggs and cheese, bread, potatoes, a chicken if they could catch one, stews and soups made with whatever was available in the nearest town.

The discovery of the food in the ship's mess was an adventure for Marco. Some of the stuff spooned in dollops onto his plate as he passed the serveries looked familiar, but it tasted exotic, and the dishes had names that added to the mystery for him. His fellow gun crew complained about the repetition of standard dishes; balloons in a fog (sausages in mash) or a train smash with cackle berries (tinned tomatoes with bacon mixed in, and eggs), but for Marco meal times were the highlight of his day. His favourite, one dish that he would risk being caught on a second run at the server for, was raisin duff with tinned cow (sweetened condensed milk). If the ship went down and he made it to the desert island alone, he reckoned he could live on that one dish for years.

But now, a week out of port, the ache in his stomach was more persistent. Each time he pulled on his anti-flash hood to begin his next set of hours in the gun room, his stomach felt like he'd bolted a meal, then sprinted all the way from the mess to the gun turret with his dinner still sloshing about. It was indigestion, an acid burning rising into his chest to begin with, but as the week went on it got worse. His guts started to churn and go into spasms, like a fist squeezing quickly and releasing slowly, while he was working. Always beginning at the start of his watch, but lasting longer each time. A definite, intense cramping when he was in the gun turret, but a building background ache when his watch was approaching. Marco's days started to revolve around his stomach.

He tried not eating some of the foods in the mess, then not eating at all before he came on watch, then not drinking any tea before he came on watch. None of that worked. He just ended up with more painful cramps and feeling weaker. From being the highlight of his day, he began dreading going to the mess, knowing that he had to eat to work, but already tasting the bile and feeling the cramps to come as he spooned food into his mouth.

Ten days after his swallow dive from the yardarm in the harbour, Marco reported sick. HMS *Devon* had just cleared Iceland, hitting the worse snowstorms and heaving seas that most of the crew had ever experienced. Men slept fully clothed as the temperature dropped further.

Two of the ship's crew were laid out in the cabin next to the sick berth, cut and bruised from slamming against a bulwark on deck during the storm. Marco had to report to Sick Berth Petty Officer, Nigel Thompson, who was the gatekeeper for the ship's Surgeon Lieutenant "Crooner" Reeves. Thompson was first aid trained, but he would only treat men who were injured or ill if high casualties were sustained in sea warfare. His main role on board, a job he had decided for himself, was as the malingerer filter for the sick berth, and he set the bar high when it came to a man being ill enough to be seen by the ship's doctor.

Whether it was to alleviate the depression of having treated, and lost, so many men in war years during his service as sea, or whether it was as a distraction to the daily grind of minor and major repairs to bodies, Surgeon Lieutenant Vaughan Reeves sang, almost constantly. He first did it during his early hospital operations, to fill the silences he suspected. But now he sang or hummed most of the time when he was not speaking. It was snatches from arias and overtures mostly. The Marriage of Figaro, Don Giovanni and La Traviata were his favourites, with volume ranging from a closed lip humming of main themes when walking about the ship, to full-blooded baritone blasts in the relative privacy of his own cabin.

"*Enter,*" said Petty Officer Thompson, when Marco knocked on the sick berth door. Marco went in, saluted and stood to attention, as Thompson turned to face him, putting aside some crystals that he had been grinding for use in the small dispensary.

"*Well sailor?*"

"*I think I've got the misery sir,*" Marco said.

Marco's vocabulary had never been a problem in the circus. Everybody who had been born there understood the jib, and the few who were incomers who joined the circus picked up the lingo fast. But in the navy, he was always behind the loop, from the day he signed up. He was embarrassed to ask what had been said in some of the training sessions when he didn't understand, and then too embarrassed *not* to ask when he didn't know a second time. Then there were posh accents, when the same words he thought he had learned sounded different. When one officer told his men that he had been a fencer before the war, Marco listened and wondered how someone so skinny could swing a sledgehammer, until the officer started talking about different type of swords that he'd used.

There were words everyone understood except Marco, and when he spoke, he could tell from the expressions on faces that there were some words that made no sense to anyone but him. He was fast on the uptake for navy words that were new to all the recruits in training, and he got the hang of mess room balloons in a fog, cackle berries and raisin duff, but there were some words he heard men using every day and it was now past the point where he could ask anyone what they meant.

When the ache got bad, he had gone first to Petty Officer Berwick, whom he trusted, trying to explain his symptoms, hoping that it was a well-known condition, with an equally well known and easy cure.

"*I'm molti naflo sir,*" he blurted out, "*sick in my guts and sick in my head.*"

Berwick sat him down and asked the right questions, but what Marco described was beyond his experience. He decided to send him onto Thompson, and hopefully to Crooner Reeves.

"*The misery, sailor? What in God's name is that, when it's at home?*" said Thompson, taking off his glasses and turning in his chair to face Marco.

"*Well, I'm off my grub, sir, right naflo like I've never been before, and my head aches nearly as bad as my guts,*" said Marco.

"*OK...and how long has this been going on?*"

"'*About two weeks solid, by my reckoning, sir, getting worse on every watch, even when we ain't firing. My guts have got me bent double sometimes, like somebody's squeezing them hard.*"

"*Wait a minute sailor,*" said Thompson, leaning back in his chair, and pointing his glasses at Marco.

"*You're that gunner who came off the yardarm aren't you? Caused all that man overboard fuss before we left port in Greenock.*"

"*Yes, sir, that was me,*" said Marco, "*I fell off the yardarm.*"

"*Ah, well then,*" continued Thompson, nodding knowingly, "*God knows what you were doing up there in the first place, but that's probably the cause of your so-called "misery", see.*"

Marco continued standing to attention, but looked at Thomson, puzzled.

Thomson took out a handkerchief and started to clean his glasses.

"*You've smacked your head in the dive and probably swallowed some of that filthy Greenock harbour water. God only knows what's in it from the ships in port, and it had been raining for two days if I remember right, so then there's all the extra muck from factories upstream being swept downriver. It was a damn fool stunt to pull, by the way and you're lucky that...*"

Thompson continued speaking and Marco continued looking at him, but he was no longer hearing what was said. His attention was retuned, like a radio dial being turned. He tuned out Thompson and focused on sounds coming from the adjoining cabin. Quiet but melodic singing could just be heard above the constant hum of the ship.

"*Madamina, il catalogo è questo, delle belle che amò il padron moi...*"

The language and the words were unfamiliar to him, but the melody hooked Marco, taking him back to the circus. It was the sound of the special introduction that brought in the trapeze act, scratchy music blasting out the speakers, paced just right for the performers climbing up to the wire.

"*...un catalogo egli è che ho fatt'io, osservate, leggete con me.*" The singer next door took the volume up a notch, holding the notes longer than necessary, just to show that he could.

Marco had heard the tune played hundreds of times but didn't know what it was called. It was always just the trapeze act music to him. His thoughts drifted from there to the music played for the entrance and performance of the Flying Brothers Craston. It was a brassy screamer, played fast, blasted out at top volume. It was the same circus theme played at the beginning of the evening and again at the end of the circus, when performers waved their goodbyes, going around the ring. So when it was played during his act with his brothers, the music was familiar to the audience and not particular to the tumblers' act. What made the music special to Marco was knowing the name of the piece. *The Entrance of the Gladiators,* it was called. It gave him a buzz thinking about it, entering the ring with his brothers, seeing the crowd clapping, soaking it up. He imagined other brave gladiators stepping out to entertain crowds long ago, thinking himself a descendant of what he thought of as the first circus performers, men of strength and honour, facing death or glory.

"*...so there's nothing much more than that to be done,*" Thompson finished, looking round at the work waiting to be done on his desk, and only looking up at Marco when the silence stretched out.

"*Seaman?*"

"*Yes sir, dirty water sir,*" Marco said, coming back to the conversation.

"*Yes, so come by and pick up the pills later, when I've had some time to put them in a bottle.*"

Marco was confused. "*And will I see the doctor then sir?*"

Thompson took off his glasses and rubbed the bridge of his nose. He looked away and then back at Marco

"*Have you heard anything I've said man?*"

He took a breath and then spoke his words slowly, adding pauses between sentences.

"*You don't need to see the doctor. He is very busy. You've picked up something foul in the water. I'll give you some tablets that will clear you out and settle you down. You'll be fine in a few days.*"

He paused.

"*Now, do you understand all of that? Do you want to ask me anything else?*"

"*Yes sir, no sir,*" Marco said.

"*OK. Good. You can report back for your next watch as usual. There is nothing to worry about. You've got a gippy belly, that's all.*"

Thompson turned back to the mortar and pestle, to continue grinding the crystals, with his back to Marco. Marco continued at attention for a moment, waiting for Thompson to say more, then turned and opened the cabin door quietly.

The dimly lit white passageway was deserted. He stepped through the first watertight door and walked to an elbow in the passageway, where he could hear anyone coming down the stairway before him and see anyone in the passageway behind him. He stopped, put his back against the cold steel wall and banged the back of his head twice on the flat metal. He knew dirty water wasn't making him sick. It was the misery. The gippy belly tablets, bottled by Thompson that day, would be useless.

* * * *

When Marco was a boy at the circus, Tuflo was a performer. Marco had watched him die and the memories haunted him.

Marco had seen Tuflo pick up single strands of straw, throw them and pick them up again, until the straw was reduced to dust, then rock back and forth where he stood for a while, then find more straw and start the whole routine again. When he was in the ring he'd do a listless run through of his tricks, the bare minimum of what was needed to avoid being hooked by his trainer, then wander off and have to be led back.

His trainer would tap his back legs with a metal pole to bring him back to the wooden pedestal, where he was to sit, stand on two legs or bow to the crowd. Out of sight of the crowd, the hook on the end of the pole would be used to tap him behind his ears and on his trunk, where he was most sensitive. In training, the pole would go for the first three times to his legs, then once to his ears, then to his trunk if he still didn't respond fast enough. Tuflo learned to do the tricks in the ring on the second tap to his legs, but towards the end his trainer was tapping him constantly in the ring, just to make him move at all.

Out of the ring, Tuflo started doing the same repetitive routine that he did with the bedding straw with his hay when he was being fed. Instead of eating it, he'd curl his trunk around a truss of hay and toss it over his back. Then he would pick up a single strand delicately and throw it, waiting until it landed before choosing another. He stopped eating and became too weak to perform, lying on his side for most of the day. From the time Tuflo started throwing strands of straw to the day he was led away to be shot was less than three months. Marco remembering him being buried in a farmer's field that had the largest sewage works in north east England on one side and the second largest one on the other side. It was a sad end for a performer. Tuflo had had the misery bad.

Marco remembered the decline of Tuflo, an undersized Asian elephant, not because he'd been shot – that happened to all the animals that were no longer able to perform –but because he had died of the misery and because the elephant had been younger than Marco. Up to that point in his life, Marco had never considered the possibility that anything younger than him could die. In his head, there was an order. Young things didn't die. They were just getting started. After Tuflo, Marco looked at people in the circus differently, wondering who might go next.

* * * *

Marco dreaded night watch in the gun turret most. It was when surface torpedo attacks were most likely. What little chance the ship's spotters had of detecting a U-boat conning tower in daylight was reduced to zero by the dark and the choppy seas.

Inside the turret, the crew worked in low or no lighting, in temperatures so cold it was impossible to stop shaking, even wearing multiple layers of special issue gear.

Marco still thought of it as a circus routine. Gearing up to fire blind into the darkness was mostly muscle memory. One man moved, another waited, the shell was loaded then, hoopla, the gun was ready to fire. Men in the gun turret were visible to each other only as floating anti-flash hoods and long gloves, appearing and disappearing as they moved about in the confined space, like white puppets on a black stage.

The pain in Marco's stomach had him stooped over, like he was carrying a weight on his back, even when he had the chance to stand and stretch between loadings. There had been German submarine activity detected at the limit of the range of the guns and shells had been fired, more to make any subs aware that they had been spotted, than to hit any precise targets. Then it was quiet for over an hour.

The crew took it in turns to get out for a fag break, going in twos or threes on deck. They were grateful for a lull in the icy squalls, which had alternated with 60 knot winds over the previous two days. As gun crew, working above deck, they had special issue, knee-length sheepskin jerkins, with shiny leather on the outside. The jackets were sleeveless, however, to allow movement. Exposed to the wind, it was only five minutes before bodies started to shake involuntarily, trying to generate heat from within. Men huddled like a colony of penguins in lee of the gun turret to light up.

Marco came out when it was his break and leaned on the rail in front of the guns, looking out to sea. He turned his face away from the wind to take a breath, to avoid the chest pain of having the cold air blown, rather than sucked into his lungs. He wasn't a smoker, but he liked to be downwind, catching faint wafts of the rich, hand rolled tobacco.

The sea was calm, a rarity this far north, and the surface had the look of wallpaper paste, thickening to ice with the cold. The destroyer was cutting through the two-foot swell at just over half speed, keeping pace with the cargo ships that were the soft core of the convoy. He could make out ships only as darker shapes in the uniform grey all around. He was bending over the rail looking out, then down the side of HMS *Devon,* where he had dived. Under light cloud he thought he could see the water, only because he knew it was there. A white spume was just visible along the line of the hull below him as the ship cut its way through the waves.

He raised his head and looked to where the line of the horizon would be ahead, the light of the day not yet beginning to show. As he looked back towards the ships behind in the convoy, Marco spotted one, then three faint points of light about half a mile off. He squinted through the tears brought on by the cold wind to bring the lights into focus, but the ship sped on and they were gone. Jellyfish was his first guess. He'd seen them before as luminescent floating mouths, feeding near the surface. Further south he'd seen other flashes in night sailing, from fish or from sparkling carpets of plankton that looked like they had individual battery supplies.

He turned his head to look north, towards the bow. His tight knit balaclava hood protected most of his head, but he felt his eyes sting again as he turned into the wind, the tears on his eyelashes in danger of freezing. There were more of the lights, strung in a ragged line, this time across the path of the ship, 500 yards ahead. He counted more than twenty. There were single white points and groups of three and four, close together, bobbing on the swell. As the ship got closer, he was puzzled that they were constant. There were no pulsing colours, no flashes, there then gone.

HMS *Devon* was on top of the lights just as Marco got the shout for the men to go back into the gun turret. His could feel the snot in his nose start to freeze as he looked over the side as the lights floated by, close to the hull. In the grey light of the cloudy pre-dawn he saw the lights being pushed aside, accelerating in the power of the bow wave. He squinted, trying to focus. They were not luminescent sea creatures, attracting partners or prey, but men, bodies burned and covered with black oil.

A few were bloated, floating horizontal, the lighter shade of distended bellies contrasting with the matt black, but most could be seen only as head and shoulder shapes, just above the surface. Their arms were thrown out wide from the life jackets they wore. Layers of ice crystals had formed on some of the upturned faces, where sea spray had frozen. In the near dawn light, the features of the men stood out as stark white circles in the black islands of oil.

Looking down, Marco was suddenly transported again back to Corbett's, squinting into a mirror, applying his thick make up, ready to burst through the curtain into the main ring. But the make-up was black, not red, and it was sticky, dripping from his hands.

There was no way to tell if the bodies were British or German.

As the ship ploughed through them, a few stuck together stubbornly in floating islands of two and three, where the oil itself had burned into a sticky solid, holding them shoulder-to-shoulder or back-to-back. The lifebelts had done their job, turning the sailors onto their backs to avoid drowning face down, and every one of the white lights, plugged into the belts, shone brightly to attract attention for rescue that never came.

Marco continued watching as the bodies passed into the churn of the ship's wake, disappearing in the white water, then emerging as a wider arc of lights, spread out wider and fading behind as his ship moved on. The ship behind ploughed through the same bodies. He thought briefly about raising the alarm. The rear ship of each convoy acted as a rescue ship, but only for the living, not the dead.

During attacks, the sound of the guns drowned everything else. When a ship went down, men in lifeboats or life jackets in the water would shout for help, knowing already that other ships couldn't stop and become a target. Orders for the ships were to proceed, orders for the men on deck were to avoid looking into the water at the floating survivors, wounded or dead.

Marco had seen bodies before, but never in this number, and never bodies abandoned. His thoughts drifted to what happened to causalities when no-one was searching for them. They would be left to float for weeks, moving on the currents. The taste of the oil would keep most sea scavengers off for a while, but eventually parts below the surface would rot, soft enough to nibble and the bodies would be reduced, bite by tiny bite, to skeletons, thin and soft enough to slip out of their life jackets and drift to the sea bed. The oil would remain on the water much longer than any of the blood.

Missing in action. In proud and sorrowful memory. Without a body, the words would be a kindness to relatives, who would never know how their son had suffered, scrambling terrified off the deck or blown from the sinking ship, swimming alive then floating dead in the freezing dark waters after ten minutes survival time. The next son or brother or father to die, on the next ship to go down would be the luck of the draw, the roll of the dice.

It was the chance that in a million square miles of dark sea, two enemies would meet.

HMS *Devon* was in the covering force, battleships and cruisers, flanked by a screen of destroyers, the outer protective line for the convoy. It would be one of the first to be hit. Gunnery crews saw more action than anyone else on the ship, incoming and outgoing fire. Being a gunner was the deadliest occupation on the ship and being on a ship in the Arctic was the deadliest place to be during the war. More crew were killed proportionally than in any land force. This was one of the first things Marco learned during training. Not from instructors, but from other nozzers who were following brothers into the navy. They could be bombed or torpedoed by a Juncker-88 from above, shelled from the surface by a German gunnery crew just like them, hit below by a U-boat torpedo, or holed by a mine. Many variations, all with the same outcome. The job he had signed up for was simple. Gunners had to kill the enemy before the enemy sunk the ship they were on.

During daylight hours, and when the sea was calmer, Marco could hear frantic whistleblowing on smaller ships in the convoy. Men stationed around the deck were spotters for the surface wash of torpedoes, speeding towards their ship. Each man had his navy issue whistle and ships that were fast enough had seconds to turn, presenting a smaller target. The wash trailed 50 yards behind the head of the torpedo and by the time it was spotted it was often too late. Men blew their whistles anyway, louder. Marco had heard the sound of the whistles rise, followed by the dull thud of the impact.

Survivors on Marco's ship, men who had been brave or numbed enough to go back to sea, told of the Luftwaffe Golden Comb, a sight which brought screech of whistles that could be heard across the whole convoy. On the German side, a spotter Folke-Wolf Condor would report the position of the convoy and an hour later there would be frantic ship to ship orders to zig zag as up to 50 Ju88s and He111 torpedo bombers appeared on the horizon, flying in formation in a wide line abreast, at 60 feet above the waves, preparing to simultaneously drop a saturation wave of torpedoes, half a mile long.

Men were killed when they were struck by the metal missiles or burned or drowned, after the torpedoes and bombs had struck, but surface crews like Marco's were just as often killed by the concussion wave from explosions on deck. The impact sent the whole deck leaping and could rip away protective bulkheads like they were wet cardboard, shocking men's internal organs into a bloody mush.

The Germans were damaging and sinking more ships with each Arctic run, getting closer to the tipping point where the destruction was faster than the allies' ability to replace the ships. Soon there would be too many wolves and not enough guard dogs to protect the cargo ships. Despite the morale boosting talks of officers and the combination of real information and war propaganda fed to navy and merchant ship sailors, crews who had completed more than one convoy began to realise how lucky they had been first time around.

Stories leaked out, passed from ship to ship. Two lifeboats of survivors from the USS Battleship *Washington* on a PQ convoy were picked up by a late following ship, the freighter *Olopana*. The men were frozen and in shock, but all alive. The men on the third lifeboat from the *Washington* refused to be rescued, choosing instead to row for six days, 250 miles to the island of Novaya Zemlya, rather than be taken on board *Olopana,* in the belief that it was likely to be torpedoed or bombed. As it was, three days later.

A phrase the captain of HMS *Devon* had used at the start of the trip came to Marco and he laughed. "*It is the circus of war, men.*" And it was. They had to sell enough tickets to make it worthwhile going out in the ring and performing, or it wasn't worth it. It was a business. When they ran out of ships or ran out of men to crew them, the circus would have to close or move to where there was more business, taking on the Nazis somewhere else.

What had he done at the circus and since he joined up? What did he still want to do? One hull breach from a direct hit or near miss that sprung the overlapping metal plates at the waterline; that would be all it would take. He would be another blackened body, floating for a while, nibbled at, then sinking slowly to the ocean floor, never found and never buried. If the war was won, or if it was lost, he would still be dead. Worst of all, he would never be missed. None of the bodies floating by his ship would be missed by anyone except their families. Nobody at Corbett's would mourn his passing. He was already dead to them.

The day he left the circus to begin his new life, the performers and circus crew he left behind started a new life too, one in which Marco Craston did not feature. Someone else would have taken his place in the ring and in their thoughts. There was no time to think about people who were gone, whether they had died or had left. That was wasted effort. Survival at Corbett's depended on thinking about those who were still there and what they needed to do to keep the show running.

Paul and Peter might wonder what had become of him, after the war, and his father too would think about him when he saw his brothers. But thinking about him and missing him were different things. Death notices would never be delivered to the circus because it had no address, so when the war ended, his father and brothers might believe that he had made it through. They might think that he had moved on, changed, found someone and decided to live in a house for the first time. If Paul and Peter went back to see Joe, they might raise a glass, wish him well, disappointed that he hadn't got in touch, sorry that they wouldn't see him again. But he wouldn't be missed.

And what would he miss? Only what he hoped would happen to him if he had lived. At that moment, there on the deck, he didn't have the strength, the energy that was such a part of him, to look forward. It was pointless to think about what might be when it could all end before the thought was finished.

* * * *

The shout came again, louder, more insistent. Marco turned and headed back to the gun tower, pulling his balaclava hood closer and folding his fingers inside the hood for the warmth. The last of the faint, bobbing lights disappeared in the distance.

Marco walked back to his post, wondering for the first time what a "good" injury might be; something serious enough to get him ashore, but still alive and conscious.

When the ship engaged, he was on autopilot. Load, ram home the shell, tamp up and fire, again and again, but each time the misery got worse. The minute the crew was stood down, he was bent over with the pain in his guts. Everybody saw it, but nobody sent him back to the sick berth. Petty Officer Berwick had orders not to, after being told he was wasting the doctor's time by allowing Marco to go back with the same complaint twice.

"It was a bad reaction to swallowing harbour water from that damn fool stunt," Berwick was told. *"A lesson has to be learned."*

The rest of the gun crew began to distance themselves from Marco. There was less chat, only gun business talk. They feared that he was building up to leave them short in the gun turret, or worse, to make a mistake that would prevent them firing and leave them open in an attack. They didn't know or much care if he was malingering, or if he was so sick that he shouldn't be there. If he missed his mark in the gun routines, the effect would be the same, no matter what was wrong with him. A rumour went around the gun crews, started by Petty Officer Stephens, that Marco was boiling up tobacco and drinking it, to make himself sick.

Marco thought more about Tuflo. Like him, the animal had been smart enough to know that something was wrong, but not smart enough to do anything about it, dying slowly. Marco found himself walking a circle of ship's passageways on C deck, to avoid lying in his bunk thinking about or feeling the pain in his guts. The concentration needed to duck and step through the steel doorways on his circuit of the ship was a distraction, enough to kill an hour when he couldn't sleep or in the time before his watch, when the pain was worst. The hour could stretch to two; once clockwise then turn and go back through the cold corridors in reverse, then repeat. The duck and step, duck and step routine as he walked was repetitive, soothing, like Tuflo and the straw.

But the time for his watch still came around.

"Tell me if I'm wrong, monkey boy, but it seems to me you're missing the trees and the jungle."

Stephens was quick to notice that Marco was not moving as he had done. He was slower and more deliberate in his walk across deck, and coming down stairs was now less of a slide, more of a heavy-footed trudge. Stephens sensed his chance, like a predator spotting a wounded animal.

"Maybe it's the lack of bananas, eh? Bit of a luxury at sea, but I thought the navy might have made an exception for you, being that's what you're used to back home."

Stephens was smart enough, once bitten by the yardarm incident, to pick his times carefully. Saying nothing unless he could name and trust every man in earshot, he would wait, then pick off a stooping Marco. He was like a sniper, firing off jibes he'd had hours to hone.

"Here comes the born sailor, walking upright but only just. Let those knuckles drag Craston, you know you'll be more comfortable."

"Passageway men, let the ship's mascot through there."

When time was tight, Stephens fell back on coughing in chimp noises as Marco passed. Marco could still ignore him, but Stephens' words made the misery worse, triggering more stomach cramps when he was not on watch.

* * * *

HMS *Devon* sailed on, making it to Murmansk harbour after another twelve days, intact, no sprung plates from near misses, no torpedo hits from above or below. Twelve days that felt like one never-ending night for Marco. As they anchored, he thought about the ships they'd lost on the way, both those carrying cargo and the protection ships on the convoy. What he knew about the losses was only from talk in the mess. The true losses, the reality of their chances of getting back, were never announced to crew doing a quick turnaround in Murmansk, ready for the return QP leg.

None of the hits on the way out had been close enough for Marco to see any more men in the water, and all the explosions had been in darkness. Just purple flashes out of the corner of his eye, somewhere off starboard, then the deep boom as the sound wave caught up. From his position he had seen the flaring of fuel burning, then five or ten minutes before what was left of the ship sank, restoring the darkness. How many ships, how many men picked up, how many bodies left floating? He had no way of knowing.

In Murmansk harbour, snow fell steadily, filling the tracks left by hundreds of shapeless men and women moving boxes and net-bound cargo as soon as it touched down on the wharf, swung from ships and dumped by cranes and simple, gin pole derricks moving at speeds that could never be safe. The lifting gear on the wharf itself was basic; leaning tripods constructed from rusting lengths of steel. There was nothing that could lift more than ten tons and cargo ships had to wait for crane ships sent from Britain to be moved around the docks when cargoes of armoured trucks or tanks made it into harbour.

Ships were tied up, unloaded and untied even as the last of the cargo was landed. It was frantic activity, always with one eye to the skies. If the snow kept up, the German bombers couldn't fly. When the sky cleared, the first signs of a bombing raid was the sound of misfiring engines of the Russian bi-planes going up in spirals, to try to gain enough height to attack the incoming bombers. There were just two British Hurricanes to add support, transported in pieces and reassembled at Murmansk.

Marco was glad of the time in harbour, lying curled up in his bunk. He went on deck once and watched the chaotic cargo transfer from a distance. Only a few officers were allowed ashore to plan the Q-P return journey and Marco and his gun crew were stood down as no ship's guns could be fired in the supposed safety of the asylum harbour, for fear of destroying other ships.

Despite his direct orders, Petty Officer Berwick sent Marco back to Thompson and the sick berth. Berwick couldn't ignore it any longer. As men moved about on deck, he had seen Marco climb the stairway and walk around like a half-shut penknife, bent over, but with his head up, neck stretched, looking over the side of the ship. Marco responded to commands and spoke only to acknowledge officers. Other men diverted to avoid him, anxious to avoid either contracting whatever illness he had, or being associated with someone swinging the lead.

To get past gatekeeper Petty Officer Thompson, Berwick took Marco to the sick berth himself. To get around the order he had disregarded, he explained to a sceptical Thompson that Marco's illness was now a different, more serious complaint. So Marco got in to see Surgeon Lieutenant Reeves for the first time. The doctor asked him a lot of questions and answered all of Marco's own questions, except one.

He first prodded Marco with his fingers, from diaphragm to groin, and ran through his standard list of checks for acute, non-specific abdominal pains. He found nothing that told him why Marco was in pain, but seeing the skin stretched across his ribs and sharp shoulder bones when Marco stripped for examination disturbed him, even before he started prodding. He could see that the man before him was malnourished, either through illness or through denying himself food.

Marco flinched a few times when Reeves pushed his fingers down, but then said that there was no pain. In the hard light of the doctor's room, Marco's complexion was more grey than pink, different too from the sunless, pasty white that Reeves saw in most of his patients. Marco had brown rings under his eyes from lack of sleep, and his tongue was coated with a white fur. During the examination he appeared uninterested, giving one-word answers. Reeves finished and told Marco to get dressed.

Over many years as a medic, Reeves had developed a method of explaining symptoms and causes of illness to patients that was effective and, just as important, saved him time before his next appointment. What he did was ask the questions that he anticipated and answered them too.

"*Well gunner Craston, I can't find the problem with your stomach, but that doesn't mean there isn't one now, does it? I think what's needed here is a complete medical once over, just to make sure everything is ship shape down below.*"

He looked at Marco to check for any reaction. Seeing none, he continued.

"Can we do that here on board? No, unfortunately not. We need to get you back to Blighty and into a proper hospital and that will take a few weeks. Are you worried about it? Well naturally you are, but we'll see about getting you on the next available transport and you'll be back in no time. Is it serious? Probably nothing to worry..."

"It's the misery sir, isn't it?" Marco broke in, now standing, eyes to the ground.

Reeves wasn't used to being interrupted mid flow and took a few seconds to get back on his track. He misinterpreted what Marco had said and continued.

"Well, no doubt you're feeling miserable. Of course you are. Who wouldn't be? Stuck out here, foreign lands, sore guts, missing the comforts and the folks back home. I'm going to give you something to help with the pain, make things easier on the trip back, see?"

Reeves sat back at his desk and started writing as Marco fastened a shirt button he'd missed. The doctor glanced up at the hunched figure in a uniform that looked two sizes too big. Reeves wondered what good it would do to tell him the truth now. Probably none. Painkillers strong enough to deliver some relief, at least until the poor bastard could get back home and be given the real diagnosis. Yes, that was kinder.

"The doctors back home will get to the bottom of this and you'll be back to feeling chipper in no time at all. You're probably wondering what we can do for you now? Well Thompson next door will fix you up with some pills that will help. Just give him this on your way out."

He handed Marco a folded note and led him to the door of his office, feeling the sharp bones as put a reassuring hand on Marco's shoulder.

Marco had asked the doctor if he was dying from the misery and Reeves, who believed he was dying from stomach cancer, had sidestepped the question. Sending him back to a British hospital confirmed what Marco's already knew. It was the misery. The doctor was just being kind.

* * * *

On the strength of the recommendation from Crooner Reeves, Marco was transferred to the Royal Naval Auxiliary Hospital at Vaenga. It was 15 miles of rough road, north of Murmansk, a stop off on the Kola Inlet. It sat on an isolated spit of land, serviced by a small dock. Set up and run on orderly lines by the Royal Navy, to cope with wounded from the convoys, it was staffed mainly by Russian doctors, who prioritised triage over bedside manner. This rankled with the few British medics at the hospital, who saw it as a breach of the Hippocratic oath to refuse to treat some wounded. For the Russians, to keep as many as possible alive you didn't expend energy on those who would die regardless of what care they were given. That was how incoming were sorted; one stream for treatment, one for death.

The small hospital was filled with those from the convoys who'd made it as far as Murmansk. Some died on the bumpy road ride to Vaenga. Marco stood out as having no injury that could be seen. The stoker in the bed to his right had lost a leg from an engine room explosion, and on his left a signalman was recovering from having had four feet of his oil-damaged intestines removed. Many men had been in the water suffering from hypothermia and had swallowed or breathed in oil in the few minutes before they were fished out. Most had primary blast and burn injuries, and there were a few, just a handful like Marco, who were classified in the least serious category. They had illnesses and crisis conditions; burst appendix and ulcers, pneumonia and bronchitis and other lung conditions brought on by the minus 30 temperatures. Marco was the only undiagnosed stomach complaint.

At night, there were rats. They would scurry from one bed to the next or jump from one patient to the next where the beds were close, looking for crumbs and slops of food. The screams of men didn't bother them, and the rats learned quickly which beds they could spend time on undisturbed. The men least able to feed themselves were the ones most likely to have failed to get everything from their plate to their mouth. They were also the patients least able to knock the rats to the floor or throw them across the room.

Marco was on a row of beds. He was fed, watered and medicated with Reeves' painkillers while the hospital waited on runners between Murmansk and Vaenga to find a ship with space willing to carry wounded. After three days Marco was helped into the back of a truck with six other walking wounded and taken back to Murmansk to join a cruiser. HMS *Cornwall* was due to sail the next day for Liverpool on the Q-P convoy, protecting the returning, empty cargo fleet.

Officers on the *Cornwall* had taken a collective decision as an act of mercy to take aboard wounded ratings and put them in officers' beds, whilst the officer slept on the couches in their rooms. In the event, most of the officers doubled up, two to a room, and slept between watches, so that some rooms could be designated as sick rooms, for wounded only, with bedding added for a second patient on the floor.

Marco carried his own supply of pills prescribed by Reeves. He took one before he got on the truck to get him from Murmansk to Vaenga and another to get him back to the port. The pains had him shuffling like a very old man as he made his way up the gangway onto HMS *Cornwall*. He eked out the remainder of the morphine-based tablets, snapping them in half with a spoon, making them last until the ship was five days out of port. The days on board were a blur of walking circles of any passageways he could find, sleeping and trying to eat tasteless food. As the morphine wore off, his first sharp memory was of passing Iceland.

After another 10-hour sleep, Marco found that he could stand a few degrees closer to upright and the pain in his guts only bent him over when he went on deck. He kept walking the long passageways of the cruiser, circle after circle, clockwise and then back, straightening another degree each day. Apart from a few flyovers by German spotter planes, and a U-boat seen off by a destroyer, the convoy avoided any enemy contact.

* * * *

By the time HMS *Cornwall* sighted the west coast of Scotland, Marco's pain had faded to a constant ache, like bruising he remembered from kicked by a horse when he was young. It got worse when he straightened up. On the day before they docked in Liverpool, he ate a half plate of sausages in mash, tasting it as he had during his first days on HMS *Devon,* but the pain came back as he tried to finish what was on the plate.

He left the ship as walking wounded, able to help carry stretcher cases down the gangway onto waiting ambulances on the dock, before climbing in for the short journey to Sefton General Hospital. Marco could feel the squeeze of the pains get worse as they arrived in front of the hospital.

The questions at Sefton were the same ones asked by Reeves and the same prodding, but at Sefton they were able to put Marco through more tests. Reading Reeves's coded notes–"*acute, non-specific abdominal pains,*" "*possible gastric lymphoma*–what the doctors expected to find was cancer at an advanced stage. They examined the results of Marco's barium meal X-rays. There was nothing. Puzzled, they ran a second barium meal with the same result. Sighting down the gastroscope made Marco gag but there was still nothing to be seen in his stomach to explain the pains. Swallowing pints of what tasted like liquid chalk and having a pole pushed down his throat made Marco's pains worse. He stopped eating again in the next days and went back to lying in bed when he didn't need to be anywhere else.

After the second set of tests, Marco started to question whether anything the doctors at Sefton could do would make any difference. Which is exactly what the doctors themselves were wondering. Sefton had almost a thousand beds, but the flow of casualties was increasing each week and the wards were filling up fast. Marco was taking up a bed without any confirmed diagnosis of injury or illness.

Without suggesting that the pains were not real, or induced by his refusal to eat, Marco's doctor sat on his bed to tell him that his illness might be better treated at the Royal Naval Auxiliary Hospital at Cholmondeley Castle, fifty miles south.

Marco had watched other servicemen in the hospital being

patched up. He saw the ones who began recovery. He knew that the other hospital was for men like him who would not recover. He'd overheard the nurses talking about patients who were, *"made comfortable"* in the days before they were taken out on the covered trolley.

As the hospital car from Sefton made its way up the long drive to Cholmondeley Castle, Marco Craston, gunner with unknown gastric illness, had his first sight of a different kind of turret, sticking up over the acres of woodland. As he got closer, he saw a dozen men, wrapped in overcoats and scarves sitting in two rows of deckchairs on the lawn. They were watching a cricket match, being played on a well-kept pitch, with the castle behind. All of the players were dressed in dark trousers and white shirts, except one, who was dressed all in white, including his shoes. Other men were walking around beyond the cricket, each accompanied by a nurse, also in white. It was not what he expected.

Just as the doctors at Cholmondeley had examined Marco's guts and found nothing from the medical books to explain his pain, the psychiatrist at Cholmondeley came up blank when testing for any diagnosable psychiatric illness that was causing Marco's so-called misery. Cholmondeley was a naval hospital, set up to treat serious or long-standing conditions. Few of the men sent there–some in leather restraints, some in adult nappies– would ever fight another German or Italian or Japanese soldier. These were men with pre-existing conditions when they joined up, who had been pushed over the edge by going to war, or men who had seen and heard too much in the short time they had been in battle.

Cancer had been ruled out and Marco had nothing that Cholmondeley Castle Hospital could treat. Yet his symptoms prevented him from being sent back to HMS *Devon* or any other active duties.

The navy had just opened a new facility for men like Marco. He was moved from one shore establishment to another.

* * * *

CHAPTER 3

DUNCAN THE DODGER

Duncan was almost 13 years old before he worked out that the story his father had told him couldn't be true. He kept the realisation to himself. He was embarrassed that he'd believed it for so long and told it to so many others.

Did they know it couldn't be true? Did they nod and look interested as he told it just to be polite, all the while thinking, "How stupid is he?" Had the boys listened, then moved Duncan in their teenage heads from one list to another? From the group that had everyone who was OK to be seen with, the group of boys who knocked on each other's doors if one of them was going out, to the group of boys you called on only if somebody was sick and you needed an extra for a game, somebody who you didn't need to talk to?

His father knew that Duncan would believe the story. Did he tell it so that his son would be impressed and proud that his dad had known so many amazing people? Or did he tell it like a joke with a punch line; something that Duncan was supposed to roll his eyes at and say, "Oh, dad, you had me going for a bit there..."

Duncan would never know. His dad was dead by then, killed by a single drop of plaster.

Billy was a big man, massive across the shoulders and chest, like a bear. Not lumbering, muscle or fat bound like some of the men he worked with, but fast on his feet, able to mix and work two handed for five hours straight, laying walls with brown coat plaster and then following it round with a smooth white coat until the wall was as flat as the ceiling. He was tall enough to do ceilings without a plasterer's box to stand on, skimming the fast-drying plaster to a perfect, smooth finish with no trowel marks. When his mother took a lunch piece to his dad on local jobs, Duncan had gone along and watched him at work, transfixed as the plaster was scooped from the board onto the trowel and spread across the ceiling in one movement, repeated without pause.

"Just like buttering toast, son," his father would say.

While he worked, Billy would sing. Nothing any of his mates recognized, just some half-remembered melody and words from the music hall or from a radio show. It had been when he was blasting out a chorus to one of his songs that one drop of gypsum plaster from a ceiling, or maybe from his fast-moving trowel, had dripped into his mouth onto a raw spot where he had bitten his tongue the day before.

A lump formed, irritating at first. Billy could feel it with his lips, but there was nothing to see. He only mentioned it to Jean, Duncan's mother, when it was the size of a pea on the side of his tongue. She told him to go to the doctors, get it seen to. She said it looked sore. But doctors cost money and money was tight. Billy told her it would settle down or burst and disappear. After a month the lump hadn't grown any more, but it had hardened. Billy tried twice to lance it with a needle, angling his head in front of the bathroom mirror. This had produced nothing except a mouthful of blood and stifled groans of pain.

When he did go to see a doctor, it was too late. The cancer had spread quickly from his tongue to the lymph nodes in his neck and from there, like leaking poison, around his body. Duncan watched his dad shrivel from a bear to an old man in four months. He was bed bound for the final four weeks, self-conscious and embarrassed about what was left of him. He resisted Jean's pleas to invite relatives to the house so that they could say "proper" farewells. In the last week Duncan got to see him, propped up with pillows, and his dad tried to show his old self one last time, croaking some of his unlikely tales through a ruined throat, but falling asleep after 15 minutes, mid-story, as the morphine he was taking for the pain kicked in.

Duncan was eleven then, so still in thrall of his dad's stories. His brother Andrew was six, too young to understand that his father was dying. Duncan understood that he was dying but he didn't understand why his father couldn't be cured, like other people who got ill, or why the whole family had to watch, helpless, as he shrunk away. His mother didn't know or wouldn't say when he asked her, hushing him with, "*Now don't upset your father with stuff like that Duncan. We have to keep quiet now and give him some peace.*"

There was no one else to ask and the same questions came back to him every day when he came home from school and looked at the closed bedroom door. When the minister from his dad's church came to the house near the end, Duncan asked him. The minister spoke in a quiet voice, while Duncan's mother made tea, telling Duncan without pauses about life everlasting and eternal peace. This confused Duncan even more and made him think that the minister had decided to answer a different question because he didn't know the answer to the one that Duncan had asked.

* * * *

Jean never re-married. She worked cleaning jobs while Duncan and Andrew were at school and got some help from her sister and from neighbours to guide her two boys into their teenage years and later both into the navy. She worked hard for her boys, trying to fill the gaps left by Billy, but there were some things that Billy did too well for her to even try, and his storytelling was one of them.

Duncan remembered some of the tales and kept his dad alive by telling them to Andrew in their room at night, making up details when he forgot them. By the time he was 13 he had all of the stories he could remember neatly ordered into ones that were definitely true and stories that his dad had made up. Duncan had worked out that his dad had a "tell" when he was performing for Duncan or at family gatherings.

The made-up stories always had some loud sound effects– somebody running up or falling down a stair, a fist hammering on a door, an unexpected explosion– that had the listeners jumping in surprise. Billy would use his studded work boots on wooden floors or thump his fist on a table for effect. The stories that were real were quieter, drawing you in, wondering where it was going, then building to a punch line that you never saw coming. It was the absence of banging noises in his dad's pilot story that had Duncan believing it was true for all those years.

A friend of his dad's uncle or his older cousin, Duncan could never remember which, had been an engineer at the local air base. It was him who knew the rich pilot. The engineer had worked with an oddball who owned four aeroplanes and was famous for making the first flight over Mount Everest in one of them, an open biplane, wearing three flying helmets, a balaclava and five pair of football socks, according to his dad. The pilot was called Wing Commander or Group Captain Farquhar Farquharson and he lived in a massive mansion, which had its own landing strip. He could go flying whenever he liked and would test himself by taking his plane up as high as he could without blacking out through lack of oxygen.

Farquhar Farquharson's one regret in life was that he had been too young to fly in combat in the First World War. He thought about it every time he went up in his favourite aerpplane, a Sopwith Camel single seater, still fitted with a front-mounted Vickers machine gun. He would spiral high above his mansion, pulling sharp turns and then coming out of the sun on imaginary and unsuspecting Fokkers of the German air force. He practised his combat flying technique daily and even thought about it in his bed at night. At this point in the story, Duncan's dad would drop his voice to a serious whisper and say, "*Which proved to be his big mistake.*"

One night Farquhar Farquharson dreamt that he was a First World War pilot, dog fighting Germans over the Somme. His squadron had suffered heavy losses and he was the only plane left, taking on three enemy fighters, including the legendary Red Baron, ace pilot of the Imperial German Army Air Service. Wing Commander or Group Captain Farquharson took down the first two Fokkers easily and looped around to get a fix on his long-term adversary. He lined up the Red Baron's plane in his gun sights, seeing the German look over his shoulder in alarm, and pressed his thumb forward on the Vickers fire button without mercy. The machine gun spat out bullets at 300 a minute, but instead of hitting the Fokker square on, they ripped through the propeller blades of Farquharson's Sopwith Camel, reducing them to stumps. Something had gone wrong with the synchronisation mechanism that allowed the Vickers to fire through the propeller blades. Farquharson stopped firing as the Sopwith went into a sharp nosedive, heading for the muddy fields below.

Billy paused at that point in the story, before delivering the jaw-dropper ending.

"It was Farquharson's butler who found him lying dead on the floor the next morning. The doctor who examined him reckoned that he'd fallen out of bed just as his plane had hit the ground in his dream. The cause of death was a heart attack."

Duncan had believed it, wondered at it and terrified himself in bed at night when he would wake from dreams in which he'd been chased and fallen off a roof or a cliff. Although he was too old to be taken in by any stories now, Farquhar Farquharson came back to him when he joined up in 1939. He wondered if the navy had been his automatic choice because the pilot's story had scared him off anything to do with flying for all those years.

His mother was proud that he had joined up and she was keen on the Royal Navy too, saying that they took only "good material".

"The air force take the posh boys and stiff necks and the rest of the scraps are left for the army."

That was the line that she gave to Duncan and Andrew, while secretly telling herself that her boys were less likely to be shot or bombed inside something as big and solid as a metal ship.

The week before he joined up, his brother Andrew sprung a wedding on his mother, marrying Sandra Evans at the Registry Office. *"Another good reason to come home,"* is how Andrew toasted his new bride, over a table of quickly made cakes and biscuits in the Cooperative Hall, to the nineteen people who could make it to the reception. Andrew and Sandra had been going out together since before they knew that's what it was called.

Duncan passed the General Knowledge test first time and was

sent with sixteen other aspiring matelots to a training camp on the Isle of Man. He couldn't wait to leave, until he did.

Then he was embarrassed about how much he missed home. It was his brother, mostly. When he met up with the other recruits it was a surprise to him that no one matched up to Andrew. He had expected to find Andrews in every group of men. A few had spark. They were good to be around, always looking for the laugh in what had to be done. But none of them had Andrew's energy. Any place, any time, Andrew was willing to say something or try something outrageous, just to see if it worked, to see if what was mundane could be made funny. He was couldn't-give-a-damn about the risk that it wouldn't, or that he would look stupid. Duncan had never once seen Andrew look embarrassed.

The recruits lived in basic wooden huts, four to a 12 x12 foot cabin, marched to breakfast, marched to classrooms for instruction, marched to the mess again, marched back to the huts, always with two drummers in front to keep them in step.

"All this training and practice in drill for these many hours will give you victory in that one hour of battle, when it matters," the Chief Petty Officer repeated every morning at roll call.

Anything that broke the repetition of the days was relief and one of the drummers leading them on marches would occasionally slip in a samba rhythm on the final march to barracks at night, transforming the precision marching ranks of men into a conga line briefly and then back on the beat, before the ranking officer could identify which drummer was to blame.

The classroom sessions were do-and-do-again communication and navigation skills, which did not come easy to Duncan at first. He worked at the dials, at the positioning, at the paper tests, mastering the devices, driven by the knowledge that if he couldn't do this stuff on dry land he would not be going to sea, but back to the wooden huts with the next batch of recruits, to start again and again until he passed.

Men were needed however and the Navy didn't give up easily, even on duffers.

* * * *

The final navigation do-or-die, pass-or-fail barrier to complete basic training was called Technique and Technology by the Royal Navy, but it was known as the Wall's Ice-Cream Tricycle Test by the men who faced it.

At the end of week eight, each nozzer was put under close observation by two navy trainers, clipboards and stop watches in hand. The test was to navigate a three wheeled ship about a series of nautical hazards on the flat calm of the converted lorry park on the training base.

The navy had six tricycles, front fitted with a compass and a pelorus, to allow relative bearings to be taken and to establish position. Each recruit had to peddle a set course, following bearings and navigate past various lighthouses (white stone pillars), reefs (green fencing) and signal buoys (old medicine balls, painted orange). A set of signalling flags in the rear "bread bin" basket of the tricycle had to be used appropriately at agreed points on the course to communicate with the other five ships on the car park, also navigating their way across the stony ocean. Any collision with another ship or more than two major navigational errors was an automatic fail. Minor errors–up to four–allowed a second and final attempt to navigate the course. No allowances were made for weather, nor for the navigation skills of others on the course.

The ships being cycled could be capsized by the wind or blown backwards. There was an additional challenge for tall men like Duncan. He had to cycle his ship forward fast enough to complete the course in the allotted time with his knees extending above the steel-tube handlebars, while trying to avoid scraping his shins on the metal.

From above, the exercise looked like overgrown children negotiating an obstacle course made with what they had found lying around an old yard.

Duncan passed. Two minor deductions for coming too close to a lighthouse and some question over which signalling flags he had raised, because a downpour had stuck all of his triangular flags to the bamboo stick on which he was trying to thread them.

Within two days he was on a packed train to Hove, where a

destroyer, HMS *Wanderer,* was his base for the final fortnight of sea training and seamanship. He wrote to his mother and signed the letter, *"Your loving son, Duncan McCafferty, Ordinary Seaman, (2nd Class)."*

After Hove, things happened quickly. The supply of men for ships had become a priority when the Germans started blockading supplies from the US and even more urgent when Arctic convoys were needed to supply Murmansk and Arkhangelsk, just to get the Russians through the winter. Getting enough men was about recruitment but getting men to do the jobs that were needed on the convoys was about training them fast and well, and having men already on their way as replacements to keep the ships supplied as casualties increased.

Five men in Duncan's new crew raised their hands when an officer brought them together to ask for volunteers for a posting to a ship docked at Campbeltown in the west of Scotland. Like Duncan, they were all Scottish and like Duncan none of them had waited for the second half of the information, about what they would be doing. Going back to Scotland was enough of an attraction in itself, even although they knew they might set foot in the country only to step from a train or a bus onto another ship. The fact that the volunteers were needed for "specialist" training was all they were told, before being sent to pack their kit and report for transport on shore.

Campbeltown had been chosen because it was on the end of a long peninsula, difficult to get to and easy to defend from prying eyes, or spying eyes. Every day, a converted yacht, HMS *Shemara* would sail down the sea loch, followed by a close formation group of training submarines, like a mother teaching her ducklings to swim. The name of the Anti-Submarine Detection (ASD) system on board HMS *Shemara* had been changed by Naval Intelligence to ASDIC (Anti-Submarine Detection Investigation Committee), inventing a non-existing committee in an effort to confuse any enemy spy interest.

Duncan did group exercises on the parade ground every morning, and games later in the day, to maintain his physical coordination and fitness, but most of the time he trained his ears.

Listening for underwater obstacles, real and planted, shoals of fish and old wrecks to begin with, he was echo sounding every day. Squinting his eyes, hands over his earphones, waiting for the distinctive pings that could mean submarine, he was like the silent prey listening for the predator approaching.

Each time the HMS *Shemara* cast off to sail up the sea loch someone gave the order to lower the oscillator dome, despite the fact that the dome on *Shemara* was bolted onto the front hull of the yacht. All training simulated combat conditions, and in battle the real dome might be retractable on a fast-moving destroyer, to avoid it being damaged at high speeds.

In the second part of his training, Duncan moved from the calm of the sea loch to sitting in the bowels of a rusty trawler in twenty-foot waves, pitched about on the Irish Sea, to test if he could still distinguish one ping from another.

His job was to send out a sweep of transmissions every few seconds, listening for any kind of echo and then, in seconds, decide what the echo represented. He could hear the propeller screws and engine noises of passing ships and even the pulsed call on a whale once, but the ping of an echo was the life-or-death trigger for action stations. A ship's ASDIC had a shorter range than radar and could only detect a U-boat if it was submerged. Duncan would be the first link in a life-saving chain that ended in depth charges being popped off the deck of the ship, aimed in the direction and the operating depth of the submarine.

On board HMS *Shemara,* then later on the rusty trawler *Pegasus,* there was a mock-up of an attack table. This had wooden models of movable convoys, merchant ships protected by destroyers but threatened by attacking U-boats, to be detected by Duncan and moved on the table as he tracked them. The attack table came with a mock Commander, who shouted orders and abuse, but never praise, as the operation proceeded.

To the background of barked orders, Duncan had to report every contact made, then classify it for type, distance and direction. If the contact changed bearing or disappeared, he had to pass on the information, still listening to the changing pings, like some kind of simultaneous translator. The Royal Navy had just one mock U-boat, a decommissioned *Argonaute* class submarine, donated by the French. It was used to put ASDIC operators through their final testing, as it sat silently on the floor of the Irish Sea, then fired up its engines and zig zagged towards the "fleet", trying to avoid detection.

The French submarine crew had seen action and had been forced to leave their country. They spoke little English, but their hatred of the Nazis was clear in any language. Duncan and the other ASDIC operators had read about the Nazi advance and heard doctored details about battles on radio broadcasts, but sitting with the French crew back in Campbeltown, Duncan came to understand what was at stake for Britain. He listened to the French and watched them pass around photos of loved ones who might already be dead.

In a strange twist, he went from hunting down a French submarine to listening for German submarines on a French destroyer.

* * * *

His first posting was on the dual crewed, *Bourrasque* on a PQ convoy outbound to Murmansk, via Iceland from Loch Ewe, the rendezvous point for the cargo ships and their protectors. It was 850 hard nautical miles to Faxa Bay, Reykjavik, but the conditions on that leg of the journey became a warm memory as Duncan went on to endure and survive the 1500 miles to Murmansk, via the tip of Van Mayen Island. The wide corridor of sea between Greenland and Norway was battered by a succession of north-east gales, force eight and above. The ten-day voyage from Reykjavik felt like a month. It was the beginning of the Arctic winter; 115 days of perpetual darkness.

Finding a routine to make the ship run meant a division of jobs on-board, with two parallel lines of command, English and French, overseen by the captain. Duncan's training had prepared him well for taking orders and for working with the ASDIC equipment for long hours in noisy conditions in rough conditions. Perhaps he had tuned out and wasn't listening when he had been at the final briefing on what conditions to expect in the Atlantic, but nothing had or could have prepared him for the temperatures and sea ice on what the commanders called the 'Arctic Convoys' and what the sailors called 'Polar Hell'.

As they sailed from Iceland, on a direct course heading North East for Bear Island, sea water that crashed onto the decks from side waves or sprayed over the ship from each dip of the bow became a problem. Ice froze on decks, up to three inches deep, on wires and superstructures. Gun barrels became tubes of ice that would explode if fired. One of the tasks that transcended the language barrier on-board was the issue of axes and steam hoses to a daily watch, who were first roped up and hooked to lifelines on iron stanchions before hacking at the ice to avoid a build-up that could capsize a ship.

Duncan took his shift on this with the other ASDICS, feeling naked in the cold as soon as he was out, the Arctic wind cutting through the thermal gear. He would come back into the mess for tea unable to move his fingers. Older men on the shift would come back inside with faces covered in blood, having rubbed their noses against the cold, pushing nostril hairs, frozen like tiny pins, into soft nasal tissue. He had seen men moaning in pain as frozen eyelashes fell out, one by one, when they came back to the heated quarters of the ship.

Conditions outside also made Duncan's real job inside doubly difficult. The mix of warmer, Gulf Stream waters and freezing Arctic currents produced unpredictable thermal layers and changing water densities in the seas. False readings and uninterpretable signals came through on Duncan's headphones as the sonar tried to penetrate the layers, searching for submarines. When the sonar did pick up mixed signals, the ship dropped depth charges as a precaution, to scare off any subs that might be there, but the walls of bubbles from the charges were impenetrable by sonar, leaving them blind to anything else approaching. Further north, the water became so cold that even torpedoes were affected. The electrics were never designed to operate is such temperatures and some German torpedoes would veer off course or turn in long circles until they sank or blew a hole in the first available hull.

Before March 1942, when the Nazis realised the full strategic importance of the PQ outbound Arctic convoys for the fight against Russia, the contact between the convoys and German ships and planes was skirmishing. The Nazis were distracted by other operations elsewhere in Europe and the food and supplies in Duncan's first convoy made it through without any enemy contacts. He listened to the long hours of silence on his headphones with relief. There were a few scares on the return QP leg, when he had raised the alarm on what sounded like a submarine that had approached then veered off, and when a German battle cruiser was sighted, but having assessed the strength of the convoy protection, did not engage.

As the destroyer *Bourrasque* cleared the Shetland Islands headed home for Liverpool on the return leg, Duncan's convoy passed the next outbound ships, fully loaded and headed for Murmansk. Duncan stepped off the gangway at Albert Dock, Liverpool two days later to begin his shore leave. It was the first dock in Britain to be built without timber. Duncan was grateful for the permanence of the cast iron, brick and stone beneath his feet after the Arctic waters. The solid construction of the dock was not enough to prevent it being seriously damaged however in the German May blitz on Liverpool four months later, by which time Duncan too was damaged. When he left the dock that day, kit bag over his shoulder, it was to be his last day as an ASDIC.

He caught the fast train north, to Carlisle then straight to Glasgow. It was rammed with army boys on leave, loud, high spirited, willing the train to go faster to get them home, into bars and into the arms of lovers and loved ones.

* * * *

As he approached his mother's house, something was wrong. He looked up at the windows. Although it was only two o'clock in the afternoon, the curtains were drawn. Walking up the stairs of the three-storey close, he should have been able to hear music. She always had music on, too loud for the neighbours. The *Light Programme,* blasting out scratchy big bands or comedy stage

96

acts, or the *Home Service*, broadcasting on the hour about the victories of the British, wherever they could be found.

He knocked on his own front door, something he had never done in his life. As a boy, he would run straight in. Later, he might shout hello first, to find out who was in. After a beat he heard his mother's room door opening and shuffling as she came to the front door. As she opened it, Duncan's first thought was that his mother had shrunk. She was wrapped in a thick grey shawl that reached to her ankles, and she was barefoot. Hunched over, her gaze was fixed on Duncan's knees. As she raised her eyes to look at him, he saw they were swollen and raw.

"*Oh Duncan, it's you,*" was all she said before she collapsed to her knees.

He tried to catch her on the way down, reaching for elbows or shoulders, but he was left with two handfuls of shawl as she slumped to the linoleum floor.

"*I thought it was him come back again,*" she said.

She said the same thing twice as he got her to her feet and she repeated it again as he walked her to the couch in the darkened front room.

"*Who mother? What's happened to you?*"

"*They tried to contact you, but the Navy said you were too far away,*" she mumbled.

Duncan panicked. His first thought was that his mother had been left too long on her own and had had a breakdown or that she had gone insane because of the war. He thought she was reliving his father's long wasting death, which was the last time he'd seen all of the curtains in the house closed.

"*He came to see me son, that's how I knew, before they came and told me. I heard him walk up to the door and knock, just like you did. You both have the same knock. Shave-and-a-haircut, yes-please.*"

"*Mother, tell me what...*"

She looked straight ahead as she spoke, smiling now, calm.

"*He said in that deep voice of his, "Mother I don't want you to worry about me, because I'm happy where I am, so I don't want you to get upset.*"

* * * *

Illuminating gas was made from the plentiful Scottish coal, dug by the miners who had been excused conscription to contribute to the war effort, and by consciousness objectors, sent down the pits as a punishment for being cowards. Heating the coal in special chambers at the local gasworks, built on the edges of Glasgow because of the smell, produced a mix of methane, hydrogen and carbon monoxide. This was piped away to burn as light and heat in the homes in the city. The coal gas burned with a bright orange flame, ideal for street lamps, and for the newly "plumbed in" gas fires of tenants in houses built just before the war.

Duncan had grown up with a coal fire in the living room, lit every morning with newspaper and kindling. He'd huddled in front of it to dry out when he was soaked from walking back from school and jostled for the hottest spot, pushing against Andrew until one of them fell over and their mother shouted at them to stop. Once a week he'd sat in front of the coal fire in a tin bungalow bath to be washed by his mother, who would heat another kettle before washing Andrew in the same water.

Stacked with coal and regularly stoked with the poker, the fire threw out more radiant heat than any new-fangled gas fire ever could. The downside was the coal dust and ash from the fire, which settled as black stoor on every surface in the room and in every family member's lungs too.

Sandra and Andrew had been lucky. The Glasgow Corporation waiting list for new build houses had been suspended by chaos of the war. Few people wanted to move away from places they knew anyway when there was a war on. Getting a space in the Glasgow underground or in a bomb shelter on nights when the German planes came looking for the shipyards to bomb became a much greater priority than moving to somewhere with an inside toilet. A one-bedroom Corporation house came up two weeks after Andrew left for the Navy and Sandra signed the lease, knowing that he would be delighted not to have to live with her mother. Their new house was 20 minutes out of the centre of town, but it was theirs.

Sandra worked at the Royal Ordnance munitions in Bishopton, travelling an hour each day by buses supplied by the factory. She spent most of her time in the new house, cleaning and decorating every room, sometimes with real paint, sometimes just with her imagination. At the factory, she worked with boiled guncotton, used, she knew with some satisfaction, to fire shells at the Germans who were trying to kill her Andrew. The acid baths for the cotton in the confines of the factory produced fumes that caused women on the production line to faint regularly. They would collapse, be dragged outside for fresh air to recover and be back at their station within 20 minutes.

Sandra worked day, afternoon and night shifts in rotation. The difference between the munitions factory and the wool mill she'd worked at before the war was that no-one complained. It was for the war effort, and everyone knew the consequences of not winning.

Andrew had been home two days. Three more days of shore leave until his ship was supplied and loaded, ready to go again. Sandra had to work all of them, but she was day shift on the Tuesday, so that was the one for dressing up and going out together. Nothing fancy, because there was nothing fancy to go to. Dancing was one of the few things not rationed, but dancing nights were as difficult to find as eggs that came in shells and not in a tin.

Once a month, two ex-miners, too old to serve, got together with two primary school teachers to become the Dancing Diamond Band. Piano accordion, two fiddles and a pastry brush drummer played reels, waltzes and beer barrel polkas in the church hall. Women danced with women, mostly, and the few men in uniform were different faces every month. The accordion player took his squeeze box to the Glasgow underground on nights when the sirens sounded, the music carrying through the tunnels, drowning out the sound of the bombers overhead.

Sandra caught the munitions bus at the end of her shift and ran all the way from the bus stop, desperate to wash the stench of the guncotton out of her hair and get dressed for the night. It was already six o'clock when she turned the key in the lock and pushed in the door open. The smell of the guncotton in her hair disappeared. The coal gas was a thick, foul breeze, drifting down the short hall to meet her. She was still breathing hard from running and she gagged as she inhaled and tasted the gas at the back of her throat.

Her instinct was to get to a window. She kept moving, wrapping her arm across her face and breathing into the crook of her elbow. The small kitchen, with its gas cooker, was straight ahead. She barged into the door, and it bounced against the wall and hit her as she came in. The metal window, with rusty, overpainted hinges juddered open in three pushes, just wide enough for her to get her head out and take a breath.

Andrew must have been in, made tea and left one of the gas rings part on, unlit. He'd done it before, putting too much water in the kettle, letting it boil over and put out the flame. She did a double take as she looked back over her shoulder at the cooker. The knobs were all vertical and the oven was closed. The gas was coming from somewhere else.

She picked up a tea towel and held it over her mouth, walking back to the hall. As she reached the bedroom door the rotten smell of the gas became stronger and she bunched the tea towel to her mouth and nose. She pushed the door. Andrew must have gone out and left the coal gas fire unlit. She was furious. A spark could have blown up their flat and their neighbours.

The curtains in the room were drawn and the room was dark. She went straight to the side of the marble fireplace, stooped down to turn off the T shaped tap. She straightened up and turned. Their bed was second-hand but with a new mattress, and Andrew was lying on it. His hands were clasped behind his head and his ankles were crossed. His shoes were still on, and even in the darkness of the room Sandra could see that he had not yet dressed to go to the dancing.

* * * *

When the crushers came for him, Duncan was easy to find. His shore leave was four days over and he had spent it all in his mother's house, not leaving even for his brother's funeral.

On the day of the funeral, his mother wept as much about Duncan's refusal to go as she did about Andrew's death. She had to be supported like a blind woman by Duncan's two cousins all the way from her door to the graveside and back.

To be buried with holy words and fairy tales on the life thereafter was a lie on top of a lie for Duncan. If there was a God, somebody who had control, as Duncan had believed, what sort of sick bastard was he to let Andrew die, less than a year married, never having been spiteful, sinful or a transgressor of any of the other death-penalty holy crimes that got you struck down, according to the Book?

If there was a God who caused the death of the young, funny people who made others happy, who would want to believe in him, or play by his rules? For Duncan, now, it was easier, to believe that there was no benign overseer and his life had been wasted in a lie for twenty years. It was all made up to keep in line all those stupid enough to believe. The death of Andrew and thousands in the war was the random spin of a wheel, not some cosmic strategy board as he had believed, with pieces being moved around according to a set of rules known only to God.

The cause of death on the certificate was given as accidental. This was as a kindness to his mother and to Sandra. The doctor and the policeman who came to the house must have seen how it looked. It came down to a question of hands or feet. Had Andrew kicked the gas tap accidentally as he walked past, on his way to lie on the bed, or had he crouched down and turned the tap on? Had the fire ever been lit, and then blown out? Could there have been anything so dark, so terrible that Andrew had seen in his short time away at war that would ever make him think that life was even less pointless than death?

These questions ran around Duncan's head, like unwanted rats scratching to get out, for the four days he spent unwashed, sleeping in a chair in his mother's house. The gas had killed Andrew, saturated his blood and starved his brain of oxygen. That was how he had died. But there was nobody to answer then, and there never would be anyone to bring the relief of knowing why Andrew had died, lying on his bed with his hands behind his head and a smile on his face.

The Military Police who took Duncan from his mother's house drove him all the way back to the Liverpool base. They were sympathetic, but they had a job to do.

Duncan's ship had long since sailed. He was formally detained on charges of being AWOL and locked in a cell for a couple of nights. The Assistant Divisional Officer, allocated to him as a "prisoners' friend" before he was court martialed, had done three desertion cases that week already.

One of them was a man who had deserted after all other members of his unit had been killed in an ambush and his own death seemed inevitable. The other two were gun-shy teenagers who would have deserted at the start of the war but had been too cowardly until now to face the consequences.

The Assistant Divisional Officer's job was to speak in mitigation for men when it was deserved, and to find out if there was any special circumstances defence to be taken into account. For Duncan there was neither because he wouldn't or couldn't speak to the officer.

By that stage, Duncan was preoccupied with what the telegram sent to his mother would say.

"*We are sorry to inform you that your son is a disgrace to the Royal Navy,*" or, "*It is with regret that we write to inform you that Ordinary Seaman, (2nd Class) ASDIC Operator Duncan McCafferty, has been classified as unfit for duty.*"

Or perhaps, there would be no telegram. The navy would not want to publicise the shame of those who would not fight for their country.

He remembered being taken from his mother's house, hearing her wailing as he was taken down the stairs by the Military Police, seeing neighbours' doors opening a crack to confirm what they knew already. He heard their sympathy.

"*That poor woman.*"

"*Does nae have her troubles to seek.*"

"*One son dead, and now the other one's gone mental.*"

The journey to Liverpool was a blur and all he remembered

about the court martial was somebody shaving him and combing his hair back, trying to make him presentable. Then it was over. He was back in a cell for another hour, then in the back of a navy van with no windows. As they drove, the vibration reminded him of the ship's engines and how he was missing the feel of the thrum below his feet. There was a stop, the doors opened and some papers were pushed into his pocket before a transfer to a Bedford bus for two more hours. Then he was at Kielder, surrounded by trees.

It must have been during his second night in the cells in Liverpool, he worked out later, that his mother died. Or it could have been early that next morning while he was in court. She was found at lunchtime by two neighbours. One was from next door, concerned that Jean wasn't taking sympathy callers and another from downstairs who has desperate to know details about Duncan's arrest. Her door was open, as it always was. Cause of death was a blood clot in a clogged artery, or a broken heart, depending on who was talking.

Duncan went to Liverpool and a death message went to the *Bourrasque,* battling through another storm in the North Sea. The message came back as not delivered. The navy were well practised in getting casualty news from ship to shore, delivered by "angels of death"–telegram boys on bikes–to relatives at home, but getting messages in the opposite direction took longer.

By the time the Navy had tracked Duncan to Liverpool, he was already in Kielder. By the time the information about his court martial and transfer to Kielder came back his mother was buried, her house re-rented and her worldly goods reduced to a tea chest left with his brother's widow, Sandra.

The news was delivered to Duncan across a desk by the chaplain at Kielder, ten days after her death.

"I'm sorry to have to tell you Duncan that we have received news of your mother's death."

Duncan appreciated the fact that the chaplain spared him any holy preamble, but he didn't like being called by his first name by someone he had never met. Before he could ask what had happened and when, the chaplain was there before him.

"The death of your brother affected her deeply, Duncan, and the grief was too much for her heart, it seems," he continued. *"She died peacefully in her sleep last week."*

Again, Duncan was grateful for the information, but resented the fact that the chaplain knew more about his mother's death than he did. And how could he know that she died peacefully, and not gasping for breath, trying to call out for Duncan, who wasn't there to hear her? How could he know that it was Andrew's death, rather than the sight of her other son being dragged out of the house that had caused her heart attack?

Duncan was numb, just punch-drunk. The image of his mother lying in her bed brought no tears. That morning and yesterday and the day before, he had to look around the room for clues to remind himself where he was and how he had got there. When he awoke each morning, he spent time ordering the sequence of events that had brought him there, then shut down for the day, content that he had worked it out.

Planning for the day, or the next day didn't matter, because that was nothing he had to do. People asked him the same questions, then told him when to eat, where to walk, where to sit and he accepted that. There was nowhere he needed to be. There was no nail biting or pacing around the room, no panic or dread, nothing other than being tired a lot.

Andrew's death by coal gas flattened him and there was little of him left standing when the news of his mother's death hit him.

Duncan looked up and realised that the chaplain was still talking.

"...and I'm sure your mother was a good woman and God will reward her with life everlasting and eternal peace."

It was words he had heard before. Did all holy men have to memorise this meaningless stuff, and spout it out when required, like being forced to learn and recite poetry at school, Duncan wondered?

Compassionate leave, because of the timing, the chaplain went on, was not appropriate in the circumstances. With no one to go back to comfort or to grieve with, Duncan made no objection.

He walked back to his bunk and fell asleep almost at once.

CHAPTER 4

MRS SEW AND SEW

As the Nazis got closer to the British coastline, the need to maintain military operational status superseded all previous directives, both at sea and at home.

Drifters, trawlers and fishing boats were requisitioned and became minesweepers, anti-submarine defence and auxiliary patrol ships. Even the obsolete biplane, the Fairey Swordfish, little more than a fabric covered metal frame, was brought back into service. The fragile remnant from World War 1 was put on aircraft carriers to carry and drop torpedoes on German ships threatening Arctic convoys. Deck guns from decommissioned World War 1 ships were stripped, oiled and bolted onto ships still smelling of whale oil. Machine parts from crippled ships were cleaned of rust and sometimes blood and put back into service. There was salvaged life-jackets, radio and ASDIC equipment from dead ships, towed back to home ports. Steel plates, cut from rusting hulls and other salvaged scrap was loaded onto ships headed for Murmansk and Arkhangelsk, together with lifting gear, to be used to patch up bomb, torpedo and mine holes in ships that had made the Arctic crossing and limped into Russian ports. The Russians still had the labour force in abundance, but virtually no repair materials and no machinery to move what they had, lying around rusting in yards. Every piece counted.

At home, household goods were likewise used to the limit, and when something was worn or snapped or broke into pieces that flew across the room, the bits would be collected and patched up, not thrown out. If it could be fixed, it was.

The message took a few months to bed in. While the war was

105

far away, and fighting was in places few people had heard of, the main challenge for families was adapting to the absence of husbands, brothers and sons. The war was there, but home was still here. Money was tight, but food was still plentiful. Then, as the Nazi blockage began to bite at the beginning of 1940, butter and sugar disappeared from the shop shelves and appeared instead on a list of groceries in ration books, quickly followed by meat, tea, cheese, eggs, and milk. The government pushed the shortages message hard, in newspapers, on posters and in cinemas: The sacrifices at home would help win the war. For anyone who doubted it, this was coupled with severe penalties, including jail sentences for anyone breaching rationing orders.

Make-up, toothpaste and soap starting trading on a new black market. Women drew soft pencil marks down the back of their calves, to imitate the seam of a stocking, and beetroot juice became a convincing substitute for lipstick, if you didn't mind the taste.

Whether it was the posters and films from the newly formed Ministry of Information that made people believe or the shortages and necessity that eliminated any doubt will never be known, but the connection between fighting on foreign fields and the war effort at home was firmly established.

What was previously pitied as signs of poverty and thrift in neighbours became instead something to be admired. Ingenuity became one route around shortages. In 1942 the Board of Trade launched the *Make-Do-and-Mend* scheme. Publicity was given to innovative sewing skills; making skirts out of the suits of the men away to war, creating wedding dresses from floral curtains, taking tips from *Mrs Sew-and-Sew,* a smiling doll who featured in booklets distributed to homes. Families adapted and new specialist skills were learned in a culture of scarcity.

Grannies who could darn took on a new status in households. Darning skill gave clothes a longer life. The first stage was to go up and down in lines across the hole, then go over and under the lines of up-and-down stitching vertically. For knitted fabrics, the second stage of stitches was diagonal, to give extra strength. *Mrs Sew-and-Sew* advised that you should not wait for holes to appear, that it was better instead to darn as soon as the garment began to grow thin. Clothes and the fabrics and knitting wool to make them were rationed from June 1941, but darning thread was not, until the government discovered that women were buying whole skeins of the thread and crocheting or knitting complete, new items of clothing. The expression, *"Have you a shirt to sew on this button?"* was born.

* * * *

Mrs Sew and Sew, Make Do and Mend, and *Make and Make Do* was keeping family and home afloat on war rations. In the Navy at sea, the holes were already appearing, even when and where it could be predicted they would. Gaps in the fighting and supplies fleet were showing at every level, moving towards a tipping point where there were not enough men to fill them.

Thirty three was the critical number. That was the number of ships sunk per week in the war with Germany and Japan and it was a number that went beyond the replacement capacity of joint shipbuilding in Great Britain and the US. In the Arctic convoys, 33 per week translated as one ship in four being sunk in every convoy. The Admiralty recommended a halt to convoys, at least for winter. The government decided that the losses were a terrible but acceptable price to be paid and overrode the Admiralty because of the danger of a Russia with no supply line collapsing and signing a peace deal with the Nazis.

In the First World War, army commanders gained 500 yards on a battlefield by the blunt strategy of throwing more and more men in front of enemy gunfire until the ground was taken. The number of lives lost in the Great War was only a part of some secondary calculation of the price of victory, because there was a ready supply of brave boys to take the place of those cut down. They were fighting for God and for country. Over ten million British War and Allied Victory medals were churned out, for the living and the dead. Inscriptions on medals read, *"The Great War for Civilisation"*; on gravestones, it was *"His Will Be Done."*

In 1939, more sophisticated calculations were needed on

personnel supply and demand. The length of the war was underestimated in the revised equation however, and the shallow pool of fighting navy recruits quickly dried up. Using or squandering lives to achieve victories measured in yards or increments, as had been done in the Great War trenches, quickly disappeared as a strategic option for naval commanders. Men became more valuable.

On land, the decision to move tanks and guns from one battle to another could make the difference between victory and defeat. The machine was the fundamental military unit, and more men could always be moved or found to operate the machines. At sea, this analysis changed. The person-machine system, rather than the machine alone, was the unit.

The number of ships or deck guns that could be built or repaired back into service was important, but they were only effective with enough able seamen to operate them. Plans were made on desks and in war rooms. The British Admiralty calculated acceptable limits for losses of men in the Arctic. Churchill promised Roosevelt that convoys could make the journey in three weeks, to support the Russians. Hitler moved more Kriegsmarine and Luftwaffe to ports in Norway and told his commanders that a single ship of food or munitions getting through to Murmansk or Archangelsk was unacceptable. Leaders on both sides had their eye on the prize and believed they would be victorious. The men on ships, being moved around maps on the war room tables were never told about acceptable losses or about their chances of survival.

Reasonable risks were calculated, together with margins of error, but the assessment of risks changed as the stakes increased. There was a calculation of enemy strength, predictions on weather conditions, ice conditions, and the likely impact of damages.

Under pressure, corners were cut.

* * * *

The casualty numbers recorded by the Admiralty for men having a mental breakdown on board warships during battle duty were low. But the non-action section of the casualty returns told a different story.

The number of seamen who had been lost overboard, or accidentally drowned was far higher than could be easily explained. The number of these deaths that were self-inflicted was not recorded, nor was any link between men who had attended sick berth, previous to disappearing into the sea.

For days lost to non-battle injuries, there was a similar story. Psychoneurosis was the most common cause, accounting for five per cent of the total. It was also the principal cause of discharge from the navy, followed by personality disorder.

In the Army, the higher the rank, the further a soldier found himself from the front-line, so rank was some protector against breakdown. For the Navy, the front line was up close for everyone on a warship and the intensity of the stresses was more equitable. Rank still played a part, but not so much. In the Navy around ten naval ratings for every one officer were referred from their warships to psychiatric units on shore. More and more men were coming back from ships without visible injuries.

For ships, the critical number was 33; for sailors the figure was one per cent. This was the proportion of *all* naval personnel being referred as psychiatric casualties. It was a tipping point. The Admiralty realised that action was needed before there were not enough men to crew whatever ships could be built.

It took over a year of war before the Navy accepted that even experienced sailors had a breaking point. The term 'fatigue' was introduced for those who earlier in the war might have been diagnosed as suffering from an anxiety state. Calling a condition "fatigue" was designed to avoid stigmatizing labels and to imply that natural recovery was possible.

The standards for selection of navy recruits were based not only on physical fitness, but on a follow up assessment of mental suitability. The Navy had to be confident enough that a man was stable and resilient enough not to be a risk to others on a ship in battle. The stakes were life and death. Psychology interviews were based on assessing probability. The Navy had to be confident and the man had to be stable. If there was any chance that a man would not succeed in the position for which he was to operate, he was rejected.

As the war progressed however, and hundreds of men ideally suitable for the positions for which they had applied were killed and injured, the criteria for "resilient enough" changed. Applicants who had been classified as too old, too fat, too thin or just too much of a risk for active duty were called back in and, in the space of a year, became "marginally suitable" for training or tasks at sea.

The challenge for the Navy became to put these second-choice men in jobs where probability was better-than-even that they would function without causing damage to the fleet. Drivers for shore supplies, heavy lifting, fetch-and-carry ship repair and maintenance work in docks was ideal for these men. The risk of injury or death to others was minimised. Some men were "marginally suitable" as clericals or telegraphers, marked out at once as odd in rooms full of women doing the same jobs. All the shore jobs were useful for the war effort.

The problem was that the men being blown apart and drowned were not working on shore. The widening gaps in the fleet personnel were at sea. Even more risks had to be taken.

* * * *

Convoys were crewed by trained Royal Navy sailors and merchant seamen. The men on the supply ships were experienced sailors who could live on a ship for months but had never been in an attack. They were not given details of their destination or briefed in any way on the dangers of the convoy. The main difficulty they faced was fatigue, an absolute exhaustion in keeping the ship going, not knowing if it would be for two more days or two more weeks. Some merchant seamen broke, but in different ways from sailors on war ships. They were reduced to sitting in bunks, babbling and weeping not from the fear of attack, but from exhaustion.

The enlisted Royal Navy men faced different demons. Some who had never been in anything bigger than a rowing boat found themselves on Arctic convoys six weeks after signing up to serve. Their role models, the men they worked alongside, were young P-Q, Q-P Arctic veterans, so psychologically damaged by their experiences that their behaviour just six months earlier would have been enough to get them discharged. But that was before men available to serve on ships became even more scarce.

Medical officers on Arctic convoy duty had recommended that no one should be on the bomb gauntlet runs from Scotland to Russia for longer than 18 months, because of the physical demands of the cold, battering sea and the psychological demands of constant threat of attack. For men on the edge, the feeling of being shadowed 24 hours a day by U-boats could be more damaging than any actual attack. Northern Flotilla U-boats were painted white, with a polar bear on the conning tower. Men on lookout duty were found other duties on ship when they reported seeing multiple white conning towers, even when visibility was zero.

That no one should sail for longer than 18 months was the medical recommendation but needs-must ruled. The only ways to be relieved at 18 months became death, serious injury or being taken off a ship because you were a danger to yourself or to others.

It was a paradox for the Royal Navy. During peace time, the standards for recruitment were strictly adhered to. During war, the same standards were relaxed, at a time when selecting the right men to serve became especially critical. Only the best men would do at a time when anybody would do.

At the end of 1939, 200,000 men had been conscripted to join the Royal Navy, all of them physically and mentally able. By 1941, either one of these "ables" might get you in. At the beginning of the war, the navy General Knowledge test and interviews at recruitment stations filtered out men with criminal records, those who had been expelled from school or had problems holding down a steady job in civilian life. When casualties increased and the need became great, very great, so-called military delinquents were looked at differently.

The Army had already suggested that in time of war these men might not be liabilities after all, but instead could make the best soldiers, precisely because of their aggressive characteristics and lack of a sense of self-preservation. With more vacancies in the naval ranks, the recruitment bar was lowered again, taking on men for the sake of having ships functional, if not fully effective.

A naval delinquent might be obstinate, might not do what was commanded of him, or not do it in a manner that the officer would have it done. He might stand still after being commanded to move, or he might give undutiful language in the presence of an officer. This caused problems for officers, for the maintenance of discipline among other men and for deciding what offences could be punished. But in crisis it was the price the Navy was willing to pay just to have enough men to crew a ship.

During the first year of war recruitment, Royal Navy psychiatrists had the time and the luxury of research. They followed up on how well their selection tests had prevented potential delinquents getting into the Navy, and how well recruits judged to be borderline-suitable for naval service had adjusted to Royal Navy life. What they found was so professionally embarrassing to the psychiatrists and to the Navy that the results were quickly buried.

Psychiatric screening was of little use in predicting performance on a ship. The tests were all sound in statistical validity, but practically useless as predictors. Some of the men who had passed with high scores went on to commit offences that had them not just discharged but jailed for years. More than half the men who had scraped by as borderline delinquent adjusted well to navy life and became model sailors.

One of the most disturbing findings in the follow up research on serving men was that identifying someone as a mental instability risk actually increased his chances of becoming one. Men who were picked out as in need of additional support from naval psychiatrists came to believe that they needed it.

By 1943 there were 227 psychiatrists in the Army. The Navy had just 35. The Navy underestimated the number of psychiatric causalities and was taken by surprise. Since the Navy and the Air Force had the pick of recruits, it was assumed that the selection process and the average level of intelligence would filter out mental instability. But nobody foresaw Arctic convoys, and nobody could predict what men on war ships would see.

That was why two years into the war one percent of all naval personnel were listed as psychiatric casualties.

* * * *

When war equipment and machinery was tested, it was taken to the limits. Steel ball bearings used in axles were heated until they expanded and jammed above 200 degrees centigrade. Piston rods in marine engines were good for ten years hard service, and the water pumps to supply cooling to the same pistons could be relied on to work for half that time. Then they broke down. Manufacturers could give the precise lifespan of a single cog or the temperature tolerances of a radio circuit because they had test beds where the pieces would be stretched, heated or pounded until they broke.

Just occasionally, two parts made by the exact same process would have very different durability. Ninety per cent of the parts would have a standard lifespan, eight per cent would last longer, one per cent five times longer than expected, and one per cent would fall to pieces after the first testing. There was no way of telling just by looking at the part.

The idea that equipment failed, predictably or unpredictably during battle was not new, or surprising. It had been known since the first archers' bowstrings snapped. What was surprising was how long it had taken before commanders realised and accepted that the men operating the equipment in war also broke. "Battle fatigue" was acknowledged in the First Word War. This was the socially and politically acceptable understanding that a soldier could become worn down or worn out by the stresses of battle. Being fatigued had public connotations of some temporary, gentlemanly interlude; a good night's sleep, some R&R away from the front line and a chap would be back to his best. "Fatigued" or exhausted was worn down, rather than broken. Recuperation was needed, rather than any major repairs. All would be well, given some time. We all get tired.

Saying that someone was unable to continue fighting the enemy because of "anxiety neurosis", on the other hand, was over the line of what was normal in the public mind. This was a special condition, not something anybody might experience. It was something that simple rest and natural recovery wouldn't cure. To the public, a man being sent back from the war with a diagnosis of neuropsychosis or psychoneurosis definitely wasn't just tired. Such a marker meant that he was irreparably damaged, to-be-kept-away-from-children bat-shit crazy.

So it was that when numbers of psychiatric casualties reached a critical level, the Admiralty had to re-think the plan to have men treated for "war neurosis" in wards within general naval hospitals at Barrow Gurney, Bristol, and Kingseat, Aberdeenshire.

Having men with a common condition treated under one roof, as might be done for burns or blindness, did have the logic of effective delivery in numbers. The volume, severity and unpredictable variety of psychiatric conditions of men coming back from the war quickly overwhelmed the side wards that had been set up in hospitals caring for physical causalities, however. Dedicated psychiatric hospitals had to be set up at Knowle, near Fareham and at Cholmondeley Castle, Cheshire. The men arriving at these hospitals would never fight again.

But amongst the thousands of psychiatric casualties coming back from war at sea, the Admiralty identified a small subset of men who just might.

They were suitable for a new form of treatment. It was time to try the Stone Frigate approach.

CHAPTER 5

THE STONE FRIGATE APPROACH

When things go wrong, everybody has a prepared fall-back position. A go-to that is a reliable recourse when it feels like the day is crumbling and everything that usually works doesn't.

For Marco in his previous life it was simple. When in doubt, tumble. Escape from difficulties in the circus ring were guaranteed. For Clarence it was, "*Three, two, one, job done.*" Turn his cap around, close out the world and focus on what was in his hands. All cares and woes forgotten. For Duncan it had been the reliable pairing of God and faith, to get him through the worst of times.

For the Royal Navy, the fall-back position had been to build more ships and recruit or press gang more men to sail those ships into battle. This simple strategy had worked for centuries, sinking any armadas put before them, maintaining Britain as the greatest sea power in the world. But now, in the space of months, that certainty had gone. The supply of men had dried up and the navy itself was in danger of being up the creek without a paddle, let alone a sail. It was time to take a lead from Mrs Sew and Sew and Make Do and Mend with what was available.

The original HMS *Standard* had been a 74-gunner launched in 1782. She was a slick two-gun deck ship, a good combination of fast and relatively cheap to build, with effective firepower. After moving into semi-retirement for harbour service in 1799, she was broken up and re-used as joists and firewood in 1816. The navy also re-used the ship's name when a respectful number of years had passed.

In 1941, the HMS *Standard* had become a Stone Frigate; an onshore Royal Navy base.

The first site considered by the Admiralty for this Stone Frigate was adjacent to an established naval base on the Orkneys, off the north coast of Scotland. Scapa Flow was a secure base during both world wars, a sheltered bay far enough from the range of German airfields.

Existing naval psychiatric units were usually set up near ports. This was a pragmatic issue to reduce travel costs for incoming patients from ships, but it was also a psychological issue. Specialist units were established near ports because psychiatrists agreed that to admit a man to an inland hospital made it doubly difficult to get him back into the right frame of mind for returning to sea.

The site at Scapa Flow was suitable for the Stone Frigate. It was also the flattest, windiest place in all of the UK. To say that the Orkneys is warmed by the Gulf Stream is a euphemism. In reality, it meant that some days in winter when the wind would normally bring driving snow, it brings driving rain instead. The average temperature was eight degrees.

Scapa Flow was a site considered precisely because it was cold, bleak and, for the Navy's purposes, testing. But it was rejected in favour of another site, equally remote and bleak, for logistic reasons. Scapa Flow might need to expand further, depending on the course of the war, and escorting and transporting men in ones and twos from the mainland to the Orkneys would be expensive in time and in travel costs. So HMS *Standard* was established at Kielder instead.

* * * *

The plan for what was to be a three-year therapeutic endeavour was developed over two short months. There was indeed a therapeutic plan, of sorts. For the men to be received at HMS *Standard,* the hard routines and challenges of life at sea experienced by other sailors were to be substituted for equally hard manual work on shore. It was to be a diversion of focus – of sorts. All of the men had a special drafting category of C(Q).

C(Q) rating meant that a man had been assessed as physically fit and amenable to training, but currently unreliable and a liability to the Navy in a time of war. C(Q) men could be removed from service on ships without being discharged. For the coffers of the Royal Navy this meant reduced claims for war pensions, at a time when invalidating men out of the Navy on physical grounds or neuropsychiatric grounds was draining the pension pot faster than it could be filled.

The layout of HMS *Standard* buildings at Kielder was V shape. There were two long rows of nine-windowed huts almost touching at the apex where they reached the woods, with shorter huts scattered in the shelter of the V, built on the driest ground, rather than in any pattern. The long huts were barracks and the others served as a clinic, two Ergotherapy, occupational therapy units, a mess hall and the main camp office and staff accommodation.

All of the huts had the same basic, barrack design. Timbers were 6x2 or 4x2 for floor and roof joints, rafters and struts. The cladding was half-inch ship-lap, treated to weather an unknown number of winters, and uniformly grey within a month of being nailed down as roof and external walls for the huts.

The original, smaller camp on the Kielder site had been built in 1933, an outpost where unemployed men were transported like prisoners and given a trade, learning the skills of fencing, road making and ditch drainage. Before the Navy took the camp on and made the huts wind and waterproof again, lumberjacks from Newfoundland had lived there, briefly, clearing swathes of the trees for building and firewood for the war effort.

Running off at an angle to one leg of the chevron of huts, a path led down a short hill to a bare patch of level ground, drained and flattened to be an exercise field. It was also used for compulsory football. Behind one of the goals, a tennis court had been marked out by thin lines, dug out and filled with sawdust. Beside the tennis court was a shed that looked like a privy, for storing the sports equipment. Around the court, lengths of tatty fishing net were held up by thin lodge pole pines, stripped of their branches, and pieces of the same fishing net with fewer holes was draped over a rope that split the court.

The huts flanked the field on one side and on the other the only road in or out of the camp ran tight against the North Tyne river, fast flowing and constantly fed by water from the surrounding moors. On a clear day, the highest point for ten miles, Garnet Fell, could be seen through a fire break in the trees.

Men were "received and processed" at HMS *Standard,* not admitted or confined. Men were patients, not prisoners, but HMS *Standard* was not a hospital ship. No-one could leave without reassignment papers and there were more frequent roll calls than anywhere else in the Royal Navy. Not all of the men had committed any naval or civil offences, but most had. These ranged from assault and larceny on shore to deserting or skulking from a place of duty, breaking out of a ship, refusing an order, and striking a superior officer while at sea.

Any attempt to leave HMS *Standard* without papers was seen as confirmation of a man's unbalanced mental state. It was thirty miles to the nearest village. There was nowhere to go. Trying to escape was as irrational as jumping off a ship at sea. But then again, the number of seamen who had been lost overboard, or accidentally drowned in the war already was far higher than could be easily explained.

There was a single gate for entry, but no barbed wire. Within a mile of the gate any runners could find the cover of wide bands of planted spruce that bordered the camp on three sides, stretching up the low hills. The dense tree cover would be a godsend for a man on the run. But then, a man could only be said to be on the run if people were actively looking for him. The few men who went out the front gate in the first few weeks, at night, had trekked a few dark miles along the road and then either turned around and come back, or collapsed, exhausted and waited for one of the passing camp trucks to take them back to camp next morning.

All of the land outside the wide strips of conifers remained as it had been before being drained by the thirsty trees. It was low lying moor as far as the Scottish border, with knee deep heather and hardy shrubs above ground. Beneath that there was deeper, unpredictable peat bog. No matter how dry the summer, the water table on the moor remained constant. The white bones of grazing hill sheep and cows that had wandered from the herd contrasted with the deep browns and greens of the bog. Tempted by growth of new shoots, the animals had sunk belly deep into the slough and died of hunger or exposure. No animals or men walked across the moor. For anything that tried, every step had to be first pushed through the thick heather, then pulled out of the mud into which it sank, until exhaustion set in.

* * * *

By the end of the war it was a navy requirement for medics who chose to specialize in neuropsychiatry to serve at least six months at sea, to gain some credibility with the men they were to treat, and to see at first hand the combat stresses on board a sea-going ship. But when the Stone Frigate at Kielder was set up in 1941, neither of the two psychiatrists in charge had ever been on a warship, although both had come from specialist navy units.

Surgeon-Lieut.-Commander A. John D. Ballard, who was in overall command of men at HMS *Standard* had been at the Royal Navy Auxiliary Hospital, Barrow Gurney. He had excelled there in adapting existing clinical treatments, making them more suited to the needs of the navy, to return men to sea as quickly as possible.

He had pioneered his own form of "Refreshment Therapy", a cut-down version of a technique used by army psychiatrists for soldiers returned from the front line in anxiety states. Selected patients arriving at Barrow Gurney with a diagnosis of operational strain syndrome, a form of sea-going shell shock, were put to sleep with an injection of Nembutal, enough to knock a man out for at least a day. When they awoke, Ballard made sure that they had a hot shower, hot food, a clean uniform and a chat with the chaplain. Some men were easily treated and back at sea within five days of arriving at the Auxiliary Hospital.

In Ballard's diagnosis, battlefield exhaustion varied only in degree, and the sooner the condition was caught, the more effectively it could be treated. The number of seamen evacuated from the front line, arriving at the hospital, could also be reduced by some psychiatric first aid at the front line. A sharp order from a senior officer, or a slap to the face would bring a few to their senses, without the need for further action. The number of patients receiving Ballard's Refreshment Therapy and returning to Barrow Gurney or other psychiatric units at a later date was not recorded.

It was Ballard's initial success rate that first attracted the attention of the Admiralty and got him assigned to Kielder. He didn't throw his hat in the ring for the job and he didn't throw his hat in the air when he was appointed. Keeping with navy tradition for such appointments, it was a short phone call followed by a longer set of orders, hand delivered from the Admiralty Executive, informing Ballard that he was being posted to Kielder, "*in recognition of outstanding results in successful treatment at Barrow Gurney, and the need for an experienced naval neuropsychiatrist to lead this new and exciting endeavour in difficult times.*"

His orders were to rehabilitate sailors whose conduct had been problematic but without any evidence of major mental illness. No targets for success were stated, but ninety per cent plus was implicit. It was a salvage operation; repair and return as many men as possible to battle, and failing that, to other duties. Through his work at Barrow Gurney, Ballard was aware of the background to Kielder.

The Admiralty had started out in 1939 with high principles. The directive to all naval neuropsychiatrists was to avoid the mistakes of the First World War, when the unforeseen epidemic of shell shock had swamped the front line and home-based hospitals, leaving no spaces for those with physical wounds.

In the First World War wards were filled with men who had lost the ability to walk or to talk for no apparent reason. There were men who lay in bed all day, frowning and grimacing, baring their teeth like chimpanzees in a zoo. In the grounds of hospitals, men with bandaged wounds and stumps limped on the same paths as men who skipped from place to place or walked like they were hooked up to live electricity, jerking and twitching uncontrollably.

The Admiralty's proposed strategy in World War 2 was

twofold; to tighten up on the type of men who were recruited to the navy in the first place, and on the criteria for diagnosing verifiable, combat-related disorders. The term shell shock was banned as unhelpful. As an extra financial disincentive, the criteria for receiving a naval pension were restricted to discourage men seeking premature discharge. All the plans to learn from World War 1, to prevent a tsunami of psychiatric causalities, went to shit in the first year of the World War 2.

All the Admiralty careful recruitment filtering of sailors, checking suitability for battle was rendered useless by the intensity of the fighting itself. No one had predicted what crews would face. Recruits on ships were rushing to be fully trained before they were killed. Naval personnel broke down in thousands. Then the critical one per cent level was reached. What was more surprising was that it was not more. The average age of sailors on the Arctic convoys was less than twenty, but photos of those who came back showed faces that looked ten years older.

* * * *

Even before the last piece of ship-lap cladding had been nailed down to make the barracks ready to receive the first patient, Ballard had split the men arriving at Kielder into three groups. In his own psychiatric classification, these groups were the temperamentally unstable, the malingerers and a third hut set aside for cases of low morale. On site there were also three cells. Ballard intended to use these only in extreme circumstances, and for a small number of resistant-to-treatment or agitated patients.

In the absence of cells in previous institutions he had found sheets and blankets to be effective. Sheets dipped in warm or cold water could be wrapped around a man from head to toe and left in place for a few hours. The technique had a calming effect and allowed agitated patients, and medical staff, to get some rest. Dry sheets or even blankets could be used in cold conditions.

Ballard had treatment planned for the three huts. These were sure-fire fixes that would either return men to active service, or move them on to somewhere more suitable, freeing up another bunk for more promising material, another sailor more worthy.

A. John D. Ballard came from a long lineage of medical men. His father had been a mere family doctor, which had disappointed his surgeon grandfather. He could trace the medical tradition back through a series of sons and brothers who had all been professional healers. There were bone doctors and stomach doctors, even a syphilologist, as well as head doctors like himself, going back many generations.

Handwritten records were kept by mothers and grandmothers and proudly passed down to each new medical man in the family when he graduated and joined the profession. Every family has secrets and somewhere in Ballard's ancestry was the physician and surgeon Dr James Dowden-Ballard, the only medic on the family tree to bring shame rather than fame to the medical dynasty.

James Dowden-Ballard had been dismissed from his post at Haslar Hospital in Portsmouth after inexplicably drowning three of his patients in a hogshead cask. Over a period of weeks, he had persuaded or forced the men to climb into the wooden barrel and then held their heads under water until they were dead. So sensational were his deeds that they were reported in *The Times* of London. Dowden-Ballard disappeared from Haslar before he could be apprehended and was believed to have left Portsmouth for the American colonies soon after, deserting his wife and three sons.

As a result of the shame brought on the family James' brother, Alexander Dowden-Ballard, a country doctor in Suffolk, shortened his double-barrelled name to D. Ballard, to avoid the stigma by association for him and for subsequent generations. If anyone asked, the D stood for David or Donald or whatever else came to mind.

A. John. D. Ballard, the latest in the line of doctors in the family, had expertise in psychiatric diagnosis, but he was being called upon by the navy to extend this to an assessment of a man's occupational readiness. All patients at Kielder would be treated with the same dignity and naval discipline. There would be therapy available from day one for each man. The Admiralty had a clear line on what conditions should be for men in Naval

Detention Quarters (NDQ): *"Places of detention must not offer greater but less attractions than service with the unit."*

So Kielder was not to became an attractive alternative to duty, but nothing so severe that men felt that they were serving a sentence which they could lie and cheat their way out, just by saying the right things. It was to be a new combination of treatment, containment and punishment, an uncomfortable mix of carrot and stick.

But above all, the purpose of the camp was salvage. Kielder was to take the cast offs and put them on the road to a particular type of recovery, the Admiralty way: *"The building up of self-respect by discipline of the right sort."*

* * * *

There was a naval commanding officer and four subordinate officers living on-site, charged with maintaining navy discipline during rehabilitation, in addition, to the two psychiatrists, a medical officer and a number of navy day staff to supervise the therapeutic activities.

HMS *Standard* was an island in a bog, rather than floating at sea. It was a unique facility in other ways too. Whereas existing treatment centres were under the control of the Royal Navy Medical Service, Kielder was managed directly by the Admiralty Executive. This made it the only place in the Royal Navy where punishment could be meted out by medical officers.

This was potentially problematic for the medics. For any doctor who took seriously the do-no-harm Hippocratic oath, punishing patients was like being a conscientious objector asked to take up arms. The staff at Kielder were carefully briefed however, willing to suspend normal rules of medical engagement to achieve what was necessary for the war effort. If there had been a traditional navy sick list at the camp, under navy regulations, it would have included every man there. So the sick list was restricted to physical injuries and ailments that could readily be verified by medical testing. Any other complaints were considered part of a man's condition and his reason for being there.

Ballard gave his induction address to the full team of staff assembled before the first batch of patients arrived and he delivered the same address, in its entirety, to individual replacement staff over the following three years.

"Exceptional circumstances require exceptional measures," was his opener.

Ballard emphasised that punishment should never be a first line of treatment. Any severe discipline was, he explained, part of the master plan for treatment and may be used only under particular circumstances. The main difficulty with the master plan was that nobody–the psychiatrists, the PT and OT instructors, the outdoor supervisors or the men who were received at HMS *Standard*–had seen the plan in its entirety.

The psychiatrists were given freedom to experiment, based on their previous successes. New treatments were to be devised to first identify, then repair damaged men, quickly. The men were for repair and re-use, as Ballard also explained in his induction.

"The psychiatrist, men, has a bag of tools and an instruction manual with many pages missing. His task is to repair the human machines put before him, to restore men to working order."

At Kielder, the usual medical ethical guidelines, which could send new treatments into the long grass of piloting and development phases for many years, could be circumvented, or done retrospectively, with the tacit approval on the Admiralty. Ballard had complete medical charge of the camp. His criterion for what was acceptable and what was not was results. If a C(Q) man could be salvaged and returned to active service by treatment at HMS *Standard,* that was the end of argument on how this was achieved. The methods used could be general or special.

For the final part of this induction talk, Ballard's voice rose, as he imagined himself talking not to a handful of dutifully interested camp staff in the middle of a North England moor, but to the nation, or at least the Royal Medical Psychological Association, where he pictured himself invited to deliver his address at the end of the war.

"In a war, product not process is what counts, men. To win well does not matter to me nor to the enemy. If we have more of

these men standing and serving their country than the enemy at the end of the war, we will have succeeded. Our mission, your mission, is to return fighting navy men to their ships."

Kielder was a test bed, a crucible where ideas could be tried and where something new could be created. Men were referred to as "the material". The outdoor work and psychotherapy under naval discipline were designed to stretch and challenge the men sent to HMS *Standard*. Just like machine parts however, any two men put through the same process might have very different durability, and breaking points. There was no way of telling just by looking at the material.

*   *   *   *

George Thurman was a civilian psychiatrist who had been persuaded to delay his retirement as part of the war effort. He had been working short term at Royal Navy Auxiliary Hospital, Kingseat, Newmachar and he was glad of the chance to return to Northumberland. Doing the job in Newmachar was bread and butter psychiatry. It didn't make his heart race or his soul sing, and Aberdeenshire had been cold, really cold. He dreaded getting up some mornings not because of the succession of broken men he would see that day, but because he could hear the howling wind, chilled by the North Sea and set to blow for 24 hours.

His experience as an asylum psychiatrist had been split between training, learning his trade, at Newcastle Upon Tyne asylum, then at St George's in Morpeth, where he was one of four duty psychiatrists for 420 patients. After the first five years of excitement and seeing how many ways the human brain could spring a surprise on its owner and on psychiatry, the work had become a grind.

Repetition; different names, same conditions, same prognosis. Overcrowded and permanently smelling of piss, the wards were just locked bedrooms where it was difficult for anyone to sleep, or to act like they didn't belong there. His job, he told nurses at St Georges, was nothing more than keeping the screaming, fighting and moaning to a minimum. And that was just among the staff, he would joke.

The prospect of being able to move back to Northumberland and have two psychiatrists for just 100 patients at HMS Standard was more like the easing down he had in mind when he agreed to delay his retirement. There was no telling how long the war would drag on and it was a chance too good to pass up. Even the thought of the wounds opened up by running into one of his two ex-wives who lived in Newcastle was not enough to keep him from saying yes.

His new mission at Kielder, shared with anyone at Kingseat who asked and many who didn't, was twofold. He would help those he could, obviously, using his vast experience of repairing human minds. But he had been chosen and was being called upon by the Navy, he believed, principally because of his particular ability to weed out the duplicitous.

Thurman prided himself on knowing when a patient was ill and when they were conveniently ill. He had already come across a steady stream of sailors at the Navy Auxiliary Hospital feigning psychosis to escape service. But Dr George Thurman knew what psychosis looked like and he had the chancers he encountered back out the door of his office and onto a ship before they could finish describing just how crazy they were. He had come across a lot of scams in his years. He no longer found it surprising how far people would go in feigning symptoms. There had been women faking hysterical fits to avoid being married off to men old enough to be their uncle, men pleading memory loss in front of a judge after being nicked for heinous crimes, and even a priest claiming to be Jesus after an immaculate conception had left two of his parishioners pregnant.

After all he had seen over the years, he should not have been surprised when he was shown the *Malingerer's Guide,* but he was. Some bright spark in London, by all accounts doing good business and lining his pockets, had put together a list of symptoms, guaranteed to get you out of having to fight for your county. The *Malingerer's Guide,* printed in tiny letters and disguised as a regular book of matches, was being sold to army and navy recruits. One of the books of matches had made it as far north as Aberdeenshire, found in the possessions of a sailor who had done a runner from the Newmachar hospital.

In the ongoing war on malingering, the Admiralty had countered the match book circulating in London with a leaflet issued to all Navy Auxiliary Hospitals called, *"The Methods of the Conscious Deceiver (A few hints as to how to examine and how to deal with feigned sickness and disease)."*

The match book and the leaflet had alerted George to the lengths to which some men would go, and the level of cunning that he would need to nail them. These were men, cowards in any battle, lacking even the courage to desert. He had already caught one rating, referred for heart problems and cyanosis. Only by prolonged observations and secret searches of the man's locker was Thurman able to discover that the paralysis and blue tinge in the man's fingers and toes was due not to poor circulation, but to the army issue Ointment Number 2 the man had been eating at night. The ointment was designed for the application to skin exposed to mustard gas in World War 1. How anyone had discovered it effects on the body when ingested was another mystery of malingering.

Bed wetters and other hysterical cases who had been given the benefit of the doubt by other medics and sent to Thurman were more difficult to catch out, but when George Thurman's malingerer antennae started twitching, he stayed on a man's case until he exposed him for what he was.

So George was ready to go back to Northumberland and to do his duty at Kielder.

* * * *

Navy routine was maintained at HMS *Standard* at Kielder. The Royal Navy ensign was raised every morning and lowered at dusk. The flagpole was over twice the height of anything else in the camp, constantly in the line of sight, as if to remind men of their loyalty wherever they were in the camp.

To keep men in touch with the navy, the daily timetable was the same, regardless of which hut a man lived in or where he spent his day. It started with turn-out at 6.45 and ended with navy pipe down at 22.00. Breakfast was at 8.00, after PT, dinner was at 12.10 and supper at 19.00, again after PT.

A man's time was only his own during the day for ten minutes stand easy at 10.45 and again at 14.45. Between supper and pipe down was the only time a man had choice. He could attend the Occupational Therapy room to draw, paint or for woodwork or plastic work, or he could do more PT. There was a discussion group before pipe down, led by the chaplain. This was restricted however, to men who had been classified as having a high eductive ability.

Work parties were sent out of the camp in trucks at 9.00 sharp each morning to do tree felling, land drainage and farm labour and these men stayed away all day. Those who remained did physical labour in the morning – sawed logs, dug drainage ditches around the camp, shifted rocks from the riverbank, or did maintenance on the camp's vehicles –and in the afternoon there was school, drill and route marches.

Each man was weighed and examined once a week and the amount of physical labour was stepped up for any man gaining pounds that wasn't muscle mass. There was church service on Sundays, and even a once-a-week rum issue to the men at the camp, miles from sea. The psychiatrists, Ballard and Thurman, agreed on the main routines, and where they differed in opinion Thurman deferred to Ballard.

While music by Wagner and Koniggratzer Marsch was being used to drown out screams and the sound of gunshots executing prisoners in Nazi concentration camps 800 miles away, the speakers on the poles at Kielder blasted out carefully chosen tunes from Ballard's gramophone in his office. What he played was a subset of what he had brought with him from Barrow Gurney and records that he had procured through his camp allowance for essential therapeutic supplies.

He didn't have much ammunition to use the scratchy gramophone as a psychological weapon in the fight for men's spirit, but what he had was enough for most occasions. Physical Therapy sessions were to the tune of Shep Fields and his Rippling

Rhythm Orchestra, making the star jumps easier with *Whistle While you Work*. For music to keep the pulses steady, and the men calm, Ballard went with the waves of soothing piano in the Warsaw Concerto.

In his interviews with new arrivals, Ballard got snippets of information from men about the music that was popular with those on the front line, and he used this information to keep the men at Kielder in touch with what their battling colleagues were listening to, so they would be up to speed when they went back to active service.

But Ballard had to be careful. His well-worn copies of *It's Been a Long Long Time* by the Harry James Band and *Ten Days With Baby* by Benny Goodman, brought with him from Barrow Gurney, were played in his office only when he had disconnected the speakers, to avoid stirring up the wrong kind of longings in men. And therein lay the dilemma for Ballard. Should he be using the music to make the men forget the experiences they had been through, or to remind them that there was still a war on, and that they were missing it, and everything else outside the confines of Kielder Camp?

One afternoon he had played just two records, continuously for two hours, just to test if the music had any effect on behaviour of men in the camp, or if anyone would complain, or even notice. The two tunes he played were *Cleanin' my Rifle (and Dreaming of You)* by Count Bassie and *Praise the Lord and Pass the Ammunition* by Kay Kyser and his orchestra. There was no reaction whatsoever, apart from one of his junior officers knocking on his door to check that he was OK.

On the same afternoon as Ballard was playing his two gun tunes, far away in Buchenwald Dutch, Polish and German Jews were being lined up and forced to sing patriotic songs about a Fatherland that was no longer theirs, and never had been. The punishment for not singing loudly, or enthusiastically enough was a beating or death. The forced singing and the choice of songs had the desired effect, demoralising prisoners to the point where submission seemed the only choice.

Also at the same time, on ships somewhere off Bear Island,

Vera Lynn was assuring men fighting ice storms, U-Boats on the PQ7b convoy that there would, indeed, be bluebirds over the white cliffs of Dover, just you wait and see.

Neither the navy nor the army fully understood why it was important to keep music close to where men were dying in battle, but the lengths to which they went to get records and radios into frontline positions acknowledged that it was a priority. Men were not as easily led into death as in the First World War, when all that was needed to make men charge to their death into machine guns and cannons was a piper, a kilt and *Hielen' Laddie* blasting out over the sound of guns. But music could still do a job.

* * * *

The rail line that ran from Riccarton Junction in the Scottish Borders south east to Hexham, linked the Scottish and English rail networks. A basic wooden platform had been built to create Lewiefield Halt station. The station was little more than a glorified hut, a waiting room and office, where trains had stopped with supplies and men bound for the original "Lewie Camp", one of the government's first job creation schemes. The camp, now HMS *Standard* at Kielder, had housed the unemployed but willing men, in the isolation of the moor. In the absence of decent roads, the rail line was convenient. The Admiralty however, had good reasons for not sending seamen to Kielder by train.

Men arrived instead in batches of between six and ten, in uniform, transported in the back of a Royal Navy Bedford bus, kit bags at their feet. The letters RN were prominent on the side of the bus, painted in white. The more usual transport between navy medical units was a covered Dodge truck, with a Red Cross painted side and top. The Navy didn't use an ambulance for transport to Kielder, to reinforce the fact that it was not a hospital.

Psychologically, the bus had other advantages too. Windows for one, so that men did not feel that they were being confined and exiled, at least until they reached Kielder and saw the huts that looked like the internment camps being built elsewhere in the country, despite the absence of a high fence.

In the early days, the RN bus attracted little attention as it travelled through the villages of Bellingham and Falstone coming north, with Marco and Clarence, or through Hawick and Bonchester Bridge transporting Duncan, south from Scotland. The Admiralty had sent local newspapers a short press release, to put them off the scent of the real story. The press release explained how the camp was to be used for conscientious objectors, who were being put to work in the forestry, to replace the lumberjacks from Newfoundland who had been there between 1939–40. Conchies were being sent there either to help the war effort, or as a punishment for their cowardice, depending on your point of view.

When that story began to be doubted by locals, the Admiralty changed tact, saying that the men were in fact injured seamen who had been disfigured and needed special treatment. After just three months, local gossip about madmen locked in cells, and deserters and shirkers at the camp were rife, spread by the few local suppliers allowed access to the camp with groceries. People in the villages around Kielder started to do double takes on Royal Navy Bedford buses so far from sea. The buses began to draw stares and pointed fingers as they passed.

* * * *

On arrival, men were billeted first in the smaller Reception Hut. The next day they went through increasingly probing interviews with the chaplain, the schoolmaster, the medical officer, then Ballard or Thurman as the psychiatrists. In the space of six hours the questions went quickly from, "*Settling in OK? Which church did you attend as a boy?*", through, "*Any problems with the waterworks?*", to, "*Did you ever get into trouble at school?*", and "*Do you get bored easily?*"

Ballard played his interviews by the book, starting with the Penrose-Raven Progressive Matrices, to test basic IQ, before more specific tests, and an interview, going through his standard list of open ended questions. The Penrose-Raven picture tests required a person to fill in the blank in a figure where one part had been missed out, choosing from four possible shapes. The Matrices gave Ballard a starting point, a measure of a man's eductive ability. By gauging a basic level of intelligence, Ballard could decide how much time he should spend in the rest of the interview and how much effort the rest of the staff at Kielder should spend working with the man.

The Navy did have the better pick of recruits from the civilian population originally, it was true, and the general intelligence test weeded out the worst, but there were still some cracked eggs that slipped through. The decision had been taken by the Admiralty not to send any defectives to Kielder, but Ballard still found himself interviewing some dull men, many without secondary education.

Rehabilitating a backward man to the point where he could be returned to navy service was virtually impossible, in Ballard's view. There is so little material to work with, and no common grounds for personal contact. Appealing to a sense of honour or motivating such a man with a dread of shame was effort wasted, because such principles required some basic reasoning abilities, absent in these men probably from birth. Ballard could detect and categorise two types in hopeless cases of low intelligence in particular, usually within minutes of meeting them.

The first were examples of the worst kind of British manhood, floating around the Navy until Kielder became a kind of sump into which such specimens would drain. There were aggressive, egotistic men, who came into his office and sat without being asked. It took very few questions to establish that they had little interest in anything except beer, betting and women. They preferred fighting with the police to combat with the enemy. Ballard noted that these men often came from mixed blood, with the Clydeside Irish especially prone to this kind of impulsive lifestyle, lacking self-control. With or without any underlying mental illness, these men were totally incorrigible, resistant to treatment. The worst of this type would laugh in his face and openly admit that he would rather be locked up, anywhere, than face a force eight gale and the Nazis.

This type of case knew no shame. One man had complained

loudly in Ballard's office when he was searched on suspicion of having stolen cigarettes. When the cigarettes were not found on him, he then boasted to Ballard that he had in fact stolen them and then hidden them. These men were likely idle and insubordinate from a young age, and Ballard assessed and dismissed them as unsuitable for treatment within minutes. They were after their ticket out of the Navy, and any way of getting it. If all else failed, these incorrigibles would even claim to be conscientious objectors and like real conchies that Ballard had come across, they were never backward about coming forward with opinions and complaints. He was forced to send such men to permanent shore services which, for them, was a second best, cushy number where they could see out the war.

The other type of backward men were the inadequates, who could be further subdivided into loafers, shirkers and non-triers. A characteristic of all inadequates, Ballard discovered, was that they had never played games at school. Even those who said they had were lying. Character and manliness in these men had never been acquired or tested. They were fussy poltroons, useless in a real battle. Typically, they could function perfectly well in dance halls, bars and cinemas when on home leave, but developed black-outs, fainting fits and other symptoms when they stood on the departure platform to return to their ship, or on when falling in for navy inspection. Ballard took some guilty, professional pleasure in the surprise of these poor specimens when they discovered that nearly every other man in Number 3 hut at Kielder had identical headaches and dizziness. Ballard enjoyed witnessing each man's utter incredulity when he discovered that the medical officers and other staff at the camp were uninterested and unimpressed with their symptoms.

Ballard searched for the potential of return to active service in all of his incoming psychiatric casualties, but he was aware that effort wasted on a hopeless case was effort that could have been put to better use on a man with character.

Some cases were beyond help by their own design and there were others with wiring that was irreparably damaged, usually no fault of their own. These cases had to be removed for long term hospital treatment almost as soon as they arrived. Ballard despaired at some of the cases that been diagnosed by his fellow psychiatrists and sent as suitable material to Kielder. One of the first admissions had been a naval Wireman, clearly delusional, who had been found with schizophrenic drawings in all his pockets. The man was drawing a world that didn't exist, except in his head. Another rating, from a very good home but with filthy habits, repeatedly disobeyed orders and struck two superior officers when challenged. Both of these cases could and should have been spotted at the depot hospitals, even by junior medical staff, and redirected appropriately, rather than to Kielder.

With more facilities and more time, Ballard concluded, it may have been possible to harden off a few of these hopeless cases and send them back to ships. But in the six-month maximum turnaround for each man set by the Admiralty, little could be done for them at Kielder that would make a difference. Ultimately, most would be prematurely discharged as unsuitable, unlikely to make a reliable sailor. It would be pointless to try to convert to better ways those unlikely ever to be of any use to their country in any capacity in the time he had available. At the same time, for such a man to gain an easy exemption from serving his country, just by refusing while others served, would only tempt malinger-waverers to follow suit. So Ballard had to be at least seen to be trying.

* * * *

Surgeon-Lieut.-Commander A. John D. Ballard prided himself on being able to assess, on the basis of his first meeting with a new rating, a man's suitability for re-drafting. He could accurately predict the likelihood of the man going back into service at his three-month review. The likelihood was written either as a zero or as a tick in very small notation in the bottom corner of the man's record. Ballard was never wrong in his professional judgement. Even in cases where men seemed ready to go back or were reluctant to do so, Ballard acted on his first meeting zeros and ticks to detain them further or to put them on the next available transport.

Marco came into the small office and Ballard pulled his chair closer to his desk, readying his fountain pen for interview notes. He was encouraged to have some promising material at last. It was his fourth interview that day and the others who had attempted the Penrose-Raven Matrices had ranged from a farmboy-thick deckhand to a ship's cook who held the pencil like he was stirring soup.

As well as the Matrices, Ballard also put Marco through the Dot Counting Test, a new measure developed by a Swiss psychologist, to root out malingerers.

As a psychiatrist, Ballard considered anything Swiss, by definition, to be unquestionably sound. Not only did they make impeccable quality watches and knives, but they had avoided having their country trampled on and bombed in war by the simple expedient of saying, "*No thanks.*"

When he read about the new Dot test while still working at Barrow Gurney, Ballard had written a personal letter to Andre Rey at the Burghölzli psychiatric hospital in Zurich, explaining the set up at Kielder, and offering to share any data he collected in exchange for permissions for use of the Dot Counting Test. To his delight and professional pride, he received a reply within the month, with a copy of test instructions, cards and a short note in French agreeing to the proposed arrangement.

Patients were asked to count a random spread of dots on cards presented to them, and then asked to count the same number of grouped dots, lined up in rows. The recorded time taken to count both sets of dots increased gradually for normal, cooperative patients as the number of dots increased, simply because it took longer to count more dots. For the malingerer, however, the times taken to count dots varied unpredictably as the number of dots increased; sometimes faster, sometimes slower. Andre Ray's test detected this variation as an attempt to feign war induced anxiety state, or *encéphalopathie traumatique*. When the malingerer's time to count grouped dots was higher than his time to count the same number of ungrouped dots, this was strong evidence that the patient was not acting in good faith and feigned psychosis was to be strongly suspected. A recognised characteristic of malingers was that they tried to suppress their true abilities.

When Ballard moved the tests to the centre of his desk, Marco looked at the papers then at Ballard's pile of instructions.

"*I should tell you up front Doc, that I don't read too good,*" he said.

"*That's OK Seaman Craston,*" Ballard replied, squaring up the papers. "*There is no reading required for these tests. You can count up to ten, I assume?*"

"*Yeah, doc, counting's no problem.*"

Marco's dot counting timings charted as a straight line; two seconds for the first set of dots, up to eleven seconds for the largest group. His times were slightly slower that the averages given in instructions by Andre Ray, but he could count the random dots faster than the ordered dots, which puzzled Ballard a bit. He had also completed the Matrices with a maximum score, flying through the matching of shapes.

Three questions into Marco's interview however, Ballard was forced, for the first time, to consider the reliability of both the Penrose-Raven Matrices and the Dot Counting Test. Was it possible for a man with low eductive ability to have high shape perception without having any trace of real intelligence, and was it possible for that man to fake timings consistently on the dots test?

Marco's performance indicated a good basic level of intelligence. But his interview answers seemed to be in response a different set of questions.

"*Now, before we start writing anything down Seaman Craston,*" Ballard addressed all of the patients as "seaman" on every occasion, a gentle reminder of where they belonged, "*can you remind me why you're here at Kielder?*"

This was his standard opener, to get a gauge of how aware a man was of his condition and environment, or how delusional.

Marco spoke clearly, but fast.

"*I reckon that I've been sent here to die like Tuflo, doc. See, I've been molti naflo for weeks now, been off my usual skran and what they all say is that the water was melalo after the dive, but me, I know it's the misery doc."*

Marco paused.

"You don't have to keep it from me any longer."

Ballard looked up from his pad, nodding professionally.

"Right...Seaman Craston," he said, latching onto the few words he had understood, *"this chap Tuflo, was he one of your shipmates? Someone that you lost in battle, someone close to you perhaps?"*

"No doc, Tuflo was an elephant see, just a young bull, hardly getting started in his life when he was gone. I've seen the misery with birds too, doc. Birds that have been locked up. First the plumage goes then sure as eggs the will follows and the bird goes feet up."

Ballard looked down at the blank sheet in front of him, not sure what to write, or where to steer his questioning next.

"I see. An elephant...,".

Ballard knew that some of the navy divisions had mascots. A bird maybe, but an elephant seemed unlikely. He stalled for time, using one of his standard reflexive replies, *"...that must have been difficult for you."*

When Ballard was out of his comfort zone with patients, his hyperhidrosis kicked in. It had started in his times as a junior, when he first moved from textbooks to real people. This was not any tell-tale underarm stains on his fresh, white shirts, or a cold, sticking stream running down his back; it was a flooding incontinence in his palms. He carried a handkerchief the size of a tea towel for these emergencies. The sheer volume of liquid ruled out wiping his hands on his uniform surreptitiously or burying his hands in his pockets. Over the years he had devised strategies to mask his condition. He produced the sheet of a handkerchief now, wiping it once across his nose for effect, then bunching it evenly between two clenched fists, under the cover of his desk, like a magician ready to produce the lengths of silk that would impress an audience.

Marco was still talking.

"It was doc. Hard to see anything go that way. And the worst was, we never even had time to bury him proper before we

moved on. Just left him there in that field by the sewage works for somebody to find and wonder how he got there."

"In a field? I see."

Ballard wondered if Marco was delusional, or if it was some trauma-induced reinterpretation of actual events. Maybe something that happened to him on his ship, or even in his childhood. Did he believe the elephant was real? Did the elephant represent a pet or a parent who had died?

Ballard knew he had to find more familiar ground and come back to the elephant later, maybe after more tests on Marco.

In desperation, he glanced across his desk at the single sheet of typed notes that had come as Marco's referral form, now clipped to a handwritten note from the Kielder medical officer, who had met with Marco earlier. Letting go of the handkerchief with one hand, he drew the papers towards him. He read that before being sent to HMS *Standard,* Marco had been considered for a re-scrub at gunnery school. But whoever had interviewed Marco had realised, like Ballard, that a simple refresher course on firing naval weaponry was not going to solve the problem with miserable elephants.

Ballard read more from the typed notes.

"I see that you have had some pains in your stomach on board ship. Let me ask you about those," he said.

Marco was slumped forward in this chair but sat upright again as he spoke.

"Well doc, the pains they come and go. Sometimes so bad that I can't straighten up, couldn't load a pistol, never mind a shell in the turret. Can't even walk, other times, except round and round the decks, like a horse around a ring, going nowhere. The walking eases it up a bit see, least takes my mind off it. The pains are not so bad now, just come and go. But I know they're always there, quiet inside see, eating me up, bit by bit."

As Marco spoke, he mimed. First bending over again, then straightening up, loading an imaginary pistol, carrying a shell, then rolling his head as he described his circuit of the decks, finally making crocodiles with this fingers and thumbs as he mimed the hungry pains, eating at him. He stopped and sat back in his chair.

Ballard was distracted for a few seconds by Marco's mime and lost the thread of his questioning. He looked at the notes again.

"*Yes, the pains must have been difficult for you too,*" he said, buying more time, keeping his head down as he read.

"*Did you have any pains like this before you joined up seaman?*"

Marco's performing hands dropped into to his lap and stayed there.

"*Some, but nothing so multi kativa as this doc. Some landings and tumbles where I missed my mark and took a sore one, but I was soon back up, tumbling again. This is different. I know it.*" He paused and then asked in a quieter voice, "*What's it say in them papers you got there doc? How long do they reckon?*"

The medical officer's note was brief. The patient had been tested for stomach cancer and later for suspected peptic ulcer before being referred to Kielder. None of the usual symptoms were present, in duration or pattern of onset. Non-ulcer dyspepsia or more likely psychogenic gastrointestinal reaction was the cause of the reported pains. Ballard knew from his experience at Barrow Gurney that a suspected peptic ulcer was one of the most common medical routes off a ship.

Medics always erred on the side of caution for unexplained symptoms, but some seamen knew this and used it. Many were genuinely ill, the combat stress of the front line having burned an acid hole in their gut. In the First World War the first sign of battle fatigue had been the shaking hand. In the Second World War it was more and more the shaking stomach. But some shirkers played the peptic ulcer card well, with textbook escalation of symptoms, timed to coincide with proximity to ports. They made the most of their symptoms, felt no disgrace at abandoning their posts, and were content to leave other men to fight in their place.

The interview was at a crucial stage. Experience told Ballard to take it slowly, to avoid confronting the patient with scepticism at this early stage, anything that indicated that the patient wasn't believed, either about his stomach pains or about his elephant.

"*Well Craston, I think it's mostly good news,*" Ballard said. "*Dr Bell hasn't found any of the usual signs for the stomach complaint that you've been having, and it sounds like there has been an improvement since you came ashore.*"

Ballard then spoke more slowly, watching Marco's reaction.

"*I think we may be able to continue the improvement by what we can do together here at Kielder. The doctor and I will keep a close eye on your condition and meet with you to see how it's going. I think we can be hopeful.*" He put his pen down.

Ballard decided that was far enough to push for now, keeping it vague, saying things were getting better, but not how. Explaining to Marco the difference between a real ulcer and a functional, psychosomatic disorder might come later, or not at all. The patients didn't need to know what was wrong with them, only that they were getting better, ready to go back to sea, repaired. Ballard would raise the idea of a return to service gradually, over the first month. Too soon and Craston's pains could return. He might be ready to hear about going back after a month, having seen other men at later stages of recovery.

"*We'll get you started on camp duties and see how you progress from there, shall we? You might like to join one of the work parties going out later, when you're up to it. And remember, my office is always open Seaman, if you want to talk with me or any of the other staff. We are here to help you get well.*"

Marco listened without changing his expression. His hands opened on his lap, as he shrugged and spoke in the same quiet voice.

"*Well, I never heard of nobody or nothing recover from the misery doc, I'll be honest, but I hear what you're saying. Even if it only slows it down for a while, that's something, eh? And I've never seen a place like this, in the Navy or out, so who knows.*"

Ballard waited for a few seconds for Marco to pick up the cue to leave, then stood to show what was required. At this, Marco looked up, got to his feet with a half salute and shuffled out of the office. Ballard bundled the damp handkerchief in his briefcase with another from a previous interview and took out a freshly ironed replacement.

* * * *

After administering the bank of tests and the first interview, Ballard was hopeful about Seaman Clarence Watson, putting him on a tick as someone who would draft back into service if not at three-month then certainly at six. His main difficulty was where to place Clarence in the treatment programme.

His bulk and strength made him a first choice for the outside parties. He could do the work of two men without complaint when directed to the trees to be felled or the ditches to be dug. Clarence's preference however, coaxed from him over two disjointed interviews with Ballard, was to work on machines. He had been written up for a trial period on truck maintenance. This had gone well. In some ways, too well.

The therapeutic aim of the machine work was process, not product. To have a man gainfully occupied for hours at a time was an important step on the road back to navy service. On the camp vehicles there were always maintenance checks to be done, plugs, oil, water and fuel levels, plus identification of rust and other wear and tear for replacement.

On his first morning Clarence had been tasked with standard checking of a truck engine. Left alone, he had stripped almost to component parts with only basic tools, before reassembly, all without reference to the workshop manual. The process had taken him three hours. The officer in charge of transport maintenance had reported Clarence to Ballard for refusing an order, although the order–to stop–had come too late, when the gasket head and radiator had already been removed and engine parts were already laid out neatly on blankets on the workshop floor. Clarence's trial period on maintenance was discontinued and he was switched to river bank duties.

Once a week, two giant tipper trucks with grabs visited the camp to collect piles of boulders that had been lifted by the river working parties and moved to the side of the road. Only boulders above a set diameter, checked with a measuring rope, were suitable for the dam to be built, further up the valley. River work, like truck work, was also process; in Ballard's scheme of treatment it was following orders and engagement in hard physical labour to run interference on whatever mental demons were distracting men from returning to their ships.

Clarence was warned on his first day about carrying rocks by himself from the river bank. All rocks were to be lifted by pairs of men, working cooperatively, he was told. Boulders may be rolled, if suitable after extraction, to the roadside by one man, but only if his partner agrees to this arrangement. In the weeks that followed, none of the men that Clarence was paired with had any objections to Clarence rolling massive boulders to the roadside by himself while they watched.

Clarence liked the endless but varied repetition of the boulder work. New rocks of different shapes and sizes were waiting in the river each day, washed down, or exposed by the flow of water changing from the removal of boulders the previous day. He liked the satisfaction of the effort in shifting the boulders, and seeing the flowing river solving the puzzle set by re-routing to accommodate the new bank. There were calculations to be done in his head, on how best to first extract, then move large boulders of different shapes. As he removed a boulder, he tried to predict how the forces of the water would re-shape the bank. But it was basic physics without technology. Something was missing. Without tools or machines to work with, he was like a musician without an instrument, allowed to listen to music, but not to play it.

He stayed with the boulder work for the first three weeks, to show Ballard that he was willing, then went to ask for a transfer back to the truck maintenance. Ballard agreed after discussion that he could do three days of river work and two on the trucks, to be reviewed if the transport officer reported that Clarence could follow orders and limit disassembly to only what was necessary.

Ballard saw this work detail negotiation as a definite indicator of Clarence's improvement. The man was still hard to draw out of his hard shell, it had been observed. Instructors reported that Clarence seldom started any conversations with staff or with other men, but he was spending more time at breaks closer to groups, listening, rather than finding the most isolated spaces to sit, as he had done to begin with. He was silent, but his work rate and general compliance with orders couldn't be faulted.

As Ballard charted his progress in his colour coded notes, he puzzled over what would constitute a return to normal for Clarence. What would be better *enough* for Clarence? Had Clarence ever been someone who felt the need for other people before his breakdown, or had he been a loner who was now functioning as he had before? There was no way of knowing from his record, but Ballard's judgement was that Clarence had never been a leader much less a follower of those around him. He didn't seem content, but then he showed none of the signs of distress or temperamental instability that had brought him to Kielder.

In past cases like this Ballard had seen constitutional timidity, a permanent emotional scar from battle experience that left a man half of what he had been. Clarence was not timid. Ballard had already discontinued red dotting his notes (new admission or incorrigible case) and moved onto black dot entries (definite and significant improvement in condition). For now, his green Eberhard Faber coloured pencil remained in its tin in Ballard's desk drawer.

Only men whose entries were green dotted for a continuous period of two weeks were passed fit for preparation to return to shore or ship duty. Some men who had had a combat role would never return to a battleship because of extent of the damage they had suffered, but they could function well doing the boring but necessary tasks of maintaining anti-torpedo nets around harbours, or dock repairs on damaged ships.

Clarence stayed on the black dots on Ballard's notes for the time being.

* * * *

Clarence watched and listened, each day learning more. He worked with the other men from all the other huts and ate with them, and at night in Number 2 hut he heard them talk with others or with themselves until they fell asleep or he did. Each man at HMS *Standard* was there for a reason. What Clarence couldn't decide was how many different reasons there might be. Two, five, ten or as many reasons as there were men? But he was not Ballard, the clever psychiatrist. He was Clarence the engineer. He looked around Kielder and what he saw was men who were worn, broken or malfunctioning.

Malfunction was different from broken. There was always a reason for what was wrong with a machine, but finding it was not always possible, even for him. A radio with a single loose connection among thousands might fire up and transmit nine times out of ten, or go silent and dead for hours, before sparking back to life. Do you replace the whole radio, keep looking for the loose wire, or just keep using the radio until it worked just six or five times out of ten? All the parts were still sound, but the connections were unreliable. To Clarence, that was Number 2 hut, or at least most of the men with whom he shared it. Everything worked, until it didn't.

Number 2 hut awoke as one, first thing in the morning, thirty-six defaulter feet hitting the floor early, anticipating the morning bugle call, up and ready for PT before breakfast. They filed out to the hoisting of the colours as a unit, straight lines, even spaces, easily distinguished from the raggle-taggle processions emerging from the other three huts, where groups of groggy men finished dressing as they walked.

After breakfast there was allocation to lorry work, ditch digging, river work, camp duties and work parties going off camp. The Number 2 hut men split off in ones and twos, to join their respective work parties. It was only then, Clarence noticed, that wheels started to come loose.

Able Seaman Barry Angel from Number 2 hut was working further up the river from Clarence. Barry had, halfway through the day, started rolling stones that had been collected by the roadside back to the water. There was no warning or any other changes in the man, he just finished rolling one stone to the road, then went into reverse. He ignored direct orders to desist and had to be physically restrained and taken to one of the cells.

James Cadogan, a ship's stoker, was restricted to camp duties after wandering off during a tree felling operation. He had been found among the spruce felled by his work party from earlier in the day, stripping a tree, needle by needle. Telegraphist Eric Murray was another Number 2 hut man. At least he was until transported out to one of the main psychiatric hospitals after digging a hole behind the Number 2 hut and trying to bury himself.

Clarence wasn't sure if it was one of Ballard's ideas or something that had come from some bright spark higher up the chain, but once a week there was an air raid drill in the camp. Men were told that there would be drills when they arrived in the camp. These drills would be at irregular intervals. The men were shown the exercise field and told to assemble there when the alarm sounded. All fine, all calm, all in keeping with what the men might experience when they returned to sea or shore duties. Everyone understood it was a drill, until the rising wail of the siren began.

The effect was like live grenades or mortars were being tossed into the camp. The men from Number 2 hut were the last ones to gather at the exercise field. Some of them had sprinted off in the opposite direction, running zigzags to dodge the incoming fire. Others were curled up in balls around the camp, and a few had to be coaxed out from under the huts, long after the drill was over.

The men of Number 2 hut malfunctioned. Clarence saw it every day. They worked well most of the time, like machinery, but broke down in ways that couldn't be predicted, under what seemed to be ordinary conditions. It could be a sudden noise. The air raid siren was the worst, but screeching brakes or a banging door could do it too. Other times it was something nobody else noticed or saw. Clarence had seen one man lose it when somebody lit a match. These were men who had jumped over the side of ships in harbour and who might just as easily jump off a moving lorry, or step in front of one. Temperamental instability was what Ballard called it in his interview. On ships it was called gang plank fever, and had been for centuries.

Whatever it was called, then or now, it came as a result of good navy training. Clarence saw it in others, and he recognised

145

it in himself too.

A navy man, a real navy man, overcame fear and horror. He refused to allow it to interfere in the execution of his duties. That was the Navy way. It was nothing that was specifically taught in training. It was learned in that first shelling or torpedo attack; a crash course on being a man. You fought the enemy and your personal demons with a face that showed nothing, so that no one else could know how shit-scared you were.

Being unaffected was expected. Not reacting to the screaming, drowning men in the water or the sight of body parts of friends on board the ship. Holding it together. On the ships, ordinary sailors were most in awe of the man who appeared totally fearless. He was spoken of as a superman in battles in the mess room when there was a break in the fighting. To appear fearless was to be admired and envied.

But to be fearless and to be courageous was different. A man who put himself in a spot where death was more likely than survival was only courageous if he felt the same bowel-loosening fear as his ship mates. If he felt no fear, then he was fearless, yes, but not courageous.

Clarence knew that he was neither fearless nor courageous, which left just one label. Any man who did not persist when he was afraid was, by definition, a coward.

To *appear* fearless was what most men did, day after day, when the next explosion could be the last thing you heard. That was the Navy way. It worked for most men. Doing what the man next to you was doing, keeping it together, even forcing out a joke or a laugh.

The Navy way worked very well up to the point when a reaction to the horror did come, as it had for Clarence and for others in Number 2 hut. Then what had been under control in the Navy way for months overwhelmed the brain, like a timed device exploding and throwing shrapnel in unpredictable directions. The damage was different for each man, but none was ever the same again.

* * * *

The reasons men broke down were the reasons they were at Kielder, but knowing that didn't help anyone. The psychiatrists knew it and the men knew it. The psychiatrists fished about, like blind men, looking for the loose connections, with little hope of finding them. The machines would never work as well as they did before. It would be a better bet, Clarence thought, not to test men because that was when things went wrong. No, it would be better to just accept what a man was capable of now and leave it at that. Knowing that a machine would break down and still choosing to use that machine every day was irresponsible and only had one outcome.

After a month taking apart the river bank, piece by piece, and doing what little maintenance he was allowed on the trucks. Clarence had seen most of the camp routines and how they fitted together. He watched and listened until he had all of the pieces. These were the component parts of the grand Kielder plan for rehabilitation and recycling of men. He could visualise it as a giant engineering drawing with dimension lines and arrows. It was a force diagram, showing the forces acting directly on the men as if they were conical pendulums or the barrels being pulled up a smooth incline. The forces to be applied by Ballard and Thurman intended to change the direction and shape of a man.

As clearly as he saw the plan, he knew it would never work, at least not for him. He would never be back in a ship's engine room, even if he spent years at Kielder. He had killed Madden and he would rather jump overboard into the propellers of any ship he got near than go back to a boiler room and the scene of the crime.

The Stone Frigate Approach was filling his day with so much activity that he didn't have time to think about what had happened as much. The psychiatrist asked him to think about it. Thinking about it, or not thinking about it; neither worked, neither changed what he had done. That was the honest truth.

Be honest. That was how Ballard always opened their weekly session.

"Be honest with me, Seaman Watson, but be honest especially with yourself."

147

It was being honest about how little Kielder was doing for him that led Clarence to insulin coma therapy.

* * * *

Since he was posted to HMS *Standard,* Ballard had been looking for a willing subject. He didn't need to be enthusiastic, just compliant. To register success, it would need to be more than one, but he had to start somewhere. Twenty should be enough to convince. Kielder was a test bed, ideal for innovations and opportunities that didn't come often in a career. He could combine the trauma that was the war with the freedom he had to experiment on the men and his previous breakthroughs at Barrow Gurney. He could create something that would have him recognised as a pioneer, perhaps even have a treatment named after him.

It was every psychiatrist's dream, if they came out from behind the false modesty and the I'm-only-doing-it-to-help-others bullshit. If they were honest enough to admit it. Psychiatrists had buildings and hospitals and even streets named after them and loved it. Parkinson, Huntington, Addison and Alzheimer had gained textbook fame by having conditions named after them, for ground-breaking work in mental disease. But how many psychiatrists had put their name not on an illness, but on a ground-breaking *cure?* The answer was damn few, and none that anyone had heard of outside medical colleges.

Ballard knew of Mitchell's Rest Cure, the starting point for his own successes with Refreshment Therapy at Barrow Gurney. Silas Weir Mitchell had been an army physician who had taken notes on cartloads of soldiers returning from the American Civil War with nervous disorders. He concluded that soldiers in continuous pain became cowards and even the strongest of men could become hysterical. Bed rest, good food and a break away from the front line had restored many men to fighting fit. But Mitchell had been too naïve and too distracted by his other interests to capitalise fully on what he had found. "Mitchell's Rest Cure" became just "The Rest Cure" and was used in the years that followed to calm hysteria in rich ladies, rather than patented as a money-spinning treatment for damaged fighting men.

Ballard's own big idea, like many why-didn't-I-think-of-that genius innovations, was simple. He would extend his own version of Refreshment Therapy and combine it with Sakel's deep insulin coma therapy (DICT). The therapeutic benefit to thousands of men with shell-shock anxiety and hysteria would be enormous and would be recognized as a major advance in naval neuropsychiatry. The benefit to A. John D. Ballard would also be considerable. He would brand his innovation as Ballard's Battlefront Therapy (BBT), making him much in demand wherever war was fought, and securing his place in medical history.

* * * *

At Barrow Gurney, Ballard read a lot. There was little to read, but little else to do on down time at the hospital. The alcove beneath his office window was the dumping ground for a tower of HMSO reports from the Board of Control for England and Wales, sent to all hospitals. They were worthy, but bone-dry scientific papers, intended to keep doctors up to date on medical research and keep the authors who churned out the reports in a job.

Ballard had picked out one of the thinnest reports in the pile one day, looking for something to ease him into his afternoon nap. It was just 61 pages, a translation of a paper from 1936, titled *Hypoglycaemic Shock Treatment in Schizophrenia*. As he flicked through the pages, he shifted his position from lounging on the sofa to sitting bold upright and thoughts of an afternoon nap disappeared. It was the figure of 88% that did it.

The Board of Control for England and Wales had paid for someone to go all the way to Vienna to look at what Sakel had been doing in his clinic and in his kitchen. Dr Isobel Wilson came back to report that the Austrian was demonstrating a success rate of over 88% for his Deep Coma Insulin Therapy, used on patients with schizophrenia.

For psychiatrists elsewhere, this was a penicillin-like hit rate. Nothing in current use was approaching 50% effectiveness for treatment for deep-seated schizophrenia. Within the year, the DICT treatment had been approved by the Board of Control for use in Insulin Centres in over thirty hospitals in England.

Sakel believed that an insulin overdose reduced the effects of a faulty adrenal system, the physiological cause of patients' delusions and agitation. Ballard didn't know or much care how it worked, or that Sakel discovered it by accident when he gave a patient too much insulin. It didn't bother him either that Sakel had tested it on just a few of his pets in his kitchen before injecting humans. It worked, and it worked on 88% of patients. That was enough for Ballard.

His own variation on the treatment was simple. If the therapy was powerful enough to bring schizophrenic patients all the way back from whatever confused world they'd been living in for months or years, it might be powerful enough to erase the memories and clear the blockages that prevented some naval men going back to war.

It was direct therapy, saving the Admiralty on resources. It would cut out the need for his staff to spend hours chatting or pretending to be concerned about withdrawn men with whom they had little in common. With the exception of Thurman, the staff at Kielder had not chosen to be there, they had been sent by the navy. When he addressed them as a group, he looked out at the faces of the inexperienced, the unfit and the plain uninterested.

The schizophrenia evidence from Sakel said that DICT would work best on functional disorders, so Ballard's initial plan was to try it out on some of the malingerers. That would be the obvious test bed. He could jump start some of them back to reality. But that would be difficult. The men in Number 3 hut were too smart to agree, too cunning to volunteer for anything that might threaten their chances of seeing out the war quietly. No-one in Number 3 hut was going to put themselves forward willingly for anything that might send them back to duty. Ballard would need five-point restraints to hold down any malingerer that he could corner for the treatment, and the screams would scare off any others. So that left Number 2 or Number 4 hut.

What might DICT do to those in Number 4 hut, the constitutionally timid, men who had lost their zip and the will to fight the enemy, if they ever had it in the first place. The most likely outcome was that DICT would add a fear of hospitals and medical procedures to those with an existing fear of war, guns, water and whatever else terrified them. The treatment, even the thought of the treatment, would cause more panic in these men, already lacking in stability and resilience. Ballard moved the pile of summary notes on Number 4 hut to one side of his desk. No point in wasting his time with that then.

Clinically, Number 2 hut patients would not be best suited for DICT, but they would be the most easily persuaded. These were men still more afraid of being labelled as cowards than of being wounded in returning to duty. The men in Number 2 and Number 4 hut might have some of the same symptoms, but they differed in how much they would do to overcome their fear. Number 2 hut patients might be ill, but they would at least try. Those in Number 4 hut wouldn't, for reasons that psychiatrist might argue about, but which were of little consequence to Ballard.

Ballard had knocked out patients for a day at Barrow Gurney with a shot of Nembutal. It was an easy procedure that could be done by nurses under his supervision. But his new Battlefront Therapy needed much more planning. It was no quick fix, 24-hour cure that he could delegate to others.

He had difficulties at first in justifying the extra insulin in his orders for medical supplies, but he had anticipated that. A phone call to the Admiralty and some harsh words to a clerk about needing the tools to do the job if he was to have any success solved that problem. Getting the quantities of insulin he needed to put patients in a coma still took a while, but stealing enough sugar to bring them back from their coma took longer.

Sugar rationing had been introduced at the beginning of January 1940, and even with the increased allowances for rationed foods for "invalids" at Kielder, it was in short supply. He despaired as he watched patients at Kielder pile it into cups of tea every mealtime. The kitchen pooled individual allowances of sugar to make cakes and puddings as best they could, and Ballard targeted what little was left. He was careful not to be seen, but even when he was, no-one questioned him. It was just the psychiatrist filling a jar from the kitchen sugar tub for tea in his office.

Checking in his dog-eared HMSO 61-page report, there were no clinical guidelines for using DICT, so Ballard developed his own protocol. Sakel in Vienna had induced comas by injecting his schizophrenic subjects with insulin six days a week over a period of two months. Ballard had neither the insulin nor the patience to do that. He needed a quicker return that could be repeated, on minimum resources, to show that the treatment worked.

He had to stay within Navy regulations in what he was doing, but with the freedom he had at Kielder he needed only to write up the successes and avoid killing anyone. Sakel had reported a mortality rate of about one per cent and a slight risk of permanent brain damage to patients "not suited" to DICT. Ballard read this and made some notes in the margins of the report. He would need to experiment with the dosage and timings at Kielder.

* * * *

Ballard sold it to Clarence. He could offer it to a handful of men only, and Clarence was one of the lucky ones, he told him, because of his strength and resolve to withstand the rigours of the treatment, over two months. Clarence was to be offered these special injections, Ballard said, because both of them knew from their weekly meetings that the Stone Frigate approach wasn't working for Clarence. Ballard was going beyond his normal clinical responsibilities, he said, to offer Clarence a highly specialized treatment. But Ballard was selective with the truth, the honest truth, that he so valued and stressed the importance of in his interviews.

DICT was rigorous. That part was true. To watch just how rigorous it was, however, was difficult for anyone who was not a firm believer in the longer-term benefits of the treatment.

Grand mal seizures started around an hour after the insulin

injection, requiring two staff to hold Clarence down on the bed until the risk of broken bones, biting his tongue and choking from the thrashing had passed. The onset of coma was unpredictable, but followed within a few minutes of the seizures ending, when the muscles went from spasm to floppy hypotonia. A deep coma state could then be confirmed by the absence of any response to a light shone on the pupil of the eye, and when a feather touched on the eyeball didn't produce blinking. Ballard followed Sakel's guidance on leaving Clarence in a state of deep coma for 20 minutes in each session, before starting to bring him back.

Without the luxury of injectable glucose, Ballard slid a lubricated nasal tube down Clarence's throat and poured down a solution a lukewarm water saturated with sugar. Clarence would come to, gagging and in state of disorientated panic each time. He was left to sleep for a few hours in the room, during which time he experienced further hypoglycaemic after-shocks, with major convulsions. Ballard would be at his office desk next door, and took to strapping Clarence to the bed, to prevent him falling to the floor during the convulsions. By the afternoon, Clarence was sent back to work, with little memory of what had happened, other than the scratched throat, and a strange feeling of being bloated.

For five days a week, over three and a half weeks Ballard injected the insulin, varying the dosage and the time spent in deep coma, keeping meticulous notes. At the end of each afternoon, he would meet with Clarence, pen in hand, always with the same opener, *"Be honest with me, Seaman Watson, but be honest especially with yourself."*

He probed for the effects of the deep coma on Clarence's memories of the boiler room and Madden's death, noting any small changes in the details as he forced Clarence to recount the incident again and again.

After the first week Clarence had gained three pounds, after the second his cheeks were puffed like a hamster keeping food for later. The overdoses of insulin in his blood system were laying down stores of fat from anything he ate, and from the flood of sugar solutions forced into his stomach through the rubber tube.

He sweated constantly when he was working and his shirt was soaked even when he wasn't. His speech began to slur when he was tired, which was most of the time. Ballard reassured him that it was all normal; part of price to be paid for the success of the special treatment. Clarence accepted it, in a daze some days, falling asleep after meals, having to walk around the camp in the evening to avoid sitting down and falling asleep.

In the afternoons, after the injections, Clarence was still able to tune into some work for short periods – reverse his cap and three, two, one, get the job done. He was restricted to working on bench jobs. Having him near engines or anything with moving parts was too much of a risk. It wouldn't be just the hairs on the back of his hands that were in danger of being pulled into machinery. But his work hours went from three per day down to one, as recovery times got longer, and Ballard waited until he was convinced that Clarence had had his last seizure for the day. By the end of week two, Clarence noticed tools shaking in his hand, and by the third week he needed one hand on his wrist to hold tools steady enough to work. Lining up parts and connecting hoses took more concentration too, and he had to give up on wiring jobs.

To be clumsy, for Clarence, was worse than losing one of his senses. To look at what needed to be done and then to fix it was what he did, and who he was. He wasn't better than anyone else, but it was what made him different. He could do something that no one else could. He defined himself too, by the quality of his repairs, and by his creation of new parts when they were needed. To look at a machine casing or a box with wires-in, wires-out and to see through the metal and understand what was happening inside made him special. He could look at a rotary valve or a boiler operating on a Rankine Cycle and diagnose what was going wrong, by looking at how the machinery was behaving. To repair, to make the components work in harmony again as a unit, all he needed was a set of precision measuring instruments and his tools, some basic raw materials and his cap reversed. Three, two, one, get the job done.

To see inside the machine. But this was what Ballard was

trying to do too, Clarence realised. Looking inside a man's head, understanding what was malfunctioning, then using the tools that he had to try to make the unit work as it should, as it had before. But what chance did Ballard have without accurate machine plans and a circuit diagram?

Clarence couldn't remember not being hairy, hairier than other boys, and he couldn't remember what he did and how he thought before he became Clarence the engineer. That was who he was now, comfortable with the satisfaction that his work brought to him and also to others. Most of the men at HMS *Standard* saw him as a Steady-Eddie. He was stodgy, slow moving Clarence, who didn't say much but got the job done. But that was OK with him. He had looked around the other men on HMS *Perseus* when he started, and even now at Kielder, and there was no-one he would rather be, long term at least, than Clarence the engineer. There were ratings and officers on *Perseus* who were smart, some who inspired the men around them, and some who could be relied upon for a laugh, anytime of the day. Clarence admired them without wanting to be them, accepting that he never could. He was embarrassed at how good he felt on *Perseus* when he first heard other men on board refer to him as Clarence the engineer. Not Clarence-that-guy-who-works-in-the-engine-room or Clarence-the-grease-monkey, or even Clarence-the-donkeyman, but Clarence the engineer. That was who he was. But at Kielder, with each day of Insulin Coma Therapy he found it more and more difficult to remember.

In the fugue of wakening from the deep comas was worst. He would clutch the sides of the trolley bed, going through 30 seconds of muscle clenching panic, waking in a room and a body foreign to him, like an adult new-born. Who and where he was were a total blank, and the panic increased with each second until he could make any sense of it.

Awareness and memories crept back, more slowly each time he was put under. The wet patch spreading across his trousers was the first reminder of where he was, the hard, familiar reality that he'd peed himself starting a sequence of other realisations as he looked around. Then, just when he had remembered enough to relax his grip on the trolley, he would feel himself falling into a pit as another seizure dragged him back to unconsciousness and the sequence would be repeated. Recovery was longer each time and he had more absences later in the day, moments when he would jolt, eyes wide and surprised, unaware what he had been doing in the previous few seconds.

Gaps appeared in his memories, parts of his life when he could only remember the before and after of what he had done. When he did remember things in detail, he realised that the events must have happened long before he thought they did. He remembered conversations that he'd had, but sometimes not the person or whether it had happened at sea or before he joined up. He was never chatty, but he became even more reluctant to speak to other men at Kielder after getting lost mid-sentence, finding himself standing with others as they looked at him, waiting for him to finish, or reply to what they had said.

His identity, his mastery as Clarence the engineer, started to go. When he knocked a screwdriver from his bench and then fell off his stool to the floor trying to catch it, alarms bells rang, loud enough to be heard even through the insulin fug that he was living in.

* * * *

"*What happens if I stop the injections now doc?*"

"*Well of course you can opt to stop the treatment now Clarence, but I have to advise against it. I know that you are having problems with the side effects, but I don't think you realise how close we are to a breakthrough.*"

"*What kind of a breakthrough doc?*"

Ballard paused, standing to look out his window, tensing one fist, then the other.

"*Let me answer your question with another one Clarence. It is a simple one. When was the last time your thought about Madden?*"

Clarence looked away, down at the floor, trying to concentrate. As he stood in front of Ballard's desk, searching his memories from the last few days, he trembled like he was hooked up to mild electrical current. No, definitely no images of Madden, screaming, banging his fists against the wall of the boiler as it was fired up. But then he had no memories either of what kind of soup had been served that day at lunch, or whether he liked it.

"*I haven't thought about him in a while, that's true, but I haven't thought about anybody else either, so I guess that's good,*" he said. "*Does that mean that the treatment's working, that I'm getting better, even when I feel this bad?*"

Ballard just smiled and nodded. He didn't ask Clarence to sit, hoping to keep it short.

Clarence clasped his hands together to make them stop shaking.

"*It's not that I'm not grateful, doc. I am. But when will enough be enough with the insulin? I don't think I can take much more than what I'm taking. I'm sleeping half the day, pissing myself like a baby, and I can't do any proper work any more.*"

Ballard's smile disappeared. He sat back down but left Clarence standing.

"*We're close Clarence, really close. I said that when we started that you were one of the few men here who was strong enough for this special treatment. I know that it has been difficult for you, but you've borne it so well up to now, like we both knew you would. Another week or so should do it. That should clear the decks, take you to the point where we can stop the injections and start to put you back together, ready to serve. You'd like that, wouldn't you?*"

"*Yes, doc, I want to go back to work, but another week and I...*"

Ballard held up a hand, cutting him off.

"*I said at the beginning Clarence that the choice was yours. It still is. If you stop the injections now we may have purged enough of the memories to get you back to ship shape, but there is a chance, a real chance in my clinical opinion, that the treatment will be incomplete and the memories will come creeping back as soon as you stop the injections. Or they may come back later. If that happens, and I'm just saying that they may, not that they will, then it will be the memories that are stronger, not you, and*"

157

to shift them again will be doubly difficult."

Clarence looked down again, concentrating on all that he was being told.

"Well, what if we stop them for just a few days, doc, see if that works? I could keep you up to date on how I'm feeling and we could start them again if it doesn't work?"

Ballard took out his handkerchief, wiped it briefly across his nose and started to wring it with his hands.

"Mmm, that is an interesting suggestion Clarence, and it might work with some other types of therapy. Unfortunately, it doesn't work like that with Battlefron..., I mean the insulin therapy."

Clarence persisted.

"But we could try it, doc, right? Just to see?"

Ballard leant forward, putting his elbows on the desk, squeezing the handkerchief tighter. He was tired of Clarence's whinging about the injections, but he had to keep him on board if this was going to work. He drew a breath, thinking about what difficulties other great medical pioneers might have had, how many doubters they may have needed to convince, before being recognised for what they were.

Clarence looked rough; Ballard had to admit. He had never seen a man gain weight at such a rate. His face was puffy and red, with eyes reduced almost to slits. The wet sheen on his skin renewed every few minutes and there were patches of sweat blotched across his shirt and all the way around the neck. His hair, normally springy, was plastered to his skull. Ballard had predicted that there would be physical changes, but the speed of the changes surprised him. He had recorded it all in his notes.

But he couldn't stop now. Clarence was as strong as an ox; that was why he had chosen him. A few more weeks, not a week or so as he had told Clarence, would prove that the Battlefront Therapy worked. Then he could find a few more willing subjects, confirm the success, write his paper, move out and move up. For now, it was important to continue with persuasion, using what he knew about Clarence. He made an effort to breathe slowly and keep irritation out of his voice.

"Well, it's complicated, but I will try to explain it to you." He

paused again, and Clarence nodded.

"*You might think about your flashbacks, about what happened like an infected wound, or like rust. If we don't clean out every last little piece, no matter how small, what is left will grow again.*"

Ballard let Clarence picture the remains of something still there in his head, something still toxic.

"*So, you stop the treatment and it might seem like everything's back to normal. You might even be back to work on a ship, your troubles behind you. You could go for weeks, even months with no problems. But then it happens.*"

Ballard paused again for effect, looking at Clarence to make sure he had him hooked.

"*Then you see someone who looks a bit like Madden, or you hear the sound like boilers firing up, or someone gets injured on board ship and the flashbacks begin. It might be just a quick blast of the memories that brought you here, and you get over it, so no big deal. But it might be something worse. The memories might come back gradually or all at once. By then, it would be too late for you to come back here. You might end up in place much worse than this, where the doctors keep people safe from themselves and from others. They wouldn't know you there, or what had happened to you, and you would be...*"

Ballard didn't finish the sentence, looking up at Clarence with a tight-lipped smile and his eyebrows raised.

Clarence said nothing for a beat.

"*I...see what you mean doc. I wouldn't want that to happen, to be in a place like that. I appreciate everything that you're doing for me, how you've gone out on a limb and given me special attention to try to help me. But even if there was some way of reducing the dose or the amount of time that I'm under, so that I can recover for more work in the afternoon...*"

Ballard drew another breath. He had maintained his professional front, nodding in the right places, a few "*uh-hu*"s and "*I sees*" thrown in to fake interest in Clarence's quibbles. But now he was quite suddenly bored by the petty details about what the insulin treatment was doing to Clarence's body and his so-called work. Who cared if he was sleeping half the day, or that he felt too dozy to fix some machinery that would get fixed by someone else anyway? He could sleep all day, every day and nobody would give a tinker's damn. These were trivial matters, inconsequential in the bigger plan of what was to be achieved for many others in the long term. Ballard decided it was time to stop pretending that this was a negotiation. It was time to assert his authority and to push onto the next phase of the injections.

He spoke more quickly.

"*Well we could reduce the dose Clarence, of course we could. It might work. But it would be a risk, like the risk I'd be taking if we stopped the treatment altogether now and you took a turn for the worst later. I could never forgive myself if that happened, you know, if I was responsible for that and you got worse instead of better. And you know more than most what that's like Clarence, thinking about how you might have done something differently, thinking about all the 'if-onlys', wondering what would have happened if you had done A instead of B.*"

Ballard paused again, to make sure that Clarence made the connection with Madden. It was sledgehammer psychology, but it worked.

"*No, I wouldn't want that doc,*" Clarence said, looking at the floor.

Before Clarence could come back with more questions, Ballard stood up again.

"*Well, I'm glad that you have told me about your worries Clarence. This is valuable part of the therapy. A few weeks ago, you would not have been able to talk about these things, so I'm encouraged by your progress.*"

Ballard came around his desk to where Clarence was standing.

"*So, another week or so should do it,*" he said, putting his hand on Clarence's elbow to turn him to the door. Touch elbow for reassurance, touch shoulder for commiseration or sympathy, pat shoulder to show who was boss; Ballard had done it for so long, he didn't need to think about it.

Clarence walked back to the Number 2 hut, lay on his bed and was asleep within a minute.

* * * *

Over the following week, Ballard ticked off the number of insulin comas induced in his meticulous clinical notes, creeping ever closer to 25; the rough and ready calculation he had made for success, based on Sakel's work. He charted day-to-day variations in the number of Clarence's afternoon seizures following the morning injections. His psychiatric supervision of other ratings in the camp and meetings with staff became an irritating distraction, keeping him away from his pioneering work, monitoring Clarence. He delegated as many weekly sessions as he could to Thurman, even asking him to do new admission interviews. Thurman was flattered by the new level of clinical responsibility, at least until he realised he was being dumped on.

Clarence had tried to keep track of how many sessions he'd done, but he became too confused after the first five. In the week following their meeting, Ballard upped the dosage from 100 to 150 units of insulin, without telling Clarence and without any complaints. Clarence went into deep coma much faster, within ten minutes, but the sugar solution still brought him back just as fast. He slept most of the day, in and out of seizures. He also started to miss meals, either because he was unconscious at the time they were being served, or because the thought of eating made him feel sick.

After 24 days of treatment, Ballard drew a line, gambling that he had done enough. In that final week of sessions Clarence had to be wakened before the injections could be administered, and Ballard had moved him to one of Kielder's detention cells after men in Number 2 hut complained that he had become doubly incontinent during the night, stinking the place out.

In one of the short periods when Clarence was awake and lucid, Ballard explained to him that he was stopping the injections. Stopping the insulin completely, rather than stepping it down, as Sakel had done, was a risk, but Ballard judged that if Clarence was strong enough to withstand 150 units a day, his body would cope with the sudden withdrawal. He still looked strong despite his lethargy and time in bed.

Ballard set out a shift pattern for his staff to monitor Clarence, watching through the open door of his cell while they sat completing other paperwork for the camp. The biggest risk was from choking or head injury during after-shock seizures. Clarence also needed sponged down every few hours, the sweat continuing to soak the bedding and anything he wore. Ballard wanted to collect data for his write-up on sleeping patterns, or anything else Clarence did that was clinically notable during the recovery.

After three days without injections, Clarence was awake longer than he was asleep in a 24-hour period and Ballard decided it was time to test him.

His plan was simple. Hook him up to the heart monitor and get him to recall what he could about the boiler incident. See how much he could remember and how he reacted to it. If Ballard's Battlefront Therapy had done its job, it would have cleared out the rooms in Clarence's head where he kept the pictures of Madden. Ballard considered heart rate as a crude, almost primitive measure in a discipline as sophisticated as psychiatry, but he knew that it was a stable external predictor of anxiety in a patient, even if it told you nothing about what was going on internally. He also knew that any psychophysiological numbers would be useful evidence for the effectiveness of his Battlefront Therapy when he came to convince others, when his paper was published.

Clarence's heart rate was over a hundred at rest and Ballard gave it a few minutes to settle. There was a smell of stale sweat and a greasy sheen on Clarence's face. Getting hooked up to the precordial leads and the uncertainty of what was to come could be responsible for that, but his heart kept racing, dipping below one hundred and then going up again when Ballard started talking or came near him. Every time Clarence shifted in his chair, Ballard caught a waft of something strong. It was more than stale stench or unwashed clothes, or filthy underwear. It was acidic, like concentrated urine. The patches on Clarence's shirt grew, as Ballard adjusted the wiring for the testing.

Soldier's Heart was a term doctors used for shell shock in the First World War. Traumatised troops had difficulty first carrying their packs, then lost the will to fight, or sometimes the will to live. But Clarence's sailor's heart, like the rest of his body, was strong, and beating fast enough that Ballard could see Clarence's chest wall move on patches where his shirt was tight to the skin, glued with the sweat.

"*Now Seaman Watson, I want you to relax. You must be honest with me,*" said Ballard in his usual lead-in.

"*I'm going to ask you some questions and I want to you tell me how you are feeling.*"

He could see Clarence grip the arms of the chair more tightly, a rictus smile fixed on his face as he nodded. His heart rate rose close to 120.

"*Tell me what you remember about your time on...*", he glanced at his notes, "*HMS Perseus. Just start anywhere you like from when you joined up with the ship.*"

Clarence shuffled in his seat and Ballard turned his head away as the smell hit him again. It was now much stronger, and he glanced down at Clarence's crotch to check if it could be real piss, or just some toxic variation Clarence's body was pumping out onto his skin. The patches on Clarence's shirt had now joined up with each other even on top of his shoulders, where his steel wool hair usually held the material off his skin.

Ballard sat at the side of his desk. He had his pencil in hand, pad within reach, concentrating on Clarence's reaction, ready to make the crucial notes for his write up.

Clarence stared at the floor and said nothing for a full thirty seconds and Ballard was about to follow up with another question when he spoke.

"*I killed Madden, doc. I know you want me say I don't remember it, but I do. He was in the boiler...*"

Ballard jumped in before Clarence could say any more.

"*Well, let's not start there, no. Let's go back to when you first joined HMS Perseus, what you remember from those times, before all of that.*"

Clarence continued as if Ballard had not spoken.

"*...the pictures are fuzzier now, but I can still see him, banging on the metal, while we were running to our positions, lining up.*

I can't remember now if it was a fire-drill or some general alarm, or where I went after it all happened, but I can still see his face in the steam, clear as day."

Clarence now looked as if he had been sitting in a jet of steam himself. Using his shirt sleeve, he wiped streams of sweat from his brow running into his eyes. His shirt that was now glistening wet in places, across his chest, where the material was unable to absorb or redirect any more sweat to the few remaining dry patches.

Ballard reached for his handkerchief, then stopped himself. Sweating was the least of his problems. It was not going to plan. He was scrabbling already, this early in the interview. He needed to direct Clarence to answers that would show what his Battlefront Therapy had achieved.

"What if we just go back to the day before all of this and take it from there? That might be a better way to do it…"

Clarence looked up and for the first time, Ballard heard irritation in his reply.

"I don't remember anything about the day before doc, and I don't remember what happened the day after. I never did remember any of that before the insulin and I still don't."

He spoke slowly, still slurring a few words, but definite in his answer.

His heart rate had jumped up another eight beats per minute. Ballard reached over to his desk to scribble the number in his notes, buying time to decide on another tact. He had to find something, anything that would take Clarence where he wanted him to go, to give him what he needed for his write up. He had passed more work onto Thurman over the previous week and he had his paper on BBT drafted already. All that was missing was a few choice quotes from Clarence, and the psychophysiological numbers that showed movement in the right direction.

Asking Clarence to go back to HMS *Perseus* had been too direct, too much of a risk. Ballard needed to temper his expectations, to lead Clarence on a longer route to the answers. He put down his pencil.

"OK, Seaman Watson, let's not talk about what happened on

Perseus just yet. I'm going to ask you about how you're feeling instead. You OK with that?"

"I don't mind doc," Clarence said, his voice flat, but clipped, not his usual eager-to-please tone.

"Good. Talking about feelings should be easier, and it should bring your heart rate down too," Ballard said, nodding at the equipment on his desk. Even as Ballard finished speaking, Clarence's heart rate came down below one hundred again. Ballard slid down further in his chair, trying to look more relaxed than he felt. He twisted the pencil as he spoke.

"I've seen a lot of men who have been to war. You know that. And sometimes men who have experienced terrible things like you get more upset remembering those things now than they did when the terrible things happened."

He checked Clarence for any reaction and glanced again at the heart rate monitor.

"The symptoms men come to me with are caused by the remembering, not by what happened to them. Do you follow?"

Clarence paused, then said, *"I think so doc, yes."*

"Good. Now, here's what I'm thinking. For some men, it's the opposite of that. It's definitely how they felt at the time that makes them feel worse, not the act of remembering it. What do you think might be true for you? Which would you say was worse Seaman Watson? Was it how you felt at the time on Perseus, or is it how you feel when you remember it all now?"

Ballard stopped, looking at the bloated and bedraggled man before him, mouth hanging open, a dribble of saliva escaping one corner, eyes half shut. Before the interview, Ballard had high expectations. Clarence would say how much better he felt, how the memories had faded, how grateful he was; all the finishing touches that Ballard needed for his paper. But now he was reduced to spoon feeding Clarence answer A or answer B questions, just to scrape together something that he could use in his write up. If he could just lead Clarence to say that it was better now, that it was easier than before, it would be a start. He could write a convincing story about his Battlefront Therapy around that.

"*To be honest doc, I don't have feelings about it now,*" Clarence replied, after another long pause in which his head fell forward, then jolted back up.

"*All I've got is those same pictures of Madden in my head and when they start I can't think about anything else, and I can't do anything else. When they start I can't stop them, and I'm just glad when they finish.*"

Clarence opened his palms and looked at them in turn, as if the pictures might appear there.

Ballard took a handkerchief from his drawer and held it between his own hands. Growing more desperate, he stripped the interview down to his one question.

"*Yes, but which would you say is worse, then or now?*"

He put the emphasis on "then", steering Clarence, willing him to the basic answer he needed.

"*Like I said before doc, I didn't have feelings that I can remember when it happened. It all just happened. I was away for a while somewhere on the ship, they said. I don't remember where. Then they found me, then I was transferred. I don't remember much about that either. I was feeling tired, I remember that. I was very tired and it was cold. I just wanted to sleep and they kept waking me up.*"

Ballard squeezed his handkerchief tighter.

"*But now, what about now Seaman, now, not then. Now that you're over all that. You must feel differently?*"

"*Well I'm still tired, like I was, even more tired now, but that's from the insulin I think,*" Clarence said.

It was hopeless. Ballard took his handkerchief in both hands and twisted it, like he was wringing out a towel. His frustration threatened to scupper the interview, to deny him what he needed from this dumb brute of a man. If he lost his patience now, it could undo all his efforts of the past weeks. He drew breath and fell back on his professional training, the need for patience and above all, resilience. In that moment, it was not his psychiatry training that kept him calm, it was the thought of how long it had taken him to accumulate enough bloody sugar for the therapy, how long that would take if he needed to do it all again with someone else from Number 2 hut.

He was the psychiatrist on a trajectory. That was what he had to remember. Seaman Watson, the material in front of him, would soon be a memory, just a steppingstone on Ballard's path to greater things. That was the situation. All that was needed was persistence for a few more minutes to get what he needed.

"*Yes, yes, Seaman Watson, being tired is an effect of the treatment, obviously. I understand that and I know that you have been through a lot. What I'm asking you about is any other feelings, besides being tired. Can you go back and try to remember how you felt then, and then tell me about how you feel about it now?*"

Again, Ballard put in the emphasis, this time on "now".

"*Think hard. It's very important for the success of your therapy.*"

Clarence had closed his eyes. Ballard wondered if he was concentrating, trying to remember, if he had dozed off, or if he was having another absence seizure. When he spoke, eyes still closed, his words came faster and in a voice that was higher, like his throat was constricted.

"*I don't want to do that doc. I don't want to go back. You see, I know the pictures are still there, just waiting, and I know they're just the same. They still come when I'm sleeping now, and that's bad enough.*"

He paused, opened his eyes and looked up at Ballard.

"*I'm not trying to be awkward doc. I want to get better and go back to work. But why would I want to think about the pictures now, when I'm awake, and stir it all up when I don't have to? That will just make me worse, not better.*"

Ballard put his pencil flat on his pad and held it there, pressing it down. The pencil was slippery with the sweat from his palm and he lifted his hand when he saw a damp patch appear on the paper, smudging his last line of notes. His hyperhidrosis was going into overdrive. He nodded to buy himself some time again, and to hide his irritation.

"*Yes, I see how difficult this must be for you.*"

He had not calculated on Clarence being not only dumb, but

stubborn too. After all his efforts, everything he'd done for him, this lump of a man was refusing to cooperate.

He was on the point of giving up. Was it worth going on? He had tried leading Clarence to the answers he needed. Short of chalking the words on a board and holding them up for Clarence to read, he'd tried everything else.

He could make it up. Why not? What difference would it make if he just invented Clarence's words to go alongside some made up numbers on his Battlefront Therapy? Who would notice? He could protect Clarence's identity. Nobody would find him. He could invent what Clarence said, throw in a few grammatical errors in the quotes from his patient to make it sound authentic. Lack of integrity? Falsification of results? Only if he was caught, and the chances of that were slim in the chaos of war.

Then, just as he leaned forward to stand up, he looked down at the smudged notes on what Clarence had said so far, and it came to him. He had one last ploy. He sat back in his chair and looked at Clarence until he had eye contact.

"*I understand why you don't want to think about the pictures while you're sitting there, if they upset you. Who would? That makes sense. I've said before that I know what you've been through.*"

Ballard picked up his pencil again and tapped it on his notes.

"*But I think we're getting somewhere Seaman Watson. I believe that you have made progress.*"

Clarence looked confused. "*Well, how do you mean doc?*"

"*Let me put it this way. When I look at my notes, this is what I see. What you're telling me is that you have more control over your feelings now than you did before the treatment. Correct?*"

Clarence looked at him blankly, his mouth again hanging open.

"*What you are telling me is that you can stop the pictures coming when you're awake now. Is that correct, yes?*"

Clarence shook his head.

"*I don't know what I'm telling you doc. The pictures are still there. Maybe they'll always be there. When they come, they come. I'm seeing Madden in the boiler room. I don't know when the pictures will come next, but I know they will come for sure if you ask me to think about them again."*

Ballard sat back in his chair and crossed his arms, wiping some the sweat on his hands under his arms.

"OK Seaman Watson, but you see, I believe that's a good sign. We can agree that's a benefit of the therapy, I would say. What I'm writing in my notebook here is that you now have more control over the memories that were causing you the problems."

"Well, I don't know if I have any more control..." Clarence started, before Ballard cut in.

He pointed at Clarence.

"But you do, Seaman Watson, you do. Don't you see? It may be that you just don't see the progress you've made as clearly as I do because of the effects of the insulin. If you can decide when the memories, or the pictures as you call them, will come then that means you are more in control now. You just told me that you could make the pictures come now, if you wanted to, yes?"

Clarence shook his head again, and said, *"But what about the times when I don't want them to come, doc? When they just come. That's always been my problem, I think."*

Ballard turned to a dry page in his notebook and wrote quickly as he spoke.

"I think that's what we need to work on next."

He stopped and looked up at Clarence. He was animated now, pointing not just with his finger, but with both hands at Clarence.

"The treatment has helped you. There have been some variations from what we both expected, some things that we didn't foresee, and I know that has been difficult for you. But overall there is no doubt in my mind that there has been a satisfactory psychiatric outcome so far."

He went back to his notepad, writing an abbreviated form of what he had said, speaking faster as he continued.

"You are now closer to being discharged from Kielder and closer to going back to your engineer work than you've ever been since you came here. You can be very pleased and proud of your progress. We both can."

For the first time in the interview with Ballard, Clarence brightened, the semblance of a real smile breaking out on his face.

"Well, that's good to know, doc. The last few weeks have been hard for me..."

"Yes, just a few more sessions with the insulin may be all we need to ensure that the treatment is successful, and that it lasts, of course," Ballard continued as he wrote in his pad, not looking up.

Clarence closed his eyes, then opened them again, looking out the window. He felt some bile rise to the back of his throat. Some of the men in Number 2 hut had been called cowards who couldn't take any more war. He was no coward, but he couldn't take any more insulin and sugar.

* * * *

There had to be a routine. It wasn't that Duncan didn't understand or accept that. He did. Without it there was no order. It was how the navy operated. It was needed on a ship and it was needed, perhaps even more, at HMS *Standard*. He had agreed as much in his first, short meeting with Ballard when he arrived at Kielder. Well, not so much agreed as accepted, since Ballard was telling him, rather than asking for his views on the importance of routine.

At sea, the survival of the whole ship's company could depend on the conduct of one man. It was hammered into recruits from the first day of training: You are a vital part of a fighting machine. Don't question, just do. A fighting ship depended equally on each man on board.

Poor morale and lack of order on a ship could spread, like rust, and rust, like loose lips, could sink ships. When a crew member went rogue, the usual strategy was to separate the man who was a liability from the others, to prevent crew mates becoming affected, or disaffected.

On land, such men might need help. On board a ship at sea, in battle, a man not pulling his weight, not doing as much as everyone else, for whatever reason, was not someone who needed help. To the rest of the crew, he was someone being allowed to get away with it. It created feelings of injustice in the ranks and the crew became difficult to manage, questioning orders, or doing just enough to get by, because they started to believe they were doing more than others. For a captain and his officers, managing such problems was a diversion from fighting the enemy.

So, it made sense to Duncan that men with morale problems were extracted from ships, taken out of the mix, to minimise damage and sent to Kielder. What he didn't understand, what went against all the method and organisation in which he had been drilled in his training, was why all these men, worn and dissatisfied, would be housed together in the same Number 4 hut. They were put together, where contagious dissatisfaction and discontent could spread quickly, like a bad dose of flu.

That was the question that Duncan really wanted to ask Ballard when they met. That, and why he was housed with these men, just for going AWOL back in Scotland? Was he being punished for missing his ship or for reacting badly to his brother's death? Was he serving time for what he had done, or housed in Number 4 hut to recover?

Duncan had listened carefully to Surgeon-Lieut.-Commander A. John D. Ballard's general welcome to Kielder as he explained to the assembled rows of men why they had been sent there. He covered the primary objective of re-drafting. There were no details in his welcome however, of just how men like Duncan were to be fixed and returned to duty.

"All of you men have been specially selected for Kielder. You have served your country in war and you will again. Although this is not a ship, it is a naval facility, run on navy discipline with all men working together for a common cause. You have been chosen for HMS Standard, just as you were for chosen for the ships on which you served. You had the skills and the fortitude to serve then and you still do now. My job as ship's captain on HMS Standard is to return you to duty by whatever means necessary. This is my mission at Kielder and you should make it your mission too."

Ballard spoke on the same theme of duty and country for another 15 minutes. Part of his welcome kept coming back to Duncan in the following weeks, "by whatever means necessary."

It rang a bell from his childhood, and it was not a happy memory.

When he was seven years old, Duncan had a dog. He had pestered his mother for weeks, until his dad had come home one night with a pup that one of his builder mates had given him. It was black and grey, just a mutt, and young enough to run around until it collapsed with exhaustion. Duncan's family lived on the edge of the town then, before rows of new houses were built on the fields behind them. There were acres of open farmland for the dog to run about, which was good, but also the risk being shot, which was not.

The sheep farmers counted their livestock in pounds, shillings and pence, and the sentence for any dog found sheep worrying, or even in the same field as the sheep was death. No questions, no comeback; the farmer with a gun was always in the right.

The same builder mate who gave Duncan's dad the pup had a brother who ran a croft farther out of town. It was five acres of scrawny hill sheep, potatoes, turnips and a bolthole for the brother to head to at the weekend. When Duncan's dad, Billy mentioned the sheep worrying problem, his workmate offered to solve it. Dead easy, he said.

So it was that Duncan had his first trip in a car when he and his dad, Benny the dog, the workmate and his brother all piled into the crofter's beaten up Rover 10 and headed out to the croft one Saturday morning. Duncan knew they were taking the pup to teach it not to chase sheep, or to "learn it" as his dad said, but whether Duncan knew what that meant, he couldn't remember. His dad had explained to him that his dog would be shot if it went for the sheep on farmland, and that was one of the worse things Duncan could imagine happening.

When they got to the croft, up a track that bounced them around in the car, the weekend crofter led them around the back of the stone and corrugated building to the sheep pen. There was a ewe in the pen, her coat matted and straggly, and suckling furiously beneath her was a lamb, born just that week.

Without a word, the crofter walked over to Duncan and took the pup from his arms, turned around and dropped the dog into the pen. The pup landed on his feet, looking first at the two sheep then back up at Duncan. The ewe glanced once at the pup, repositioned herself in the pen and back kicked the dog into the air. Benny flew five feet across the pen and slammed into the rough boards on the other side, whimpering as he landed. The ewe followed up with her head, but the crofter was faster, grabbing the pup by the scruff of the neck and pulling it out of the pen before the sheep could connect. He handed the shaking dog back to Duncan.

"*There ye go, son. That dug'll no be chasing any sheep for a good while now,*" he said with a laugh, and a nod to Billy.

It was quick and permanent fix. For the next three years, when they took Benny for a walk he ran in the opposite direction when he saw a sheep, or a cow or a horse, or any light-coloured dogs. It could take hours to find him, cowering behind a rubbish bin, or in bushes, or returning home exhausted after hours.

In that first week at Kielder, Duncan thought about Benny being thrown into the sheep pen. What means would be necessary to affect a permanent fix for the men with whom he shared Number 4 hut?

During the day, some men would talk and at night and some would scream. It took only days for Duncan to hear enough from the 17 men of Number 4 hut to know why each of them was there.

Most had developed a fear of enemy action. They had lost the will to fight, worn down by incoming shells, the dark, the flashes and the inevitability of death, though not necessarily their own. Some were still brave enough to fight but had simply lost faith in the navy and what they were doing to win the war. A few, just a few, had caught a fear of the sea itself. They were the midnight screamers, with recurring dreams that came with the smell of freezing seas.

Did the Admiralty have a quick solution at Kielder for these men that could undo the fears, something that would last?

He was not afraid of the battle or of the sea like the other men, but Duncan didn't want to go back. After a couple of weeks, he realised what he had in common with the other men in Number 4 hut. Put on a ship in the face of the enemy, none of them would fight. In the eyes of the Admiralty they lacked moral fibre. They no longer believed in what they were being asked to do.

He was like them, yes, but was Number 4 hut where he should be? He had lost faith in more than just the Navy. Why was he fighting? He had asked questions and got no answers. If his life was all just a random spin of the wheel, what was the point of living by a code that he had believed in since he was a boy? What he did today or tomorrow or the next day didn't change what would happen to him in this world or the next. So why try so hard?

God was some old blind man stumbling around in a room full of delicate glass figures, stepping on them and sending others smashing to the ground, oblivious or indifferent to the damage he was causing. There was no celestial points tally, no holy accountant at the gates of heaven, balancing good deeds with bad as part of some admissions policy. The names of the next men to die at sea were being drawn daily in some unholy lottery. His brother and thousands like him had been taken for no reason.

* * * *

The routine of HMS *Standard* was to win hearts and minds. It didn't matter which came first. During the day, hard work, carefully planned, exhausted the men and time restrictions left no space for deviant thoughts. Ten minutes of stand easy, morning and afternoon, was enough to rest tired muscles but not enough to allow men to think about what was happening to them or why.

The Admiralty, the working navy and the Royal College of Psychiatrists all agreed that discipline reinforced courage. By extension, more discipline reinforced more courage. Every available minute in a man's day and every available thought was to be filled with rehabilitation by persuasion, so that thoughts of *not* returning to naval duties were never an option.

Courage in battle was persisting in the face of danger, despite being afraid. The men who had been sent to Kielder had not kept going when they had faced fear, indeed some of them had given up just at the thought of what they were about to face. This was what the Admiralty wanted to change, using all available waking time.

* * * *

By the third or fourth week, he couldn't remember which, Duncan had succumbed to the relentless routine, almost. He didn't give up and decide to go along with it all. It was just easier to work, eat and sleep with the herd, than to raise more questions and be picked out for special attention. Routine was necessary. But still something rankled him about sleepwalking his way through the days. The evening that sent him on another path started like any other.

He watched as the men like him who had chosen PT over OT for the first part of the evening were ushered into the OT room by the hut officer, for the second activity of the evening before pipe down. The men leaving the room after a woodwork session, those considered unsuitable for the discussion group to follow, slowed or stood outside the hut looking in, curious about what they were missing, but accepting of the fact that it was not for them. Being denied inclusion in the group made it intriguing and attractive, even when the alternative was an extra half hour in bed that night.

The chaplain's half hour discussion group was part of the educational scheme of the camp. The topic for the evening, led jointly by the chaplain and the Number 4 hut officer was, "*No man has a right unless another has a duty*," already chalked in capitals on the blackboard in the chaplain's neat lettering.

The men were split into two groups and the groups were flipped after fifteen minutes. The therapeutic objective, barely disguised, was to get the men thinking and if possible saying that freedoms in Britain depended on everyone, including the idle, cowards and shirkers, like them, all doing what they were supposed to in a time of war.

The discussion was a pincer movement. The hut officer's tack was, "we-are-all-in-it-together-men", while the chaplain hammered away from the angle of, "Jesus-died-for-our-sins".

Two sides of the same coin, a strategy designed to generate guilt in men not at the battle front in a time of war, men not performing their duties.

Duncan bored quickly of the hut officer's soapbox lecture. The man led and monopolised the talk, avoiding the possibility of any real discussion by filling the time with tales of his own bravery in the face of the enemy. If the officer was half the war hero he claimed to be, Duncan wondered, then why had he washed up at Kielder, a sheepdog for the navy, instead of inspiring men at the front? He might have asked him that, if there had been any chance for anyone else to speak.

The groups flipped, changing seating and speaker. Duncan had already given up, deciding on the path of least resistance for a quiet time. Keep his head down, study the rain running down the window and mutter basic answers if asked any questions to show that he was listening. He would let the preaching wash over him and volunteer nothing. But only three minutes into the chaplain's session, Duncan heard himself interrupt, speaking out even as he was telling himself to shut up and see out the session.

He tried hard to hold back, but it was like a geyser blowing. He heard the question bubbling up and he and was powerless to stop it when it reached his mouth, bursting out. The Padre was on about the sacrifices of Jesus, one of his favourite rants. That's what did it.

"*Sorry, 'scuse me Padre,*" Duncan said, half raising an arm to attract attention.

"*If Jesus died so that we could all get to heaven, and if God is watching over us until we get there, then how come he's letting so many people die in this bloody war?*"

He tried for a reasonable tone. It was hard to keep the anger out of it and the volume rose as he got to the end of his question.

Men who were stuck at the front of the group craned their necks to see who had decided to talk, rather than listen, silently cursing Duncan for dragging the session on, possibly beyond time. It could have been over in half an hour and they could have been out, in their bunks and asleep. The chaplain smiled, showing no sign of irritation at Duncan's interruption. The pulpit rhythm in the rise and fall of his voice continued in his reply.

"*Now that is a very good question and one that I've often asked myself in my service to God and service to my country. You can call me Charlie, by the way son, there's no need for the formality of "Padre" here.*"

Duncan watched the chaplain as he spoke. He didn't look at Duncan directly, swinging his eyes instead between the left and right ends of the back row of men, like a tennis umpire.

"*It is a difficult question and it needs a full answer son.*"

Duncan saw men in front of him slump down further in their chairs. Whenever the chaplain said the words, "full answer' it meant he was moving into sermon-mode, holy guns blazing.

"*If we all had just one chance to ask God a question, your question might be the one that most people would ask. Let me answer it in this way. Firstly, we learn in Corinthians 13 that although some things, like wars, are puzzling to us now, unclear, like hazy reflections in a mirror, we will see everything clearer later.*"

The chaplain paused to point skyward.

"*We cannot as mere mortals know the bigger picture for what has been planned. Only the Almighty is privy to that.*"

The other men in the group had listened to the beginning of the chaplain's answer, but everyone except Duncan had tuned out when he got to "*Corinthians 13.*" After that, to a man they were looking anywhere but the front, finding something more interesting up their nose, or a loose thread on their uniform.

But the chaplain didn't need an attentive audience; rows of faces in front of him were enough to power his sermon.

"*We only see through a glass, darkly, until we enter into glory, later in life when we will know more. We also know that God has decided to give his subjects the freedom to choose to do right or wrong. While most of us have chosen wisely to follow the word of Jesus, a few have made bad decisions, which have started wars that have led to the death of many. Faith too, is important...*"

Duncan had been too distracted at first by the idea of someone called Charlie the Chaplain to follow the beginning of the answer he got, but the mention of bad decisions brought him back from picturing the padre with a small moustache, swinging a cane.

He heard himself interrupt, again, beginning to speak before he knew how he would finish.

"So, because Hitler made a few bad decisions, but God doesn't have the power to stop him from making more, God can't prevent other men dying?"

He paused, clenching his fists to stay calm.

"Is that what you are saying padre?"

The chaplain stopped, mid-flow, fixing his gaze on Duncan for the first time. He was surprised that his usual, boilerplate answer to the why-is-God-doing-nothing question had not been enough to satisfy or at least silence Duncan. He looked at his feet, then moved up a holy gear, lifting a heavy, leather-bound bible from the table behind him.

As he did, men in the group sat up. The 15-minute session was going to be strung out even longer, but now it was getting entertaining. Would there be a fight? Would the chaplain throw the holy book at Duncan?

"Some men do evil things son, but only God in his infinite wisdom can judge them or forgive them. For our part, as men of God, we must do what we believe to be right and just, in the knowledge that we too will be judged."

The chaplain had both hands on the bible, held in front of him. Duncan listened to the words, but couldn't tell if the chaplain was quoting from scripture, or making it up as he went along.

"In Matthew 7 we hear the word of Jesus. Judge not, that ye be not judged, for with what judgment you judge, you shall be judged and with what measure you mete, it shall be measured to you again."

Duncan listened, trying hard to concentrate. There were far too many 'yous' and 'judges' in what Charlie the chaplain had said for Duncan to make any sense of it. It was like a labyrinthine biblical riddle. It was not an answer to Duncan's question, or even another question to his answer.

There was a brief silence in the room as the chaplain stood, bible in hand, his gaze now upwards. No one moved.

It was the exhaustion that told Duncan he had lost the argument, if it ever was two sided. He felt himself go limp suddenly and became aware for the first time that he was sweating, the smell of defeat, produced by his body especially for the occasion.

Every man in the room except the padre was now staring at him, wondering if he could come back off the canvas for another round, throw another punch, but willing him to stay down, take a count of ten and let it end. He gave up. He had lost, no match for the chaplain's practised, bamboozling holy-speak. Everyone in the room had listened and the message of the evening was clear: To argue with the padre was to argue with the word of God and there would be only one winner, every time.

That night, Duncan didn't sleep much. Every time he rolled over, the words of God, as spoken by the chaplain came to him, repeated over, reminding him that God didn't have much to say to him.

It was that night, in the long stretches as he lay awake, that he started the planning.

* * * *

During the day, Marco worked in the kitchens. He was fast and able and Ballard heard no complaints from his staff about 'call-offs' or 'sore guts' as he had feared when he put Marco on peeling spuds and cleaning plates and pans.

Ballard had tested Marco further, sending him outside the camp on work parties. Supervisors reported that Marco was willing but just didn't have the muscle mass for moving rocks at the riverbank or for sawing logs all day. The report from the drainage ditch crew was short but positive. Marco was capable of digging ditches.

All of the reports were a first for Ballard. Every other Number 3 hut patient he had sent out on work parties had reacted predictably to anything that smelled of physical labour by trading on imagined symptoms, being brought back to camp before the end of the day.

Ballard kept Marco on the same daytime regime of kitchen duties, fresh air, exercise and physical work, the psychiatric bread-and-butter treatment for the camp, to see if the ulcer or the dead elephant would re-appear. Marco was easily directed to activities and uncomplaining. Ballard added brief notes on his record sheet, discontinuing the red dots and beginning days of black dot entries.

In contrast to programming his days, filling Marco's evenings with therapeutic activities was a struggle for Ballard, or more accurately for the instructors.

The regular evening education classes were not for Marco. For most men, instructors were able to pick up where school had finished, but for Marco there was no pick-up point. He could read most words, given the time to sound them out, but instructors just didn't have the time to practice writing letter shapes, which was the school level he would have been at, if he had attended school. He wasn't schooled enough for the discussion group, and he spent most of his time at the woodwork or plastic work classes asking what time they would be finished.

Marco worked hard at being a good patient. He did whatever he was asked, whether it was peeling spuds, scraping carrots, scouring pots or digging ditches. He wanted to meet with Ballard again, have him read in reports how well he'd been doing and ask him when the treatment would begin to help Marco with the misery.

It was after he was moved from the river crew to the ditch digging crew that Marco realised Ballard was putting him through some kind of test, to see if he was ready for the treatment. Marco pushed himself hard at the ditch digging, to make a real impression. He'd had enough of living in Number 3 hut and he was ready to try whatever Ballard had in mind to move him on.

Marco's father, Joe, would have called the men in Number 3 hut a bunch of Martin Harveys. Marco had seen just a few of these in the circus and they didn't last long. They were novelty acts, mostly. The two that Marco remembered were a trainer who could make his dogs dance on two legs and bark out a song, and a clown who kicked a donkey around the ring before doing another circuit when the donkey did the same to him. It wasn't that the acts couldn't perform and entertain; some days they just didn't want to.

Joe had worked with the original Martin Harvey and added his name to his vocabulary before any of the Craston brothers were born. Harvey was a sword swallower who could also hammer a nail through a conveniently pierced hole in his tongue. Joe could work himself into a froth, recounting circus shows when Martin Harvey stayed in his wagon, saying that he didn't feel like it, or wandered off into town, drinking. He was famous for it.

In the Navy, Marco had seen shirkers, swinging the lead and good at it. The Navy seemed to have picked the best ones and brought them all to Number 3 hut. He was in Number 3 hut too, but he was no Martin Harvey.

* * * *

In Number 2 hut, before lights out, there was a gathering. The only rules were that you stood behind the line when you threw, and there was no rolling allowed. That was it. There were no restrictions on how high or how low you threw or even if you hit the wall. Clarence knew it as pap, it was 'keeley' to Duncan and, until he could make out what others were saying, Marco thought it was called pigeon toss.

Some men went down on one knee, swaying back and forward like cobras before launching their coin in a perfect arc. Others went for power, trying to throw the penny with such force that it flattened against the wall and slid down, exhausted, into a winning position.

The number of pennies in the camp available for pitch-and-toss only increased when a new man arrived. Men already there had only what was in their pockets. There was no fortnightly Pay Parade, no wages in envelopes paid out and there was nothing to buy. There was the rum ration and a cigarette allowance for men who smoked, but that didn't involve any cash.

Pitch-and-toss started outside with a few bored men one day and then moved into Number 2 hut as a spectator attraction when the cold weather set in. The man who threw the penny that landed closest to the wall scooped all of the pennies already thrown.

That was the game. To keep the game alive, the men worked out a system, playing until there were only five men left with pennies. Other men, for a threepence, a sixpence or cigarettes could buy some pennies back, to allow them back into the next game. *"The pennies are round so that they can go around,"* was the call at the end of every game.

The time after painting, plastic work and PT, before pipe down at 22.00, was half an hour, sometimes less but it was precious; the only time in the day apart from stand easy at 10.45 and 14.45 that was not spoken for with camp routine.

Marco was drawn from his bunk to Number 2 hut by the cheering, a bubble of circus memory rising. It was the first crowd noise of any kind he had heard since arriving at Kielder.

There were few common causes in the camp to unite the many. Hoisting of the colours, bringing everybody together, was done in silence. It was another reminder if any was needed that each man was far from the sea and had fallen well short of what was expected by the Royal Navy. Even the compulsory camp football was a joyless, silent pantomime. Men in coloured bibs ran about to instruction until exhausted, directed by instructors on either side of the pitch. The men were repeating experiences as adults that had first alienated them to games as children.

The penny tossers in Number 2 hut were just loud enough to keep a comatose Clarence awake. His bunk was at the pitch-and-toss end of the hut. He lay on his stomach in a state of threshold consciousness, the sound of the coins and the men's cheering jerking him back from sleep each time. He could feel his bunk move as men climbed on the end to get a better view of the action.

Duncan would have turned up, gladly, to watch men playing cards, chess, dominoes, or any form of distraction to let him forget, and fast, after his nightly encounters with Corinthians 13 and Charlie the chaplain. In the discussion sessions he felt like he was punching at a wet blanket thrown over him. No matter how many times he swore he would say nothing, and then cursed himself for speaking, he was drawn in. The chaplain would just absorb everything Duncan could throw, with his smug smile, slowly suffocating Duncan with the scriptures and the unknowable mysteries of God as a back-up explanation to cover anything else.

So the penny-toss was a welcome simplicity. Someone threw, someone won, rules agreed and understood, no divine explanations or excuses.

Marco picked a spot behind Clarence's bunk where he could see the men throw, but not where the pennies landed. When he asked if he was blocking Clarence's view of the action, he got a mumbled reply. It was only when he asked a second time that he realised that Clarence wasn't lying flat on the bunk to get the best view of the game.

"*You look knackered mate.*"

"*I can't keep my eyes open long enough for a whole game,*" Clarence said, the words spaced out in an effort to make them clear.

Marco could tell how close to the wall the pennies had landed from the reaction of the throwers and the crowd. He watched the show from the side-lines for three nights, seeing men from all three huts united in the excitement of nothing more than a pile of pennies. His need to be close to the drama, to watch from the edge of the ring, was strong and he changed his position on Clarence's bunk each night, getting closer. Eventually his urge to perform was too strong.

When he started playing, one of the men nicknamed Marco "the tup" and it stuck. The other man told him he looked like an angry sheep the first time he used his technique. But the sheep noises from the crowd stopped when Marco started to scoop up the pennies.

It was timing. Too soon and the board shook before the coin landed; a millisecond too late and the coin was already dead. The force of the foot stamp and the half second for the shock wave to travel along the wooden boards had to be factored in too. Marco had it nailed.

The vibration in the floorboard from his stamp killed the penny dead where it landed. He stood on one foot as he threw and then planted his shoe flat on the floor an instant before the coin landed, flat, as near as was possible to the wall. A bit of fine tuning to begin with, then he had it every time. A couple of the other seaman tried to copy his technique, stomping or even jumping in the air, making more noise, but no more money.

So it was that pitch-and-toss, rather than serving their country at sea in a time of war that first brought together Clarence, Duncan and Marco.

Marco made it a habit to sit on the end of Clarence's bunk and chat before the game started. It was part nervous, pre-performance routine, part morbid curiosity at what kind of misery could knock out a man of Clarence's size, day after day.

Duncan was fascinated by Marco, initially by his skill with the pennies and later by how he brought the same high-energy enthusiasm to everything he did in the camp, a place where most men were soul-dead. He was wary when he first started chatting to him. Duncan wanted to know the secret of Marco's energy, his irrational vitality in this place, yes, but without asking him directly. He didn't want to use up what little energy he had left finding the source of Marco's if the answer was, as he dreaded, something that involved having Jesus or one of his many holy pals in his heart.

After a week, the three men would meet at Clarence's bunk before the pitch-and-toss, Marco talking, always nervous before his performance, Duncan listening, entertained, Clarence staying awake, just.

* * * *

Two nights a week there was a short slot for letter writing, to keep men in touch with families. The session wasn't long enough to write a whole letter, but men could gradually put together the one letter home every two weeks that was allowed. All letters going out or coming in were first censored by Ballard or his fellow psychiatrist Thurman, for reasons of security, the men were told. Ballard and Thurman met once a week, to discuss if there was anything in any of the letters going out that might sink ships, or indicate improvement, or regression in any of the men.

Before he came to pitch-and-toss, Marco worked on his letter for fifteen minutes. That is, he dictated halting sentences, building to what was to be sent. It took him four weeks to put together his letter. One of the men in Number 3 hut, Geoff Wilkins, formerly of HMS *Daring,* now of Kielder with debilitating stomach complaints, had no family, or none that he wanted anyone to know about. He did, however, have a liking for an extra dollop of potatoes when Marco was on kitchen serving duties, and extra handfuls of salt from kitchen stores, for times when he needed to be too sick to go on a work party. So Marco traded; potatoes and salt for Geoff's secondary education.

Marco wanted to let his father and his brothers to know that he was OK. That was it. Why Geoff couldn't write just that and send it, he wasn't sure. He didn't need a reply. Marco saw other men in the hut, hunched over tables, tongues sticking out in concentration, adding word after word. Some men wrote three and four-page letters. Geoff told Marco he had to say more in a letter but didn't help much. When Geoff stopped scribbling or Marco stopped talking all Geoff would say was, "*OK. What else?*"

It was always Joe, never Dad or Pop. Marco pictured Joe reading his letter and wanted it to sound right.

Dear Joe
It's Marco here. I am OK. Everything bona. Hope you are good and Peter and Paul are good. I am not in jail or anything multi kativa, but I am not on a ship no more either. Living with a bunch of jossers for now. Most of them are Martin Harveys, but not me.
Nanti letters, because I will be out by then.
Your son
Marco

When Geoff asked him where it was going, all Marco had was, "*Joe Craston, Corbett's Circus.*" Geoff wrote this in block capitals on the envelope and handed it over. Marco thought it would be enough, since there was only one Corbett's circus and one Joe Craston who worked there.

After three weeks of waiting, Marco had his second meeting with Ballard. It turned out to be his last. Marco was ready to hear about starting his treatment for the misery. Sure, he was nervous; who wouldn't be? When he found out the reason that Clarence was laid out in bed was because of *his* treatment, he wondered how much pain he himself was willing to go through to get rid of the misery. The answer was whatever it took, of course it was, because he didn't want to end up like Tuflo, and if Ballard had some magic cure he would take it, to get rid of the misery and to get out of Kielder. Maybe there were some new pills that had been invented in the war, or something Ballard could do that no one else could.

But Ballard didn't want to talk to Marco about the misery or his treatment.

"It's this letter, Seaman Craston," he said, not looking up as Marco came into the office.

Marco looked at the torn envelope on Ballard's desk, beside a stack of letters, all on the same standard issue, buff-coloured paper. Ballard had Marco's letter on a space cleared on the desk. Marco stared at the writing, embarrassed at his words. Embarrassed too, that the words covered less than half a page.

"It can't go out like this."

Marco looked from the letter to the envelope. Why did Ballard need to take out his letter and read it, just to tell him that?

"But there's only one Corbett's circus, doc. The letter would find him."

Ballard sighed.

"It might find him eventually with this ridiculous address," Ballard said, tapping the envelope with his pencil, *"but that's not why it can't go out,"*

He leaned back in his chair, keeping Marco standing at attention.

"It's not the address. It's what you've written in the letter that's the problem."

Marco hung his head.

"I know there's not much there, doc. I'm not too good with

words, and I can see from those other letters that you might want a bit more, but see that's all I've got. Maybe for the next one I could tell him more..."

Ballard held up his hand, cutting him off.

Pinching the bridge of his nose, he said, "That's not it either Seaman Craston. Let me explain it to you in plain terms."

He smoothed the crumpled letter out in front of him.

"You see, I'm responsible for all the men in this camp. I'm responsible for their welfare, and for their security, and this is especially important because we are at war. This camp is still part of the Royal Navy and anything in this camp that threatens the security of the Navy is my responsibility."

Marco was listening, but he was already lost.

"So that is why you see this pile of letters here," Ballard said, patting the stack beside him.

"Information. Information has become the most valuable currency in our battle with the Germans..."

There had been times in Marco's training, in classroom sessions, when he found himself tuned out, like a radio dial that had moved off the station frequency. Some of the times that was OK, because half the class were also tuned out, being told something that had to be said by their instructors, something that they had to sit and listen to. "Don't put your head inside anything that closes... yadda, yadda, yadda...don't drop any shells...yadda, yadda, yadda...don't do stupid things...yadda, yadda, yadda."

Other times, he had lost the thread of something important being said and couldn't find his way back onto the radio station, no matter how hard he tried to concentrate. This was one of those times.

He watched Ballard's mouth move and he heard the words, but they could have been in any order for all the sense that they were making.

"...and if I am not able to guarantee that the information going out poses no threat to naval and national security, then I am not able to send that information out. You can understand why that is the position, I hope?"

Ballard made eye contact with Marco for an acknowledgement

but saw only a blank stare.

"*Which brings me to your letter,*" he continued, tapping an index finger on the few lines Marco had dictated to Geoff.

"*I've looked for these words that are in your letter and they are not in my dictionary, which raises my suspicions.*" He stopped, put his hand to his chin and left a long pause for Marco to fill.

"*What words, doc?*"

"*Well let's take a few examples, shall we?*" Ballard ran his finger over along the lines.

"*What about this one? Kativa? Or this one here, which my colleague Dr Thurman found especially puzzling. Who is this chap Martin Harvey?*"

As Ballard spoke, Marco wondered how many other people, beside Thurman had read the letter he'd written to his father.

"*That's, that's just something I say doc, when I'm speaking. Kativa is something that ain't too good. Martin Harvey was a sword swallower, he was a circy who didn't like working, least that's what Joe told me, and ...*"

"*Let me stop you there Craston. This all sounds very well and I'm sure that you would be able to give me an explanation for all these words, now that you've been asked about them. But how do I know that any of what you are telling me is true? I only have your account of what all this means.*"

"*But I can tell you what they mean doc, if that's the problem?*"

"*The problem Craston,*" Ballard said, tapping his finger on the letter again, "*is that I can never know, really know, what they mean.*"

"*But...*"

"*We don't have a lot of time, and this is a busy day for me, so let me be frank here Seaman Craston,*" Ballard said, leaning forward in his chair.

"*I've met many people in my years as a psychiatrist, and as I've moved all around the country. I know and you know that your people, circus types and gypsies and the like, use some words to keep outsiders from knowing what is being said. Correct?*"

Ballard didn't wait for a reply.

"*You may be using these words because you want your*

conversation to be private. That is fine in a personal letter. However, what is not fine, what is not in any way fine, is when these words are used as code, as some kind of secret language, to send information that may fall into the hands of the enemy."

Marco could feel the radio dial moving off station again, the sound of static increasing. He was trying to make the link between his letter, Joe and the Nazis, but he couldn't concentrate on how that might work and continue listening to Ballard at the same time. Joe wasn't a Nazi and nobody at the circus was German.

"I'm not saying that you would, deliberately, disclose secrets about what we are doing here at Kielder. Of course not. You might not even be aware that the information that you are sending out is of a sensitive nature. But as a representative of the Navy, with security responsibility, I cannot take that chance."

Ballard rose from his chair, folding Marco's letter as he did so.

"The Yanks have an expression for it that you can bear in mind when you are writing your next letter Seaman Craston. Loose lips might sink ships. That's what they say. Loose lips might sink ships. Think carefully about what you are writing."

The radio dial in Marco's head was spinning. He was lost, picturing American sailors in uniform with flapping lips creating massive waves, swamping battleships, and wondering how he could have caused it.

"Keep your letters light. Tell your father about the weather, let him know that you are keeping busy and enjoying your food, that sort of thing. Most of all, write it in the King's English, then we won't need to have this conversation again."

Ballard moved around his desk as he saw Marco open his mouth to reply.

"All clear?" he said, ushering Marco to the door.

Marco found himself standing outside the main camp office before he settled on what he was going to say in reply and realised how pointless it would be to say it.

There were many times since he'd joined up when he felt dumb, not just different from the other men around him, but missing something that they all had. These were times when he'd been the only nozzer in the classroom who didn't know the answer to

189

the question being asked, or the only crewman in the mess room who didn't get the joke that had just been cracked. Even on HMS *Devon,* when he was the butt of Petty Officer, First Class Stephens' jokes, there were times when he heard what was said about him, but didn't get why men were laughing with Stephens, only that he was the target. Ballard had made him feel dumb, confusing him with talk of secrets and Nazis and sinking ships, and then dismissed him and the letter it had taken him weeks to write to Joe.

And there was no treatment for the misery. He would have started on it by now, for sure. Ballard would have mentioned it in their meeting. The treatment had been a lie by Ballard to keep Marco quiet, to keep him digging ditches and serving in the kitchen, and to keep him at Kielder.

CHAPTER 6

GARNET FELL

There was no digging of tunnels with spoons or clambering over barbed wire fences on a moonless night. There were no wire clippers, no machine gun turrets with spotlights or barking dogs to avoid. It was just a walk, straight out the main gate when it got dark. Each man had a pack, half a bed sheet filled and knotted as planned. At the arranged time, doors opened quietly in the three huts and Clarence, Duncan and Marco felt their way to their stash, collecting what they had each agreed to carry. They met by the exercise field to pick up the final items, then back up the path, through the huts, keeping quiet and low, and out.

No alarms sounded as they walked down the road in darkness, guided by their knowledge of the curve of the first bend, and following the sound of the North Tyne river on the right. The water was noisy, in spate after recent rains.

After a mile, they slowed, the first adrenaline rush over. Marco had taken the lead at an Olympic walking pace, head up, keeping one foot on the ground at all times, but only just. Clarence brought up the rear, looking over his shoulder every hundred yards, expecting to hear a shout and the crunching of tyres or the sound of boots clumping down the road behind them. Duncan was in the middle, keeping his eyes on Marco's back, adjusting the weight of his pack, trying to keep it centred between his shoulder blades.

The route they had decided on was straight across the moor, heading for Garnet Fell, as the nearest landmark and the furthest and highest point they could see from the camp. After that, there was no plan. The prime objective was escape, not final destination.

"*We'll figure it out,*" Duncan had said, and the two others had agreed, complicit in the lie. Difficult questions and planning beyond Garnet Fell would delay their departure, so they were avoided.

* * * *

"*But what if we could get away?*" It was Duncan who had first floated it, and he was the one who spent most time thinking how it could be done. Yes, he had been to first to say it out loud, but when he did it was like a damn bursting. Clarence and Marco would have gone with him that same night, without any preparations and Duncan would have gone alone anyway if either of them decided that escape was crazier than staying.

Clarence was still groggy for most of the day, but wide awake for the first time in weeks when they started talking about it for real around his bunk. The noise of the penny-toss was good cover. Nothing about the plan was written down, which suited Marco. He needed only the when and where.

When he had been at the circus Marco took each day head on. He had tried to do that even at HMS *Standard*. When he woke each morning, he had no worries about the day before or the day before that, because nothing that had happened could be changed, no matter how good or bad it had been. The meeting with Ballard had changed that. Every morning since, he woke remembering Ballard's deception and how he had been trapped like a rat, condemned to spend whatever time he had left at Kielder, with nothing better on offer. Then came the meetings with Clarence and Duncan and the chance to run, to get out, to anywhere.

Because it was Duncan who had been brave enough to suggest it, the other two were depending on him for the plan, when there could be no plan. The leap into the unknown gave Duncan a gnawing headache. There were more questions with no answers each time they met.

Three deserters on the run with no money and no place to hide? Three mentally deranged deserters, as the Admiralty would be keen to emphasise when they put the alert out to the public. The questions with no answers would push to the front of his thoughts when he was planning, building his escape stash, and he would push them back. Getting out and clear; that was what mattered, and they had to focus on that. All planning was for the breakout and they blinkered themselves to the obvious, gaping hole in the plan. What the hell were they were going to do after the first hours?

With no destination in mind, they had taken what they thought men on the run would need for the journey, rather than for any arrival elsewhere. Hidden around the camp under huts were tins of meat, stolen from the kitchen, packs of biscuits and handfuls of potatoes. Duncan had also taken matches, a tin opener, a knife, and a bible. The Holy Book was a compact source of paper to start a fire. His simple reckoning was that the more food they could carry, even although it was heavy, the further they could get from the camp. Each of the three had also stored a rubberised overcoat, issued to men on work parties going outside the camp. These were bulky, taking up more than half the space in their improvised packs, but Duncan persuaded the other two that being soaked by rain would slow them down even more than the extra weight of the coats. The choice had been between the rubberised coat, waterproof, but cold and standard-issue navy duffel coat, which was warm, but more difficult to steal and four times its weight when wet.

Each man slipped out of his hut at the agreed time, taking the blanket from his bed, wrapped around shoulders and worn as a hood. It was effective camouflage, blending with the weathered timbers of the huts. They were difficult to see. Or they would have been, if anyone had been looking.

* * * *

In the moonless darkness, the firebreak in the conifers at the side of the road was no more than a change of shade, a long stretch of dark grey between the solid, black masses of trees either side. Where the rows of trees had been planted, the sitting bog water had been sucked from the ground beneath over the years for tree growth and transpiration. Across the width of the firebreak this left a dry carpet of spruce needles with peaty soil underneath. The smell was of soil that had been ploughed. Beyond the soft ground of the firebreak were seven hard miles across the treeless moor, just to reach Garnet Fell.

In Duncan's plan, there were just a few fixed time points. One was to get out before midnight. The other was to get to Garnet Fell before sunrise. After that, they would be spotted easily from the camp, as the only movement for miles on the hill. If that happened, they wouldn't be chased, just watched through binoculars, then picked up by police and brought back to Kielder from the nearest road. Game over.

All the way along the length of the firebreak, Clarence had regrets about taking the rubber. It was already rationed, and to him it felt like theft.

After the Japanese invaded every major producing country except Ceylon, the supply of rubber to Britain stopped. HMS *Standard* had no special certificate, because it was not front line, so lorries at the camp were limited to five tyres a year, like other vehicles. The Navy had to patch up any punctured tubes, just like civilian cars and vans. Make do and mend. Government advice was to drive at "victory speed", which was 35 miles per hour, to preserve the tyres. Clarence had taken an inner tube that was already punctured, not a new one, so he was less guilty about that. But it would still have been patched up and put back into service, probably by him. Sand down the hole, rubber glue, patch, chalk to dry it out; ready to go. He could do it in less than 20 minutes. But instead of fixing it up, he had destroyed the tube beyond any repair, which went against his engineer's oath to resuscitate whenever possible. In the workshop, with no one around, he had taken a shard of broken glass and a length of wood to keep his lines straight and cut out long strips of rubber.

He now unravelled the long grey snake of rubber around his waist, and began loosening the knots between the rubber strips, as they stopped at the end of the firebreak, on edge of the moor.

There were some parts of the escape plan that they knew would work. They had done a dummy run, coming out of the huts late at night and walking around. There was nobody to notice. They had planned a rendezvous at the sports field and walked back to the huts, even up to the front gate without a challenge. These were the parts of the plan that could be rehearsed. Getting out and getting clear was easy.

"*We'll figure it out,*" they had agreed. Now came the first jump into the unknown. This part of the plan had to work, or they would all be back in their bunks before breakfast, or each in one of Kielder three cells.

Clarence passed four strips each to Duncan and Marco. The two men stretched the rubber strips between their hands and waited, watching Clarence.

"*Tie them tight, but not so tight that you cut off the circulation,*" he said, sitting down on a tree stump.

"*One around your ankle, and one at the front of your foot.*"

As he spoke, Clarence took the first of the tennis racquets, stolen from the sports shed, from his pack and threaded the rubber through the sheep-gut strings. His size-ten foot covered the length of the face of the racquet, with the toes of his navy boot resting on the wooden rim at the front. Clarence carefully tied on both his racquets, double knotting the strips, and got to his feet. Duncan and Marco stood close to him in the darkness, trying to make out what he was doing and how it looked when he had finished. Duncan sat down next and Clarence waddled over to help him. He started to explain the knotting, but then decided it was quicker to do the job himself and bent down in front of Duncan. He linked the strips of rubber on Duncan's foot and ankle so that they could move, the action pulling up the front of each racquet when Duncan took a step. Marco was quicker on the uptake. He had worked out his own arrangement for fastening the rubber strips to give him a spring in his step. He was practising walking along the track as Duncan stood up.

"*Seems easy enough on the flat,*" Marco said, lifting and planting each foot like he was walking through deep snow.

The rims of the wooden racquets were bent, warped from sitting in the damp of the games shed without braces, and the men spent another five minutes deciding whether it was best to secure them to their feet concave-up or concave-down.

In the end, it didn't matter. The bog on the moor didn't care which way the racquets were tied on.

* * * *

Marco found his rhythm within the first hundred yards, picking his steps as his eyes adjusted to the dark. He used the spring in the clumps of heather when he could, to minimise the energy-sapping mud. When he hit flat patches of bog, he still needed to strain, but his improvised snowshoes kept the worst of his sinkings to ankle depth.

Clarence started off with giant, Fee-Fi-Fo-Fum strides, which was a mistake. He took long strides to reduce the amount of time he was in contact with the bog, but each time he came down on soft ground, his weight slammed the racquet on his foot deep into the mud. While he stopped to pull one foot out, the other was sinking deeper. Within the first mile his shirt was soaked in sweat and his legs were feeling heavy.

Duncan took a different approach, trying to pick out the clumps in the gloom and stay on top of the heather and firmer ground where he could see it, using the bounce like Marco. He tried walking sideways, crablike, when they hit stretches of bog too wide to go around. It used different muscles and he didn't tire as quickly, for the first few miles at least.

The whole moor was like a shallow lake of mud with islands of hardy vegetation dotty across the surface. If you stood, you sank. In some places Clarence went ankle deep in seconds. Sometimes it was instant, like stepping into a cold bath, but elsewhere the mud was thicker and it was a slower, creeping process, only noticed as feet went cold as the water crept up over the collar of boots. Duncan and Marco spent less time in contact with the ground, but they sank down like Clarence too.

The bog was half water, half saturated peat, sucking down any animals heavy enough to break the surface of the water. The sporadic islands of woody heather and moss banks floated rather than grew in the poor soil, any nutrients being leeched away. Other plants that survived, butterworts and sundews, had to trap and kill insect prey to get enough nitrogen and phosphorus to live.

In places where the bog looked flat there was layer upon layer of absorbent sphagnum moss, laid down over hundreds of years. The knee-deep green sponge absorbed eight times its own weight in water. There were lighter greens and ochres, isolated, swollen islands, looking like geysers getting ready to blow. Here the moss had become saturated until it could hold no more water. When one of these green islands burst it could suddenly become a pool, two metres deep.

From high above, and in daylight, it might have been possible to plan and pick a route where one step would support the next, a join-the-dots on tufts of more stable ground, with only brief scuttles across muddy pools. But at ground level and in the dark, the landscape was a just a patchwork of black and greys. Testing out each step ahead meant less sinking and fewer falls, but it was too slow for men on the run.

They plodded on, blindly, tripping, getting wetter with every yard they gained, cursing as they went down and the racquets on their feet tripped them a second time as they got up. By the end of the fourth mile, they were all feeling it, even Marco. Clarence was falling behind, so far that the other two had to take stops until he was close enough that they could hear him breathing heavily. Only his reserves of strength and his bloody-mindedness were keeping him stomping on, his arms now in front of him, like a bear walking upright.

"*Stop here,*" Duncan said, feeling in front of him with his hands and testing for a clump of heather that was not going to sink when he sat on it, or make his arse any wetter than it already was. They had one water bottle, filled from the North Tyne. He took it from his pack and passed it around. They had counted on being able to refill it from faster flowing streams higher on the moor, and they were still gambling on that as they finished the water in two rounds.

Marco followed Duncan's lead and sat. When Clarence caught up he remained standing, panting.

"*I didn't think it would be this hard,*" Duncan said, head down. "*I'm on my chinstraps here, already.*"

"*I'm not going back,*" Clarence said, between breaths, before Duncan had finished speaking. Marco looked toward where Duncan sat in the darkness. Clarence didn't just mean he wasn't turning around. After what the insulin therapy and Ballard had done to him at HMS *Standard,* he would walk himself to a standstill and die on the moor, rather than go back.

"*Maybe if we find a gully we can follow that to Garnet Fell if we don't make it before sun-up. If we keep low we won't be spotted from the camp,*" Duncan said.

There was no reply. Finding gullies or any other contours on the moor was unlikely when they couldn't see beyond the next pool of black mud.

"*We just have to keep going. The sun will be up in four hours, and then we're fucked,*" said Clarence, adjusting his pack. He was still standing, ready to go.

"*Let me go in front,*" he continued.

"*I've been holding you back, but I can pick up the pace. We have to push it, even if we're chockered.*"

Clarence looked towards Duncan, then repositioned his pack on his back and started walking.

"*I can keep going. Just tell me when I'm dead,*" he said.

Marco stood first. He could make it in a straight dash, he reckoned, head down, not looking up until the gradient changed and the other side of the hill told him that he was beyond Garnet Fell. But they were in it together. He would go at their pace. He would stick with them until it was hopeless. Then he could still make a run for it on his own if he had to, if it started to look like they would be caught.

The day before they left, Marco had killed ten flies. So that was OK. He had started it out of boredom, then made it more interesting by setting himself a daily target. Looking for the flies stopped him thinking about the misery so much, about whether it was growing and how long it would take. It was getting to him. He had started with three a day, but that was too easy. Over a week, he worked it up to ten a day. Nobody noticed. He swatted, or shot out a hand and caught them, mid-air. They jumped backward as they took off, so he knew where to be. After his last meeting with Ballard he decided to make it twelve a day. It would be harder, but he could do it. The problem with twelve was that he would have to keep them somewhere, so he could count at the end of the day, just to make sure. It would be too easy to cheat. After his meeting with Ballard, he thought of ways to keep himself sharp. He could eat all of the flies he killed, or even half of them, as a punishment if he didn't meet his daily target. That would get him through the days. Or he could up it to twenty a day. That would keep him busy.

Lying on his bunk on his last night at Kielder, he worked out that he had never been in one place for so long in his life. It had been the right time to go.

* * * *

"*And I'm ditching this,*" Clarence said, after walking just another hundred yards.

He pulled the rubber coat from his pack and threw it on the ground, then walked back and forth, waiting for the other two to catch up.

"*It's slowing me down, and I'll be sweating like a racehorse if I have to put it on.*"

Marco was close enough to Duncan, to hear him sigh. He looked at him, then at Clarence's coat splayed on the ground as they caught up. Clarence waddled on the spot on his tennis racquets.

"*OK, maybe you're right. We can travel faster without them.*" Duncan unpacked his own coat, rolled it into a tight ball and stood on it in a patch of deep mud.

"*But let's not make it too easy for them to track us. At least bury the coats.*"

Marco followed suit, and Clarence went to where he thrown

his coat and bunched it up. Duncan watched as both men sunk their bundles in the mud. He took the bible from the edge of his pack and added it to the muddy grave in the bog. The pages had been soaked through the first or second time he tripped and went down. A wet bible was the last thing he needed weighing him down. Its only use dry had been to start a fire.

Clarence continued standing in the same spot, moving from one foot to the other to avoid sinking.

"OK, we go on to Garnet Fell," said Duncan. He got to his feet, feeling his calves complaining.

"But we try it in close single file, and we do it peloton."

"Who's peloton?" said Marco.

"It might help. It was something I learned in my training," Duncan replied.

Then he made up the rest.

"On the bikes we had, you could cut down on peddling by slipstreaming behind each other, taking a turn in front."

"Bikes?" said Clarence.

"Yes, we had to ride bikes to show that we could take bearings and establish our position."

Clarence laughed, *"That sounds good Duncan, but I can hardly stand without sinking here, and I don't see any bikes."*

Duncan held up both hands, although no one could see them in the dark, *"No, no, I'm maybe not explaining it well. We've all been ploughing through the moor by ourselves here, strung out in a line and getting knackered. We'll each take a stint in front, finding a path and the other two can follow. See if that works any better."*

"And this was something you learned becoming an ASDIC?" Marco said, still fascinated by the bikes.

"Well, sort of," Duncan replied, deciding not to tell then that all he knew about pelotons was what he had overheard from one of his navy instructors who was a cyclist. There wasn't much call for riding in peloton as he circled around the wet lorry park doing the Wall's Ice-cream Tricycle Test.

* * * *

The distance they could see ahead across the moor increased a few yards. It was just enough to remind them that the point of maximum darkness, when they had greatest cover, had passed. They talked more as they walked. The point man shouted instructions over his shoulder; where to go, left or right, or what he had just stood in.

"*Boggy dip, step fast.*"

"*Keep left, deep water.*"

"*Up on top of the clumps, follow me across.*"

They took half an hour each on point, or as close to it as they could judge on Clarence's watch.

The novelty of the walking peloton got them through the next two miles of bog. As they climbed higher, there was less water running off the hill and fewer mud patches that were too big to circumnavigate.

With two miles to go, Garnet Fell appeared as a dark line ahead defined by the first grey light of the day. Clarence was leading when they saw it. He was still looking over his shoulder every few hundred yards, even when it was pitch black. If they could see the ridge, anyone looking from Kielder could too. Clarence felt his heart beat faster as stepped up the pace on point, taking longer strides.

It was another mistake. He went thigh deep in mud as he tried to make an impossible jump from one clump of heather to the next. It took five minutes of Marco and Duncan pulling and Clarence swearing to get him out and another five minutes of searching, shoulder deep in the mud for the tennis racquet that had been sucked off this foot.

The serge bell bottoms and knee-high black socks that each man wore might have been specially designed to absorb and wick water. After the first ankle-deep plunges, when they had cleared the fire break in the trees, the cold water from the bog had been seeping upward. Capillary action Clarence said, as they stopped to change positions in the peloton. Both of the others looked at him blankly. The cold damp crept another few inches up the trouser legs each time water splashed over the boot laces or up and over the boot collar. In contrast, the thick serge jumpers, over cotton flannel shirts, topped with a blanket had them dripping sweat. With each mile, the bottom half of each man got colder and the sweat ran down their backs to meet the bog water coming up.

Garnet Fell became a sharper line on the horizon, a series of brown and grey hillocks now as the light increased. Despite pushing themselves harder, the pace was slowing. Clarence was falling behind again, forcing himself to plant one foot in front of the other, frustrated with his lack of strength and panicking more as the contrast between the dark moor and the morning sky became more pronounced.

They stopped again and without saying anything Duncan slipped the tennis racquets from his feet and pressed them down into the mud, hidden like the rubber coats from any improbable trackers. The other two followed suit.

Duncan had weighed the risk of being spotted from the camp with the chances of ending up in a muddy hole like one of the dead sheep and deer they had passed. They had to get to the ridge before it was light and they couldn't do that with the tennis racquets. He didn't know if they could do it without them but he had to gamble.

It was when Marco took over from Duncan as point man that he started the humming. He had the tune in his head for the last half mile, and only realised he was humming out loud when Duncan joined in. It might have been the last one of Ballard's records that day, blasting over the speakers, an earworm that had stuck with him, or a tune from much further back that just surfaced in his head to match the rhythm of his steps. He didn't know what it was called, only that it fitted the plodding through the bog.

It had originally been a heave-ho shanty, composed by seasonal workers, to distract them from the pack animal work of pulling barges on Russian rivers. That was before Glen Miller and his band gave it a jazz-swing makeover and had it playing in dancehalls and on frontline radios, and on ships headed for battle. Marco didn't look back when he heard Duncan pick up the tune, but he did when he heard the bass trombone of Clarence join in, humming quietly at first, but then trying out sounds in his throat to imitate other wind instruments, then the whole brass section. The light increased suddenly, like the flick of a switch, and the whole landscape of browns and the dark green of mosses came into view. Marco was able to make out the reflection of the light on the bigger pools and he could see patches of solid ground that gave them more platforms to move across. Their next mile was their fastest, and driest, covered at route march pace as a three-piece acapella orchestra doing the Song of the Volga Boatmen.

* * * *

They pushed on at a pace impossible to sustain for any more than a few minutes, more desperate with each step to get over the ridge of Garnet Fall, before someone waking in the camp spotted movement on the moor and went for a pair of binoculars. It was light enough for the point man to lead without shouting instructions over his shoulder. Marco had just looked back to make sure the other two were close enough to see where he was stepping when he went down as if he'd been shot.

Duncan and Clarence heard the loud splat as he went spread-eagled and black mud flew up around him. The thick goo glued him to the surface. He pushed up into a kneeling position, and the mud flowed up and over his calves instantly. He was elbow deep as the other two reached him and, taking an arm each, got him back on his feet. Marco scraped the worst of the thick sludge off his front and his face, then looked down at where he had tripped. He reached down and tugged at a round edge sticking out of the mud. As it came free, it looked like a metal wheel but as he scraped lumps of mud from it he felt rather than saw that it was an old Brodie steel helmet, used by the army.

"*Now how the hell did that get up here?*" said Clarence, as Marco rinsed the last of the mud from the helmet in the surface water.

"*Must have been army training,*" said Duncan, "*before Kielder was built or it might even be a left over from the last war.*"

Marco rubbed his arm across the dome of the helmet.

"*I'm going to take it with me,*" he said, turning in over in his hands.

"*Might come in handy.*"

Duncan looked at him, then again at the helmet.

"*Handy for what? Last time I looked, we were well clear of any enemy shelling or shrapnel up here, I think,*" he said, scoffing.

They had ditched the coats and racquets to travel faster and now Marco wanted to load himself up with junk.

They all stared at the helmet, a shared and unwelcome reminder of the men elsewhere who were wearing them and fighting a battle that they were avoiding. Duncan definitely didn't need any more reminders.

"*Toss it Marco. It's just something else to carry and you don't need it.*"

Marco pulled off the remnants of a disintegrated leather strap from the helmet.

"*I'll just keep it for a while I think. It'll squeeze in my pack.*"

Clarence looked back to Duncan, then to Marco, wondering if they were going to fight about a metal helmet.

"*But it will just slow you down...,*" Duncan started, then stopped himself.

"*Let's get going. I'll take the front for a while,*" he said.

He turned and walked off, not waiting for a reply.

They cleared the ridge at Garnet Fell, wet with mud below and sweat above, just as it became light enough to make out true colours on the moor. None of them looked back to see how much of the camp could be seen, because it was better not to know.

They heard a faint hiss, carried on the wind. It was one of the blacked-out goods trains, passing three miles away, winding its way downhill towards the main station at Kielder, and on past Lewiefield Halt.

The plan, such as it was, had come to an end. The primary objective of escape had been achieved. But it was not the exhilaration of escaping to something better that had driven them clear when their legs were heavy after the first few miles, it was the memories and the dread of being spotted and taken back to face more time in the camp. Like animals being chased by fast prey, they had gone full out on energy, knowing they couldn't sustain the pace but ignoring the consequences because of the alternative.

Within minutes of cresting the ridge, exhaustion set in. The last peak of the adrenaline rush of getting there, getting clear before dawn, combined with the sudden weight of water-sodden boots and clothes brought them to a dead stop. They went down like deflated balloons. Marco leading, collapsed on his haunches, head down, and Duncan sprawled across one edge of a boulder. Clarence remained standing, hands on his knees, leaning against the same boulder. They were on a slope of heather in a clearing of scattered rock and some gorse. They were now hidden from the camp, but more visible with each minute of growing daylight to anyone who was looking from the other side of the ridge.

At the bottom of the slope they could see a line of rowan trees, skirting the edge of a thicker wood of older birch and oak. The wood was dark beyond the first few yards, the daylight absorbed by the trees fighting for space.

"*One more push,*" Duncan said, pointing between hoarse gasps. "*We're still out in the open here.*"

The other two nodded. If they could just drag themselves to the cover of the woods, collapse there and rest, hidden from view. They could stop for an hour and plan what to do next.

Another lie agreed.

Each man fixed on a point in the woods and started walking as the crow flies. There was no talking, eyes ahead, each of them tripping and getting up, wetter each time, no longer searching for solid footing.

* * * *

The wood was deeper than it looked from the slope, a heart shaped patch half a mile across. It was one of the few areas of native woodland left on the moorland, a rear-guard action against the bog. The trees had grown on a drier mound of earth, a left-over dumped by retreating glacial melt. The soil was rich enough in nutrients to sustain the older trees, but most seeds falling to the woodland floor died through lack of light. One edge of the heart-shape woods was darker, broad oaks marking the limit of the old trees, abutted by the ubiquitous Sitka spruce, marching past in straight lines into the distance, cutting out the light on that side of the heart.

Each man found a spot with his back to a tree, emptied water from his boots and peeled off mud-saturated socks. They wrung out as much as they could from their bell bottoms, wrapped the damp blankets tighter around shoulders and tried to sleep, each of them slammed by the exhaustion of the walk. Even Clarence, still with a reservoir of unwanted blood sugar, was sapped. It wasn't the distance. He could do that and more most days, insulin or no insulin. It was straining to pull each foot out of the mud, over and over, and constantly looking over his shoulder for who might be coming from the camp.

The three men slept off and on in the unfamiliar silence of the wood, moving position every few minutes to stop shivering. After an hour, the exhaustion trumped even the shivering.

It was as light as the day was going to get on the moor when the sound of Clarence throwing up woke the other two. There was nothing left to come up but green bile. Clarence was on all fours, his face puce and his eyes watering. His pain was front and back. His stomach clenching and his liver bruised like it had been punched, the aftermath of the beating the organ had taken during the insulin and sugar overdoses. His vomiting went on for another fifteen minutes, until there really was nothing left to come up, although his stomach kept trying. He clenched handfuls of wet leaves with each spasm of pain, then used them to wipe his mouth.

They had escaped and got beyond Garnet Fell. That was the end point of the preparations. Only Duncan had really believed they would get this far. The other two, like him wanted out but chose escape, likely capture and punishment over more time in the camp. To plan, to store the supplies, to talk secretly during the pitch-and-toss games, to pick a date and a route had got them through the final days of what they were suffering at the camp.

Even to get beyond the gates and to be dragged back an hour later would have been better than not making a break, better than doing nothing, and being in the camp another week, or another month.

Soaking it up. That's how the men in Number 3 Hut told Marco it should be done. Just seeing out the days, playing whatever game the Admiralty wanted to play, saying the right things to Ballard, or the wrong things, until you were discharged as unsuitable, unlikely to make a reliable sailor, or invalidated out onto a war pension. But Marco couldn't do it that way and neither could Clarence or Duncan.

They had served, trying to be honourable and honest and their answers to Ballard were straight, even when they meant more time at Kielder. Each day passed more slowly, feeling more like a sentence, from reveille to lights out, stretched until hours dragged like clocks had stopped. A return to service, a discharge or an invalidity pension became less likely each day. Transfer in a locked van, to a different type of prison, became more probable.

Now they were clear, beyond the plan, but there was no congratulating each other because walking out had been hard but simple. Getting away, or what happened the next day had never been in the plan. They were exhausted and aching, wet and shivering. What little sleep they'd had didn't change how things looked.

* * * *

The moor was covered in a deep bank of mist again, up to the edge of the heart shaped woods. The fog condensed on the hairs of their damp blankets. Burying the rubber coats in the mud had been the right thing to do at the time, but waterproofs made sense now. Duncan's shoes squelched as he squeezed them back on, stuffing his sodden socks into the makeshift back pack. The bog water had leeched another few inches further up his serge trousers during the early morning, sticking to his legs and adding to the weight to be carried.

With nowhere else to go but forward, the three men walked

deeper into the wood, in single file, Duncan leading. Low branches pulled at his pack, snapping back on Clarence. The trees were dense and in clumps, not planted in neat rows like the spruce. Duncan felt his way with his hands out in front, stopping when there was just enough light from above to pick a change in direction. They might have been the first humans to walk in parts of the isolated woods since the trees that had once covered most of the moor had been systematically cleared for grazing and cultivation, until it was too late for either.

A branch that Duncan had pushed aside sprang back and slapped Clarennce in the face, leaving a red welt across his cheek.

"Bugger! This can't go much further."

Duncan froze as he pushed through the next curtain of thin branches. There was an outline of a roof, less than twenty yards ahead. In an attempt at a tactical hand signal he threw up his arm at a right angle, fist clenched. Clarence walked straight into Duncan's fist, taking knuckles square on the chin.

"Bloody hell man. What are you doing?" said Clarence, reeling back.

Duncan turned and clamped his hand over Clarence's mouth

"Quiet!", he whispered.

Clarence straight armed Duncan in the chest, pushing him off easily, and raised his hand to nurse his chin. As Duncan fell to the ground, Clarence saw ahead to the low slope of the roof. Marco emerged from the thicket and both of the others pointed. Marco stopped dead, seeing the danger.

Anyone living in the house, out there, was bound to know about the Kielder camp, their nearest neighbour. Three men in uniform, wet and bedraggled, coming off the moor would be reported or maybe just shot, as dangerous. They backtracked quietly into the wood, keeping eyes on the side of the building, watching for movement, praying that Clarence's surprised shout had not been heard.

After five minutes silence, Marco said, *"No smoke."*

The other two looked at him. He pointed to the roof of the building.

"Up here? No fire when it's this cold? I don't think anybody's home."

Clarence stayed hidden while Duncan and Marco went left and right. The agreed sign was to be a two-tone whistle if anyone was spotted. At that time of year, there was little bird life for miles. In the silence of the wood, a man whistling would sound like nothing except a man whistling, but it was the only signal they could think of.

The building was smaller than it looked, much smaller. From the woods, where Clarence still stood, it looked like the gable end of a long cottage, but closer up the end of the building they could see was actually the windowless back of the house, its longer side. They could have skirted around it, cleared the woods and kept going, who knows where. But the attraction of dry land and a roof after a night on the sodden moor was strong. Strong enough to block out the risk that they would be walking in on someone, even someone with a gun.

When he got close enough to see the front of the building, it was clear to Duncan that if anyone was inside they would be even more desperate than him. Sheep had broken in the bottom half of a crumbling wooden door and sheep droppings were squashed like beads of putty along the line of the door where it once met the rough plank floor. The door was hanging open, and the single window on the front of the bothy had one pane remaining from four.

The abandoned shepherd's hut was on the lighter edge of the wood, south facing. It was solid, with walls constructed from the stones cleared from ploughed fields elsewhere and stuck together with lime mortar. The corrugated iron roof would be noisy in wind, in rain and even when it was heating up and cooling down on the few days with sun. The rough wood on the floor was dry in places and protected from the worst of the north winds by the woods. In one corner of the floor the edge of a massive boulder, another glacial left-over, jutted into the hut. The side wall of the hut had been built around it. A flat shelf had been hacked out of the smooth stone of the boulder, and it was thick with the melted wax from years of candles.

The squat building had one box bed, with a thin straw mattress, set on a wooden base. The bed looked like it had been nailed together from wooden pallets scavenged from the farm. There was a single wool blanket, which was more holes than blanket, on a high rack behind the door. The shepherd would have used the bothy during lambing, or if he had failed to find lost sheep and had to wait until the next day for light. Any shepherds in the area young enough to fight had joined up or gone to work on lowland farms. All of the sheep, even the rangy hill sheep kept just for wool, had been taken for stringy chops, tripe or boiled down as tough mutton during the first year of the war.

* * * *

They had swapped one hut for another. Resting there was another plan agreed readily. It was another beginning with no end. With the relief of something to focus on again, they set to work.

Duncan had matches, cadged from smokers at Kielder and stored in a tobacco tin before they left. The pervasive damp of the moor had found its way through the smallest holes in the tin. He sifted through the matches, picking out the few that had survived dry. Clarence took two chunks of wax from the boulder and started by kneading them until they were soft. Using strong hands, he shaped two makeshift candles, using as wicks strands of brown twine he found lying about in the hut. They used the candles only to give enough light to see each other until it was late enough to sleep.

Marco was modest enough not to mention that he was right to dig it out of the mud and carry it. Their multi-purpose pan and bowl was his prized Brodie helmet. In it, he was able to carry water from a hill stream now free of sheep shit since the beginning of the war. There was a low table in one corner of the hut, made from a pallet and fencing nails. The shepherd had used brown twine to try to bind the legs more securely to the table top, but it still swayed under any weight.

By far, the hut's best feature was that it could not be seen until you were almost on it. It had been built in a slight hollow for shelter from the wind, shielded by the bank of gorse bushes behind and a copse of thin alder trees on two sides. There were no drove roads within a mile, no path leading past it, and any tracks that the shepherd and sheep had worn across the hillside had been reclaimed by the couch grass, heather and more gorse.

Marco volunteered to take the first full day on lookout, after finding a route back through to the north side of the woods to a spot where anyone coming over the ridge of Garnet Fall could be spotted.

At night, with cloud cover and the added blanket of mist, the darkness was total, like being shut in a basement. It was possible to move only by touch. After the three days of posting lookouts, they started to believe that no search parties had been sent out after them and they relaxed just a little as they spent their days at the hut.

They used their time making it cleaner on the inside and invisible from the outside. The spiders who had made webs across the angles of wall and ceiling retreated to holes in the wood and stone. Duncan used broken wood from the door to scrape a layer of soil and sheep droppings from the floor. Marco took the threadbare blanket they had found and hung it over the inside of the door to cover the gap at the bottom. Clarence stuck a curtain of branches, as thick as was possible to snap off, into the soft ground at the front of the hut. From twenty feet it was obvious the branches were not growing there, but from five hundred feet the hut could only be seen if you were looking for it.

They threw piles of lighter coloured stones and strips of rusty metal at the side of the hut into the woods and looked for anything else that might catch the eye from a distance. The camouflaging activity was good distraction. It prolonged the pretence that they could live there and put off the time until one of them voiced what they were all thinking. What next?

In their back packs they had the five small tins of army-issue meat, three packs of biscuits and two handfuls of potatoes. As they laid up in the hut, first drying out then recovering from the escape, all that they had carried was eaten in two days. The biscuits were dry and hard, and could only be eaten with mouthfuls of water, supped from the helmet. A fire for boiling the potatoes, also in Marco's helmet, was only safe after dark. It was like Ramadan for Christians, waiting until the sun, somewhere above the clouds and the mist, went down. They were so hungry by then that they ate everything, boiling the potatoes then mixing in the fatty meat for some flavour. For those two days the food was delicious. Then it was done.

They had to get by on what they could find for the next few days, as September became October. In the wood there were handfuls of berries that the birds had missed. They could only be reached by lying flat and sliding under thorns to get to them. Some stubborn crab apples, shrivelled and pitted, pecked but edible, clung to branches of isolated trees in the woods. Of the three, only Clarence had kept his regulation silks around his neck, and he knotted his black scarf and used it as a carrier for the apples.

But berries and apples cost them more energy than they gave back. They had to push their way through the woods, forage for hours for the fruit, eat some, carry some and then fart their way back to the bothy, to eat what they had carried. Within an hour they were hungry again.

They scouted further from the hut, trying to catch small fish from slow moving sections of the stream cutting through the valley. Like the fruit, this brought meagre returns for long hours of work. Marco was the most successful and even then, it wasn't much. He would stand like a heron, or squat on a rock midstream, still and silent for long stretches, then strike and scoop in one movement. About one splash in ten, he was able to throw a thrashing fish onto the bank. Not the size for photographs with the proud angler, but usually big enough for a few bites. Clarence and Duncan took turns with the trusty helmet near the bank of the stream, scooping tiddlers out the water, dumping them on the grass and picking out fish big enough to eat, bones and all. It was half a day's work to get enough for a meal, or what passed for one. By dusk the fire was built, ready to be lit, by which time all three of them were hungry enough to be thinking about how the fish they had caught would taste raw.

* * * *

The bothy smelled like wet dog, the damp fug mixing with smoke from the fire and the linger of cooked fish. All of that became background to the nostrils over the first few days, as each man's sour body odour grew stronger, until each of them became inured to that too.

The stripe with the purple insert on Clarence's old navy uniform had verified him capable of raising steam. When the dry matches ran out however, raising fire was beyond even his abilities. It was Marco, ex-gunner and acrobat who had the secret of fire. To him it was what you did when you had no matches; to the other two men what he did was some kind of traveller's witchcraft.

There was a pile of dusty ashes outside from the final fire that had gone out. Marco scooped a handful of these in a piece of bark and dried them in the bothy. From deep in the woods he picked some stalks from dried nettle that had grown under a broad-leafed oak, protected from rain. After flattening them out, he rolled the stalks into a thin cigarette, with the ash as the tobacco. The first time he saw him do it, Duncan and Clarence thought Marco had lost it. Maybe some delayed reaction to what had happened to him on HMS *Devon,* or something else at the camp. Marco was making roll-ups with nettles and ash, to smoke with matches they didn't have. Marco didn't explain, because he took their silence as an assumption that they understood what he was doing.

Next, he took two pieces of pallet from the table they never used. Then it was just the right amount of speed and pressure, rolling the cigarette he'd made steadily between the two pieces of wood until there was smoke. Some gentle blowing on the embers and presto, smoke and flame, every time. To keep the flame alive, Marco had collected lumps of chaga mushroom, cancerous lumps of fungus growing on the birch trees. Crumbled up, it was perfect for a base in the main fire, or for a portable flame that could be carried in the helmet when the weather meant they had to start the fire off inside the hut.

Clarence the engineer was in awe of the primitive technology and Marco's casual mastery of fire making. Even watching it a third and a fourth time, he couldn't understand how Marco could produce live fire from dead ashes and dead plants. Given enough time, Clarence reckoned he could have engineered some means of making sparks from rocks, striking metal and lighting dried grasses. Maybe. But to do it on demand, in rain and wind would have been tough. Duncan was even more impressed. With his own limited survival skills, he knew that he would have had to wait a very long time to get any warmth from a fire, probably until lightning struck a tree.

There was enough dead wood around to keep the fire lit for some heat before they went inside to sleep. Most mornings it was the same view from the front of the bothy. By sunrise, a grey blanket of cold mist encroached to within a few hundred yards, getting lighter for a while as the sun got higher, but never thinning enough to bring any warmth. They were tempted to light the fire. Who was going to see anything, smoke or flames, through the permanent hanging mist? But they resisted, knowing that the fire would stand out like a lighthouse to anyone watching if the mist suddenly burned off. Nine days into their stay, that day came, if only for an hour. The curtain of mist lifted and they felt the sun on their faces.

What surprised Duncan was just how far they were from anywhere. The horizon was farmland. They could tell from the speck of a tractor, just a dot, crawling in a straight line. One half of a massive field was ploughed, the other half still straw coloured. Between the tractor and the bothy, the land was a patchwork. Closer, there was more moorland and in the distance were irregular, four-sided shapes that might have been crops, or areas fenced off as too wet, to keep the beasts out. It was too far away to tell. There were no cows, sheep or humans to be seen, apart from the tractor driver. Small darker blocks, far off, could have been farm houses.

In that single hour of sunshine, Clarence and Marco pointed and speculated about what might be fields of potatoes, what might be barns with crops stored, and the straight lines that could be roads. There were flashes, reflections off glass, that must be farmhouses. On the space in front of the bothy, Duncan tried to take a bearing on the nearest houses, laying arrows of stones on the ground, different lengths to indicate distance. There might be food there, to be begged, stolen or in exchange for labour.

For most of the hour of sunshine, Duncan watching the tractor. What he would give for that simplicity. To have to concentrate only on ploughing straight furrows and having no worries tomorrow except how much more of the field could be ploughed. Plough, plant, harvest, repeat; it had satisfying and obvious purpose. There was no deeper meaning to be fathomed, no unknowable master plan.

Two years ago, driving at six miles an hour across a field in the middle of nowhere, with nothing to do other than drop down a gear if the engine was smoking, would have pushed Duncan to the mental state that got him incarcerated at Kielder. But now, he looked in envy at the bright green speck in the distance, turning to begin another straight line.

* * * *

The first snow came early that year, and the trees behind them offered no barrier to the east wind that brought it, finding the holes in the brickwork of the bothy. They used handfuls of mud, mixed with grass on the inside and beads of sheep droppings on the outside to plug the smaller gaps, but the wind rattled in where the walls met the corrugated roof. The water that had soaked into the wood of the door and floor turned to ice and the single window pane frosted up inside. The cold brought back memories. It was painful, but it was relative. At least there was no morning watch needed to axe ice off the focsle to prevent the bothy capsizing.

At night, the blankets they had carried from the camp were too small and too thin. They had a rota for who slept on the box bed. The two on the floor huddled together, sharing warmth in the one corner of the hut least chilled by the wind. The risk of sweating was low. With feet wrapped in thick black socks and knees pulled up, it was possible to sleep, a couple of hours at a time, until an outstretched arm or leg gave a reminder of the cold. As Duncan faced the nightly dilemma of whether to cover his ears or his feet with his blanket, he remembered the luxury of a ship-issue balaclava.

Each man warmed up in his own way in the cold morning. Marco was movement. He was up first, gathering firewood and fungus for the evening, then up and down the hill, scooping pans of water from the stream for the others to drink and wash. Duncan and Clarence both stamped around, still wrapped in blankets, getting the circulation going, checking the weather.

Duncan had a routine, circling the stacks of dried wood, wondering whether a fire would be seen, but never risking it, getting close to the wood, imagining the heat it would bring. Clarence's first task in the morning was checking the curtain of branches he had stuck in the ground in front of the bothy. He removed branches that had lost their leaves, then warmed up by breaking off green branches from the woods as replacements. Keeping his curtain of camouflage as thick as he liked it was getting more difficult with each day of falling leaves.

After washing, the three men went longer each time around the edge of the woods, looking for anything still edible on trees and bushes. Marco warmed up fastest in the frost of the morning, covering the distance a dog the other two men had taken for a walk.

After two weeks, the apples and berries were all gone and they were reduced to collecting brown coloured mushrooms and then being too scared to eat most of them in case they were poisonous. The water in the hill stream was running lower and there were no more fish. They were forced to scavenge further afield for food.

Their fear of being spotted and captured was constant, but the gnawing hunger pains were stronger, pushing them out in ever widening circles from the safety of the shepherd's hut, trying to remember the most promising spots from what they had seen in that brief hour of sunshine, using Duncan's arrows on the ground as a guide.

The safest time to go was in full moonlight when there were no clouds, which was rare, when they could see and the risk of detection was low. Even then, they were searching in a world of black and white, unable to pick out flashes of red or green or any other colours that might mean food.

They compromised. Before it was full light in the morning, Duncan and Marco started going on recces, searching. Possibilities were identified from a distance. They identified farmers' fields, barns, even farmhouses as they got more desperate and walked further out. They mapped the area, using drystane dykes as reference lines and as cover as they moved, always vigilant for any line-of-sight points on the higher hills.

Following the morning recce, Marco returned with Clarence at night to the most promising food spots that he and Duncan had identified in the morning. They carried a hessian sack they had found, blown across a field and snagged on barbed wire.

Their first bag was loose potatoes, shaken from trailers onto the tracks, or missed when the main crop had been dug up. It was only when there was more light that they could see which of the spuds had been burrowed into by insects, gone soft or were green. One mouthful was enough to convince Clarence and the other two that green potatoes were poisonous, cooked or not. Their best haul in those last few days at the bothy was from a field of turnips, two miles away.

They were careful to smooth over the foot holes left in the field, worried that the farmer would spot them and report the theft. They decided that one raid on the turnips was enough, but then returned for a second night, having found nothing better.

The mist on that night was thick and almost luminous, with no wind to move it on. It allowed Marco and Clarence to walk upright on farm tracks and along the length of the drystane dyking, with no fear of being seen, instead of crouching like miners down a pit. To Clarence it seemed that they were walking past the same gateposts again and again, but Marco's mental map of the drystane dykes was dead on and took them straight to the turnip field.

Clarence was shaking the wet earth off a turnip he had just

pulled when he first heard the slurp of footsteps. Feet were pulled out of mud and squelched down again. It was a familiar sound to him after their walk across the moor. First in the distance, but then louder, coming towards them. He turned full circle in the mist, trying to get a fix on Marco and on the sound. Moving closer, he grabbed Marco by the shoulder, but Marco had already heard it and was pointing along the edge of the field. They stood stock still. Marco lifted a finger to his lips. Clarence nodded and released the grip on his shoulder. The footsteps stopped.

Attack or retreat? That was the battle decision to be made, silently. Standing and waiting for the enemy to advance was not an option. From the sounds, they were two against one, so chances of victory were good, especially with the advantage of Clarence's bulk and power. If they retreated, the sound of their own steps on the wet ground could be followed back to the bothy, even in the mist, and then it might be over for all three of them. If they only injured the stranger who had found them stealing the turnips, he would report it and they would be hunted down. If they killed him, they would be hunted and it would be murder charges they faced, not just desertion when they were caught. Marco rejected both ideas in the few seconds that he and Clarence stood frozen in place in the mud. It left just one way out.

They would jump him, take him back to the bothy and tie him up with the twine before they made a run for it. Get him on the ground first, then force him to walk back. Clarence could carry him, if it came to that. Then they would need to get away fast, leaving him tied up, but they could leave a message somewhere so that he would be found.

There was the sound of a single, wet footstep coming closer.

Marco turned face on to Clarence to make sure that he could be seen. He mimed his plan of attack as best he could. Clarence nodded at the point in the silent show where Marco swung his fist and feigned being knocked out, so he was confident that Clarence understood at least that part of the plan.

Moving back, he pointed at Clarence and waved his hand right, in circle motion. He then pointed at his own chest and started to move, silently, left. He ground one heel into the soft soil, as far as it would go, only then putting his weight on that foot, lifting his other foot at the same time, before repeating the process. He checked where he was stepping, peering down at the ground in front of him for anything that might give away his position. The only sound he made was that of small crumbs of earth falling a few inches to the ground from his boots.

Clarence tried. In the ploughed field, he tip-toed from one ridge of soil to the next, feeling for firm ground in the dark. His size was a problem for stealth. Marco could hear the crunch of each step that Clarence took until they were far enough apart to be invisible to each other in the fog.

As they circled, Marco and Clarence heard the sound of another two cautious steps from the figure ahead, then a snapping sound, muffled by the mist. Both men froze again. To Clarence, it was the sound of a gun being cocked. The same sound came again, this time followed by a wet rubbing. Clarence listened, hearing the man shifting his arm from the side of a wet rubber coat to point his gun out in front. The figure took two more steps forward, no longer quiet now, emboldened by the gun. Marco moved his position, judging the man to be directly between him and where Clarence would be.

It became darker as thick cloud moved across the sky. Marco and Clarence had moved ten yards, left and right. Marco judged that the stranger would now be standing on the spot where he and Clarence had split up, close enough to see the half-filled sack of turnips they had left.

The odds were not going to get any better. If they rushed him now, he couldn't get two shots off and they might both get to him before he could swivel, left or right with the gun. Ten yards, fifteen maximum, Marco estimated, and they could be on him. Shouting through the darkness and the mist to Clarence would reduce their chance of success. The gunman might start shooting and hit at least one of them coming in. Marco made the decision to rush the gunman alone and shout just before he hit him, alerting Clarence and give him the chance to follow up when all of the gunman's attention was on Marco. Even if the man fired, chances were that the shot would go wide.

He braced his feet in the mud and pushed off like a sprinter, covering the distance in under five seconds. Just as he made out the dark shape in front of him, he yelled, *"Now, Clarence now! Take him!"*

It was like running into a wall. Marco threw himself forward in the dark and just bounced off. There was no head and neck to grab, no hand or gun to grapple with, just a wet solid mass. By the time Clarence came barging in five seconds later, the cow, a black Angus, had kicked its back legs out and charged off across the field, terrified, sounding more like an elephant than a cow.

Like Marco and Clarence, the cow had been stealing from the field of turnips under the cover of darkness, and like them it was a fugitive from justice, an escapee from a slaughterhouse bolt to the head. Whether the Angus knew that beef was rationed, or that capture meant death, was doubtful but as the last of its herd it knew by instinct or from experience that survival meant finding food and avoiding humans in daylight hours.

They backtracked, found their sack and finished filling it. On the way back to the bothy, Clarence fantasised about the cow and how good it would be to cook the turnips with an enormous steak of beef, oozing juices, covered in gravy.

"But you and me chasing that cow and trying to kill it would be like cavemen going after a mammoth without spears," Clarence laughed.

Marco didn't know what a mammoth was and was too embarrassed to ask, but he laughed along with Clarence and nodded agreement in the darkness.

* * * *

At night in the bothy, after they had eaten whatever had been found that day, the choices were watching the spiders or talking. There was plenty of shared chat to begin with, about walking out the gates of the camp, getting across the moor, falling and racing to avoid being seen and the relief of finding the hut. When talk of their escape dried up, they went further back, sharing what they wanted to remember about the other men in the camp, and what Clarence could remember. Then going as far back as the convoys. Talking about the cold, the Arctic winds and frozen nostril hairs made the hut seem just a few degrees warmer.

Like their memories of the convoys, what each man remembered about the treatment at HMS *Standard* was incomplete. Clarence remembered the pain of the first insulin injections, the taste of the sugar, then little else. He had flashes of sweat being sponged off him, being trolleyed from one room to another, faces above him, then lying on his back paralysed and terrified, not knowing where he was or why he couldn't move. His only other clear memories were going back to engine maintenance in the afternoons, shaking, and the beginnings of the penny toss in his hut.

Even after the time spent resting at the bothy, Duncan still had the exhaustion of the daily work parties in his muscles. As the least fit of the three when he arrived at Kielder, he took the long days logging and ditch digging hardest. He saw more clearly now the Admiralty treatment regime, such as it was. Wear the body down, drive a man until he was barely awake, then target his mind. It was clearing the decks, making space, to then fill the space created with the special kind of thinking needed for war. These were thoughts to be carefully planted, nurtured and grown over the weeks and months. Conflating good and bad with God and the devil, linking it with bravery and cowardice, to make a man realise how lacking he was, and how many people he had disappointed. Then, when a man was at his lowest, flattened with the daily despair of his guilt, dangling a path of redemption, all sins forgiven. A chance to be re-drafted into the navy, for God, King and Country, with the chance to do it right this time.

Duncan understood more clearly now why and how it was done, and with that understanding he resented it even more. Each man at Kielder had been judged guilty without trial, sentenced for the crimes of weakness, of seeing or feeling too much. The sentence was time to be served being belittled and humiliated. It was Duncan's resentment that had kept him walking across the moor when his body wanted to fall forward into the knee-high heather and sleep, when each step was only been possible when he looked down and willed his feet to move.

The three talked in the dark, first about what they had done and what had been done to them, or what they could remember of it. Then later, as they opened up, what it felt like. Each of them passed a point when it didn't matter how much he shared. Whatever came next couldn't be any worse and talking about what had come before wouldn't make any difference. After all, it was just talking. What was going to happen would, regardless.

Duncan broke the dam, by telling them how he'd gone AWOL after his brother Andrew's death. Marco and Clarence waited their turn and then each dug out what they could remember of what had brought them to Kielder. From that point, no-one was embarrassed about the unmanliness of his honesty.

The stories of how they came to be hiding in a hut filled the days of waiting, not knowing what was next. When one man spoke, the others listened, nodding unseen in the candlelit gloom of the hut. There were silences as they waited to see if the speaker would say more, then someone else would jump in.

Clarence left out some of the details about James Madden's blistered death in the boiler, but gave them enough, his voice choking in his throat as he told what he could remember, and what he had put together later.

Marco told his story. Like Thompson and Reeves in the sick berth on HMS *Devon* and Ballard at Kielder before them, Clarence and Duncan were confused, thinking at first that Marco had contracted a disease called the misery from an elephant. He spoke quickly, leaving nothing out, telling them how he thought he would die and then thinking out loud about whether it was possible to recover from the misery, when no one ever had. The other two listened. They heard all that he said and understood most of it by the end.

"*All those jossers and flatties–no offence, lads–don't get it. I'm in the pit, with the misery, bad, and all that doctor tells me is that I've swallowed some parni that's dirty. I knew he was wrong that first day and I told him, but he's the gaffer on the ship, see, so what he says is right, and what I know don't matter. He's the big cheese on board, with all them medicine books in his office and his fancy glasses. He knows stuff that I don't. But I don't care what he knows, until I know that he cares. And he don't. Of course, he says he does. When I finally get past Petty Officer high and mighty Thompson and Reeves turns down his music so we can speak, I know that he's looking through me 'cause I'm travelling stock in his eyes, one of those who didn't have the smarts to avoid the draft."*

Marco remembered all of it and told his story like he was reading from some diary in his head. It was raw, but rich in detail. Clarence and Duncan held their stomachs as he told them about the pains in his guts, and laughed out loud at his climb up the yardarm, as they pictured the jaws dropping on deck when he dived.

What they shared in those weeks at the shepherd's hut got the three men through what was to come.

* * * *

Kielder moor and plantation was 250 square miles of perpetual bog and long rectangles of Sitka and Norway spruce planted to drink from that bog until they were tall enough to be harvested and replaced. There had been no maps on display at HMS *Standard*. It was one more way in which the Admiralty reinforced the point that men were at Kielder getting ready to serve at sea again. Anything else, including local geography, was distraction and irrelevant. Clarence, Duncan and Marco had no way of knowing how far it was to the nearest road or town, other than what they had seen on the bus on their way to Kielder, or in the one-hour window of sunshine at the bothy. Marco and Clarence deferred to Duncan for his navigation skills.

He took on the responsibility willingly at first, happy to use what he had pieced together to get them out of the camp. In the final days at the bothy Duncan was patient with Marco's questions about their location. Rather than admit he was as clueless as the others, Duncan tried to explain his best guess about what might lie east or south or north.

But rather than satisfy Marco's curiosity, Duncan's answers

just led to further, more detailed questions. He was like a two-year old who had just learned the word "why?", barely waiting for an answer before peppering Duncan with another question. After a long day, when they had failed to find enough food, there was one question too many and Duncan's patience snapped.

"Last time I checked, I was employed by the navy as an ASDIC operator Marco, not a fucking homing pigeon, so I just don't know!"

He regretted it as soon as it was out.

They were sitting outside the bothy as it got dark, eating small green turnips that had been boiled in the Brodie helmet, flavoured with some tough sprigs of rosemary to disguise the bitter taste. They had learned on their very first night-time raid that eating mature turnips straight from the field was for cows, but not for sailors, no matter how hungry you were. Only Marco had vomited that night. Clarence and Duncan lay clutching their stomachs for hours, wishing they could.

It was October and a wind from the south had brought some rare respite from the biting cold. Marco and Duncan sat with their backs against the hut, while Clarence tended the fire, keeping the smoke to a minimum, still wary each day of being spotted.

He pushed the burning sticks around, keeping the centre burning as hot as possible, not looking up. Duncan's outburst didn't faze Marco. He paused and then was back in his stride, directing his question to Clarence.

"D'you think the Navy have a special, brutto camp for deserters who've run away twice?" he said, between mouthfuls.

"Or a special navy punishment, reserved just for the likes of us?"

He kept going, not waiting for answers.

"In the old days it would have been keelhauling, or carrying a capstan on your shoulders on deck for a whole watch, walking fore and aft so that everyone could see you. But at least it was over fast then."

"I doubt it," Clarence replied, staring at the flames.

"What, no special escape-proof camp, or no special sentence?" said Marco, turning to look at him.

"No. *Just more of the same, if we're caught,*" Clarence said without expression.

Duncan finished his turnip and rubbed his hands together.

"*Thirty-nine lashes,*" he said, stretching his legs in front of him, "*that was the most the Navy could give you. It comes from the Bible. New Testament, I think. Strange what you find in there, what you remember.*"

The other two looked at him.

"*The cat had three tails, see, and thirteen lashes was the most a man could stand, so Jewish law said that forty stripes minus one was the most it could be. That's where the Navy got 39.*"

Clarence used a green branch to push in the wood on the edges of the fire, drying it out before it was forced into the flames.

"*Sounds cruel,*" he said.

"*Stoning and burning people, they were big on that in the Bible too,*" Duncan continued, "*in between all the bits about the love of a kind and merciful God.*"

He laughed quietly to himself.

Marco looked over at Duncan. "*Well I think we're safe here from being striped with the lash. They won't send us back to the camp either, I reckon. The worst we'll do is hard labour, or time in a cell.*"

"*I'm not going back,*" said Clarence.

It had been his mantra since they walked out the gates of the camp. He had said it before then, Duncan remembered, when they were planning, talking about not going back even before they had left. In the bothy at night, Clarence spoke not about being spotted or being found, but about being caught. He nagged the other two daily about the need for vigilance in everything they did. When they went out on forays for food, he still told the other two to creep behind the cover of drystane dykes, even when they could see nothing but mist or moor for miles. He would stop dead, standing for minutes, listening for sounds in the darkness.

"*I don't think they're looking for us any...*" Duncan started.

Clarence spoke over him. "*They might not still be looking for us, but that doesn't mean that they won't find us,*" he said.

"We're less than a day's walk away from the camp."

Duncan and Marco did think about being found and taken back, every day, but with Clarence it was every hour. He was as careful as a fox in everything he did, but it was a fox being hunted by some cruel predator that would kill its prey slowly. The only time he was not on his guard was when he had to sleep. Where he sat when they were inside and where he stood outside was always with the best line of sight for incoming. Marco and Duncan acceded to his orders, like he was the superior officer, when they left the bothy for any reason, foraging. Despite being the one who made the most noise crunching along the paths, he drilled them on not stepping on branches that would crack and give away their position, and avoiding the long spruce cones that would crunch underfoot.

Duncan and Marco would have done their time if caught, despondent but resigned, but Clarence wouldn't. The little he remembered about the insulin therapy made it worse. The flashbacks, when they did come, still flooded in as one endless day of tormented panic. He was waking terrified, crashing in and out of seizures, with the constant smell of the rubber tube and sickening taste of the sugar. The therapy had done nothing for how Madden's death made him feel. It had just added another room of memories on which he fought to hold the door shut.

The other two didn't speak about it. They hoped Clarence's memories might fade, the longer that they were clear of the camp. But they didn't. What he would resort to, to avoid capture, was unspoken. Clarence would choose a high window, or a belt tied to bed, or even a broken cup and an artery rather than confinement. He would find any way out to avoid forced time and somebody else digging in his head again for his memories. Marco had joked about how any punishment coming their way wouldn't be so bad because it couldn't be worse than Kielder. Clarence would just smile and say nothing or, *"I'm not going back."*

Clarence's daytime blackouts had passed, but he still had dreams in which he was being dragged down into seizures. When it happened at the camp during the therapy, there had been five seconds of desperate panic when he realised it was happening. In his dreams, the five seconds was stretched out for the length of the dream. Clarence would struggle, like a blind wrestler trying to break free from unseen hands pulling him down into darkness, but he never escaped.

* * * *

It was the two days of constant rain that did it, finally. On the first day, Marco went out alone looking for food and came back with nothing, soaked through and shivering. Clarence went the second day, with the same result. On the third day, they built a fire inside the bothy, breaking two of their rules, but desperate for warmth and some way of drying out. It took Marco almost 30 minutes to get it going. The constant damp in the bothy, fed by the rain permeating the walls, left him just a few dry nettle stalks to work with. Hunched under his wet blanket, he mumbled to himself, or perhaps to the two slabs of wood as he rubbed them together, getting more agitated each time the ash and stalks disintegrated into wet clumps without smoking.

Duncan had never seen him this way. Marco pointed and talked as if to threaten or curse his fire making equipment.

"*Te kurel, te kurel,*" over and over; muttering it first, then getting louder with each failed attempt.

He was down to his last handful of nettle stalks. Moving slowly, he took a scoop of ashes from deep in the small pile where it was driest, and wrapped them in all of the stalks he had left. He rolled the flat pieces of wood together, keeping the pressure constant and increasing the speed, pausing to sniff for any sign of smoke. Finally, there was a whiff. He had some dried grass ready, with some crumbs of chaga and two dry pine cones. He blew gently across his hands. There was a red glow, then a gentle "pop" as the flame he had been willing appeared.

As he walked the flame across to where a pyramid of twigs waited, Duncan heard Marco continue to mutter under his breath. The small pieces of wood started to burn and Marco stood back and pointed at them, keeping his hand tight against his hip. Duncan was never sure exactly what he said, and he never did ask him, but what he thought he heard was, "*Never niffle a nettle-monger, you bastard,*" in a victorious tone that invited no reply from the growing fire.

The days of rain were the end of pretending and putting off what had to be done. It was a final reality check on the fantasy that they could live there, undetected. With no food, they would die, and with no fire that might be by freezing as the winter took hold.

When it was time to go, they had little to carry. Just as they had escaped from the camp with no plan beyond that, they tidied up and left the shepherd's hut with a bearing, using Duncan's arrows of stones still on the ground, rather than a destination in mind.

They agreed that heading to the sea was right. Ports were familiar territory, busy with possibilities. Even if one of those possibilities was being caught there by military police as deserters, or as cowards and deserters, or even as escaped lunatics. The alternative was trekking back to Garnet Fell and across the bog-factor ten moor, into the unknown. So, going to the coast was agreed without much discussion.

In their short time at the bothy, one thing they had learned was the difference between the resident mist that sat on the moor, like an extension of the boglands, and the fresher-smelling haars that swept across the moor as warmer air passed over the cold North Sea and became a mist, blown inland. Both types of mist covered the ground in a wet blanket and could reduce visibility to 30 feet or less. The ability to differentiate between mist and haar didn't make them outdoor experts with fifty different words for snow, but it did tell them that the coast was east, and walkable, probably. Duncan took a final compass point as they left, sighting on the sun as a dimmed light bulb above the clouds. The distant click of trains, two per day, travelling south east to Hexham or north west to Scotland was another moving trig point.

They had less to carry when they left. There were no tins of meat, potatoes, rubber coats or bibles, and each man was a belt size smaller. The remaining pile of small turnips was thrown into the woods. It would take more energy to carry them than the turnips gave back. Duncan had his blanket tied in a roll with twine, while the other two wore theirs as cloaks. Marco's final act was to bury his Brodie helmet in soft ground behind the bothie.

Clarence delayed their departure, taking extra time to kick about all the dead ash from fires they had made, until he was happy they had left no trace for the search party he still watched for every day.

* * * *

Keep going due east until they hit the coast. That was the plan. They would follow the line they had set, going straight, ignoring the walking logic of going around hills, going over them instead, through tree plantations rather than skirting the edges. For the first leg of the journey however, there was no straight line without being caught. They had to follow a long horseshoe loop around the original route that had taken them to the shepherd's hut.

After an hour's walking, they caught a glimpse of the roofs of the Kielder Camp huts through a break in the trees on their right. This made them even more determined to ignore the temptation of easier tracks they could see drifting south east. The bearing that Duncan had taken on the last clear day before they left was a hill, shaped like a giant face, heavily planted on one side and rocky on the other. This was their heading. The hill came and went on the horizon as they dipped in and out of hollows, and as showers blew through, testing their ability to keep walking on a straight line without a fixed point to guide them.

The hill with the face was their pole star, just as Garnet Fell had been before. Eyes on the prize. No thoughts about what to do when they got there, or what lay beyond the hill, because those thoughts only distracted from their mission to get there. It was enough to go over, through and around what was in their way, in the knowledge that each step took them closer to the hill.

Sticking to the plan, they criss-crossed streams that snaked through the landscape. They got wet when they could have followed the bank, crossed further downstream and staying dry. They only detoured for the widest stretches of mud, keeping the hill in sight and lining it up again as soon as they could. The biggest pools of surface water were not necessarily the deepest, as Duncan found out when he stepped in a puddle no bigger than a chess board and sunk to his waist in black mud. Marco and Clarence took an arm each and pulled him clear. There was no time to stop. The next shower blew through, rinsing off the worst of the clag, and Duncan looked cleaner but still dripping wet.

As they moved further east, the landscape changed. Their feet found more traction on slippery slabs of stone, just below the wet surface. But the walking was harder on the knees for muscles expecting cushioned ground on each step.

After three hours, a bank of thicker cloud rolled in from the east and the hill disappeared behind another curtain of rain. The light faded and they were soon walking on memory. Trying to fix on due east and where the hill with the face had been, Clarence and Marco took their lead, as always in matters of direction, from Duncan. The walking went from heads up, eyes on the hill, to heads down, following the heels of the man in front. After another mile, Duncan stopped when they passed trees, checking for moss growing on the north side of trunks, and adjusted the line they had been following, still the unspoken Johnny-on-the-spot for keeping them on a bearing. He checked the direction of the wind before darkness fell and tried keeping it in the same place as they walked. It was a gamble, but the only guide he had by then. As it grew dark, memories came back of that first night tramping out of the camp.

Without the urgency of escape that had driven them or the imagined pursuers close behind, they trudged on, slowing by the mile, through a mix of heath, bog and ankle knocking rocks. The patches of muddy ground were fewer, but soaked away their energy faster, a reminder of how weak they were after their days of desperate foraging for food around the shepherd's hut. Without a fixed point, they veered from east to south east in the darkness, a degree at a time, pushed by the contours of the land, their commitment to going over every hill rather than around it wavering with the fatigue.

When the moon rose after midnight, three-quarters full, Duncan came good again. He knew the illuminated side of the moon was east and at last he had a bearing to straighten up their route. But by that time, they were miles further south than they had intended.

By two in the morning all chat had died and they were walking on empty. Duncan was still at the front. The black water from his immersion in the mud hole earlier had wicked its way as high as his chest and on every step his clothes stuck to his skin, stretched and then released, sapping his energy further. Some alarm bell in his head impelled him to walk faster, to try to generate heat from within and dry himself out. On the convoys, he had seen some men pulled out alive after hours in the sea, shivering like him. They smiled, relieved that the worst was over, then went still and quietly died. He pushed the pace as fast as he could, despite the sucking of his wet clothes.

In the end, it was their inability to maintain a bearing straight east that was their salvation. It was the diversion from their original route to a line going south east that saved Duncan from exposure or from walking relentlessly until all three men were so weak that they collapsed, died or were captured.

They followed the Tyne Valley, pushed by the contours of the hills like the water flowing through it, towards the spot where the North and South Tyne rivers met. By that time, each of them was drained, leg muscles searching the body desperately for anything that could be burned for energy. Of the three, Marco was closest to collapse. In his usual walking style across the moor, he moved like a locust, in jumps. Each step seemed to come after a spring was pushed down and then released, sending him further than seemed possible from a standing start. Now he dragged behind Clarence, the bounce gone, caring less about getting wetter and more weighed down by his pack and by more mud with each mile.

As they got closer to the confluence of the two rivers the land funnelled them deeper into the valley, where the banks were steeper, covered in long grass, blown flat. The north facing ground was permanently wet from the river spray, year-long. Their muscles ached with the effort of slipping down the bank toward the fast-flowing water with every step, and having to clamber up to get back on a line to transverse the slope. Their black navy boots were made for tramping across roads, gravel and parade grounds and gave no grip on the slick, matted grass.

At the wide entry to the valley there had been old sheep tracks and narrower rabbit trails, picked out as lines in the moonlight, to guide them across the slopes. Now these were gone. As they worked their way around another bend in the river valley, the bank became so steep that they had to go from walking to scrambling. They could only move crab-like, facing the slope, to avoid sliding into the water below.

Duncan grabbed a handful of grass before taking another sideways step, kicking his toe into the wet ground beneath. He edged his way across the slope for another twenty yards and slowed to a stop. He pulled himself flat against the slope, his face pressed into the wet grass. They were nowhere. Clarence and Marco had trusted him, as their compass, to get them out. To where didn't matter; just far enough away from the camp that no-one was coming to bring them back. He had got them clear, but had led them into a dead end. They were soaked and struggling to move forward, the slope too steep.

Duncan had stopped shivering. It was taking him longer with each step to close his cold hands on the grass and drag a foot across the slope. The wind whipping down the valley was stronger now, taking any body heat from his head and reminding him with every blast of his wet clothes, slapping at his skin.

In the gloom, he could just see the shape of Clarence behind him. He could hear the heavy breathing. Like Duncan, he was holding on, flattened against the grass. As Duncan watched, Clarence began pointing with his free hand, up and down the slope. Maybe talking to himself about the best way to go, maybe just on the edge of losing it, Duncan thought. Behind Clarence, Marco was a silent curiosity. In the months that he had known him, Duncan had never seen him go so long without talking.

They had not eaten in twenty hours. Apart from muttered

cursing following trips and slides down the bank, none of them had spoken since they started along the river bank an hour ago. In the pre-dawn darkness, there was no way to see beyond the next rise in the undulating grass ridges as the river cut its way down the steep valley. In the last hour, they had covered less than half a mile.

If the slope got any steeper, they could go no further. Only Duncan knew how close they were to stopping even if it didn't get any worse. They had no energy for the steps to go back the way they had come or to climb higher up the slope on the rock scree above them, to more unknown moorland. Duncan wiped the water from his face and looked back. Clarence and Marco had trusted in him and he had let them down. He had to keep going until he couldn't.

Their progress across the slope slowed to the point that only one man was moving at a time in a stuttering relay. Duncan would edge a few feet along, moving one limb at a time, then rest, pressing himself flat on the grass against the slope. Clarence would follow, until he was close enough to Duncan, then Marco would move.

Duncan stopped moving again. He was fighting the urge to let go. How long would it take? To release his hold on the grass and slide down into the water feet first on his belly, and let the river do the rest. The water below sounded like it was fast and deep enough to do the job, although it was difficult to tell what was the rumble of white water pounding over rocks and what was wind, now constant.

There would be the sudden blast of cold to take the breath away, then he'd be under. Telling his muscles not to resist and forcing himself to breathe in enough water in the first few seconds, to make himself a sinking ship, would be difficult, but how much harder than this or what was to follow? The other two would believe that he had slipped. There would be no shame.

After another minute, he thought he was passing out. The combination of hunger, the cold and the strain would make the decision for him. He would black out and slide down into the water without pain. There were spots in front of his eyes, which became curly worms, lit up, glowing, turning. He closed his eyes, shook his head and they disappeared, then came back when he looked at his hands, tightening on the wet grass on the slope. It was a final effort by his body to resist the inevitable. The spots came again and he stopped. It was a pause for some last thoughts.

If he was going to go out this way, he wanted his final memories to be good ones, not the disappointment of failing in the war, then being arrested and bringing shame on his mother, then botching the escape from Kielder, letting down even more people. He went back to good times with his brother Andrew, listening to his dad's rambling stories, his dog Benny running about the room, times in the house with his mum after his dad was gone. One memory evoked another and in just two minutes he was back home, in front of the fire. It was blazing, the coals glowing in a slowly collapsing pyramid, the ash falling through the fireplace grate. He could feel the heat coming off the fire and a warmth inside. The sound of the water and the wind faded. Just as he was settling down to nap in front of the fire, Clarence grabbed Duncan's right shoulder so hard that he pulled out the tuft of grass he was holding and had to adjust his left-hand grip to stop himself from falling.

"*Lights,*" Clarence croaked.

Duncan came back to the cold reality of the hill, kicking in another foothold to steady himself. He turned to look at Clarence. His first thought was that the curly light worms were getting to him too. Clarence was pointing along the slope. When Duncan looked he saw at first only the worms. He shut his eyes tightly and opened them again to focus and he could make out a nest of lights, real lights, in the distance. It was Hexham.

They had veered off course by miles. It was a long diagonal of the straight line they had planned and the hill with the face that had been their marker was now far to the north. Travelling due east, they would have been in another twenty miles of rough moorland in the darkness, missing any villages or towns. On that route, all three of them would have died from exhaustion or exposure. Sticking together or striking out alone would have made no difference. They would all have died.

* * * *

The lights and the promise of sleep, maybe even somewhere with a roof, was enough to snap them out of the exhausted stupor brought on by the cold. They dug deep, knowing they were still far from any buildings, but closer with each painful step. Duncan started shivering again.

In the dawn light, they were able to work their way down off the slope to the valley floor, edging along the narrow bank of the river, and wading in shallows where the bank disappeared. Seeing the rise and fall of the water in the centre of the river, Duncan saw that he was right. If he'd let himself slip, the river would have taken him in minutes. They dragged themselves on, looking more with each step like a zombie invasion on Hexham, the lights pulling them forward.

After falling for the third time, collapsing mid-stride rather than tripping, Duncan had no choice but to put up with the indignity of being propped up by Clarence, an arm around his shoulder, hip-to-hip as they put on a final burst of near normal speed over the last mile.

Feet dragging and heads down, they made it to the outskirts of the town and a hay barn, isolated from its farmhouse further down the valley. It was open on one side, built in rough timbers, rotted through in places. On the side of the barn, a trough was filled to the brim with rainwater from a drainpipe. The farmer had finished storing his hay for the winter that had begun, slanting thousand-pound ricks stacked around the barn, four high and three-deep. The remnants of bales, or maybe even last year's hay, was ankle deep on the floor.

As they entered the dark barn, every aching muscle was begging Duncan to collapse into the first soft spot, to lay down anywhere, spread-eagled in the hay. He resisted, an alarm bell ringing in his head about men pulled from the sea and how much faster they died if left in wet clothes. Grunting with effort, he stripped off everything that was dripping wet and climbed on a bale to drape his clothes over beams in the barn. Clarence stood watching, then followed his lead, but Marco had to be lifted from the floor where he had collapsed and peeled out of his wet clothes, limp and semi-conscious. Their final act, directed by Duncan again, was to push loose bales together into a shelter. If they were children, it would have looked like they were making a fort. There were some torn sacks hooked on one wall of the barn. They used this to brush the loose hay into the hollow they had made, extra insulation against the wind that blew through the open side of the barn. Within ten minutes they had each made a nest and were more unconscious than asleep.

* * * *

They awoke around noon the next day and laid up, seeking out the warmest spots in the barn, out of the wind, limbs aching, waiting for everything hanging on the beams to dry out. They took turns sitting out in the cold water of the trough, making a joke in the hay barn about drawing straws for who went first. After washing the mud and grime from their bodies, they were able to rub themselves almost dry with handfuls of hay, then retreat back quickly to the warmth of the barn.

Hexham looked closer than it had in the dark, but still too far to make out how long it would take to get there, or what they would be walking into.

"*We can't go into town like this.*"

Duncan stood up, looking up at his thick bell bottoms and serge jumpers on the beam, still stiff with dirt in the fibres.

He couldn't see the other two because they were each huddled in separate nooks of the barn, but he knew they were listening.

"*And I don't mean buck naked,*" he continued.

"*One of us in a dirty navy uniform might be somebody injured, or just some oddball discharged early. But three of us, walking about in uniforms looking like this? We'll be clocked as deserters in minutes.*"

Clarence had taken down his clothes and had them on the hay beside him. He was holding his trousers, rubbing at a patch of dried mud, but not making much of a difference. Although he had spent most of his time on board HMS *Perseus* wearing little more than a set of sweaty overalls, it did bother him how he looked now. He thought back to the first time he had put on his dress uniform, with his straight stripe and purple insert, and didn't want to take it off. The uniform let everyone know who he was, without asking. He was Clarence the engineer.

One of the first lessons he learned on joining up was the navy difference between may and shall. Ranks *may* wear work wear for operational, training and manual work when appropriate but, ranks in uniform *shall* be well groomed with smart and properly pressed uniform.

"*May is permissive; shall is imperative.*" That's what the navy instructor said, over and over. Clarence didn't know what the words meant, but if it said 'shall', you did it. That was easier to remember. And that was the bit that bothered him now as he rubbed harder at the grey patch on his bell bottoms.

Ratings in uniform *shall* be well groomed and smart and reflect credit on the navy and on the individual. He remembered that bit, word for word. As he looked down at his filthy trousers and his jumper, now limp and shapeless after so many soakings, he wondered if he could be a credit to anyone, ever again, even to himself. Using one cuff of his jumper, now stretched wider than the rest of the sleeve, he tried to rub some shine into one of his shoes.

Duncan had stopped talking and moved to another spot in the barn, where he could see Clarence and Marco. They were waiting for him to take the lead, again, and he was trying. He was having trouble thinking straight, deciding what came first. They couldn't last much longer without food. Looking around the barn, a line from a poem he been forced to learn at school jumped into his head. "*Water, water, everywhere, Nor any drop to drink.*" Something about a sailor being thirsty at sea, he remembered. The barn was full of food, but it was animal fodder. Duncan had already seen Marco take a handful of the cut grasses and chew on it in desperation.

Looking now at the other two, he decided on the new priorities. Getting a change of clothes for everyone, finding food and getting Clarence a shave.

Duncan and Marco looked rough, but without a razor, Clarence's face had become two eyes peeking through a black carpet. Hair covered his cheek bones, making his hairline seem even lower, and the white band where the hair on his neck finished and his chest hair began had disappeared. Duncan's bedraggled reflection in the water trough confirmed that he himself would not pass muster, but any stranger opening a door to find Clarence on his doorstep asking for work, asking for anything, would remember him for a long time, and might report him, after they had closed the door as quickly as possible and checked the phases of the moon. So leaving Clarence in the barn for now was necessary, while Duncan and Marco went to the nearest farms, asking for jobs needing done, payment in food or in cash.

Duncan laid it all out to the other two, explaining why it was clothes before food, despite their aching bellies. First Marco, now Clarence had been chewing on strands of hay. Duncan tried it in desperation, finding that he had to work his jaws in an unnatural figure-of-eight movement to grind down the coarse grass. It tasted of nothing but fooled his stomach into believing that something was on its way, if only for a few minutes.

All three sat chewing and Duncan repeated the need to replace the giveaway uniforms with something less conspicuous.

Clarence spoke first.

"We could pinch some stuff from a washing line at night, but we'd need a lot of all three of us."

"Well, we could," said Duncan, "I thought about that too. But it might get reported, or we might meet the farmer in town when we're wearing his stuff, and then we'd be in the shit."

"What about breaking into a garage or a factory?" Clarence said. "There's bound to be some overalls we could take."

Duncan nodded, "That might work, but it would be risky because we don't know the place and we might get caught."

They were quiet for a moment.

"A chovie," said Marco quietly, now dressed again but still curled up in nest of hay, "that's what we need to find."

Clarence looked across at Duncan. Neither of them was sure if Marco was talking to himself, or who chovie was.

238

* * * *

Marco had carried them in a pouch, tied to his waistband at the back. Across the wet moor on that first long night and then on the longer journey from the shepherd's bothy to the farmer's hay barn. When he was trying to bounce from one patch of dry ground to another, the pouch slowed him down, like a handicapped horse carrying weights on a long race over hurdles. But he kept it slung behind and centred so that he was at least balanced. When he found the Brodie helmet, the other two told him to dump it, but he kept that too, just knowing it would be worth the extra weight to be carried. And it was. Duncan and Clarence both told him to dump the bag of pennies, as soon as they were clear of the Kielder gate, when they first heard the chink-chink of the coins. They were too heavy to carry, they said, and the noise might give them away. How were they going to spend that number of pennies, Duncan asked. Every movement Marco made came with a dry rattle of the coins. But now his denari would come good. Back at Number 2 hut the games went on, but they were over sooner, with only the pennies that Marco hadn't won on that last night in the camp remaining.

When he was washing himself down, he rinsed the coins in the trough and laid them out to dry. He counted them out into rows on the floor of the barn, where they still lay. He had forty-five; just under four Bob.

Clarence and Duncan looked at them now.

"*That would buy us plenty of eggs and beans,*" said Clarence.

"*It might,*" Duncan said, "*but people might wonder why we don't have ration books like everyone else. And if we got the grub, we might be full for a while, but we would still be stuck in this barn, skint and hungry again the next day.*"

Clarence stood up and started pacing around.

"*But four Bob won't be enough to get us kitted out with new gear, will it?*" he said.

"*So maybe we would be able to at least think straight if we had some decent grub?*"

Clarence was hungry, really hungry.

239

They all looked at the pennies in silence for a moment.

"Four Bob might get enough kit for one of us at a chovie," said Marco, *"and then he might look respectable enough to get some work."*

At Corbett's, when a clown's costume wore out or became more patches than costume, the boss would send someone into town with some of the circus takings to find an old clothes shop, a chovie. Clothes that people gave or threw away doubled as clown pants and jackets, with a few alterations. Bell tent size trousers with a waist band tied at the chest and stitched tight at the ankles, or a suit jacket with sleeves too short, or an old pair of bloomers always got a laugh. Tattered hats, and anything with feathers, fur or frills to catch the punter's eye were also good.

Clarence and Duncan listened as Marco explained. When he had finished, Duncan went back to the water trough with handfuls of hay, soaked them and rubbed again at the worst of the mud still showing on his uniform. He put it on and set off walking into Hexham in search of a chovie, having never seen one before in his life.

* * * *

The war had produced a new kind of chovie. Clothes rationing had hit hard all over the country. *"Use it up, wear it out, make it do,"* was the message broadcast on posters, in the face of a short supply of raw materials coming into the country and the need to use all available factory space for military production.

The Red Cross Gift shops that sprung up in 1941 were donated clothes that ranged from posh to rags. There were rails of colourful clothes with minimal wear, gifted by the rich as no longer suitable to be seen in public, and there were tables piled with clothes, uniformly sludge in colour, that had been truly used up, worn out and chucked out, the remnants that in better times would have been collected by the local rag-and-bone man riding through streets on his cart and ringing his bell to attract custom.

The Red Cross Gift shops also had some of the first Government utility clothing. These were cheap but reliable coats, dresses and trousers made with whatever materials were still available. Nothing fancy, designed for civilian wear, and stamped CC41 to guarantee a basic standard. Because of teething problems in early production, however, the basic standard was very basic. Some of the clothes fell apart.

* * * *

After half an hour wandering around, trying to look like he was going somewhere, Duncan found Hexham's Red Cross Shop down a narrow side street. It was hidden like a dirty secret, so that proud but poor people in Hexham could pick their time to visit, unseen, in the hope that neighbours had picked a different time.

The bell above the door announced his entry. Duncan was the only customer in shop. A woman in uniform behind the counter looked up from the book she was reading and nodded to him. Duncan went first to a rack of good quality coats, jackets and furs on a rack and flicked through them, feeling the material, playing for time, before moving over to the table of clothes he had targeted when he first came in. A scrap of paper, labelled simply, "*Mens,*" had been tacked to one leg of the table. It was a tangle of clothes with a mishmash of colours, none of them found in a rainbow. After sorting through the knot of clothes in the top layers, Duncan extracted a pair of utility trousers and put them to one side. They were split on one seam with no pockets or turn-ups, to save on material. After another few minutes he found a thick woollen jumper with the elbows darned. He held it up against his chest, then put it on top of the utility trousers. The Red Cross volunteer stood up as he brought the clothes to her and hoisted the bag of pennies onto the counter in payment.

"*Just got demobbed, did you son?*" she said, folding the trousers.

"*Yeah, that's right,*" Duncan said, smiling. "*Still waiting for my pay to catch up with me, and no ration book yet either.*"

"*So it looks like you've broken into the piggy bank here,*" she said, as she counted off the pennies into stacks, smiling back and looking down at his scuffed boots, the shoelaces a mass of knots. He could see that the woman in her neat Red Cross uniform didn't believe a word. She was willing to go along with the charade because he was also in uniform and looked like he had done his bit for his country. In the absence of any physical injury, she probably had him down as a mental case, which suited Duncan. It was better that than a deserter, and it got him more sympathy than suspicion.

"*I'll just tie these up for you,*" she said, producing a ball of string and a pair of scissors from under the counter.

"*While I'm doing that,*" she continued, "*why don't you have a look over there?*"

She pointed towards another pyramid of clothes on the floor in a darker corner of the shop that Duncan hadn't noticed when he first came in.

"*If you see anything you like in there, just help yourself, for free,*" she said. "*That lot's just going to be cut up for rags or patched into blackout curtains.*"

Duncan hesitated, decided that he was long past the point of maintaining his dignity or pretending he had a choice and walked over to the pile in the corner, as she was tying up his bundle.

"*Thanks. I'll just have a look,*" he said.

The shirts and trousers he had raked through on the *Mens* table at least allowed people in Hexham the illusion that the clothes they were buying, to be seen in, might, just might, have been bought by them new, long ago. The pile on the floor had no such pretences. They were clothes that nobody wanted, even in the back of their wardrobe. He went through the pile systematically, lifting what was on top, examining each item and then moving it to a new stack he built on the floor. After ten minutes he had enough.

"*Find what you need?*"

The Red Cross woman had cleared the stacks of pennies into her till. She continued with a stream of chat as she tied up his second bundle of clothes and Duncan played along as the recently demobbed serviceman, saying how much he was looking forward to getting home.

On his way back to the barn, Duncan stopped a few times, beside dustbins in the town, making as if he was resting from carrying the heavy bundles. He scavenged what he could, but it wasn't much. He had what was left of a cooked chicken carcass and some potato peelings. He covered them with a discarded newspaper from the bin and wrapped the bundle in his holy jumper.

* * * *

When he got back to the barn, the combination of the mystery parcels and the smell of chicken had Clarence and Duncan circle around him like excited dogs.

For Clarence, Duncan had found a brown jacket that had been let out at the back with a wide stripe of material that almost matched the colour of the jacket, and trousers that were a size too big, patched on both legs. For Marco, he had brought back a "siren" suit with a zip that was jammed. The belted, one-piece romper suit was designed for people to jump into quickly in the dark, to make the run to the air raid shelters. It fitted Marco perfectly, making him look like an oversized child. A couple of safety pins held what was left of the zip together. Neither man complained, happy to get out of the navy clothing that had been wet, dirty or both since they had left HMS *Standard*.

Duncan had found another safety pin, to hold together the seam of his utility trousers. He tucked his holy jumper into the trousers and saved the need for a belt to keep them up. As he looked at Clarence and Marco in their new getups, he wondered about the matching boots they wore. This was less obvious, though, and probably the last thing anybody would notice if the men were seen together, given the ragbag sideshows that were going on above the boots.

With stomachs cramping from the lack of food, or from chewing grasses, they picked at the bones of the chicken, sucking them clean, and ate the slivers of potato peelings that didn't have mould on them.

They were keen to get started on the new plan, for Duncan

and Marco to get food or money from piecemeal work at farms on the edge of town, but it was too late in the day to start. As darkness fell, the three men bedded down in the barn for a second night, using their old navy kit for extra bedding.

* * * *

The new plan lasted less than half a day.

Farmers, on their isolated tracks, were cautious, bordering on paranoid. As the war went on, there were more and more displaced wanderers turning up on their doorstep. A series of travellers, tramps and odd bods, all looking to sell their labour for a meal. There was work to do, but the farmers had also listened to their radios and heard the planes flying overhead. There were stories of German parachutists and disguised Nazi spies being sent as the first wave of invasion from France.

On four of the five farms that Duncan and Marco got to on that morning, they didn't get as far as the farmhouse door. Farmers met them outside in the yard with shotguns, loaded and cocked. On the fifth farm, the farmhouse door opened a crack and they were told to fuck off.

"*Try further afield tomorrow,*" Duncan said, without enthusiasm as they walked back to the barn.

"*We just need to find one farm, just one.*"

Marco knew that further afield was going to be further than the two-mile radius they had walked that day. He had been reduced to lifting muddy ears of wheat from the edge of fields, rubbing it between his palms and chewing on the grains. His guts had started aching again, for the first time since they had left Kielder. He couldn't decide if it was from hunger, from eating the hay and raw grains, or the return of the misery.

Clarence spent some of the time waiting for the other two to return improving his nest in the barn. He had moved up a level, to a sheltered spot on a corner where two hay bales met. His arse was insulated and the loose hay that he had dragged up with him was an effective blanket. The journey from HMS *Standard,* then from the shepherd's hut had brought his weight back to what it was before he started on the insulin treatment. He walked around inspecting every corner of the barn, looking for anything he had missed and distracting himself from his stomach, which was making gurgling sounds, like a sink draining.

Duncan was last to fall asleep that night. Farm work had been a good plan. He still believed that. The flaw in the plan was that it was out of date. The farmers in Duncan's head, those in his plan, no longer existed. One of the first things he noticed as he and Marco walked the farms was that every farm had a pig. Just one. Even if there was farm work to be done, there would be no scraps or spare food left over as payment. As they walked between farms, he saw women and children working in the fields and farm buildings. Women doing the work that the farm hands might have done, and even children driving tractors. Farmers putting their wives and kids to work. It was reliable and cheap, with no need to pay for day workers, and probably no money to pay them anyway.

Duncan realised that he was out of touch with the war and with how fast things had changed. It had been only a few months, but he was like a man released from prison after a long stretch. He'd seen the changes as he walked around Hexham, looking for the chovie. The people he passed in the streets moved around with purpose, focused on what needed to be done. There were no clumps of shoppers, yakking on corners, or neighbours laughing together across fences. Children were dragged by the hand from one place to another, no time to play. Surviving the day, and worrying about how much worse tomorrow might be occupied thoughts and showed on faces. Those who glanced at Duncan passed quickly, intent on their destination or duty. What he'd seen in town gave him an idea for what he, Duncan and Marco could do, had to do, next to survive. It would be risky, but once more on their journey they had run out of options.

* * * *

Hexham was a market town, and there was still food on the shop shelves for sale, if you had cash or the right ration books.

A pint of milk was tuppence, a dozen eggs or a tin of beans three times that. There was also the Shambles stalls on market days, which was every day except Sunday. Duncan had been drawn by the swell of noise from the market, diverted for a moment in his search for the chovie.

The town had a pinched feel about it. In the First World War, newspaper headlines had assured citizens that the war would be over by Christmas. Nobody in government was putting out such assurances this time around and the people of Hexham were dug in for the long game, doing what the radio broadcasts said was necessary, and sometimes a bit more to get what they needed to survive. When a German bomber was shot down and crashed outside the town, a miner from the nearby coal pit was first on the scene, after a night shift. He took the boots from one of the dead bodies and ended up in court for his actions. He was accused of theft from a corpse, but the court admonished him. Stealing a pair of leather boots from someone who had come to kill dozens, maybe hundreds of Britons, was not grave robbing. It was a crime that was only just over the line of what was acceptable in the fight against the Nazis.

There was fast and noisy trading at the Shambles market, all the way from Parliament Street to the narrow cobbled vennel that gave the market its name. Established stall holders had the prime spots in straight lines in the main market building, a length of the double-pitched slate roof held up by stone columns. Other stalls were set up in the open, higgledy-piggledy, down either side. Stall holders hawking their wares did their best to disguise the fact that what was on show was basic and repeated every four stalls. Vegetables and fruit were not rationed, nor was bread, but what was on sale at stalls were the remnants of what farmers and households had grown or baked for themselves. All that was left to be thrown away at the end of the day was the discarded scraps of those remnants, leftovers of the leftovers.

On the main stalls there were potatoes and carrots that would have been stored over winter, shrivelled parsnips and apples, both cookers and eaters, all washed and rubbed to make them look as shiny as possible. Some stalls had stale cakes or other cooked food that had been cobbled together from what little was left over on rations. Vegetables, eggs and salted spam dressed up as wartime pies, fritters and turnovers from whatever could be frittered or turned over. At the end of each market day, barrows and canvas canopies were stored in alleys and against walls.

At either end of the market there was a pig-bin. It was marked, *"We Want Your Kitchen Waste."* It was all part of the war re-cycling effort. It was from there that Duncan had grabbed the two handfuls of potato peelings, trying to look like he was putting them in, rather than taking them out. He had dug his hands deeper in the bin and came up with only mush; food so rotten it was difficult to tell what it might have been. Not much to eat, but enough to give him an idea.

The trick was timing, and being in the right place. There was a pause in the market day, no more than ten minutes, between the stalls closing up for the day and left-overs being dumped into the pig bins. It happened when buyers were leaving and sellers were busy boxing up what they could sell tomorrow.

Begging or asking the stall holders for scraps would raise suspicion. To be seen digging in the pig bins would be worse. Walking through the market, at the right time, wearing the right clothes was the only way to do it. On the first run, Duncan came from the south end, Marco from the north, taking one side of the street each. They then swapped sides and did the same in reverse. With one eye on the stall holders and one on the leftovers, both men mingled with the thinning crowd, stooping without stopping and storing what could be carried up their sleeves. Clarence stayed in hiding at the far end of the market and collected what was emptied from bulging sleeves into an old fruit crate, found behind one of the shops, then covering the crate with some sackcloth. Duncan and Marco were limited to scraps that would not squish when shoved up a sleeve, but there was enough of those.

Duncan took a risk by doing an extra run from the south end on the second day. He had spotted a rusty safety razor on the edge of a table of old tools and garden equipment. On his first pass he brushed the razor off the table with his sleeve and nudged it out of sight with his foot. On his second run he bent to tie his lace and the razor went up his sleeve.

They each took a different route back to the barn at night as it got dark, still wary of being spotted as a group of strangers in town. They ran the same routine for four days, scavenging by day, eating and planning at night. Their pickings from the market were repetitive but edible and there was enough. The open barn gave a clear view of the road and they were on lookout, but the weather stayed kind enough that the farmer didn't need the hay to supplement his animals that week.

They were clear of Kielder, clear of the shepherd's bothy, now rested, stomachs no longer making noises that could be heard across a room. Marco started to believe again that he had beaten the misery.

"*Maybe shook it off,*" he said to Duncan on the way back to the barn on the third night.

"*Maybe you just need a full belly,*" Duncan said. He never understood what the misery might be, or how anyone except Marco might have it.

Every day without the pains was another good day for Marco. Most of the time he worried about little beyond whether the sleeves in his jumpsuit could hold more food, or when the cows would be coming to the barn.

Clarence was back to getting through the nights without sweats and screams. He could still taste sugar on the back of his throat whenever he was eating, but the smell of the rubber tube had gone. Without work, real work, creating and repairing with his hands, he was getting jittery, hanging about in Hexham with a fruit crate, trying hard not to look like he was waiting for someone, when he was. Shaving had helped, though he still felt conspicuous, trying to keep his back to the wall to hide the wide stripe running up the back of his jacket where it had been let out. The stripe of contrasting material was a light brown colour. He knew it wasn't yellow, but with too much thinking time on his hands in Hexham he started to believe that others might make that association and start asking questions about why he was standing on street corners instead of fighting the Nazis.

Duncan was happy to have put some distance between the three men and Kielder. Since their break out, they had been reduced to hunter-gatherers, like cave men in muddy uniforms. Now they had some time to think beyond the next trig point, beyond the next turnip or potato field. The next plan, he knew, was going to need more than just a break in the trees, a hill in the distance to aim for, or some faint lights in the darkness.

* * * *

After they had eaten on the fourth night, Duncan asked the question again. What next? They started with the pipe-dreams and worked back to reality. Clarence's idea was to escape to America on an ocean liner, create new identities and join up with the Yanks to fight again. The best Duncan could come up with at first was stealing cigarettes from Hexham railway station during the blackout and selling them at the market and around pubs to make some travelling cash.

Clarence had given his idea some thought. "*I could get us on a ship, if we could get to the west coast,*" he said.

"*Three more bodies going up a gangplank are never going to be noticed. The ports are going to be as rammed as the Shambles market.*"

"*And if we get there?*" Duncan said.

"*To the west coast?*"

"*To the coast, yes, but to America as well, I mean. What are we going to do?*" Duncan replied.

"*Last time I looked, we were three penniless deserters, dressed like hobos. We'll stick out if we move, even more than we do in Hexham, and we'll still be skint if we get to America.*"

"*Well, we could...,*" Clarence trailed off.

He could see them walking off a dock onto a ship as stowaways, but he hadn't figured how to get to a port without being caught. If they made it across the Atlantic, he could find work. Engineers were engineers everywhere. He didn't know what Duncan or Marco would do, though, and that would be on him.

They sat quiet for a minute.

Duncan had another idea, a better one than nicking fags from the station. It had come to him first when he'd been walking about in Hexham, seeing the chaos that had become normal life for most. Maybe there was a way to make the most of the lack of order. He floated his idea, to see how it would sound out loud.

"*We could fake who we are. Just turn up and join up again in Hexham or Newcastle.*"

He looked at the other two, testing the water.

"*Doesn't have to be navy. Christ, last time I checked, the army were taking anybody that could walk upright. They must be desperate for men by now. Nobody's going to knock us back just because we don't have proper ID. Just go in, say we were bombed, lost everything, all our paperwork.*"

Clarence and Marco kept their heads down and said nothing.

Duncan pushed it. "*OK. We could go to different recruiting centres, Newcastle, Carlisle, so nobody sees us together.*"

He was trying to convince himself that it would work, and more than that, that he wanted to do it.

"*We'd be signed up, guaranteed,*" he said, "*and we wouldn't have to go back to sea.*"

He looked for eye contact from Duncan or Marco but got none.

The silence stretched on, and Duncan got his answer.

Marco spoke first, feeling obliged to come up with something. He started talking up Duncan's first idea.

"*Breaking into the station, that could work,*" he said. "*Nobody who buys fags on the quiet is going to report it, are they? If we can get enough, we could make a few hundred quid. That would get us most places.*"

As he spoke, Duncan and Clarence were shaking their heads, picturing just how many cigarettes they would need to steal to make that much.

"*What about a stall in the Shambles, then?*" Marco went on, without pausing.

"*We nick some stuff from the goods yard in the station, to get us started, then buy other stuff, legit, to sell on the stall? That could work.*"

250

Neither of the others replied.

Duncan stood up and started to walk about the barn and Clarence pulled out strands of hay from a bale. Marco continued talking, outlining another plan, even crazier than the others. He repeated it and got no response from the other two.

In the dark, they kept talking for another half hour, flying then shooting down schemes to stay in Hexham or to get away. The ideas became more desperate and reckless. Nothing was off the table. After all the planning to get them this far, they were forced to concede that their next move was the endgame. They had been on the run, ridden their luck and survived. At best, running again was only going to bring them to where they were now, looking at each other and asking the same question.

Maybe if they had been back at HMS *Standard,* planning their escape, they would have convinced themselves that at least one of the schemes they came up with would work. Even at the shepherd's hut, they would have believed in more possibilities. But the reality of trekking across the moors and living hand to mouth, scavenging for food, cold and wet for weeks had made them less hopeful, more cautious. The confidence that their escape would all come good if only they were willing to take the bigger risks was gone, replaced by the growing realisation that what came next was more a question of when, rather than what.

In the end, as they fell asleep that night they came down to just two options. They could surrender at the Police Station in Hexham or go with Marco's cockermamie plan.

Without ID cards, pay books or money, it was only a matter of time before one of them was stopped in town and matched to a list of deserters or escapees, and then it was over for all of them. They agreed on that. It would be better then, to hand themselves in and hope for leniency and a lesser sentence as a result. They agreed on that. Nobody would be stupid enough to send them back to HMS *Standard,* knowing that they could walk out the main gates again anytime. They agreed on that too. The war couldn't last for ever, and when they had done their time, wherever they served it, they would be free men, able to start a new life, not looking over their shoulder every day, like now.

Agreed. Handing themselves in would be hard, but it was the best option. Agreed.

So it was decided. They talked themselves to a stop and settled down to sleep a final night in the barn.

In the morning, they put on their navy uniforms, still stiff in places, stained and sagging in others, but still worn with pride, despite all that had happened. They ate the last of the food they had taken from the Shambles market the day before. Clarence sat by the trough and shaved himself human again with the rusty safety razor, sharpened on a stone. They were ready.

All three stood in the doorway of the barn for a final time, looking back at the old clothes from the chovie, folded and left for the farmer. Marco and Duncan turned and walked out into the sunlight.

Clarence stood, hesitated and sat down again on the nearest clump of hay.

"*I can't go back.*"

Duncan looked at Marco and they went back into the barn slowly, sitting either side of Clarence. He sat with his hands clasped tightly in front of him.

After a moment, Duncan said, "*OK Clarence, we started this together, and we'll finish it together.*"

"*I can't go back,*" Clarence repeated.

They sat on the hay and nobody spoke for a full minute.

"*That's fine. We do it the other way,*" said Duncan, looking at Marco, who nodded in agreement. What had seemed the only rational way forward just a minute before didn't any more.

It didn't take much. Clarence's fear of being taken back to Kielder was enough. Duncan didn't need any more persuasion not to hand himself in. Clarence was an easy get out, and a relief for him. The decision on what to do next had been made by someone else this time. He would go along with it, happy that he wasn't responsible for Marco's slap-arse-crazy plan. But this time was different. Marco's naivety and his plan were as likely to get them killed as captured. Success was only the third most likely outcome.

"*It will work,*" Marco said, because he couldn't see why it wouldn't, and because he didn't see any other way out.

The previous night, Duncan had disagreed. *"It will get us shot."*

Now, ten hours later, he would go along with it, as the only remaining game in town. As the three of them sat on the hay, all dressed up and nowhere to go, Duncan's dilemma became whether to jump in and take over, or to let Marco run his own show, despite his serious doubts.

For Marco, the only dilemma, the only part of the plan that needed sorting to make it work, was whether to wait for their lifeline to arrive, or to go looking for it.

* * * *

To the south of Hexham, on the edge of where housing ended, was a patch of land 800 feet above sea level. This was the obvious spot. The racecourse buildings were being used as an ammunition depot, but the flat oval of green where the horses had raced before the war was ideal. The lights from there would be seen from the town and there was plenty of space. So, Marco decided they could wait. But for how long?

Or he could follow the marks. A circus left a trail. He knew the signs, like a tracker who'd once been part of the tribe but had left, gone over to the other side. Looking around a town he could tell where the circus would set up. From there it would be easy. If there were remains, discarded cartons, sawdust still in the grass, he would know. He didn't get down with his ear to the ground or feel the temperature of the campfire, like some injun you'd see in the cinema, but he could tell from the signs how many moons had passed since the circus had been. The holes left in the grass at the racecourse, from metal spikes driven in to rope up the big chapiteau told him.

When he first checked the racecourse at Hexham there were no clean sided holes in the grass, which meant the trail wasn't fresh. It had been weeks since a circus show there. He knew where they would be headed. The migrating performers rarely varied their route, like heavy beasts moving between water holes.

To wait, or to follow and catch up? Duncan had made the big decisions up to now and Marco had gone along. Now Duncan and Clarence would be counting on him. If he got it wrong, they would be stuck in Hexham for too long and one of them might be caught in town or trying to get out of it. Finding the circus fast, that was all he needed to do.

Marco was pretty sure there would be work for all three of them as trailers, being fed for piecemeal work, selling tickets, peddling balloons. That would be enough for now. He could show Clarence and Duncan the ropes, at least until they found something better. Nobody would be looking for deserters in a circus.

"Pick up the trail and follow it." That was how he explained his plan to Duncan and Clarence. *"Get work, get fed."* He made it sound easy. But it wasn't. There were risks he didn't tell them about.

The easiest kind of circus trail to pick up was from the worst kind of circus; fireball outfits. Marco had seen it from his time with the Brothers Craston. It had happened only once, when Corbett's circus was setting up outside a northern town on their usual route. The locals came out at night and threw stones and cow dung at the tent, and one of the ropes was cut. A fireball outfit had passed through the previous week and Corbett's paid the price.

Corbett's was a Sunday school show, one of the best. A clean show with no rigged games on the side to fleece the flatties, no dirty girl side tents with booze. It had real acts, no dogs dressed as lions or acrobats too old to tumble. Mr Corbett would stand for no dodgy stuff. The previous stick and rag show had come through town, some cheap shysters with no history, sold tickets, put on a show with farm animals and a few freaks, and stolen from houses in town while the people were at the show. They had burned up the pitch for anyone coming to town behind them, and Corbett's had suffered. Fireball outfits were parasites, living on the routes established by clean shows. They would keep one day ahead, even sending night riders on ahead to tear down or cover up posters of clean shows.

The other danger was that he might pick up the trail of some fleabag outfit, so run down and ragged that there would be no work for any of them and they would have burned their boats catching up and be left stranded, even worse than they were now.

There was no way of telling just from the trail. To wait was safest. To follow would be like trying to jump on a train as it passed, not knowing what kind of train it was. With the war, circuses would be moving faster, stopping just a night or two in one place. That would be enough stopover time to get any punters who could afford it into the tent. Ration books wouldn't get you a ticket and any cash that was around could be better spent or saved. There would be slim pickings and rows of empty wooden seats. Mr and Mrs Wood and all the little Woods, as his father had called them.

But each day that they waited made capture more likely. Nobody at the market had given them a second look so far, but they soon would. If the same three men became daily fixtures, walking through, again and again in the same outfits every day, somebody would ask why. Everyone was on the look-out for strangers. One suspicious stall holder or one eagle-eyed shopper, that would be all it would take. It was chancy to wait.

The circus trail would go west, towards Carlisle, anticlockwise on the circuit that Marco knew. If it had been to Hexham it had come from Newcastle, up the east coast, cross county and then back south on the west coast, maybe as far as Preston, then east and back around again. It would take three or four months for the full loop, but if times were hard like now, much less. Pitch up, do the show, pack up and move, faster and faster as the money in each of the towns ran dry. The circus might gamble, detour and set up in a smaller town, like Haydon Bridge or Scotby. It was something new to take folks' mind off the war for an hour or two. For the circus it was a risk, knowing that they might be pitching an empty tent, but always a chance that the lights and the sight of the circus in a new town would bring a crowd, even if it was only once.

* * * *

Train tickets were not being inspected much at Hexham station, but faces were. Two police officers and the station master walked the platform. The station master nodded or doffed his cap to familiar faces and lifted his chin up as a greeting to strangers. The police officers walked together, ten feet behind the station master, casually looking each person up and down from under the brim of their helmets.

Duncan, as the best dressed of the three, had been sent first, while Marco and Clarence continued with the Shambles market routine for one more day to get food for the journey. Duncan was trying to mingle at the station, straining his neck above the clouds of steam with each train, searching for some imaginary relative getting off, while checking how easy it would be to get on. Those passengers carrying bags or leading a child by the hand, and those in uniform were invisible to the two policemen.

Duncan watched from behind a pillar as the police targeted an olive-skinned man travelling alone with no luggage, touching their helmets to him before asking a few questions, blocking his way to the train, all the while looking over his shoulder for anyone else worthy of their attention. Unlike the police Duncan had spotted and avoided in the town, these two were armed, leather holsters with Webley and Scott revolvers on their belts. Tightened security at stations had started in London and crept north as the Nazis got closer to the English Channel and invasion fears grew. But it was not just Nazis that the two policemen were looking for.

The Newcastle and Carlisle railway line carried troops, goods and civilian passengers, with that order of priority given to what moved and when. With rationing, blackouts and the black market, the number of thefts from goods trains had escalated since the beginning of the war to a point where it was more than the total number of all thefts from buildings reported in England and Wales combined. Carriages parked in railway sidings were emptied overnight and even trains leaving Newcastle to travel non-stop to Carlisle turned up with half their load. And it was getting worse. The armed police were at stations looking for characters more difficult to spot. They were searching for spivs, drones and racketeers on the make, as well as Aryan-looking spies, or anyone carrying a German parachute.

Most of the racketeers who were able bodied were wanted for other reasons too. They were men AWOL from their units, men who had thrown away their identification tags, survived and avoided service by stealing and selling. In Scotland, Glasgow was the biggest refuge for deserters. It was big enough to absorb hundreds of anonymous bodies to the city and suburbs, living with sympathetic families or under false identities. In England, it was the "L-Triangle", the roads and railways in and between London, Leeds and Liverpool, that had the biggest concentration of deserters. Over a hundred thousand men across the country were on the trot, having walked off their posts, or unaccounted for after leave.

Black market goods, off the ration books, came north from Newcastle in trucks, cars and carried in suitcases. There was timber and petrol, cigarettes and stockings, cans of condensed milk and swanky clothes, all for sale at right price or in exchange for anything else that could be traded. The police were struggling to cope with growing number of people being drawn into thefts, but the bigger battle was against complicity in the crimes.

Law abiding citizens were doing everything they could for the war effort at home. Making sacrifices, tightening belts, hoovering, shaking and ironing blackout curtains to avoid having to wash them and make them thinner. They were helping neighbours in their time of greatest need, taking in the old and children who had been evacuated from the cities. But when it came to the chance of extra meat from the butcher in exchange for a few extra eggs from the farm, or looting city shops during blackouts, most of those very same law-abiding citizens turned a blind eye.

Where rationing made the ordinary valuable, the black market boomed. Everybody knew somebody who knew somebody else who could get you what you needed, or what you wanted most. Nobody referred to what was on offer as stolen. If you had the money, or something to trade, the only price of making life a bit easier at home was keeping quiet about where your luxuries came from. Even the Ministry of Food was complicit. Faced with a mountain of bomb-damaged goods they had requisitioned from around the country, the Ministry had no way of getting rid of them, other than selling to interested black market profiteers. It seemed everyone was at it.

* * * *

Duncan knew little about the boom in thefts from the railways, but what he learned from his time spent recceing the station platform that day was that if he, Clarence and Marco tried to board a train at Hexham, the only decision for the two policemen on the platform would be who to question first. Even if they each tried getting on different trains, the chances of getting past the police, then travelling without a pass, a ticket or the money to pay for one were slim. The odds were certain that one or more of them would be stopped on the platform or the train.

For Marco's plan to work, it all came back to that same question. Whether to wait for the circus to arrive again in Hexham, or to go looking for it. That day, the question was answered. They couldn't wait any longer.

Marco and Clarence had done their scraps collection at the Shambles without Duncan, using a box hidden down a lane at either end of the main market. They were more watchful than ever, trying to keep an eye on all those around them without drawing attention in their chovie clothes. Some people at the market were now on nodding terms with Marco as he passed in his pinned-up overalls. He had a face that made people smile, with or without circus make-up. Most assumed that he was a stall holder who wore unusual overalls.

When Winston Churchill had appeared in public in his own pinstripe onesie, especially made for the fallout shelter, he had legitimised the look and given it adult dignity. But Marco in his shabby romper suit with the busted zip, walking through the Shambles, stood out like a lost child in pyjamas. He was being recognised, and it wouldn't be many days before the friendly nods became, "*Good mornings,*" and then more curious enquiries.

They went back to the barn for one more night. Marco laid out the plan, in all the detail he could muster, making up some of it to plaster over the cracks. Next day was long. They waited until it was almost dark, conserving energy, before walking into Hexham again to the railway station, where they hid.

They would jump a goods train and then Marco would spot the circus somewhere along the line between Hexham and Carlisle. They would get off. It was a simple plan. Too fucking simple, Duncan thought. All three of them had to find space on a train, possibly a moving train, without being seen or being cut in half between the wheels and the track. Then Marco had to spot some blacked-out tent that might be miles from the line, before they jumped off the train, avoiding killing themselves. Duncan just nodded as Marco explained it all and said nothing. He had already stepped off the ledge with Marco's plan. There was no going back.

* * * *

They found a spot in knee-deep weeds, behind an abandoned passenger carriage that had been shunted into a defunct siding. As they crouched there in the dark, Marco listed the stations, speaking quietly, either to memorise them or to convince Duncan that he knew what he was doing.

"*Haydon Bridge, Bardon Mill, Haltwhistle, Greenhead, Rose Hill, Wetherall then Scotby,*" he repeated over and over.

"*I reckon we'll catch them before Scotby.*"

"*Does the train stop at them all?*" asked Clarence, the most he'd said since they left the barn to go to the station.

Marco paused, then said, "*Well, it's a goods train Clarence, so it…*"

Duncan swung around and looked at Marco, wide-eyed, shaking his head imperceptibly, to cut him off. Clarence didn't need any more details now about their chances, or lack of them.

"*We'll have enough time to get off Clarence, as soon as Marco spots the circus,*" Duncan said.

"*Yes, we'll find it soon enough,*" said Marco, playing along.

259

"I've a good idea of where they might be in each town that the train goes through."

The plan was going to be over before it started if they were still crouching there in the weeds in the daylight next morning. They needed to get lucky and they did.

It had been a consignment of four hundred bottles of whisky, waiting in a Newcastle rail yard. It had been, until thieves snipped the seals on the carriage and loaded the crates onto a lorry. The loss wasn't noticed as the carriage was hooked up again and moved north, bound for Carlisle. At Hexham the train stopped to let the east bound train through on a strip of single track.

They were crouched in the dark, looking for an empty carriage with all doors open. Marco said they would be able to pick one out in the dark by the light flickering through as the rake of carriages came past. But as the first train of the night squealed to a stop in the darkened railway yard, all carriages for the length of the train remained dark. They spotted two porters working their way along the track, trying to read labels on the freight by candlelight, and then match them to lists on clipboards. The only other light was from a pale blue blackout bulb on the main station.

Clarence, who was tallest, watched through the dusty windows of the rotting carriage in the siding as the goods train stopped. The other two peered around the carriage, trying to stay hidden.

"There! That one's open."

It was Clarence who noticed the goods car that was different. The faint light from the station caught the bare metal on the door seal where it had been cut.

They waited until the candlelit lamps of the railway porters had moved further up the long train before they made their move. Looping around to the back of the train they walked silently, stepping on the railway sleepers until they reached the carriage. Clarence grabbed the heavy door and slid it on its runners, an inch at a time, stopping and listening for the porters. Duncan reached past him into the carriage when the door was far enough open.

"Shit, it's full," he whispered.

Clarence put his shoulder to the door and pushed it back another three feet. A row of wooden crates was stacked the length of both doors and all the way to the top of the carriage.

"*Get back. We need to wait for the next one,*" Duncan said, waving them away from the door.

He was frustrated by Marco's plan going predictably wrong, and by his own inability to shut up and let Marco run his own show. As the other two turned, Duncan slammed his hand against the stack of crates, cursing under his breath. The crates wobbled. The top crate swayed then banged against the top of the carriage door as it came to rest, with the clinking of bottle on bottle. He heard the crunching footsteps on the railway ballast stop, further up the track. All three men froze, listening as the porters talked, then swung their lanterns back and forward, trying to cast light further. The footsteps started again, walking towards the front of the train.

Duncan stretched his arm around the crates. The thieves at Newcastle had taken the whisky, then re-arranged the stacks of crates, to give themselves more time before discovery. There was space behind the two stacks by the door; not enough for three men to sit, but enough to stand, nose to nose, or back to back, undetected.

They had to move the front stack, pushing it into the carriage, climb in, then get the door almost all the way shut. They repositioned the stacks just as the train started to move.

Standing in the dark as the train gathered speed, Duncan peered through a gap in two of the whisky crates, watching for the first station. What he saw was a dark blur that might have been a station house and a single light bulb, or a house that had no blackout curtains. Then it was dark again.

"*Haydon Bridge,*" Marco said over his shoulder.

"*How do you know?*" Duncan said.

"*Just do,*" said Marco.

Two more stations flashed past the same way.

"*What's the first stop?*" Clarence asked, quietly.

No-one answered.

They were on a train. Duncan didn't believe they would get

this far. But what now? There were a lot of flaws in Marco's crazy plan and Clarence's question had just exposed the biggest one, the one that he and Marco had chosen to ignore and the one that they had both kept from Clarence. Squinting through the gap in the crates, Duncan could see nothing in the blackout. Even if Marco could see the lights of a circus in one of these backwoods towns, to get off they were going to have to get the door open, push the crates out and jump from the speeding train into the darkness, because this was a goods train and it wasn't stopping at any of the stations that Marco had memorised.

As the train gathered more speed, the stations became fleeting flashes of light. As they passed through Haltwhistle, Clarence had the answer to his question. There would be no orderly stops, as he hoped, no chances for Marco to ease the door open a bit more and look for tell-tale, muted circus lights somewhere in the distance. There would no circus work for him or for Duncan. Marco's plan wouldn't work. They were back to running, escaping again with no destination in mind. They were avoiding being caught, for now. But they would be caught when the train did stop. There would be more porters and police checking the carriages. He wasn't going back.

As he stood in the darkened carriage, with Duncan in front of him and Marco behind, Clarence abandoned hopes of finding a circus. He closed his eyes and concentrated instead on Newton's Second law of motion and a man throwing bricks down a well.

It wasn't the speed that would cause the injuries, it would be the acceleration, his change in velocity divided by the change in time to fall. He would have horizontal velocity, the speed of the train, but also vertical velocity from gravity, so he would be moving down and across as he jumped. In the darkness, the numbers appeared on a blackboard before his eyes.

The train was doing over forty miles per hour, maybe slowing to thirty-five on inclines and bends. He could do nothing about that. If he had more space, he could start his run inside the carriage to cut down the difference between his speed as he jumped and the speed of the train. But crammed between crates, there would be no running. Acceleration on impact at thirty-two feet per second squared was survivable, but he would be flying out the carriage and hitting the ground at much more than that. If he had a good landing on soft ground, on his shoulder, and rolled, he might live.

Doing the calculations calmed Clarence, even though the numbers told him that his chances of standing or walking after he had jumped were not good. The acceleration was too high and might kill him, but it was just as likely that sudden deceleration on a rock or a tree by the side of the track would end his life as he jumped into darkness.

Duncan had begun to stretch his leg muscles as much as he could in the confined space between the crates, getting ready to jump and run, wherever the train did stop. No point now in staying together. The best chance for all of them was to split up, give the police or the MPs three targets, rather than one. Maybe that had been true from the start. They had plotted the escape together, stored the coats and the food and the tennis racquets together and walked out together. That was the right thing to do then. One man trying to walk across that moor would have been sucked into the mud and drowned, or turned back in the first half hour, defeated. Together, they had dragged each other through that first night one way or another and survived. Three was better than one at the shepherd's hut too, only because one man alone there would have starved or frozen to death or gone insane. In Hexham, the three-man scheme at the Shambles market and Marco's chovie had fed and clothed them.

Marco's crazy join-the-dots circus plan was never going to work. Duncan knew that from the first time Marco had laid it out piece by piece in the barn. In pieces because it was obvious that Marco was making it up as he went along. Worse, because he started his plan at the end and worked backwards. He told them how easy it would be to get work and hide in a circus. That part of the plan he was sure of, and that was probably all he had, before Duncan and Clarence quizzed him about how they would get to the circus. They would ride on a train, he said. And how would they get on a train? Well...they could pretend to be sailors who had lost their papers, or they could hop a goods train, or they could wear disguises as clowns... And how would they find a circus?

Apart from his knowledge of the circus, and what they could all do there, every part of Marco's plan was shaky, each link in the chain weaker than the last. Despite all that, Marco's plan got them clear of Hexham and for that at least Duncan was grateful.

* * * *

It has been over an hour since they left the goods yard at Hexham. Clarence was making his final calculations on whether to jump in the same direction that the train was moving, or reduce his acceleration slightly by jumping against the direction of travel, and Duncan was stretching his Achilles tendons, thinking about whether the first one out the door was most or least likely to be caught, and then feeling guilty about trying to increase his chances of getting away at the cost of the other two.

The train began to slow again, as it had done for bends in the tracks, but this time there was a louder squeal of brakes. It happened quickly. With no loose passengers to be thrown about, the engineer used the throttle to bleed the steam, stopping the pistons, and threw on the brakes at the same time. The train shuddered as it decelerated quickly to a stop. The three men were thrown together, and only the tightly-packed whisky crates prevented them from falling over.

The train had reached Carlisle, London Road station, the end of the line.

As they eased the door open, ready to run, Marco smelled, rather than saw the circus through the gap.

CHAPTER 7

CLOWNS ALL AT SEA

Outside, Clarence, dressed as a bear, was doing what was necessary as best he could. He threw himself into the role, but he was no circus act. He was not big enough to be a strong man, and too big to be an acrobat or a clown, even if he had hopes of being either, which he did not. He was just a trailer, filling in. The stake bites on his ankles were a painful reminder that he was a josser. Only true circus crew, performers or circus by birth, could walk across the site where the main tent was pitched in the dark, avoiding the ropes and the metal stakes to which they were tied.

One of the clowns had given him the bear costume, found at the bottom of a painted trunk stuffed with left-overs nobody wanted to throw away. It had belonged to Bosco, a clown long since dead, who became a roller-skating bear for part of his act. With Clarence's shape and bulk, playing a bear was not a great stretch, but it was for the costume. The feet and hands had been cut off so that he could get into it. Even then, he was only able to move without bending his limbs. The suit looked like it was glued on, rather than buttoned, and he walked like a child taking his first steps.

"*Peanuts and popcorn, right here. A crackerjack prize in every pack,*" he shouted, again and again, through the holes of the bear's snout.

The other new trailer, Duncan, still dressed in his own raggedy jumper from the chovie, manned a booth, selling tickets to latecomers, bringing in some money to pay for his food and to keep the circus afloat.

Clarence was also a strong pair of hands, putting up and pulling down the tents, loading and unloading gear into trucks when the circus moved. It was enough for him that he could earn his keep, like Marco. The only time Clarence was needed in the ring was for a rare run-in and walkaround, when the timings of the show was off. Between acts, to fill the gap, he was sent to walk, stiff limbed around the ring, stopping only to give his best bear roar for adults and wave to children in the front two rows, which was as far as he could see in the costume.

Like selling the peanuts and popcorn, he gave it his best shot. All the circus crew treated him well and he was grateful. Anybody could put on a bear suit and shout and roar for a couple of minutes, but not anybody could perform in the ring. Clarence knew that others on the payroll of the circus, the real acts, did something that only they could.

While Clarence did the necessary with peanuts and popcorn, lifting, moving and occasionally roaring, Marco sat on the grass in clown alley, the backstage area of the ring, checking over his new and special prop, built by Clarence.

It was too big to put anywhere else, and it had to be hidden from the audience until it was time to go on. It had been Marco's idea from the start. He had impressed the circus boss from the first day with what he could do in the ring with just some make-up and a pile of old chairs. From that first performance, he had pestered the boss for the time and new props he needed to develop his act into something more. Clarence was delighted with what Marco asked him to do, but Duncan at first refused point blank to have any part of it. That was until the circus boss told him that selling tickets to latecomers wasn't bringing in enough money to feed the circus animals, let alone the crew. To stay with the circus, Duncan was given a choice between helping out Marco or feeding and mucking out the animals to earn his keep. He became a reluctant performer.

Clowns All at Sea was squeezed between the two wire acts. Johnny Juarez, with his feet and legs in constant motion, trying to keep the slack wire below his centre of gravity, was on first. His three sisters, Dolly, Molly and Polly, fifteen feet higher,

266

balancing poles, metal rings and each other on the high copper wire above the heads of the audience, came after. The running order had been shuffled around to keep the crowd watching. In the unwritten book of ring craft, it was decreed that there had to be something moving in the ring at all times. The set-up time between acts was cut to a minimum and lights were used to distract attention elsewhere as the trampoline was rolled in, or as the rope was hooked up to the roof in preparation for Alice and her aerial acrobatics on the Spanish Web.

Times might be hard with the war, but the circus would be back the same way again. If any of the crowd remembered them, it was important to be remembered well. A Sunday School circus outfit had to deliver plenty of bounce to the ounce for the paying punters.

Before the war, the closing ring spectacle would end with the ringmaster encouraging the crowd to tell all their friends what a great time they'd had. But things had changed. Their friends wouldn't be coming next night because more often than not the circus would be moving on the next day. Instead, the performance closed with a patriotic speech, thanking everyone for coming, God-blessing the fighting forces, including circus performers serving in the forces, and ending with an acapella God Save the King from the performers and the punters.

* * * *

As the clapping for Johnny Juarez died down, the spotlight operated by Clarence did a ballyhoo, swooping across spectators in a figure of eight pattern, to build anticipation. The beam of light came to rest on the entrance to the ring, where the ring curtains parted.

It looked first like the bow of a ship, then, as it came in the audience saw that it was mounted on three wheels. A strip of L-shaped angle iron on the front edge joined the two, curved wooden sides, painted with colourful fish. The deck of the truncated ship was plain white, giving no hint of what lay below decks. Where the bow of the ship broadened to become the deck, a steering wheel, much too big for any car, was mounted. A gear chain linked it to the third wheel of the tricycle behind. The leather saddle, which rose up with every rotation of the pedals, was the size for riding a horse, not a tricycle. The profile of the machine as it rolled out from the side of the ring was the Stop-Me-and-Buy-One, Walls Ice Cream bike, a shape familiar to the crowd, but the size and modifications made it like a child's drawing of the real thing.

Marco had the build-up in the act timed to rotations of the ring. First time around just to let the crowd get a look at the contraption, what it could do and raise a few laughs. Duncan pedalled, dressed all in white with a navy captain's peaked cap that doubled as the Walls Ice Cream vendor's hat. Every few yards, he goose-honked the horn, mounted on the steering wheel. The pull of a lever clashed a pair of beaten-up high-hat cymbals on one wooden side of the tricycle and thumped a drum beat on the other. Second time around, the crowd were surprised when jets of water shot high in the air from the bow of the ship, spraying the front two rows. Then half a circuit to build the surprise, as the deck of the ship opened slowly, showing first a hand, then an arm, waving to the crowd.

Marco emerged in full white clown make up, white sailor's cap pulled down over his ears and a baggy black and white striped top. He closed the deck behind him and stood up shakily at the bow, shading his eyes with one hand, looking out to sea. The crowd "*Oooed*" as the tricycle sped up over two more circuits and Marco wobbled, looking like he might fall off any second. The circuits gave him time to identify a likely child and to quieten the crowd in preparation for his oration.

The poem was familiar to schoolchildren in the audience but was better known by their parents in its many bar room variations. Casabianca was the boy sailor who died at the Battle of the Nile, still at his post as his ship caught fire. He had heroically refused to leave the ship without permission from the admiral, who was also his father. It was the story of a tragic death, fated by its popularity to become a limerick.

Marco did one circuit first for the parents, working his

diaphragm and projecting his voice to the back row, standing, hand on heart at the bow of his ship.

The boy stood on the burning deck
His legs were all a' quiver
He gave a cough
His clothes fell off and left him there to shiver

With the final line, Marco whipped off his baggy top, to reveal a skinny, short sleeved version of the same stripy pattern, wrapping his arms across his chest and shaking at the knees. That brought the first wave of laughter and applause from the adults.

His next circuit was slower and his words clearer, aimed at the children.

The boy stood on the burning deck
His feet were full of blisters
The flames licked up and burned his pants
And now his bloomers are his sister's

The navy white trousers came off in a single movement, thrown overboard, and a pair of oversized silk bloomers sprung out, knee length and red polka dot. The wave of noise from the audience this time was high pitched delight, at the naughtiness of mentioning underwear in public, and the sight of man wearing women's bloomers.

Marco next produced a Jolly Roger flag from within the tricycle, tied it to his foot and began a series of handstands as a human flagpole on the tip of the bow. The music picked up to a circus gallop as the tricycle sped up again and Marco hand walked down the deck. Then, just as it looked like he had lost his balance, he flipped upright onto Duncan's shoulders, standing there for a half circuit of the ring. Then it was a donkey kick onto the handlebars of the tricycle for another handstand before a final flip back onto the deck.

The finale began with a simple set up. Marco took a board and a wooden log from inside the hatch of the tricycle and, after several fake attempts, stood on the board as it balanced on the log, while Duncan continued to peddle, now at full speed. The music got louder still.

From the darkness of the performers' entrance tunnel, a red

and yellow ball came bouncing then rolling across the ring. As it rolled in front of the tricycle, Duncan braked hard, bringing the contraption to a sudden stop. Marco went flying through the air and there was the sound of open-mouthed gasps.

When in doubt, tumble. It had worked for Marco then, and it still did. He hit the ground rolling, did one somersault there and converted it into a punch front, planting his feet and somersaulting in the air. The distance to the edge of the ring was crucial. He landed, tripped over the low boards at the side of the ring and stumbled into the front row, landing sprawled on the lap of his target. All the while, Clarence tracked Marco's passage with the spotlight.

Front row customers passed a notice in the way in, warning them that sitting at the front was at their own risk. Parents with excited children were least likely to read it. When Marco had dusted himself down and mimed his apology to the mother, he turned to the child, the volunteer he had already picked out while circling on the tricycle. He needed to work quickly now, to keep the momentum of the act. While he made his introduction, with a rubber-armed shake of the child's hand, up and down, he spoke quietly to the mother, asking permission to take her child into the ring, promising nothing to worry about, no danger, and a safe return. Getting the child to agree was never a problem. When he realised that he would get to be in the show, he was out of his seat, ready to go. Five or six-year olds were ideal. Any younger and the child got scared, and older children were too heavy.

Hand in hand, Marco walked the child into the centre of the ring, turning to each side of the seating and scooping his other hand to invite applause. Then the chase began.

First Marco tried an exaggerated flag-down of the tricycle as Duncan passed. This was followed by pursuit of the tricycle, child in tow, as Duncan lapped him in a circuit of the ring. Finally, after appealing to the crowd and wiping an imaginary tear from his make-up, Marco gathered up the child, lifted him to sit on his shoulders and swung onto the tricycle behind Duncan as he slowed.

Despite what happened next, that was the riskiest part of the manoeuvre. He kept one hand behind the child's back at all times. Clambering over a still-smiling Duncan, knocking his hat askew, he put his hand over Duncan's eyes as the tricycle swerved on its path. Marco reached the deck again and stood with the boy still on his shoulders to much relieved applause.

The finale, the big schtrabat, in the Flying Brothers Craston act had been Peter at the bottom of the three-man tower as Marco sprung and landed on Paul's shoulders. For Marco's young Pimpo clown act, it had been his Humpty Tumble onto the bentwood chairs. Marco, Clarence and Duncan were never going to be the Flying Brothers, but Marco still had his sense for working the crowd, building to the big finish, working with what they had.

As Clarence tracked the tricycle with the spotlight on its last double circuit, Duncan slowed and Marco bent down and lifted the balancing board and the wooden log again, holding them up to his audience. He signalled with his painted eyebrows, asking them if he should do it, if he could do the balancing, with the child on his shoulders. This brought hands to faces in alarm, and some parents to their feet, at the thought of the child falling with Marco from the speeding tricycle.

When he had let the tension build a bit more on a final circuit by allowing the loose log to roll about dangerously, he took the board, placed it flat on the deck and stood on it, extending his arms and pretending to balance, tightrope-style with the boy on his shoulders, while the log sat harmlessly at the side.

With a farewell wave from Marco, Duncan and the boy, the tricycle left the ring to loud, applause, and stamping feet, followed by the waft of sulphur, as members of the audience dug out and lit matches, an appreciation of the act being a highlight of the evening.

* * * *

When the war ended three years later, Duncan and Clarence, without any papers, were barred from proper jobs and not eligible for coupons for clothes or food. But they still had the circus. Marco never had any papers to begin with. In navy records, the three men were on a list of deserters, because when they walked through the gates of HMS *Standard* they had still been on active service. The list of deserters was a long one.

In the relief and chaos of repatriation and rebuilding, accurate records on the number of deserters from the army, navy and air force took years to catch up with the staggered stream of men coming home from around the world, those who chose not to, those with no one to come home to, and those whose papers had been burned or lost. The Admiralty gave the official number of navy deserters as 863. The best guess by historians in later years was 200,000 men from all three forces, unaccounted for, on the trot.

Ultimately, it was not the number of men who were listed as deserters when the fighting was over, but what they were doing that persuaded Churchill to declare an amnesty for them. With no legitimate means of earning a living, many men took to making money in ways they would have been shocked by five years earlier. Burglary from houses, robberies from banks and businesses and thieving in the street all increased, as did black market trading, and violence with fists, knives and guns as gangs fought each other for territory. Chasing and catching deserters who were criminals, criminals who were deserters and just plain criminals was overwhelming the police, already depleted by deaths in the war.

Churchill used the feel-good smokescreen of the new queen's coronation celebrations to call off the manhunt, granting an amnesty to allow deserters to come out of hiding and go home. Sins of absence without leave, failing to report, avoiding capture and fraudulent papers were all forgiven. But by 1953 it was already too late for many to return to the lives they had lived in civvy street. The amnesty didn't cover the string of criminal offences they had committed to survive in the meantime.

It was too late also for Clarence the coward, Duncan the dodger and even Marco the malingerer. They had signed up to serve, with plans when the war was over. They had faced danger when they were afraid. More than twelve years later, how they would live the rest of their years was set, first by the war and then by their experiences at HMS *Standard*.

At the circus, their lives had been on pause, while, ironically, the lives of those in the towns that the circus visited were able to move on. They saw the changes, but only from the window of a truck, as they arrived or left town, or in the changing styles of people sitting in the big tent. Still looking over their shoulder, even when the war was long ended, neither Clarence nor Duncan would go into town for fear of recognition and capture. Marco was bolder, knowing which towns and where to avoid in the safer towns when he did go for supplies.

Clarence was first to leave, when news of the February 1953 amnesty reached the circus the following month. He followed procedure, set out in the amnesty for sailors, by writing to the commodore of his first barracks, then heading home to receive the protection certificate, posted out to all deserters.

He went home not knowing what to expect and found devastation. His parents and the neighbours either side had both been killed, buried beneath tons of bricks when a German bomber mistook the water reservoir near their home for the River Clyde. He found digs for a few days, walked the streets and visited pubs, trying to find familiar faces. The place had changed so much that he had to ask directions. After five days he gave up waiting for the certificate and returned to the north of England, which had become his home as much as anywhere else.

Looking the part in the second-hand overalls he had bought, and telling garage owners that, yes, he had worked on most type of engines *got* him the jobs, but once more in his life he then had to learn to *do* the jobs. For years he had kept the circus trucks and machinery working beyond their normal life span. It had been the first time that those circus trucks had been maintained, rather than repaired. But garage work was different. In the years he'd been away, there had been a mushrooming of ten and twelve horsepower affordable cars. The engines now started with an ignition key, the cars had independent suspension, turn signals, tubeless tyres, all new to Clarence. But he learned fast, because he was, despite all that he had been through, still Clarence the engineer.

Duncan went back to Scotland and back to sea. He picked up work in Glasgow, first on the workhorse supply boats, sailing freight up and down the west coast, in all weathers. To Oban, then stopping off at the smaller isles, all the way to Stornoway. The boats, mostly built during the war, were Victualising Inshore Craft (VICs), although most people called them puffers, after the sturdy, steam puffers on which they were designed. Duncan operated the deck crane, offloading coal, timber, and food supplies to see coastal villages through the hard winters. The summers were stunning on the west coast and one girl he met in Mallaig was so beautiful that Duncan decided to stay, moving from puffers to fishing boats.

Marco stayed at the circus. He was a great admirer of Alice and her rope acrobatics and they married a year after Clarence, Duncan and Marco joined the circus. When Clarence and Duncan left, Marco and Alice's twins were already practising somersaults.

* * * *

Of the 842 men received and processed at HMS *Standard*, 680 were re-drafted into the Navy, certified fit for some kind of service again. Not all of those seamen were fully rehabilitated. Some were deployed to onshore or restricted duties, some went back onto ships, operating inshore. Some men did recover fully and went back to sea and to battle conditions. In a follow up, the navy found that 105 of the men from HMS *Standard* who returned to service had been written up for misconduct of some kind after they resumed duties.

Of the men who were not considered suitable for redrafting, 60 were discharged for neuro-psychiatric reasons and 102 were discharged as constitutionally unfitted for the Royal Navy. Three men remained recorded as deserters from the service, unaccounted for.

CHAPTER 8

WHAT REMAINS

The broken white line on the road was still as thick as good quality cake icing. There were no potholes in the dark tarmacadam, which had been laid in a time when there were few potholes and local authority budgets didn't limit how many could be repaired each year. As the road entered the wood, the dense thicket of older trees on either sided had pushed young saplings forward, as if daring them to run across the road. Sitka spruce, seeded from the original forestry planting, and a few native oak trees had grown up through the base rock and clinker of the road, breaking the clean lines that had once been the straight edges. The young trees now leaned over the grey road surface from either side, touching their top branches in places and making it dark as night, even on a bright day. Broad-leafed trees dominated near the centre of the woods. There was more oak, some birch and willow and alder in the wet areas. Walkers looking down the long dark tunnel of trees were further discouraged by gates, and signs advising them that the road was private. The gates were closed but not padlocked.

As Clarence emerged into the light, clear of the trees again after a mile, he switched off the lights on his Standard Vanguard. He'd seen a lot of advances in car design in his time working at the garages. Some were cosmetic, but some were real advances in engineering. The Vanguard was a bit of both. If it had running boards, it could have been in American movies, with slick haired actors jumping onto the side of the humpbacked getaway car.

He bought it for the engine though, believing that he might

275

have come up with some of the ideas himself, if his life had not been interrupted by the war and the death of Petty Officer James Madden. The cylinder head had wet liners, less weight and less space, less fuel to start-up and heating for the inside of the car much quicker. An engine so well designed and adaptable that it was used in everything from grey, workhorse Ferguson tractors to Triumph Roadster sports cars. He also liked the private joke, that the car was called a Standard.

The pristine centre line markings, still fresh enough to reflect the sunlight, were bright. The two lanes ran straight again, between two piles of half bricks that had once been bus stops on weed-free ground. There were no further warning signs as the road sloped down suddenly and into gently lapping water. The white line disappeared, covered by green algae, but the black strip that was the road was still visible, like a slipway that had been built for amphibious traffic.

Looking across Kielder Reservoir on the line of the submerging road, the clean white line could again be seen as a strip as it surfaced from the water briefly on the opposite bank, before disappearing into another grey thicket of trees.

"*Tell us the story now,*" a small voice in the back seat said, as Clarence eased to a stop, just feet from the water's edge. Clarence glanced across at Cathy and raised his eyebrows, smiling. They came to the same spot about once a month, and each time he added a bit more detail. It wasn't a true story he told his granddaughter, but it was a good one.

"*A long time ago, there was once there was a village where people lived happily, farming and looking after cows ("moo"), sheep ("baaa"), chickens ("cluck-cluck-cluck"), donkeys ("hee-haw") and even some dogs (meow)...*"

"*Dogs don't say meow Granda!*" the girl squealed, as delighted at the mistake as she had been the first, second and third times that Clarence had told the story.

"*Oh, right, sorry...the dogs went woof, woof, woof!*" Clarence turned and barked loudly through the space between the two front seats, eliciting more excited squeals.

He continued.

"Then one day is started to rain. And it rained, and it rained, and it rained, and it rained even more and the village started to fill up with water. The people in the village were worried that the water would come up right over their heads."

Clarence gave a naval salute, to indicate the height of the water, blowing out his cheeks.

"Now there was one very clever lady in the village, and her name was Nancy."

"Granda, Granda, that's my name!"

"Oh, so it is. How strange, eh?"

"So Nancy thought about the rain and all the poor people in the village. To save them, she decided to make a giant, giant biscuit so that all of the villagers could climb onto it and float away..."

Clarence looked out as a curtain of rain swept down the valley. The reservoir created by flooding the valley was the largest artificial lake in Europe, almost six miles long with 44 billion gallons of water. What was worth salvaging from the camp at HMS *Standard* had fitted into two trucks after the war, before all the buildings were pulled down. It took two years for river water to fill the dam to capacity.

Over many years, local people's memories of what had actually been in the valley faded, and long after the reservoir was opened in 1982 stories began about whole villages, still intact beneath the cold water. At first it was small time, local folklore, but with the coming of the internet in the 1990s, existing stories were added to and more were invented. There were grainy photos showing mysterious underwater lights and the tip of a church spire sticking out of the water after a hot summer with little rain. The ghost village beneath the water was referenced on websites featuring Bigfoot, Nessie and Roswell.

None of it was true. Some of the internet photos showed not Kielder Reservoir, but Derwent Water, further south-west, where a village had indeed been flooded when the dam was built.

The ships that Clarence, Duncan and Marco had worked on had long ago been decommissioned and broken up for scrap. All that remained of HMS *Standard*, 170 feet beneath Kielder Water, was an outline of bricks in the deepest part of the reservoir, and the memories of those still alive who had been sent there to be re-cycled.

* * * *

THE END

AUTHOR'S NOTE

The locations and other details in this story are real, based on historical and naval records. But this is a novel. The main characters and their experiences as depicted are a work of fiction, a reimagining of real events.

During the period of the Arctic Convoys (1941–45), there was an unprecedented level of death, physical and psychological injury in the Royal Navy. The British Admiralty introduced several new psychiatric programmes, including the Stone Frigate Approach, in attempts to rehabilitate sailors.

In researching Sailor's Heart, I used a number of sources, including those listed below. I can recommend these if you would like to know more about the issues covered in this book.

Beaton, T. (1915) Some Observations on Mental Conditions as observed amongst the Ship's Company of a Battleship in War-time, Journal of the Royal Naval Medical Service, 1, 447–452.

Burnett, W. (1842) National Archives, ADM 105/28, Papers relating to the state of the lunatics in the asylum at the Royal Naval Hospital at Haslar in September 1824, 2, App. 7.

Curran, D. & Mallinson, W.P. (1940) Wartime Psychiatry and Economy in Man-power, Lancet, 2, 738–743.

Glass, C. (2014) Deserter: A Hidden History of the Second World War. William Collins, Glasgow.

Harrison, T. (1945) The British Soldier: Changing Attitudes. The British Journal of Psychology, 35, 34–39. National Archives ADM 116/5559, Ministerial Committee on the Work of

Psychologists and Psychiatrists in the Services, Report of the Expert Committee.

Jones, E. & Greenberg, N. (2006) Royal Naval Psychiatry: Organisation, Methods and Outcomes (1900–1945) The Mariner's Mirror (The Society for Nautical Research) 92, 2, 10.

Le Gassicke, J. (1982) A Submerged Site of Therapeutic Endeavour, The Psychiatrist 6, 8, 135.

Prewer, R.R. (1945) The Kielder Experiment, The British Journal of Psychiatry 91, 385, 481–494.

Scott-Forbes, H. (1944) The Rehabilitation of Neuropsychiatric Cases at a Royal Naval Auxiliary Hospital, Journal of the Royal Naval Medical Service, 30, 206–214.

Scott, J. (1842) NA ADM 305/102, Journal of the Lunatic Asylum of the Royal Naval Hospital Haslar, 11 Nov 1830 to 28 Feb 1842.

Wailing, M.J. (2016) Forgotten Sacrifice: The Arctic Convoys of World War II, Osprey Publishing, Oxford.Wortis, J. (1958). In Memoriam Manfred Sakel, American Journal of Psychiatry, 115, 287–88.